Praise for Emma Denny

'Tender and gallant, this story was everything I wanted in a knightly tale. Beautiful and romantic'
Ashley Herring Blake

'A beautifully thoughtful and deliciously sweet romance about getting lost in order to find oneself. I loved every moment spent with Penn and Raff'
Freya Marske

'*One Night in Hartswood* is a thrilling, heart-stealing historic romp and achingly romantic'
M.A. Kuzniar

'A beautiful love story and journey of longing until your heart is torn apart and rebuilt'
Liz Fenwick

'A heart-wrenching, spellbinding love story'
Cressida McLaughlin

'Utterly bedazzling . . . a compulsive page-turner rich in historical detail'
Kirsty Capes

'*All the Painted Stars* is wonderfully romantic and heartbreakingly tender. I wanted to stay in Emma Denny's world for another thousand pages'
Cat Sebastian

'A delightful friends-to-lovers slow burn romance'
M.N. Bennet

Emma Denny won the Mills & Boon and RNA Romance Includes Everyone competition in 2021. They submitted their first manuscript to a publisher when they were eight and a half and were astonished when it was rejected. Thankfully, that didn't put them off. Living on the edge of a forest, Emma enjoys exploring the wilderness while thinking through their latest plot tangle, scouting out exciting craft ales and indulging in historical romances. In 2025, *All the Painted Stars* won the RNA's Popular Romantic Novel Award.

Also by Emma Denny:

One Night in Hartswood
All the Painted Stars

a VOW MADE TWICE

EMMA DENNY

ONE PLACE. MANY STORIES

HQ
An imprint of HarperCollins*Publishers* Ltd
1 London Bridge Street
London SE1 9GF

www.harpercollins.co.uk

HarperCollins*Publishers*
Macken House, 39/40 Mayor Street Upper,
Dublin 1, D01 C9W8, Ireland

This edition 2026
25 26 27 28 29 LBC 5 4 3 2 1
First published in Great Britain by HQ,
an imprint of HarperCollins*Publishers* Ltd 2026

A catalogue record for this book is available from the British Library.

ISBN: 9780008622473

This book is set in 11.8/15.5 pt. Centaur by Type-it AS, Norway

Printed and Bound in the United States

To Luke,
because he asked nicely.

A Vow Made Twice contains a character who is nonbinary/genderqueer. Because this book is set in the 1300s, they do not have the language to describe their experience as we would today. After careful consideration and research, I have chosen to use binary pronouns for this character.

For content warnings, please head to my website, emmadenny.com.

'My friend, Patroclus, whom I loved, is dead.
I loved him more than any other comrade.
I loved him like my head, my life, myself.
I lost him, killed him.'

HOMER
(TRANS. EMILY WILSON)

Prologue

France

Steel striking against wood. Horses whinnying. The dull roar of a hundred men.

Three men – three *knights* – stood alone in a tiny clearing, the rising sun casting their shadows in long, strange shapes across the grass. Little flowers, which surely had a French name that none of them knew, bloomed amongst the blades.

Soon they would be trampled.

War was upon them. Not their war, but their battle all the same.

Two of the men stood a little away from the third. Their hands were linked.

'You did not need to come,' the blond one said. 'You should have stayed in England. You should have gone *home*.'

'I go where you go,' the other replied. He had dark hair, dark eyes. A sombre expression. '*You* are my home.'

'Ash—' The blond shot a look towards their companion, who was looking away. He pulled the other man into a kiss.

'Olly . . .'

'No one else is here.' He kissed him again. 'And I do not know how many days I have left where I can do that.'

Ash's sombre expression did not change. 'Do not say that,' he muttered. 'Do not jest about such things, Olly.'

Olly gave him a half-smile. It didn't quite reach his eyes, too clouded were they with fear.

'Father knows I am useless,' he said. 'He and Hal will ride at the front. We will be positioned at the rear of the charge. The men say it is only a small scuffle. A few days rolling in the mud . . .' He rubbed at Ash's hands. 'And then we will be home.'

'You stand by what you said?' Ash wore a pleading expression. 'You will come home with me? To Dunlyn?'

'Where else would I go? All we must do is see this out, and then . . .'

'Then we can go home.' Ash smiled, finishing the sentence.

'What a grand future it will be.'

'You are not the one destined to be an *earl*.' Ash scowled.

'But think of the things you will be able to do! The people you can help, the lives you will better . . . and you *will* make them better. I know you will.'

Ash looked doubtful. 'Only with you by my side.'

'I will be.' Olly gripped his hands tighter. 'Forever.'

There was a polite cough from the other side of the clearing.

'Are you ready?' the third man said, looking between them.

Ash glanced back at Olly. '*Are* you ready?'

'Of course I am. I have been ready since the day I met you.'

'I hated you, the day I met you.'

Olly grinned. 'Not for long.'

The third man approached. 'Well?'

'I believe so, Sir Everich,' Olly said. 'Thank you for . . . for this.'

'It is not my first, lad,' Everich said. 'Nor will it be my last. Now, take hands . . .'

Ash clasped Olly's right hand, holding it tight. Everich laid his palm down too, pressing their hands together. The ceremony was ancient: older, some said, than the bonds of marriage between man and woman. A trothplight – a sworn oath of brotherhood and fidelity, a vow of eternal devotion. Of love.

'Unions of brotherhood and kin,' Everich began, 'bless us in these times of strife and war. Two knights, pledged to each other above all else, a bond unlike any other. Ashwy Barden, Oliver Coppard, I ask you both: will you become one, sharing with one another all your worldly possessions, living with each other as one?'

'Yes,' Olly said, so eager he nearly spoke over Everich's final words.

'I will,' Ash said, swallowing.

'And will you remain at the other's side until the end of your days, in prosperity and poorness?'

'I will.'

'Always.'

'And will you love each other for all that time?'

'Yes.' They spoke together, voices mingling.

'Then I bless this union, and from hereon you shall be called brothers. You will share all your goods, and live as one, and never be parted from one another. Seal this bond, and mark your agreement, with the kiss of peace.'

Ash's face reddened. *The kiss of peace*. It was traditional, after all. Many men – most men, Ash assumed – who pledged themselves to their kin did so as *just* brothers. But not all. Perhaps Everich did not know the truth of what spurred Ash and Olly to vow themselves to each other.

Judging by the glint in his eye, he did.

Ash allowed Olly to pull him into a kiss. For a brief, blissful moment, the sound of battle preparations died away.

Marshal Everich left them, his skills needed in the lord's tent as he readied for battle. They were alone at last.

'I had something made,' Ash said. 'For you. For us.'

He reached into his gambeson and under the tunic beneath, pulling out a tiny leather pouch. He tipped the contents onto his palm. Two simple gold rings, both marked with an inscription within: blocky Latin punched into the metal.

The rings were far from traditional. It had taken much thought from Ash before he chose them: tokens to be worn upon their persons, not easily lost, not easily stolen. Quickly hidden, should circumstances demand it. Sturdy and shining and infinite.

Olly peered at the inscriptions.

'*Tū et non alius,*' he read aloud.

'You,' Ash translated, 'and no one else. I cannot be – *we* cannot be all I would want, but this . . .' Ash looked down at the shining rings. 'This could be enough?'

Olly grabbed his hand and slid one of the rings onto Ash's finger. He pressed the second back into Ash's hand so he could do the same.

They glinted in the sunlight like twin stars.

'This could be enough.'

Chapter I

Ash
Yorkshire – 1364

Earl Ashwy Griffin Barden stood beside the grave of his father and clenched his hands into fists.

How could you?

The fresh mound of earth, stark against the dewy green grass, did not respond.

His father was dead, and everything had changed.

His eyes stung. There *was* grief there. But wrapped around the grief came anger, hot and uncontrollable. It burned in him. As he stared at the turned earth, he knew that the wrong man was buried beneath it.

The air was full of early spring mist – a drizzling, cloying rain that soaked the fur collar of his cloak. He wanted to rip the garment off. He wanted to tear the ceremonial chain from around his neck and stamp it into the dirt, to crush the newly forming spring shoots and curse the ground itself.

'Ash?'

He turned. Raff, his younger brother, was watching him with an intent, worried expression. Rain clung to his hair. Beside him stood Lily, their little sister, face wet with silent tears. She was furiously twisting an enormous daisy between her fingers. On the grave rested a garland of flowers; more daisies, delicate and tiny primroses, fragrant herbs, picked that morning by all three of them from Dunlyn Castle's garden. The cheerful blooms lay bright upon the dark earth.

'Are you well?'

It took the last dregs of Ash's self-control not to throw his brother down and beat some sense into him.

His hands shook. 'Yes.'

Raff said nothing.

A little way back stood the de Foucart siblings, Penn and Johanna. Their presence, while welcome, made the twist in Ash's stomach tie itself into an even sturdier knot. They were there not for the late Griffin Barden, but for Raff and Lily. When the sun set and they retired to their chambers, his siblings' grief would be soothed by the gentle presence of their chosen companions. Raff would fold into Penn's arms, the family's hostage in name alone, and spend the night in his embrace. Lily would likely drag her long-suffering partner into the armoury where she would exhaust herself until she could no longer *think*, let alone *feel*.

And Ash would be left alone, the master of an echoing keep that was far too large for him.

Behind his siblings stood his remaining family. Lord Griffin's younger and only brother, Lord Hugh, and beside him his son, Simon. He was the eldest of Hugh's children and the only boy – the younger two, both girls, married off years ago. Hugh had assured Ash that he had informed them of Lord Griffin's death, yet their absence at the funeral made Ash suspect that had been a lie.

He should have known, he thought bitterly, both as an earl and as his father's son. Hugh was not trustworthy, and certainly not reliable. Hugh had always felt the rift between his and his brother's statuses. As Griffin's younger brother, Hugh had been the recipient of a considerable inheritance: but not so considerable to compare to the title and lands he so clearly craved.

Ash suspected that Hugh's failure to pass on the word had been deliberate. A choice powered by spite and little else, disgust that the title he craved was passing to someone else.

It was another blow to Ash's pride, and his suitability. *He* was the heir. Now, he was the earl. He should have sent word to them himself, not relied on his uncle.

Ash stepped away from the grave, unable to look at it. Beside it were the graves of his mother, his grandfather, his great-grandfather: a lineage of Bardens that led, irrevocably, to him.

He caught Raff's eye, who gestured minutely with his head – an indication to join the rest of the group – but Ash couldn't. He couldn't stand there, drowning in their shared grief, knowing that they all had something to cling to when he was destined to sink.

He turned away, making for a group of noblemen. He knew every face, if not every name – many of them had known him since he was a boy. They'd seen him in his nursemaid's arms, as a toddling child, as a dirt-covered lad. They'd seen his brutal return from war and witnessed his refusal to take on his duties as heir.

He ought to keep away so they were not forced to look at him or talk to him like an equal. It would be an insult to them all to pretend that he was anything like them.

But he had run out of excuses. He stepped forwards. At his approach, the group immediately widened to let him in; regardless of their true feelings towards him, he was the lord and protector of these lands. It would not do to snub him.

'A good sending off,' Lord Roland said as Ash stood beside him. 'He would be proud of you.'

Ash forced back the denial.

'Thank you.'

Lord Roland had been one of his father's closest allies, lord of the manor in Skeldale town in the dip of the valley. Ash could not remember a time when Roland had not been in their lives. When Ash was a child, Roland had seemed a giant: a huge, red-faced man who always had gingerbread to spare. As a man, Ash was most in awe of Roland's ability to consume full casks of wine without falling over.

'A difficult time for the family,' said Roland. 'How are you faring?'

'As well as we can.'

That was the truth, in a way. They *were* faring as well as they could: which was extremely poorly. It had all been over so quickly.

Ash had become earl in an instant, given no time to privately grieve or come to terms with the title before being thrust into organising the funerary rites for his father. The others had helped – it had been some wild luck that Lily was at Dunlyn, and not in Oxford – but the bulk of it had been on him.

And so his pain had been buried and resentment built above it. He clenched his hands at his sides.

'It will ease, in time,' Roland said, ignoring Ash's terse silence. 'He was a powerful man. And loved, too. We all miss him.'

Ash knew what that meant. *You are a poor replacement.* It was a sentiment he agreed with, although to say it so boldly and make it clear that he understood the implication would be in shockingly poor taste.

'As do we. He leaves a great deal of space behind him.' Ash sighed, putting voice to a thought that had been prickling at him since his father's sudden death: 'At least now he is with Mother.'

'Aye,' Roland said. 'Reunited. I always envied them – excuse me, Barden – if this is too bold?'

'Go ahead.'

'Griffin and Marion were so devoted to one another. I know there was talk that Griffin should remarry . . . I always thought it brave of him not to. She was irreplaceable. And now they are together again.'

Ash stared at his feet. *Now they are together again*. Sourness coated his ribs once more.

'How goes your own search?' Roland said, turning to him jovially.

Ash's stomach sank even lower. Why here? Why tarnish an already spoiled day with such talk?

'We are waiting,' he managed. 'Until after the funeral.'

'Of course.'

The topic of Ash's marriage was one that had dogged him for weeks, now. One which had been dropped but not forgotten upon his father's death. It was not Lord Griffin's final request that he marry – nothing so romantic – but finding Ash a wife had been one of his final projects. Ash would see it through, if not for the reasons his father had hoped.

A brisk breeze picked up, breaking him from his thoughts. Spring was upon them, but the last remnants of winter seemed keen to cling this year.

'Come.' Ash gestured towards the waiting mourners. 'The keep is far warmer than this.'

The family went first, Ash uncomfortably at the lead with Raff and Lily by his side. Their companions had once again split off – trailing behind with the rest of the group, that deliberate distance returned once more. For the first time, Ash looked at the mourners who had not been summoned by blood or duty: local merchants, farmers, peasants, clerks and bailiffs. He could not count the number of people amassed for Lord Griffin's funeral, but he suspected it was within the hundreds – perhaps more.

As they passed through the churchyard gates, Ash paused. They were missing members of the family: his uncle and cousin. He groaned, so quietly that only Raff and Lily could hear.

'What—'

'Hugh and Simon.' Ash sighed, shaking his head.

'I can—'

'I will go.' Ash spoke first. 'I have allowed them too much leniency as it is.'

He turned, leaving his siblings and the rest of the party waiting behind. He could see Hugh and Simon lingering beside his father's grave.

Something about their posture set Ash ill at ease – something about the way they loomed above the dirt.

'. . . terrible shame, of course,' Hugh was saying. His tone did not match his words. 'And what a mess he has left behind. What a *family*.'

Simon huffed in agreement. 'Indeed. The madman, the cripple, and the little whore. How the Barden name has fallen into disgrace.'

'They cannot even marry the girl off,' Hugh said, shaking his head. 'What a pity.'

'She needs someone to force her into marriage, curse what the rest of them think.'

'Force her?'

'You understand.' Simon laughed. 'Dark corridors, night-time wandering . . . there will always be a man willing to take a pretty girl.'

Hugh was laughing along with him, now. 'A moment of pleasure for a lifetime tied to a bitch like her? Poor man.'

Ash could not stand to listen to any more. He strode forwards.

Simon turned. 'Ash,' he said, the picture of polite surprise. 'What can I—'

Ash swung his arm around and connected his fist with Simon's nose with a satisfying *crunch*.

And then everything happened at once.

Hugh shouted – Ash didn't hear what he was saying, too busy with Simon, who was swinging back with such force to Ash's temple that they both went stumbling backwards. Ash twisted them around, keeping Simon close enough that he couldn't land another punch on him.

He could hear others approaching. Shouts, gasps. It was all a ringing rush; he couldn't hear them over the pounding of his heartbeat in his ears.

It was a messy, chaotic fight. Ash hadn't had a fight like this in years, not since—

There was mud beneath his feet. Grey fog blinding him. There was shouting; shouting and wailing and the visceral, awful sound of death. Steel. Horses. He was surrounded.

He slipped. A shout from far away – *Ash! Behind you!*

Another fist collided with his face. He tasted blood. He could smell smoke, hear yelling – no, *screaming*. His neck and jaw suddenly burned in sharp, bright pain, his face hot and slick, his mouth full of blood.

He lashed out again, hands scrabbling desperately at his attacker. He needed to get out, needed to fight, needed to *win*—

'Ash!'

There really was mud beneath his feet. Through the haze, he

looked down and saw the fresh earth of the grave staining his boots. The garland was trampled beneath his foot.

And then there were hands gripping his shoulders and he was being pulled backwards.

'Ash, *breathe*.'

He couldn't. His lungs had been torn out. He collapsed to the ground, barely missing the grave. A body sagged beside him – and for a shining, brilliant moment, he had done it. He twisted himself around, pulling him into his arms, burying himself in that messy, straw-coloured hair and the smell of home.

'Ash?'

He took a great, shuddering breath. And pulled back.

Blond hair turned dark. A sun-reddened face turned pale and freckled. Worried eyes stared at him, not the laughing ones he knew.

Of course. *Of course*. Raff's anxious face emerged, his hands gripping Ash's shoulders.

The fog lifted. Across the grave, Simon was also being restrained, blood seeping from his nose and bubbling over his mouth.

'You *bastard*,' he snarled, spit and blood foaming at his lips.

Hugh hauled Simon to his feet. His expression was worryingly calm.

'Now, Simon,' he said, helping Simon steady himself. 'Remember, your cousin is not in his right mind.'

Ash raised a single shaking hand to his face. He did not find the deluge of blood he expected as his fingers brushed against his jaw and chin and lips. The open wound he sought was no more than furrowed, tight skin – poorly healed and long-since scarred. Confusion mingled with the panic still swirling in his chest.

He managed to grab Raff's wrist. 'Raff?'

Raff looked pale and scared. 'Let's get you inside.'

✡

Ash leaned against the wall of the buttery, a spent jug of wine dangling uselessly from one hand. He had gone to fetch it; the one on their table had run dry. He had seen it off in the darkness before he had even realised that he was drinking it. The others could cope without him – and the damn wine – for a few more moments. Spare him their judgemental gazes, and allow them the chance to gossip about the mad earl without him present.

He could hear the wake. People talking, musicians playing. It was like trying to eavesdrop on a dream. Every so often there'd be a voice, a crash, the sound of a dog, and he'd jump. But then it would pass.

When Ash closed his eyes, he could still see him. His terrified face, his wild blond hair, his pleading blue eyes. He could hear the shouting, feel the cut of the knife.

He wondered for how much longer he would be plagued with these episodes. Respite was brief, and their return was always vicious and fast, leaving him unsure what was real and what was not. They tormented him, both awake and asleep.

His life felt like a long path, carved into the earth. There was ruin behind him, and fog ahead of him. Soon, the road would run out.

Ash took another breath. The horrible memory of the battle faded, leaving a new one in its stead: the scene he had made at the graveside.

He had crushed the flowers beneath his boot. They had chosen them specially, plucked from their mother's garden. And he had ruined them.

Beneath his undershirt, the golden ring he wore around his neck burned against his skin, the cord about his throat heavy as a noose. He pressed the heels of his hands against his eyes, watching the swirl of shapes and colours in the dark. He could hear the thud of his own heartbeat in his ears.

If only it would stop.

Would anyone notice if he left? If he crept out through the servants' quarters and escaped into the dark? If he let the slope of the hill from which his father's keep was carved beckon him down, down into the valley below, to the bank of the fast-moving river? It would be black, now, the water like tar under the moonless sky.

He would open his mouth. Breathe the cold water in, let it fill him. Watch the bubbles pour and flutter and pop. Let it all out. Stop that ceaseless noise at last.

And then it would all be gone. All that *pain*. Worse than the pain – the well of emptiness that came alongside it. There was no fear to the thought. There never was, not anymore. Just relief. The release of a long-held tension. A hope, ephemeral and uncertain: perhaps he would see him again, wherever their shared sins had left him.

Something cold and wet urgently nudged against his palm.

He opened his eyes. Litillwitte, the enormous, shaggy deerhound, was staring up at him.

Ash looked around to see Raff closing the door behind him. Ash hadn't even heard it open. He sighed. The sense of relief burrowed itself away once more.

The dog was one of several things he had inherited from his father. Raff must have fetched him from the kennels – a kindness, unearned. Lord Griffin always had a passion for hounds, and for as long as Ash could remember he had brought them into the keep to train.

Litillwitte had been the last such undertaking before his death. After he found him wandering in Skeldale as a pup, Lord Griffin had brought the beast home. He'd intended to train him as a hunting dog, but while Litillwitte did prove to be a reasonably adept hunter, it was clear he much preferred to remain indoors, resting by the fire or hidden beneath a table at his master's feet.

And then Lord Griffin had died, suddenly and horribly. That day, Litillwitte had been like a ghost. He'd lingered in Griffin's chambers – never moving too much, never getting underfoot – simply watching the comings and goings of the physician and chamberlain and family. That first night, he'd howled until the sun rose.

The next morning, Ash had found him waiting patiently outside the door to his own chambers as if summoned there. Unsure what else to do, Ash had let him in, and the animal had plodded inside and sprawled next to the fire, legs all at angles.

Somehow Ash hadn't had the heart to force the beast to leave. He allowed him to come and go as he pleased and accepted his presence beside him as a second shadow when Ash wandered the grounds or walked around the keep.

He was not a particularly keen or useful dog, with all the manners and appearance of a well-used sheepskin rug. But as Ash stroked his head, tickling behind his ears, he felt his heart calming, his mood shifting so he could better see past the panic.

Finally, he turned to speak to his brother.

'What do you want?'

'I came to find you,' Raff said. 'People are asking after you. You ought to return.'

Raff had been kind to him earlier. Ash should have known his tolerance would not last.

'And if I do not want to return?' he spat. 'You may leave.'

'No.'

'You refuse?'

'I do.'

'I am the *earl*.' Ash's tongue was heavy around the word. He forced himself on. 'I could have you removed.'

He could feel Raff staring at him.

'Do it, then,' he said at last. 'Remove me.'

They both knew he wouldn't. When Ash fell into silence, Raff walked over and settled against the wall beside him.

'So,' he said. 'What in God's name possessed you to punch Simon?'

Ash examined his bruised knuckles. 'He deserved it.'

Raff sighed. 'I'm sure he did,' he said, 'but Ash, at Father's *funeral*? Why? You need a better reason than—'

'He insulted Lily.'

Raff went quiet. 'What?'

'They were talking about us. *All* of us. Then they started on Lily, how she is unwed, how *wild* she is.'

'Both true, you must admit.'

'He – Simon – he was saying that someone ought to put her in her place. By *force*.'

'By force?'

'He was saying she needs a man to . . . to *force* her, Raff. That she ought to be taken by some brute of a man and forced to wed and forced to be a wife.'

Raff had gone very still.

'It was horrible,' Ash continued. 'I do not care if Hugh claims I am a madman, but to talk about Lily like that . . . I could not stop myself.'

Raff shook his head. There was nothing more to say. Ash had failed to enact justice, merely given his uncle more ammunition against him.

'We are awaiting your return,' Raff said gently. 'Come, you cannot remain here forever.'

Ash rather thought he could. But aware that Raff would not take no for an answer, he followed him back into the hall. As he entered, people gawked at him. Did the chattering stop as he walked in, or had he merely imagined it?

The rest of the afternoon passed in a haze of grief and wine. People called him *Earl Barden*. Sometimes he remembered to respond to the title. He was asked again and again about his hunt for a wife. His answers got shorter, his grip on his mug tighter.

It felt like an age before he was alone again, sat at the long table upon the dais with the remainder of his family. The great hall buzzed not with the sound of guests, but with the staff clearing away the remnants of the feast, piles of food to be given away to the poor. His head was numb, a veil between him and everyone else.

Raff sat beside him. Penn sat on his other side, holding him up.

'Thank God that is over,' Penn said.

Ash could only agree. 'If anyone so much as *utters* the word "marriage",' he muttered, 'I will have them locked in the tower.'

'I suppose they wish to know who will be joining you,' Jo said.

'That and they all crave gossip,' Lily added. 'It is a more diverting topic than Father's . . . than Father.'

Ash grimaced. It was an impossible choice: given the chance, he would prefer to talk about neither.

'Do you still intend to head north this week?' Penn asked.

'I warned you about the tower, de Foucart.'

'I did *not* mention "marriage", *Barden*.'

Ash grunted. It was a fair question: he was supposed to head out to meet his potential wife that very day, but his father's sudden death had put those plans in disarray. It was a good excuse to call off the journey altogether, to claim that the matchmaking would be over until he had found time to grieve.

But musing on Roland's words about his parents being reunited made him even keener to get it over with.

'I do,' he said. 'It is too important to delay. I shall set out in a few days.'

'So,' Penn said, rolling a mug in his hands. 'Agatha, is this one?'

'Agnes.'

Ash didn't look at him as he pulled the wine jug closer. Penn knew her name. He was being baited, like a hare.

'I am surprised you have seen fit to actually speak to her,' Penn said. 'You have refused more women than I can even remember.'

'I am not to blame if they are unsuitable.'

'There was that woman Roland suggested,' Penn said. 'What was her name? Ruth?'

Ash scowled. Ruth had grimaced at his scars and spent the evening carefully looking away from him. 'I recall.'

'And of course we cannot forget Lady Louisa,' Penn continued gleefully.

Raff shuddered. 'I wish we could.'

'She *loved* you, though,' Penn said. 'I still recall her expression when Michael informed her she had laid her attention upon the wrong brother. Is this why you intend to travel to Lady Agatha—'

'Agnes.'

'—this time? So she does not fall in love with Raff?'

Ash sighed. They had, in fact, extended her the invitation to visit Dunlyn. And she had refused. She was a *widow,* she reminded them. She had no heirs, and no family. She would not leave her lands without better reason, especially not when she knew that Ash could leave Dunlyn Castle in the hands of a capable brother.

Michael, his father's steward, had scoffed at the perceived rudeness. He had intended to send another letter calling off the potential union, but Ash managed to stop him.

'She seems to be a good match,' Raff said, eying Ash from across the table.

Ash gave a half-nod of agreement. Agnes *was* a good match. Her influence as a widow was stronger than if she had been unwed, and she was more experienced than many of the women he had been introduced to despite being a little younger. She was Scottish, too, which while largely unimportant – save for the still-rumbling tensions that flared between the two countries – Ash appreciated. It reminded him of his mother's family, and he liked the idea of maintaining those roots in some way given how unlikely it was that his own blood would run in the veins of his heirs.

She intrigued him. No one else had turned him down in such a manner. Part of him wondered what may happen should she refuse him in person, too. Part of him wanted her to. It would prove he was a lost cause.

'I suppose,' he said. 'Michael seems to think she may be what the family is looking for.'

Penn glanced at him. 'But what are *you* looking for?'

'What?'

'There must be specific qualities you look for in a wife, elsewise you simply would have married the first eligible woman you could find. I assume there must be certain traits you require?'

Ash winced. 'You make it sound as if I am going to buy a horse.'

'If it helps at all, I am sure that she is having the same thoughts about you.'

'That does *not* help.'

'Assume I am asking for entirely selfish reasons. Whoever you wed will become a fixture in the keep, and as I happen to live here I'm keen to know what sort of person you intend to introduce into our lives.'

Ash glared at him. 'Why did I allow you to stay, again?'

'Because you cannot be bothered to look after the birds,' Penn countered. 'And Raff would be unbearable without me.'

Ash huffed. 'Fine,' he spat. 'Fine! I need . . .' He hesitated. He had tried to imagine the sort of woman who would fit his needs: the sort of woman who would care for Dunlyn until any children came of age. The sort of woman who would have those children, with or without his involvement. He had not spoken her into existence before. 'She needs to be intelligent. I need someone who understands running a keep and managing lands.'

'A partner, then?' Jo put in.

'Exactly. I would not strike up a trade deal with a clueless lord. So I should not marry a woman who will not be able to manage the keep.'

'What else?' Penn said.

'She must tolerate the Barden family's . . . oddities. She cannot mock Lily's choices, or force you two to hide your feelings. Although . . . Although I fear that may be impossible.'

The low noise of agreement from Raff made it clear that this was a thought he had mused on, too. It would be unthinkable for him and Penn to continue their relationship quite so blatantly with a stranger living beside them. It would be difficult to find anyone so tolerant as the rest of the Barden family.

They lapsed into silence. Penn broke it first, shattering through it as he so often did.

'What else, then? What about *her*?'

'How do you mean?'

'You will be spending your lives together. Surely you have an opinion on her personality? Should she be, I don't know . . . curious, funny, serious?'

'Does it matter?' Ash said.

'I should think it does, yes. I understand you won't *love* her, but it would be good for you to be friends.'

Ash peered down at the table. Penn was correct in one way: he would not love her. He had only ever loved one person. His heart had since calcified too much to love another.

He would not love her – was incapable of it. But he didn't need her friendship, either. He needed her skills, and her ability to provide him with an heir. Striking up a friendship with her was unnecessary: she would not be subjected to him for long.

He made a non-committal noise. He could sense that Penn was about to launch a rebuff at being so ignored, so he stood, swaying a little.

'I need some air.'

✡

Ash took himself to the garden, placing himself on one of the benches beside the high wall. The garden had belonged to their mother. Just thinking about her assailed him with the overwhelming scent of roses and earth, the smell that had seemed to follow her everywhere she went. She'd attempted to cultivate a love of the garden in her sons, although Raff was the only one who ever held any sort of affection for flowers. Ash had simply enjoyed spending time with her, listening to her sing and tell them stories.

She'd tended it even in the days leading up to Lily's birth, always moving with rushing, unspent energy. It was one of the last memories he had of her: the day before Lily arrived, she had plucked a strong-smelling herb from the bush beside her favourite bench. She'd become obsessed with herbs those past few months, and had bidden Ash smell it. It was betony. She'd smiled at him and told him it could be used to ward off nightmares.

Two days later, she was gone.

The garden had always been a poorly organised, chaotic affair. She grew whatever took her fancy, not caring about colours or seasons or themes. She fell in and out of love with different flowers so quickly that it was always changing, always blooming with something new and interesting. It was the perfect garden for the former Maid of Kerr: the daughter of a laird who had thrown her family's plans into disarray by marrying an English earl.

After her death, their father could not bear getting rid of the garden, but nor could he stand to keep it himself. It passed into the hands of the housekeeper, Ellen, and the gardener: tended but never loved. Raff had taken it over after his injury. At first, it had been a way to keep himself busy when the wound on his shoulder flared, but soon he had fallen in love with the gardens as well. He was by nature more serious and practical, yet he allowed the garden to grow in the same wild disarray that it had while their mother was alive.

Penn had also been drawn in, although was more likely to be found sprawled on a bench with a book purloined from whichever noble they had visited most recently, or attending to one of his birds as he flew them around the grounds. It was . . . *sweet,* Ash supposed. If a little sickening.

They loved one another. Ash had never seen his brother this happy. By marrying, Ash was sacrificing himself *for* that happiness.

Between the three Barden children, none of them had married, and so none of them had produced a suitable heir. Raff was their one other chance to pass on their father's title, but doing so would force him to toss his true love aside – the love he had fought so hard for. Ash would not allow it.

He was not so cruel as to hate his brother's happiness, no matter how much he teased him. Besides, the circumstances that had led them here made Raff an unsuitable marriage candidate anyway; his shoulder never truly healed from the horrible injury he'd suffered at the hands of his lover's father. Raff was happy to accept his fate as a crippled second son. Indeed, if almost entirely losing the use of his right arm meant he could stay with Penn, Ash suspected it was a choice he would make again.

But he also knew that, if given no alternative, Raff would force himself to wed and bed a woman he had no love for to maintain the family line and prevent their lands from moving into the hands of someone who would not care for them.

Ash thought of the close comfort that had made him so jealous at the funeral, of the way Penn stared at Raff, of the way they linked arms when they thought no one else was watching. He thought of the pain they had both endured to ensure such closeness.

He thought of Oliver. Olly, with his huge smile and messy hair like spun gold, like autumn straw, of his endless promises.

He could not damn Raff like that. Like *he* had been damned.

Ash sighed. He deserved this. Raff had sacrificed *years* of his life for him. When Ash had returned from France, delirious and determined to die, Raff had stayed by his side. He'd *forced* him to survive, even though Ash had fought him every step of the way. He'd held Ash down when he'd tried to flee the keep, desperate to bring home the body he'd never been permitted to find.

Afterwards, all anyone else saw was the miraculous recovery and the awful scar on his face. Raff saw the rest: the fractures beneath, the fog that had descended over Ash's mind, the listless, endless sea of grey and the consuming, half-formed memories.

Another brother might have pushed him back into the role of heir, injury or no. Raff hadn't. He'd allowed Ash's wild moods and furious tempers, and had all the while taken on his role, too. He'd gone with their father to visit nobles and villagers alike. He'd worked with townspeople to see to trade routes and harvests. He'd *mingled* at banquets in Ash's stead, and Ash had let him, even though he was aware of how much Raff hated being around such crowds of people. Raff would return anxious and exhausted, and Ash would thank him, but not relieve him of the duty.

He owed Raff too much to blame him. It wasn't surprising he'd finally reached for what he wanted rather than what others needed. A worse man would have done it *years* ago.

Through marrying and ensuring an heir, Ash could finally repay him those years of tolerance and undeserved patience. He felt a little guilty that Raff's hard work would ultimately be for naught – that Ash's fate would remain the same as it had done when he'd stumbled back into his brother's life years ago – but at least he was leaving Raff with more than he would have done then.

His death would hurt. Ash wasn't stupid enough to think otherwise; the death of their father had been a sharp enough pain. But the funeral had proven what Ash already knew – that Raff, and Lily too, would be all right. That they had others to lean on – others far more reliable than he ever could be. In time, they would heal from the loss.

He was watching a moth land on an overturned bucket when the sound of footsteps caught his ear.

'Ash?'

Raff had appeared in the garden archway. He weaved between the overflowing beds and came to sit beside him.

'I thought I may find you out here,' he said. 'I am sorry, Ash. About the marriage. I know it must be difficult, after . . . well.'

Ash wanted to deny it. But the wine moved his tongue unthinkingly. Raff was the only one he could talk to about the ghost that was still trailing him, after all.

'I am betraying him,' he admitted.

Raff pressed closer, saying nothing.

'At least I am not marrying for love,' Ash said. 'This is just another choice I must make as earl. Making trade agreements with Roland is not a betrayal, doing *that* does not break my vows. This is no different.'

Raff's answering silence was not an agreement. But nor was it a denial.

When he finally spoke again, he was looking at his feet. 'Surely you planned for this? With Ol—' A sharp intake of breath, the word swallowed. 'With him? You knew you would one day inherit the title, after all.'

Ash had half-hoped Raff would say the name aloud. He was thankful that he had not.

'We . . . we did,' he muttered. 'But, in truth . . .' He gave a sharp, uncontrolled bark of a laugh so sudden it made Raff jump. 'Frankly, we had rather assumed *you* would deal with the problem.'

'Me?'

'Oh, come.' Ash rolled his eyes. 'You are kind, and thoughtful, and not *entirely* hideous . . .'

'High praise indeed.'

'What I *mean* . . . I— *we* had assumed that Father would marry you off to some noblewoman and you'd have so many children that the issue of *issue* would no longer matter. We could do as we liked and the title would pass to *them,* in time.'

'Oh.'

'Oh indeed.'

'I could still—'

'*No.*' The word came out stronger than Ash had intended. 'No,' he fixed himself quickly. 'You could not. Do not even entertain that thought.'

Raff seemed poised to argue, before thinking better of it. He could not know that Ash had accepted this a long time ago, even before their father's death.

The acceptance still stung. At least it would be over soon. Ash itched at the cord looped heavily around his neck.

Soon.

Chapter 2

Agnes

The dress was wrong. It was a good dress, a well-worn dress: one of her favourites, in fact, that she had worn countless times.

Yet still, it was wrong.

Agnes Forrett held carefully still as Sara, her lady's companion, made swift work of the ties at the back.

She turned to look at herself in the mirror. The dress fit exactly as it always did. It was as comfortable as it always had been, the fabric still soft and familiar through overwear. But wrong.

'Is everything all right?'

Agnes tried to catch the wince before it showed on her face.

'Yes,' she lied, hoping that Sara had not seen her expression. 'Yes, fine. Thank you.'

Sara raised her eyebrows disbelievingly. 'Is it one of those days?'

It was impossible to hide much from Sara.

'Yes,' she said. 'But there is nothing at all to be done about it.'

Sara was the daughter of one of her father's innumerable allies, and Laurence Forrett had hoisted her upon Agnes as a lady's companion when they were both far younger. Agnes's parents had insisted upon it: she required the company of another woman, someone who was not a nursemaid, and her sisters Muriel and Ada were too young for the role. It was time Agnes learned to *behave*.

Sara was a little older, with soft, light brown skin and waves of thick dark hair, which Agnes had delighted in plaiting when they were young. Her father was a Moor, an accomplished knight who had journeyed to Scotland after winning favour in battle. A lady in her own right, Sara had been picked to ensure compliance, to guard Agnes against sin, and to keep her from unwomanly habits.

The endeavour had been entirely unsuccessful. Sara had been more of a mentor to Agnes than any of her tutors. They were both strong-willed, and had found friendship in a shared sense of alienation. Their bed in Agnes's chambers had played host to all manner of experimentations and explorations, of touches both light and fierce. It had never meant anything, but Agnes's eyes had been opened under the tutelage of the more experienced girl.

When Sara began a brief dalliance with one of the family guards – who was, Agnes had to admit, very pretty – Agnes had hidden their affair. When Agnes had defied her parent's wishes and begun to once again sneak from the home in her men's attire, Sara had assisted.

When Sara had appeared in their chambers in messy tears after missing her bleeds, Agnes had been the one to calm her. She had been the one to risk her own reputation by procuring the right herbs. She had brewed the tincture and held Sara long into the night, until the pain stopped.

When Agnes journeyed across the border to marry her late husband Nicholas la Cleve at nineteen years old, it had only been right that Sara joined her. Sara had been Agnes's strongest ally in those times when her soul and body were at war. She knew what it was like to feel other, even if not in the same way.

Sara gave Agnes a tight smile. Agnes kept her head down, avoiding the metal of the mirror. She could not bear to look at herself again – it would only make her head reel and reignite that horrible, itchy feeling that she was so familiar with. The terrible urge to step out of her own skin.

With luck, the feeling would pass soon enough. Earl Ashwy Barden – the man who would, in all likeliness, become her husband – would be arriving at the keep within the next few days. She dreaded the thought of entertaining him and assessing his suitability whilst she still felt like this.

Sara got to work wordlessly on Agnes's hair, brushing it out in a long, red cascade that reached past Agnes's waist. Agnes was quite fond of her hair, and settled herself on a stool patiently as Sara combed it before tying it in a tight, looping crown around her head.

She had barely finished slicking back the final loose strands when there was a knock at the door, and a familiar voice from without.

'Agnes?'

Agnes sighed. 'Come in.'

The door opened to reveal Agnes's sister, Muriel. She had arrived at la Cleve Castle some time ago. There was barely a year between them – Agnes older – but oftentimes it felt as if it were the other way around.

Agnes had hoped that her family, and Muriel especially, would leave her *be* during the drawn-out process of finding a good match. Her luck had not won out. At least Muriel's visit would soon be over: she would be returning to Scotland in a few days.

Muriel looked worried but determined as she entered the room. Agnes's heart fell.

'That will be all, Sara,' she said, smoothing out her skirts. 'Thank you.'

Sara gave her a knowing look. 'My ladies.'

Another wince smothered. Sara only used the title for Muriel's benefit, yet it still stung. Sara curtseyed to Muriel as she walked past, quietly shutting the door behind her.

'Muriel.' Agnes regarded her coolly. 'Are you well?'

'I am. I . . . I have come to speak to you. As a matter of some urgency.'

Agnes was sure she knew why Muriel had decided to talk to her. She raised her eyebrows. 'Yes?'

'I have heard . . . worrying rumours, about the man you are to meet.'

Muriel was talking cautiously, as if to speak too boldly may shock Agnes into hysterics. Agnes, of course, had caught wind of the rumours a day or so ago: there had been a fight during the funeral of the late Griffin Barden. She wondered how Muriel had come to know of it.

'Oh?' she prompted, feigning ignorance, keen to see how their stories differed. 'What kind of rumours?'

Muriel's face paled. 'Very concerning ones.'

Agnes made a *do tell* gesture, silently waiting for Muriel to continue.

'It may not be anything,' she said, hands clasped tight in front of her. 'But I was talking to . . . to a friend, and . . .'

'Muriel. What word do you have?'

Muriel stopped twisting her hands together.

'There was a fight at Lord Griffin's funeral,' she said. 'Between Lord Barden and his cousin.'

Agnes paused, hands impassively in her lap. She needed to know *precisely* what her sister had discovered.

'A fight?'

'It was awful apparently,' Muriel admitted at last. 'Quite a sensation. The cousin was badly hurt.'

'And Lord Barden?'

'Cuts and bruises mostly.'

'And did anyone mention *why* there was a fight? Or who threw the first fist?'

Muriel's anxious look only deepened. 'Lord Barden started it,' she said quietly. 'As to why . . .'

'Muriel?'

'I am not sure—'

'Why would a newly titled earl start a brawl at his own father's funeral?'

Muriel chewed on her bottom lip.

'Rumour will suffice,' Agnes added.

'The word is that the new earl has taken his father's death very poorly,' Muriel said at last. 'That he was already a volatile man – he was at war in France, and badly injured, which I'm sure you already know – but he returned, ah—'

Agnes waited.

'*Wrong,*' Muriel concluded darkly. 'Aggressive. Cruel. Unpredictable.'

Agnes nodded solemnly. 'And where did you hear this?'

Muriel's expression wavered for just a moment. 'Everyone is talking about it,' she said.

Agnes's first instinct was to distrust her sister. But she was not wrong; word spread fast, especially amongst their staff.

She *had* known that Barden had suffered in France, and had been equally made aware that his nature was not, perhaps, the most placid. But neither was hers, not *really*, and more so: something felt off about the rumour. Something she could not place her finger on, no matter how many directions she turned it in her head.

Not *all* the reports of Lord Barden had been poor ones. He

had been *recommended* to her, in fact, as a good match, even though he was far past the age where he ought to have taken a bride. But that was before the funeral, before these new tales had sprung up.

She was determined to work him out for herself, and not have her mind made up for her by people who were equally unacquainted with the man.

Her sister seemed to be taking her thoughtful silence as nerves that equalled her own.

'Are you *sure* you wish to go ahead with this?' she asked.

Agnes took a quick, sharp breath. 'I am.'

Muriel pouted. 'You *know* you do not have to. If you would just listen to Father, Francis cares for you ever so much, and—'

'I *tire* of hearing that man's name in my home, Muriel. I *know* I do not have to meet Lord Barden. But I intend to do so all the same, even *if* you all believe I would be better wed to Francis.'

'We're just *worried* about you, Aggie.'

This wince was not suppressed at all. '*Agnes.*'

'Agnes, then.' Muriel swooped on her, taking her hands in her own. 'We are worried about you. *I* am worried about you. I worry what sort of man you may be tying yourself to.'

That, too, was a thought Agnes had mused over. But if she acquiesced to their parents' demands and *did* return to Scotland to marry Francis mac Cainnich, she knew already what sort of man she was tying herself to: one fuelled by spite, who would never allow her freedom. A man she wanted very little to do with. At least Lord Barden – no matter what rumours followed him – was a chance for something else. If Barden *was* as violent and mad as the rumours told, then she would break off the arrangement before it had even been made.

If his invitation to the keep, even after hearing news of the scandal that had erupted at his father's funeral, irked her family, well . . . it was a hardship she was willing to live with. *Eagerly* willing, perhaps. She would not have them dictate her life for her. She had been married once already. She had run a keep, both when her husband had slipped into his all-consuming illness and after his passing. She was more than capable of dealing with an earl with a temper.

Muriel was still looking nervous. 'I will prolong my visit and stay with you, at least, whilst he is here.'

Agnes set her shoulders. 'And why would you do that?'

'So you are not alone, of course! You do not have to suffer him without support.'

Agnes rather suspected that her greyhound, Qwippe, would make a better companion for Earl Barden's visit than Muriel.

'I will be quite all right.'

'*Please*, Agnes.'

Agnes huffed. She had faced her sister's stubbornness too many times to know how this conversation would end: with Muriel dragging their parents into the argument to get her way.

'Very well – if you *insist* on staying longer, you can meet him. And then you can ride off home and tell Mother and Father that he is a *perfectly fine husband*, and cease your worrying.'

This seemed to placate her. Muriel gave another smile, gripping her hands once more. Agnes had to steel herself not to pull away.

'Thank you,' she said. 'Really, we do all only want you to be happy and safe. You know that, don't you?'

Agnes swallowed, feeling Muriel's sweaty fingers curled around her own. 'I do.'

✡

Agnes heaved shut the door to her bedchamber, leaning against it with her eyes closed.

After a moment, she stepped back and bolted it. That went some way to making her feel a little better.

Agnes already regretted allowing Muriel to stay. She hovered, noting her worries about Barden or extolling the virtues of Francis so regularly that Agnes had given up attempting to silence her in favour of simply ignoring her. She invited her on a hunt, which Muriel had refused, so Agnes had been forced to find other ways to entertain her.

In the end, she had settled for several walks of the grounds before leading her back inside to challenge her to a few games. Spring was struggling this year, and the air was still chilly, so while Agnes would have preferred to remain outside with Qwippe at her feet and a bow in her hand, she couldn't begrudge an afternoon spent at the fireside.

She had finally returned to her bedchamber not long after the sun had set, keen for some much-needed privacy and silence. With the door bolted and at last alone, Agnes shucked off the maddening dress and the shift beneath it, letting it drop carelessly to the floor.

The cold bit at her bare skin. Still avoiding the figure in the mirror, she pulled an oversized tunic, hose and braies from the clothes chest at the foot of her bed. She dressed quickly, already feeling the relief wash over her, then slid beneath the thick covers.

After a moment, there was a soft thump as Qwippe joined her, curling into a tight, white ball at Agnes's feet. At least Qwippe didn't need attentive entertaining; she was happy to snooze, occasionally raising her head and peering at Agnes as if to ensure she was still there.

Finally granted some peace, Agnes could think clearer about her future, and the man who was causing her sister such dreadful anxiety.

Agnes had known she would need to remarry the day she had become a widow. It was what was *expected* of her by society as a still-young woman, no matter her own feelings on both her marital status *and* her apparent womanhood. But she had waited too long. She had sought advice from allies and councillors as to any men who may make a suitable match, but she had assessed them too minutely, scrutinised them too hard.

Barden was the third or fourth potential suitor she had met – and, with luck, he would be the last. She had hoped she would be granted more time to seek out a husband, but since her dismissal of her last suitor – an elderly baron who had slapped her on the backside – her family had resumed their nagging for her to marry Francis.

If she did not wed soon, they would attempt to force her. She could not let them, and the longer she drew out her decision the easier it would be for them.

Her previous marriage to the English Lord Nicholas la Cleve had been a hasty match, a union bartered by important men shouting at each other in dark rooms. A small skirmish, an argument over land, settled before too much more blood could be shed with a hasty marriage between two powerful – but not *too* powerful – families, one from each side of the border. Her parents had intended to wed her to Francis mac Cainnich, the son of a nearby laird – in fact, the agreement had all but been made – but the threat of war had scuppered their plans.

Agnes had no sorrow for the ruined match. The sudden marriage to Nicholas had been as convenient for her as it had been inconvenient for Francis.

Nicholas, as it transpired, was as much a pawn in the game of others as she was. He was a baron, old enough to be her father – perhaps her *father's* father. He was a widower, and she quickly learned that he would not have been seeking a wife had it not been for the incident that forced their union.

He was, under the circumstances, as good a husband as she was likely to have. He mourned deeply for the loss of his wife, which had been many years previously. While other men may have leered and rejoiced at being tied to a young, untouched woman, he did not. There was a gap in his heart – in his *soul* – that no one could fill. Agnes certainly couldn't, and they had fallen into a friendship.

They had only been married for a short while when the illness took his mind. It took his body sometime later. They had no children together: it had caused suspicion at first, but after the illness set in that suspicion was allayed. It would have been impossible for him to sire children. Perhaps it had *always* been impossible: despite what had sounded like years of valiant efforts, he and his wife had produced just one child, who died just before his mother, a victim of the same illness.

They *had* lain together a handful of times, but more through a sense of obligation than much else. Neither wanted the other as a bedmate.

'The problem of love,' he told her once, 'is loss. She was half of my soul. No one can replace her. They could send me a dozen beautiful girls like you' – he took her hand, and she had pretended not to notice that his fingers were shaking – 'but none of them would ever be her.'

Her second marriage would be different. Whether or not she accepted Lord Barden's offer, she would be tied to a younger, more virile man. It was a little thrilling to think that she may find a husband who *excited* her, one who she wished to lie with beyond the need for making children.

The idea of children themselves did not overly worry her. She loved her elder sister Clara's children and felt the room in her heart for where her own would sit one day.

It was the rest that concerned her: the *having* of children, trapped in a changing body that did not feel like her own. True enough, she loved Clara's children, but even being around Clara in the months preceding their births had made her feel unpleasant.

Nicholas had come closer to understanding her than her family, but still even he had not known it all. Only Sara knew the extent of it – how her mind rebelled against her body. She could only imagine what that rebellion could swell into were she with child.

No one would know. She could never tell her husband how she was. But perhaps she could find a man who would give her the space she needed to breathe, either through kindness or disinterest. It would be a trial, she knew. But she would see it through.

Marrying was an awful risk. She had mere days to assess Barden before giving him a firm answer. At least it was longer than many got. At least she had a choice. She would need to trust her instincts, and ignore the rumours swirling around him, no matter *what* her sister said.

She cursed the uncertainty into the still air of her bedchamber. Qwippe stirred, looking up at her. Agnes reached out to scratch her behind the ears.

'Let's get up early,' she said, as the hound blinked at her. 'We'll go for a hunt.'

Qwippe's ears pricked up at the word *hunt*, and she sat up with her paws outstretched.

'Tomorrow,' Agnes insisted. 'Good lass.'

Qwippe huffed, and feeling certain that the creature could understand her perfectly, Agnes settled down deeper beneath the covers.

Chapter 3

Ash

Dawn brought with it a clear, bright sky. Ash peered out across his father's lands through the chamber window. He could see across the whole valley on days like this. He pulled the shutters closed, disappearing back into the shadows.

Today, he would leave his father's keep and head even further north to meet the woman who – by their best estimations – would become his wife.

Cool dread prickled the back of his mind. He forced it down, sinking into the comforting nothingness he usually felt.

They had decided that Raff would remain at Dunlyn. It was the more practical choice, especially when the death of their father was causing ripples in the previously still waters of the Barden family's lands. He would be the only Barden present: Lily and Jo were returning to Oxfordshire that morning. The brewery would not run itself. Ash did not begrudge them that: he, too, would have rather left than endure courting and a wedding.

Ash would not be alone, at least. He was travelling with a small retinue: his steward, Michael, a handful of guards and servants, and Litillwitte. Should the woman he was meeting prove entirely unsuitable or, more likely, a dreadful bore, he could at least take the beast out on the hunt. Litillwitte, of course, was the only one among their numbers whom he would truly relish spending any time with, but it was better than floundering in a stranger's keep alone.

He was lucky that the journey was an easy one. It would take perhaps a week or so to reach la Cleve Castle, along well-used and well-tended roads, and the visit itself would be brief. Most courting periods were: a scant few days to ensure they did not *entirely* loathe each other and hammer out the legal details of merging their two houses. If all went well, Agnes would be returning with Ash to Dunlyn where they would be wed as soon as the banns were read.

It was strange, considering the haste with which it would be carried out. But necessary: Ash needed to do the right thing, for once.

He headed outside to where the carts were being readied. He greeted and said goodbye to Lily and Jo, then found his horse and began to prepare it for the journey. He wasn't sure when Raff and Penn arrived, but could sense them lingering behind him.

Finally, he couldn't stand it any longer.

'Are you going to follow me to la Cleve, too?' he snapped, spinning around. 'Or will I manage to shake you off by then?'

To his annoyance, they both appeared nonplussed by his outburst.

'We only wish to say goodbye,' Raff said, infuriatingly placidly.

'To make sure I really *do* go?' Ash spat. 'Worried I will follow in your footsteps' – he nodded towards Penn – 'and ruin the match before it's even begun?'

Penn raised a single eyebrow at him. That, apparently, was all the response Ash was going to get.

'Is it unwarranted to wish to say goodbye to my brother?' Raff continued, 'Especially in such circumstances?'

Ash wanted to tell him it *was,* in fact, unwarranted. But he relented.

'Fine,' he said. '*Fine.* But stop staring at me like that. It is not as if I am—'

He cut that thought before it reached his tongue. He didn't want to think about it. He went to mount his horse, but was stopped by Raff's hand on his shoulder.

'Ash.' He pulled him into a hug. 'Good luck.'

Reluctantly, Ash hugged him back. 'I fear I will need it.'

Raff chuckled in his grip, then let him go. To Ash's surprise, Penn stepped swiftly forward and took Raff's place, wrapping his arms around Ash's shoulders.

'Do not insult her too greatly,' he said. 'Perhaps . . . just a little, though, or she will be horrified once you return and she sees your true nature.'

Ash shot him a half-smile. 'What sound advice.'

Penn grinned at him as he mounted the horse. Ash thought again on his words after the funeral.

It would be good for you to be friends.

*

Ash found himself growing more anxious the nearer they got to la Cleve Castle. Each step was drawing him closer towards something he didn't want, yet couldn't escape.

The road had been easy, quiet and entirely bereft of bandits and vagabonds. It appeared that nothing deigned to stand between Ash and his own future. They had made better time than they had dared to hope, and Ash felt like a few days of freedom had been snatched from him.

They were riding through managed woodland split with yellow gorse and fields. He had let his mind go carefully blank for most of the journey. But now, so close, the marriage – the *idea* of the marriage – poked at his thoughts, barbed and dangerous. He had sworn that he would never exchange vows with another person. Yet here he was, each step taking him closer to betrayal.

It couldn't be a true betrayal, he tried to remind himself. The man he had vowed himself to was dead. Hundreds of people retook vows. Agnes herself measured amongst their numbers: she had taken vows with her late husband, and if they saw this match through, she would take them again with him.

But that was other people. That was people he did not know, people's opinions he did not care for. After their mother had died, his father had never remarried. When he was young, Ash had thought it showed a certain kind of nobility. After he'd returned from France, he understood. His father had carried those vows with him, lodged in his heart, until he too died and returned to be with their mother.

Ash wished he too could remain faithful. People questioned why he was not married, whereas they had been happy to allow his father's grief. This was something he *had* to do. He had no choice in it: just as he had no choice in becoming earl.

Forgive me, he thought. *Please, forgive me.*

The wind picked up, catching the leaves around his horse's hooves. They passed under the shade of the trees. Bathed in darkness, Ash shivered.

He was apologising to a ghost. And yet he could still feel Oliver beside him – his presence, the heat of him, the trill of his laugh upon the sound of the wind.

He pulled the horse up short, coming to a halt. He was shaking. He could not risk another attack – not so close to Lady Agnes's keep, certainly not in her presence.

'My Lord?' Michael turned in the saddle.

'I need to clear my head.' Ash swung himself down. It was good to have his feet on solid ground. 'Ride ahead. Here.' He passed the reins to the nearest guard. 'I shall meet you at the keep.'

'My Lord—'

I am the earl. Ash didn't say it out loud. He gave Michael a curt nod, lips tight shut, and walked away.

✡

Ash crashed through the undergrowth, stamping through piles of leaves. He hated forests. He hated the dirt and the grabbing branches and the endless brambles snagging on his clothes.

He had intended to clear his head. But the shrubbery and cloying soil was doing very little to calm his spirits. Each step only made him more frustrated, his mind more tangled. The soft silence of nature wasn't a soothing balm, but an echoing cavern that loudened his already turbulent thoughts.

He was making his way back towards the road when there was a scuffle ahead of him. Unperturbed, he strode onwards, and suddenly a great bird burst from the bush beside him in a cacophony of feathers and flapping.

Ash leapt back out of the creature's way, heart pounding.

'What *are* you doing?'

A man emerged around a sharp bend in the path.

He was dressed in hunting gear: a padded gambeson with a cap pulled tight around his head. Ash could see wisps of bright red hair peeking from the edge of the fabric, framing the hunter's brown eyes. His face was long and pointed, with a mole on the height of his cheekbone below his right eye. At his hip was a quiver of arrows, in his hand a well-made bow. He could almost have been described as *pretty,* were it not for the fact that the bow was notched, arrow aimed directly at Ash's chest.

Ash immediately raised his hands in surrender. Even he could not deny that he looked more like a bandit than an earl.

'Do not shoot!' he cried. 'I am not a poacher.'

The man looked unconvinced. 'Oh aye?' he said, in a thick Scottish accent. 'Then who *are* you, sneaking around in our lands?'

Ash clenched his jaw. The man readied the bow. He was a good head shorter than Ash, but no amount of strength could win against an arrow through the heart.

'Ash Barden,' he said, quickly. 'I am—'

Now the bow lowered. 'The *earl*?'

Ash watched as the man's eyes searched his face, settling on the scar. Even in a keep full of strangers, he would be recognisable by that alone.

'It is dangerous to explore alone here if you are unfamiliar with these lands.'

Ash did not appreciate being chastised. 'Is that not true of all lands?'

The man looked unimpressed. 'True,' he said, 'but *our* lands are full of deer traps. You best tread more carefully, my Lord.'

Ash scowled at him. The hunter was too young to be speaking to him in such a way.

'Then I shall watch my path,' he drawled. 'Now *move*.'

He went to push past. The man followed. 'I must insist—'

'Insist? Need I remind you that I am an earl?' Ash did not stop or turn back. 'Run back to your mistress and inform her I have arrived.'

'I do not think—'

'That much is immediately clear.'

'My *Lord*—'

Ash walked faster, better to get away from the irritating man. He kicked his way through a sharp gorse bush, and then—

For an instant, he was suspended. Then he was falling, branches and stones scraping horribly down his back, scratching at his face. He landed with a thud.

Ash stared up. Leaves gently fluttered down around him.

A deer trap. He'd run right into it. The hunter's face appeared over the edge of the hole.

'I did warn you, my Lord.'

The man's expression betrayed what sort of person he thought would be stupid enough to fall into a deer trap. Ash's patience, already worn thin, snapped entirely.

'Clever bastard, aren't you? Are you going to help me out?'

'Not if you call me a bastard.'

Ash smirked. 'I can call you a whoreson, if you'd prefer.'

The hunter vanished. *Shit.*

'Wait!' There was no response. 'Sir?'

After a few moments, the hunter's face reappeared. 'What?'

Ash tried to hide his relief. 'Were you going to leave me?'

'I was considering it.'

'I am sure the lady of the house wouldn't appreciate you leaving me here to die.'

'With the rumours that follow you? I would not be so sure of that.'

'If the *rumours* are so dire then surely the threat of what I may do to you should you refuse me is enough to tempt your hand.'

'Are you threatening me, my Lord?'

Ash glared. It did not have the intended effect.

'Beat me black and blue, if it pleases you,' the hunter said. '*If* you can get out of that hole. I shall wait.'

He folded his arms in a relaxed pose, shifting his weight onto one leg.

'Are you going to help me out of here, or not?' Ash demanded. 'For if you *do* intend to leave me I'd rather you do it already, so I may rot here in peace. Or you could shoot me with that' – he glanced towards the bow – 'to speed up proceedings, if you like. I shan't tell anyone. Although it would truly prove you *are* a bastard.'

For a moment, Ash thought he really would shoot him. 'Do not call me that.'

'It would be easier to call you by your name, if you gave it to me.'

The man sighed. He slung the bow onto his back and got to his knees at the edge of the trap and reached down.

Ash wasn't quite sure how he managed to scramble from the hole. The hunter was significantly smaller than him, but together – the man tugging at Ash's arm as Ash struggled for purchase on the side of the pit – they heaved him out.

They both tumbled gracelessly onto the grass. When Ash looked up, it was into the face of a white, long-haired greyhound. It tilted its head to one side as it examined him. There was a neatly embroidered collar around its neck, and blood on its muzzle.

Ash stood. Beside him, the hunter did likewise. His red hair had slipped from his cap, and he pushed it back, leaving a streak of dirt along the side of his face.

'I will hear *nothing* of this,' Ash demanded. 'Do you hear me? *Nothing*. I do not want word of this spreading.'

The hunter wore a sly smile. 'Of course.'

'And for God's sake, do *not* tell Lady Agnes.'

The smile twitched. 'I would not dare, my Lord.'

'Now—' Ash straightened his tunic as best he could, brushing leaves from his shoulders. 'Show me the way out of this *damned* wood before I twist an ankle.'

They made their way back through the copse in silence. The trees quickly gave way once more to gorse, over which Ash could see the path and the rest of his retinue.

'I shall leave you here, my Lord,' the hunter said. 'There are no traps in the fields, unless you stumble into a gorse bush. I will inform the staff that you are here.'

'See that you do.'

Without bidding him farewell, Ash made his way towards the retinue. It wasn't until he was back on his horse that he realised the hunter had never given him his name.

✡

By the time Ash finally arrived at the gates of la Cleve Castle, his guilt had cleared, but his nerves had not. The hunter had told him he would not inform the mistress of the keep of his fall, but how much could his word be trusted? What if he told the rest of the household? There would be *hilarity* once they were freed from their duties and given the privacy to gossip.

Despite the man's reassurances that he would tell Lady Agnes of Ash's imminent arrival, she was not at the gates when they entered. He was greeted instead by her steward and housekeeper. Trusting Michael to deal with their things, Ash allowed them to lead him indoors to a side room, set for greeting guests. There was a fire roaring in the tiny hearth, a table set with wine and a plate of tarts. Ash sat in the chair closest to the fire, staring at the flames as Litillwitte leaned against his knee. He wondered if his host was keeping him waiting on purpose.

Finally, the door opened.

The figure standing in the doorway could only be Lady Agnes. She was wearing a deep-green gown with sweeping sleeves. Her hair – which was a vibrant red colour – was tied into a tightly woven braid that wrapped around her head like a crown. Her features were thin and pointed. She watched him with the intensity of a fox.

When she stepped into the light of the fire, he could properly see her face and her sharp, brown eyes. There was a mark below her eye, almost like a little heart.

She seemed familiar, somehow. And then he realised – she resembled the man in the woods. He must have been her brother.

Ash suppressed a curse. Of *course* he had made a fool of himself and grievously insulted the brother of the woman he was here to marry.

'Lord Ashwy?' she asked, in a broad Scottish accent.

The use of his full name startled him. 'Aye,' he said. Then: 'Yes. Lady Agnes?'

She gave him a tight smile. 'Indeed. It is a pleasure to finally meet you, Lord Barden.'

His resolve faltered. She was *so* damned familiar. He found himself looking at the sharp angles of her face, the mark beneath her eye. The tone of her voice.

He stood. She raised her eyebrows at him but did not back away. There was a little patch of dirt just above her temple.

He didn't think. He took a step closer, grabbed her by the shoulders and pulled her into the light.

There was no mistaking her. *Him.* The hunter from the woods.

'It was you. Wasn't it?'

'I have no idea what you mean.'

Ash would not be made a fool. 'You've the same mark beneath your eye,' he said. 'And you've mud on your face from where you fell.'

He reached out. The dirt came away beneath his fingers. Agnes swallowed heavily, saying nothing.

'I thought at first perhaps a brother . . .' Ash said. 'But . . . no. That was you out there, wasn't it? Dressed as a man?'

Finally she found her tongue.

'You ought to more carefully watch your words, Lord Barden. I do not know—'

Ash was being made a fool again. He did not have patience for this.

'Yes,' he insisted, 'you do.'

She gave him a long, hard look. His prediction that she would refuse him seemed suddenly like it was going to come to pass: the match abruptly ended. She took a deep breath, never once taking her eyes from him.

'I *told you*—'

'Agnes!'

They both froze. In the open doorway stood a woman with her face stuck in a look of horror.

'My God, Agnes— I will— I will fetch—'

'Wait!'

Agnes shrugged off his grip and gave chase. But she was too late. The woman dashed away, the door shutting heavily behind her. Agnes flung it open, peered into the corridor, then sighed. She did not turn around.

'I am going to find my sister.'

And then she left the room, shutting the door behind her.

Chapter 4

Agnes

On the opposite side of the door, Agnes allowed herself a heartbeat of time to calm. No one had discovered her so easily before.

Something told her that Lord Barden would not go down without a fight. Neither should he, she thought ruefully. He knew what he had seen, and she knew that he had been right. Their match – whatever it may have been destined for – was already over.

When he had pulled her towards him, she had thought, for a strange, dizzying moment, that he was about to kiss her. Which would have been *absurd*, of course, and terribly offensive.

So why had it made her heart beat out of time?

Forcing those thoughts aside, she quickly hurried down the corridor to find her sister. Muriel, it seemed, had vanished. Agnes made a quick search of the lower floors and, being unable to find her, had headed towards the guest chambers.

She nearly collided with a groom halfway down the corridor. He gave her a startled look, bowed, and then dashed on. There was a folded piece of paper gripped tight in his hand.

Agnes pushed the door open without knocking. Muriel jumped from the table at which she had been sitting. There were ink stains on her hands.

'Agnes,' she breathed, rushing over. 'Are you well? Here, sit—'

Muriel guided her to the bed, forcing her down.

'What—'

'Agnes, *please.*' Muriel was desperate. 'I need you to come home. You do not need to marry him.'

'I know I do not need to marry him.'

'Then—'

'But I am not returning to Scotland.'

'But you *must.*'

'I must?'

'You can come home, and marry Francis, and *all will be well.*'

'I will not marry Francis.'

'*Why?*'

Agnes swallowed. Muriel stared at her. Both remained silent.

Muriel backed down first. 'This is because of what happened between you when we were young.'

There was an icy lump in Agnes's stomach. 'I do not know what you're talking about.'

'Yes, you do. You *still* hold that against him, after all these years!'

Agnes bit her lip to keep her words locked behind her teeth. *I will always hold it against him.*

'He was only doing what was right for you. He was only doing what was *best*, Agnes, please—'

'What was *best*?' The words battered through, unstoppable. 'He— he—'

'You still resent him after all this time. Did you learn *nothing*? Are you willing to tie yourself to a man like Lord Barden just so you can avoid Francis?'

'If I tie myself to a man like Lord Barden it will be because that is my *choice*,' Agnes said. 'Francis mac Cainnich has nothing to do with that.'

It was a lie. Muriel knew that too.

'I love you, Agnes, but this *cannot last. Please* come home.'

'No.' Agnes straightened her back. 'I will not. If you think Francis is such a fine choice, then *you* marry him.'

Muriel made a soft, startled sound. Her eyes filled with tears. She turned – hesitated – then fled from the room. Agnes sat down heavily on the bed, her head in her hands.

She had no doubt at all that her siblings and parents loved her. But they didn't understand her. They didn't know her as she wanted to be known, as she knew herself. And try as she might, she couldn't make them see that person, either. They could only see the person they had raised or grown alongside, the person they expected her to be.

Her family loved her. But oftentimes she wondered if they loved *her*, or just the person they imagined her to be.

She headed back towards the room in which she had left Barden. If she could not deal with the problem of her sister, she could deal with him, at least. And Muriel was not entirely wrong: her first impressions of his character had been very poor. At least he was unique, she supposed. Unforgettable in his own way. He had been the first of her suitors to call her a whoreson.

And . . . *well.* She was not blind. Were he not being difficult, he would be handsome. *Very* handsome. He was tall, far taller than herself, and his dark hair and eyes held a certain intenseness. His shoulders were broad, his arms wide. He was scruffy – his red beard unkept and hair shaggy – in a way which her mother would have hated but she found very appealing.

She found it difficult to blame him for his poor mood. He was grieving and embarrassed after making a fool of himself. What sort of idiot fell into a *deer trap,* for God's sake? To add to all that, the insult of discovering the woman he had come to meet was a degenerate? She would be impressed if he remained in the keep at all.

As she approached the room, she heard shouting – several men, the clanking of armour, a dog barking.

What in *God's name* was happening? She dashed around the corner and into a scene of chaos. Barden was on his feet, flanked by a pair of household guards. His dog – the huge, grey deerhound – was barking at them.

'Good God, men!' At her voice, the guards turned. 'What is going on here?'

'Your sister called for us, my Lady,' one said, chin high. 'Said that you needed assistance with this brute.'

'Will you *unhand him,* please,' Agnes said, trying to keep herself calm.

'But Lady Muriel said—'

'But *nothing.* Lord Barden has done nothing to warrant such behaviour. Unhand him or I will have you both removed. Now!'

The guards shared a look, then took a swift step away from Barden, who looked deeply relieved.

'Thank you,' Agnes said. 'You are dismissed.'

The two guards hurried away. Barden gave her a strained look.

'Shall we sit?' she asked.

He followed her back into the side room. She resisted the urge to bolt the door behind her.

'I am sorry for worrying your sister,' he said, as soon as she had settled into a chair.

Agnes was surprised. She had not expected him to apologise.

'It is . . . fine,' she said slowly. 'And I must apologise to *you* for her taking such drastic action. Had I known what she intended to do . . .' She deflated. 'I am very sorry, Lord Barden. I do hope you can forgive her.'

'Of course,' he said. 'She was worried for your safety. Any worthwhile sibling would do the same.'

Agnes could not help feeling a little bitter. 'We are currently struggling with some . . . differing opinions.'

'Oh.'

'About this arrangement.' Agnes gestured between them.

'*Oh.*'

'It is not your fault,' she clarified. 'Not *entirely* your fault.'

Barden barked a laugh. 'That is cheering to hear. Most things *are* entirely my fault.'

Some of the tension left Agnes's shoulders. At least Barden was not offended at the mess with Muriel: many men would be, taking her behaviour as an accusation against his character. It did not, however, lessen her other concern of how he had discovered her in the grounds.

'Lord Barden,' she began, already dreading what she knew she needed to say. 'I must confess. Our discussion before Muriel interrupted us . . .' She took a deep breath. She would not insult his intelligence. 'You were correct. It *was* I who found you.'

He winced. She steeled herself, ready for the rejection.

'In that case, my Lady,' he said, 'I must apologise again.'

Agnes stared at him. '*What?*'

'For the things I said to you! My God!' He dragged a hand down his face with a laugh. 'I called you a— Oh God's teeth, I called you a—'

'Lord Barden.'

'Truly, my Lady. Had I known it was you . . .'

She raised an eyebrow, amused. 'You would have said those things to another man without apology, I take it?'

'Quite plainly I would have, yes,' he said. 'I did not mean to offend you. Or rather – I did, of course I did – but . . .' He stuttered over his words, eyebrows tightly knitted together. 'I apologise. Truly. It has been a difficult time.'

Agnes paused before responding. She truly could not understand him.

'Lord Barden,' she began, speaking slowly, 'you are worried that I am offended because you *cursed* at me?'

He nodded. She could have laughed, were she not about to ruin everything.

'I am sorry to say, it is *you* who ought to be leveraging offence.'

'Whatever do you mean? You pulled me from that pit, and you *tried* to warn me of it, but I was being too damn stupid to listen to you. How could you have caused offence?'

Perhaps he had hit his head during the fall. Perhaps he was mocking her.

'Any other man upon finding the *woman* he has ridden so far to court dressed as and behaving as a man would be . . . shocked,' she said. '*Appalled*.'

Barden blinked. His mouth opened – slow, brutal realisation. 'Oh.'

'If you wanted to turn around and return to Dunlyn you would be well within your rights.'

Barden drummed his fingers on the table. He peered into the fire, deep in thought. Agnes could not stand this waiting.

'Lord Barden?'

Finally, he spoke. 'It will take more than that to shock me, my Lady. And frankly . . . it would be within *your* rights to have me removed for insulting you.'

'I do not intend to do that.'

'And *I* do not intend to leave.'

For the first time in a long time, Agnes felt out of her depth.

'Lord Barden,' she said at last, 'I have heard many interesting things about you. May I ask you something?'

'You may,' he said, cautiously.

'Did you start that brawl at your father's funeral?'

He barely even hesitated. 'Aye, I did.'

'Why?'

'... my sister,' Barden said, after a long pause. Agnes waited for him to continue. 'My cousin insulted her. Said she ought to be— to be forced.' His voice was stony. 'He said that was the only way she would be made a wife, if someone *forced* her. I could not let him talk about her in that way.'

Agnes's stomach clenched. She found herself agreeing with him. The confession cast the incident, and the other whispers that followed him, in a new light.

'Thank you for telling me,' she said. 'I know it is difficult, but those rumours ...'

Ash nodded. 'I understand. You would be mad not to seek the truth.'

Agnes relaxed into the chair. Despite it all, it felt easy.

'Would you care for a tour of the grounds?' she asked.

He grinned. 'Only if you swear not to lead me into any more traps.'

'You led *yourself* into that trap.'

'In my rush to get away from *you*.'

'Barden, you are truly unique.' Agnes laughed. She stood, lingering beside his chair. 'Thank you again. For being honest with me.'

He looked genuinely relieved. 'Thank *you* for giving me the chance to *be* honest. Lead on, my Lady.'

Chapter 5

Ash

Ash waited in the hall as Agnes went to fetch her sister to chaperone them, as it would be improper for them to tour the grounds alone. This was good sense, and besides: he needed to apologise to her.

He was surprised, then, when Agnes returned from the upper floor looking red-faced and flustered and completely alone.

Muriel had gone. She had left while Agnes had been speaking to Ash, vanished without a word. The grooms confirmed it: she had taken her guards and fled.

'I . . . am sorry, my Lady,' Ash hazarded, unsure what else he could say.

Agnes appeared more frustrated than distraught. 'As I said . . .' She took a deep breath. 'We have had some disagreements these past few weeks. Perhaps it is for the best.'

It would not behove him to pry. Instead, he was introduced to Sara, Anges's lady's companion. She was straight-backed and serious, with dark skin and darker eyes. He wondered where her family hailed from. She eyed him closely and critically.

'My Lord.'

Ash bowed to her in greeting. She did not seem impressed.

Agnes also sent for her hound: the beast from the woods. When the kennel master brought her in, she sat in perfect poise at Agnes's side, clearly waiting for a command. By contrast, Litillwitte had plodded into the hall beside Ash and was now doing his very best impression of a dead sheep at Ash's feet.

'Shall we start with the grounds?' Agnes said.

The la Cleve grounds were nowhere near as fine as those around Dunlyn, but they provided ample space for hunting. As they reached the expansive gorse that edged the keep, Agnes looked down at the hound at her feet.

'Go on, then.' She gave a sharp whistle. 'Away, Qwippe!'

The dog, who had been calm and still until that moment, dashed into the undergrowth in a blur of white.

'Good God,' Ash muttered.

Beside him, Agnes smiled. 'She is a wonderful creature. *Marvellous* hunter. She'll run around in there for a while, flush out a few hares, then spend the rest of the day asleep beside the fire.'

There was another white blur as Qwippe emerged from a thicket of heather before vanishing again. Ash could not help but watch as the beast ran, born for the hunt. A grouse suddenly burst from the bushes, shuddering up into the sky and up and over their heads. Agnes watched, looking pleased, shielding her eyes from the sun.

'I should have brought my bow,' she said to Sara thoughtfully.

Ash looked down at Litillwitte. 'Do you not wish to go and join her?' he said.

The beast tilted his head to one side, then sat unceremoniously on Ash's foot.

'I shall assume that means *no*,' he said. Beside him, he was sure he heard Agnes snigger.

It was some time before Qwippe emerged, her pristine fur full of twigs and the limp body of an enormous hare between her teeth. Agnes greeted her effusively, praising her skill and passing her a scrap of meat from the pouch at her hip.

'I shall have to take the hare to the kitchens,' she said. 'I am sure they'll have use for it, even if it's only for feeding the dogs.' She paused. She seemed uncertain, and Ash realised she was not used to having to entertain. 'Do you wish to join me,' she asked, 'or remain out here?'

Ash peered around. It was bright and clear, and the walk had done him good, although he was loath to admit it. But he was not here for nature walks. He was here to wed.

'I think I'll join you,' he said. 'Come, Litillwitte.'

Litillwitte gave him a long look. Then rolled onto his back, tongue lolling obscenely from his mouth.

'He is a curious thing,' Agnes said, watching him.

Ash laughed sharply. 'He's a damn *idiot*,' he said. 'Father named him Litillwitte, but frankly I doubt that he has any wit at all. He's a good hunter, if you'd believe it.' They watched the dog roll in the dirt. 'When he wants to be.'

Agnes's hound was observing Litillwitte from a careful distance. Ash had never seen such a look of disdain on an animal's face before.

'He attached himself to me when Father died,' Ash continued. 'Now I cannot be rid of him.'

'He seems very . . . loyal,' Agnes said.

Ash snorted. 'That is certainly one way to describe him. Come on, you beast, or I shall leave you out here.'

Litillwitte only looked at him. Ash sighed, keen not to admit defeat to a dog.

'Here.'

Agnes was offering him one of the scraps of meat she had used to reward Qwippe.

'Oh. Thank you.'

Ash took it from her gently. Their fingers brushed. The meat had been warmed by her hand, soft beneath his fingertips.

He held it out towards Litillwitte. At the prospect of food, he sat up, sniffing.

'Oh no,' Ash said. 'Come. You *come*. And then you may have this.'

He held the scrap of meat higher. It seemed to work – with a huge sigh, Litillwitte heaved himself to his feet and came to stand at Ash's side.

'Good boy.' He dropped the scrap of meat into Litillwitte's mouth.

Wiping his hand on his cloak, Ash looked up. He caught Agnes looking quickly away as he did.

✡

'No,' Ash looked down at the chequered board on the table in front of Agnes. 'No, absolutely not.'

'Afraid I will beat you, Barden?'

'I *know* you will beat me.'

As the morning had melded into afternoon, thick clouds had rolled in, and the ensuing rain had forced them all indoors. Sara had settled herself beside the fire with some embroidery, Ash's steward was poring over account books, and Agnes had set up a game of chess. She smiled at him, that fox-like expression back.

If he were at home, he would refuse. He *hated* chess, if only because he was so bad at it.

But he was not at home. Thankful that he had a mug of ale to soothe him through the process, he sat opposite Agnes and gestured for her to begin.

'I warn you,' he said, 'I am very bad.'

Agnes rolled her eyes at him and made the first move.

Barely any time had passed before she leaned back in her chair, arms folded across her chest.

Ash glanced at her, the mug upon his lips. 'What?'

'I am trying to decide,' she said slowly, 'if you truly *are* this poor at chess, or if you are simply pretending to ensure I do not ask you to play again.'

He spluttered on the ale.

'Ah,' she said. '*Not* pretending, then.'

'I told you I was poor at this.'

'Yes, but not *this* poor.'

Ash glowered.

'I could teach you.'

He looked up. He was expecting her to be mocking him, but her expression was sincere.

'What?'

'Surely you get bored of dice and draughts?'

'Well . . .'

'You truly *are* afraid,' she said mockingly. 'At least *try*.'

She was challenging him. His resolve snapped, and he was suddenly on his feet. The table wobbled. Even Sara stopped her embroidery to look at him, the dogs curled at their feet raising their heads in surprise.

Ash's mouth opened and shut stupidly. Then he whistled towards Litillwitte and strode from the room.

✲

That had been a stupid thing to do.

Ash stood beside the gorse in the rain, feeling unutterably foolish. At his side, Litillwitte looked up at him wetly.

'Stop it,' Ash said. The dog did not look away. 'I know!' he shouted, startling a bird from the nearest hedge. 'I *know*.'

He needed to get a grip on himself. Agnes didn't need to be his friend, but she had to at least tolerate him, and she never would if he continued walking this path.

He sighed, running his hand through his wet hair.

If he returned now, he would look even more foolish. But more foolish still would be to remain out here, in the rain, cursing the world and himself. There was no going back to what had been. There was only now.

He wiped droplets from his eyelashes, turned heel, and headed back towards the shape of the keep.

He returned to find Agnes making her way across the courtyard, wrapped in a thick wool cloak. She eyed him, waiting for him to come to her.

'It is raining,' she said.

Ash shivered. 'I now realise that.'

She gave him another of those assessing looks. 'Go and change. I'll have the cook warm some wine.'

When Ash returned in fresh clothes, his hair dried as much as he could manage, he found Agnes sat at a table in the side chamber she'd met him in on the day of his arrival. Beside the fireplace sat a pair of steaming wooden mugs on a small table, and in front of her, a chessboard, ready to play.

Ash sat and took one of the mugs.

'Show me, then.'

✡

The days in la Cleve Castle passed with surprising swiftness. Ash *still* hated chess, but it kept him busy.

He needed to keep busy. Much of their time was for them alone – what Penn had called, all cheek, the *courting period*. Ash was not very adept at courting. Olly had just happened, as easy and as unstoppable as falling.

He was trying not to compare the two circumstances. Olly had been want, and passion, and *love*. This was nothing like that. Yet still the thought of Olly crowded him when he and Agnes were together. This would have been so easy, were it him.

After that first day and his pointless tantrum, Ash was learning that Agnes was the sort of person he could get along with. The sort of person his *family* would get along with, too. She had absolutely no tolerance whatsoever of his moods, but neither was she cruel – just firm, with little patience for his sourness. When she laughed at his cynicism or along with his boorish jokes, his chest tightened to realise he had pleased her.

He found that he liked her, and that alone was enough to leave him perturbed. Neither of them had confirmed the match, but he had promised that the visit to la Cleve Castle would only last a week at most. His time was running out.

He thought on it that evening during supper – roasted pheasant, caught that morning. The food was good, and as Ash picked tender meat from the bone he wondered if Joan, Dunlyn's cook, would resent having another in her kitchen. She almost certainly would: she resented having *him* in her kitchen, and he could only imagine the sort of war that could be waged by two cooks battling for space.

They would need to discuss who from Agnes's household would be coming with her should they merge their houses, and who would remain at la Cleve. There were so many things to consider – people, wages, lives. The castle and land would be his by law, and they would need someone to look after it.

He was sure they would be able to find some way to deal with it. Perhaps after their marriage Agnes would want to return; no doubt she would resent being tied to Ash for so long and would want her own space. He would grant her that much – it would no doubt cause talk, but rumours had shadowed him for so long that he couldn't find the room to care for one more.

It was strange, thinking so plainly of his own future. He was making choices for a man who did not exist.

The evening waned. As had become customary, Agnes challenged Ash to a game of chess – and as was equally customary, he groused about the offer for several minutes before refilling his mug and joining her.

It was tricky to focus with the fire burning so warmly and the ale swirling his head. Trickier than usual. But he was getting a better grip on the game in just these few days, and Agnes – for all her sarcasm – was a patient teacher.

Reasonably patient. She knew, somehow, when he was pretending to be bad and when he truly was being inept. It was infuriating.

She went first, as always, and for some time the game passed in contemplative silence. But when Ash, his mug empty and his eyes drooping, went to grab for the nearest piece and move it whenever the damn thing fit, she gave a small, pointed cough.

He looked up at her, hand poised above the piece. She didn't say anything, just raised her eyebrows and pursed her lips.

Something shivered down his spine. Ash flexed his fingers, sat up straighter, and tried again.

She beat him, but she had a smile on her face as she did. As he passed her to retire to his chambers, she stood, placing a warm hand on his shoulder.

'Very good.'

Something tightened within him, something that felt familiar yet foreign.

'Are you going to pat me on the head and feed me a scrap of meat from your skirts as well?' he teased.

She didn't remove her hand. The feeling grew, seeping lower.

'Only if you think it will improve your chess skills.'

'It certainly cannot make them worse.'

She shot him a smile, gave a brief nod, and left him to head back towards his chambers. He took the stairs quickly, feeling strangely untethered. It was an odd, floating feeling – one that he couldn't define. He slumped onto the bed. He was too warm, his face and skin flushed, fingertips tingling. It was the ale, he thought, and the heat of sitting so close by the fire. Nothing more.

Litillwitte settled himself into his usual place against Ash's leg, peering up at him.

'I am all right,' Ash muttered, more to himself than the dog.

He readied himself to sleep, splashing his face with cool water then scrambling beneath the coverlet. Litillwitte heaved himself up beside him, his warm bulk comforting, even if he made the whole room stink of wet fur.

Agnes flicked back into his memory, unbidden. The look she had given him across the chessboard. The heat of her hand against his shoulder. The smile. The teasing. Something new and slithering coiled in his belly, a feeling he knew. A feeling he didn't.

Slowly, Ash passed into the dark. And then—

A low voice purred in his ear, almost melodious, almost like thunder.

'Ashel . . .'

Hands gripped his wrists, his legs, his ankles. His head was buried in pillows, face pressed against the linen, mouth open in a gasp.

'*God,* Ashel, my Ash—' A delicious hardness pressed against his backside, teasing him. '*Yes.*'

There were slippery sheets beneath his hands, ones that he couldn't quite grasp, no matter how he tried. The voice came from everywhere: behind him, under him, right beside his ear in a warm rasp.

Ash sunk lower into the bed. The person behind him still gripped him, digging fingers into the most tender of flesh. He ground himself down against the sheets with a groan that formed in his throat but never escaped his mouth, his words caught.

'You're so good, Ash, so good—'

Ash tried to open his eyes, but when he did, all he could see was red-tinged darkness.

'*Please—*'

The word came out with no sound at all, his mouth opening and closing in a silent beg. He didn't know what he was asking for – to be entered, to be granted release, to be able to open his eyes and *see* . . .

He needed to see him. He tried to twist around, but his arms were stuck to the sheets as if pinned there, as if the bed and his flesh were carved from the same immovable stone.

'I am here, Ashel.'

Ash knew he was. He could hear him, he could *feel* him, but it wasn't enough. He had to see.

He wrenched harder at his arms. There was a sound behind him. A touch, light as a cobweb, to his face.

Ash forced his eyes open.

Woollen blankets. White-knuckled hands. He pushed himself back, turned in the grip that still held him, wrapping his legs around a waist more familiar than his own.

Oliver stared down at him, his expression all dark lust and glowing devotion. He looked like he always had.

Except the right side of his head was a tangled mess of blood and hair.

'There you are,' Olly said. 'I thought you'd forgotten me.'

Ash's heart thudded unpleasantly in his chest. 'Never.'

Olly sighed, then leaned closer, till their lips were brushing.

'Olly?'

'I love you.' Blood smeared across Olly's lips.

'I love you too,' Ash whispered. 'Of course I do.'

The blood seeped lower, spreading across his face. 'Do you?'

He heaved Ash up, then took his hands. His skin was like *ice*. He placed a frozen kiss to the backs of Ash's fingers.

When he pulled away, there was something nestled in Ash's palm. He unfurled his hand.

Olly's ring. Ash looked up at him. 'Olly . . .'

The blood oozed further, coating him, covering him thickly in darkness. He jerked back, as if something had hooked around his middle.

'Olly!'

And then he was gone, flung backwards into the blackness. Ash lifted himself up, ready to give chase, but his legs were wrong and twisting around each other as he scrambled down the bed. He pulled himself to the edge, using all his strength. Below was nothing but a huge, dark void.

'Olly!'

Chapter 6

Agnes

The letter arrived while she and Sara were playing dice in her solar. Agnes took it from the serving girl curiously but tossed it aside as soon as she recognised the handwriting.

This was the *third* letter Muriel had sent since leaving. Agnes's first thought was to throw it into the fire. She didn't want to know what Muriel had to say.

But that was foolish. Instead, she picked it up, tossed it into the wooden box within which she kept all her correspondence, and snapped the lid shut.

There was a rap at the door. Beneath the table, Qwippe sat up. Agnes, too, stilled. If it was yet another letter, they could go hang.

'Enter.'

The door opened. It was not another servant but Barden.

'I did not see you in the hall,' he said. 'You appear to be busy. Apologies, I will—'

'No, no.' Agnes stood, beckoning him inside. 'I have received another letter.'

'From your family?'

He was sharp. He tried to hide it, but it was there.

'Indeed.'

'Are they well?'

She wondered if that was the question he really wanted to ask. She considered lying to him, but relented quickly. The marriage seemed more likely every day: he needed to know the truth.

'I cannot say,' she said, leaning on the table. 'As I have not read their letters. I *know* what they will demand of me, and I have no desire to capitulate to them.'

Barden raised his eyebrows. 'Oh?'

'They do not want me to marry you. They have their hearts set on a . . . a family friend. Francis mac Cainnich.'

'Who is he?'

The truth of *that* was too painful: Barden did not need to know it.

'I have known him since we were young,' she explained. 'Rich, powerful. Scottish. We were promised to each other when we were babes. And then of course I married Nicholas, and now that he is dead, Francis – and my family – think that I belong to him.'

'Hence why they do not wish for us to wed.'

'Precisely. And since Nicholas's death I have come into lands and wealth that Francis would sorely love to call his own.'

He scowled, scratching at his scar. 'Of course.'

Agnes wanted to reach up and stop him – she could only imagine what sort of damage he did to the poorly healed skin with all his picking. She did not: it would be far too intimate.

'Why were you looking for me?' she said instead.

His expression slipped. He looked worried.

'I wondered if we may talk.'

He looked *very* worried. Anxiety hardened in Agnes's stomach. Had he come to refuse her? If he did, it would make her family's determination even stronger.

'Of course,' she said, cautiously. 'Sara . . . would you give us a moment?'

Sara gave her a knowing look before seeing herself out of the room.

'Would you care to talk over a game?'

She waved a hand towards the chess set. It would do her good to have something else to focus on, a way to channel her thoughts, if Barden really *was* here to refuse her hand.

He nodded, but said nothing. Agnes quickly set up the pieces, gesturing for him to take the seat opposite her. The game started slowly. But it was clear that Barden was showing his usual impatience from the outset.

'Are you—'

'Agnes.' Barden moved a piece with unthinking swiftness. 'When we wed—' He made a strange, strangled noise. '*If* we wed . . . I need you to understand that our union will be a contract above all else. An *arrangement*.'

Agnes made her own move. That was her understanding of the matter, too. She thought he was aware of that.

'Of course.'

'I—' Ash stilled, his hand floating over a piece. 'I have made vows before,' he said, staring at the chequered surface.

Something was being offered. The fear that Ash had come to call off the match began to fade, something more sinister beneath.

'I thought you were unmarried?' She curled it into a question.

'I am.'

'A widower, then? I thought someone would have told—'

'I am not a widower.' He moved another piece.

Agnes kept her eyes on the board instead of Barden's face. There was more here. She shuffled a pawn forward – a useless move, designed to buy more time.

'We promised—' Barden said, at last. A sentence with no ending.

'You made vows, which you could not see through?'

Barden said nothing, just moved another piece. His silence was an admission, heavier for its stillness. She wondered what unsuitability had stopped those vows from turning into something more. He did not seem the sort of man who would rush into marriage with a stranger if he had no choice. If he'd made a vow to another, he would uphold that, she was sure.

Which meant that the vow had broken, in some way. Through parting, or time, or—

She moved her piece. 'And now? What happened to her?'

Something cracked in Barden's expression. Without pause, he grabbed his king and shoved it towards Agnes's knight – a clear forfeit.

'Dead.'

'Ash—'

He was on his feet and was gone. The door slammed behind him with such force that the knight toppled over.

Agnes picked it up and rolled it between her fingers. She wondered who the woman who had inspired such devotion had been. And it *was* devotion – there was no mistaking the pain in Barden's eyes as that single, horrible syllable had fallen to the board between them.

Quietly, she set the pieces back into place.

✡

The conversation with Barden had unsettled her. She left the room sometime after he had, keen not to appear as if she were chasing him, and paused at one of the windows.

The sun was high and bright, the air crisp and clear.

It was a good day for a hunt. It was a good day to be *her*. She needed the relief of it, especially after that conversation. She could already sense the unsettled feeling beneath her skin. Back in her chambers, she swiftly undressed, replacing her shift with hose and undershirt before reaching into the very bottom of her clothes chest for her cuirass.

To call it a cuirass was not quite accurate. It was a thick garment that finished just below her ribs with ties beneath her arms, somewhere between an arming doublet and a gambeson. It was sleeveless, secured with straps over her shoulders. She had sewn it herself: a layer of linen, a thick layer of wool, and a layer of boiled leather all held tight together with sturdy thread. As she pulled it out, she fiddled at the seams. It was becoming loose again – the leather growing too supple. She would have to make another.

She slid the cuirass on over the undershirt and began to tighten the lacing. The tightness and padding transformed her, the curve of her breasts, which had never been particularly large to start with, flattened.

She'd made the first of many iterations of the garment when she was still young, fashioned haphazardly out of a stolen gambeson. She'd started the project in a moment of desperation: she had been binding her breasts with cloth bandages for years, and it *hurt*. She had needed a better solution.

Since then, she'd tweaked the design every time she outgrew it or wore it out until she had landed upon something that seemed to work reliably. She reused as much as she could, repurposing the boiled leather when it wore out or changed shape.

She ran her hands over her chest and down her sides with a soft, easy smile. It was tight around her chest, but she could *breathe* for the first time in days. She pulled the rumpled disguise of her dress back on, then headed from her chambers into the yard to fetch Qwippe and her bow.

No one attempted to stop her as she walked from the manor towards the woods. Once beneath the canopy of trees, she made her way to the disused woodsman's hut.

The hut had not been fit for purpose since before Agnes had arrived. Where it once contained food and supplies, now all that was left were a few half-decayed chairs and the wooden chest that Agnes had dragged there herself.

It was full of clothes – things she had bought and stolen and, in some cases, made herself, hidden away where no one would find them. After tossing aside her gown, Agnes pulled on a tunic – old and faded, perfect for hunting, with loose fabric that finished the job of hiding her silhouette. She slung a belt low around her waist and then after a moment's pause grabbed a thin walking cloak; this early into spring there was still a chill in the air. She grabbed her cap, too, using it to cover her hair and tying it beneath her chin to hide some of her face.

There. She stepped through the ruined doorway of the hut and out into the woods, smiling as the spring sun hit her skin.

Like this, she could relax. Very rarely was she seen, and by and large those who did see her overlooked her.

The first time she had been spotted by a servant she had hastily constructed a tale about running into Lord la Cleve and his wife, and had claimed that Lady Agnes had given her – *him* – permission to hunt in the grounds: a show of camaraderie with a fellow Scot.

It had been a risky lie, and she had been forced to rush back to the hut and quickly return to her woman's clothes before the servant could come to find her to verify the tale. She had confirmed that she had met a young Scotsman in town, told the staff that he was a member of a neighbouring lord's household, and ensured word spread that they grant him use of the grounds and lands. Nicholas had watched her with a close, amused eye.

When the housekeeper had turned to him to confirm the story, Agnes's heart had lodged in her throat. And yet, to her great surprise, he had verified her account.

Afterwards, he'd given her an arched smile and said, in that teasing way of his: 'What are you up to, wife?'

It had only been later that Agnes realised he must have assumed the mysterious Scotsman was her lover. And it was later still – *much* later, just before his sudden illness – when he discovered the truth of the thing.

She didn't know if it was his nature or his illness that made him indifferent towards the revelation. He didn't truly understand it – as far as he was concerned, she was just swapping clothes. Dressing up like a child in their parent's things.

Now, she was rarely interrupted when wandering the grounds. She was adept at keeping out of the way regardless, and until Barden's quick discovery the only one who recognised her when she was dressed like this – besides Sara – was Qwippe.

Her quiver bounced against her hip as she walked, Qwippe a little way ahead sniffing out scents. This was how things should be: this was the freedom she craved. It was the freedom she would *lose*, if wed to Francis. It was not even a fear: it was a fact. He would find out, he would stop her, he would punish her.

She swallowed the thought down, keeping her eyes up at the treetops. They rustled pleasingly in the spring breeze, the sound like a mighty wave crashing.

She sent Qwippe out and away with the smallest hand gesture.

It took mere moments before there was a discordant bark. She readied the bow.

The tension in her body seemed to flow into the weapon, down the string, filling it with the coiled, unshakable energy running through her bones. With each arrow loosed, each one notched, each shot made – even when they flew through the trees, hitting nothing – the tension eased, channelling out.

The sunlight dappled against her skin, warming her, soothing her mind. A hare bounded through the brushes ahead of her.

She took aim.

Chapter 7

Ash

Another mistake. Another mark against his name.

Ash stared out of the window of the guest chamber. He should have been more patient, should have allowed Agnes more time to ask questions. But he'd been assaulted with the memory of Olly's face on the edge of that field in France, and it had overwhelmed him.

A shape in the field beyond the window caught his eye: a flash of white amongst the green and brown. Qwippe. There was no mistaking the hound's speed as she dashed across the gorse. Sure enough, there was someone out there with her, a lad in hunting gear with a bow in his hand.

Ash looked closer. It was Agnes. She really *did* look like a young man. It was remarkable. He remembered her anxieties when he had confronted her, her quick denial and eventual acceptance. She had insisted that he should be offended, but such a response had not even *occurred* to him. It would be unthinkable, given Lily's nature – and his own – when it came to blurring the confines of one's sex. Given all he had done with Olly, and what Olly had done *to* him, it would make him a hypocrite of the worst sort to damn her for such choices.

God curse him, he needed to speak to her. He rose from his spot by the window, called to Litillwitte, and hurried outside.

*

'Agnes!'

Ash jogged across the gorse, already breathless by the time he reached Agnes's side. She spun around with a shocked expression, speaking before he could.

'Barden. Is everything all right?'

'Yes,' he said, realising she must have assumed he was in some panic. 'I spied Qwippe from the manor and thought I could join you. If you allow me, that is. I wished to apologise for leaving so . . . abruptly.'

She gave him a knowing look.

'It is clearly a difficult subject,' she said diplomatically. 'You need not apologise.'

'Yet I could have behaved a *little* less like a cur,' he said.

'Perhaps.' She looked around. 'Do you hunt?'

Ash shook his head. 'Not typically,' he said. 'I am invited on hunts often enough, but rarely do I truly partake. My brother, now, my brother *loves* it. I leave such things to him, where I can.'

She was watching him closely. Too closely. He could not help but ramble, filling the silence with empty words.

'Although of course, now his arm—'

'Barden.'

He shut his mouth. 'Yes?'

'You are *truly* not shocked by this?'

Once again, he was lost. 'By what?'

'By *this*—' She gestured at herself.

Oh. 'Not at all,' he said. 'It would be – *well,* considering my own—' He quickly stopped himself. 'My *sister*—'

He had nearly given himself away. Agnes had not seemed to notice, instead now looking deeply intrigued.

'Your sister . . . ?' she prompted carefully.

How to even begin?

'It is rather complicated.' Ash sighed. 'And it is not a tale she – or *any* of us – wish to spread.'

'I understand,' Agnes said quickly. 'Do not feel as if you must tell me.'

'Although . . .'

Ash paused. If they *were* to wed, Agnes would meet Lily soon enough and see her for herself; it was not as if Lily was adept in holding her tongue.

'A while ago she vanished from the keep,' he explained. 'She stole some men's clothes and old armour, cut off her hair and disguised herself as a knight. She entered a *tournament*. Did very well, by all accounts,' he added, with pride.

Agnes gaped at him. '*What?* Why?'

'She was trying to save her friend from marriage. She did it, too. I think . . .' He laughed, unable to help it. 'I think you two would get along, truly. Although she is very busy with the brewery, so it may take some time for you to meet.'

'Your *sister* runs a brewery?'

'She does.'

'But you are an *earl*?'

'That I am.' Ash grinned. 'It is . . . God's bollocks, it is complicated. *Very* complicated. You know, I assume, of our problems in Oxford?'

They had never discussed it before, but *everyone* had heard tale of their scuffle with the de Foucart family and their bartering for Raff's freedom.

'Of course.'

'It is all to do with that, and Lily's marriage . . .' He dragged a hand down his face, picking at his scar. 'God, but it *is* complicated. When you return – when *we* return . . . I will explain it all. It feels wrong to talk about it without them here. I . . . I apologise.'

'It is quite all right,' Agnes said. 'I understand. You do not wish to spread rumours?'

'Quite. I wonder if we *both* fear rumour, my Lady,' he said, chuckling. 'Or is it my Lord? My Lord Forrett?'

Agnes's face fixed into an odd little expression, her lips parted. And then she laughed along too, the sound bright and loud.

'What would that make *you*, if we wed?' she said.

'Lord, I cannot say.'

Ash shook his head. She seemed pleased with him. He wanted to maintain that, he realised – wanted to give her something to compensate for being shackled to him.

'You enjoy dressing like this?'

She took a moment to respond, as if he had asked something more difficult.

'Yes,' she said at last. 'Yes, I . . . I do.'

'And your late husband allowed it?'

'He did.'

Ash nodded. 'I want this to *work*, Agnes, I think we both have our reasons for needing to wed. For marriage, and heirs, and the whole damn mess of it. I know you do not need my permission to do . . . well, to do anything, if I have judged you right. But if – when?' He made it into a question, looking at her. 'When we wed . . . I do not intend to force you to stop . . . this.' He gestured at her uselessly.

She stared at him. 'You will not stop me?'

'I will not. I doubt I *could*. But I will not try, either.'

She swallowed. Her silence was deafening.

'*When* we wed?' she asked, eventually.

Relief, smooth and easy. 'If you agree to the match.'

'You're a surly bastard with too many secrets who drinks too much,' Agnes said, failing to hold back a smile.

'And you're a snappish fox of a woman who dresses as a man,' Ash countered, grinning.

'What a fine pair we make.' Agnes extended her hand. 'Yes, then. I agree.'

He took her hand. Her fingertips were calloused. At their feet, the dogs sat side by side, watching them with interest.

'I think we make a good match, Barden.'

Ash squeezed her fingers. 'I think we do.'

Chapter 8

Noll

A song in a language he had tried to forget. The smell of blood. Pain that came in like a huge, slow wave.

He was trapped in a tiny room. Stone and wood. Rust on the walls. Damp on the floor, seeping into his bones. Above, a tiny window.

His hands were tied. His head was ringing, a horrible pressure throbbing around the right of his skull, behind his eye. His mouth tasted of blood and dirt. He spat. One of his own teeth fell out. It sat glistening whitely on the half-obscured floor like a star.

'Noll.'

The voice invaded, clambering in through the window. The room shifted, blurred.

'Noll!'

There was a hand gripping his arm. He turned to look at the person shaking him, but his face faltered and swirled.

'Wake up!'

With a horrendous groan, Noll rolled onto his side, his eyes cracking open.

The room was gone. He was back in the tiny loft that had served as his living space this past year or so. Beside him, kneeling at his side and already fully dressed, Pepper was shaking his arm.

'Good,' he said, finally letting go. 'Get up. You're to see John, remember?'

Noll blinked sluggishly as the memory dragged itself across his mind. Yes. John. He had sent one of his boys to summon Noll a few days ago. There would be consequences if he did not go.

He stretched out on the cot. His arm twinged, the tight skin sending a bone-deep pain shooting down to his fingers. He shook out the feeling as he sat up, the world slowly coming back to him as the curtain of sleep lifted.

Pepper stood up and began to busy himself around the room, combing out his messy hair and chattering.

'What do you think John wants with you?'

Noll scratched at himself and stood, kicking the bedclothes aside. 'Lord knows,' he grumbled, tugging on his tunic. 'It would be far too easy for him to simply *tell* me.'

He walked over to the window, leaned out, grabbed the canvas sack hanging from the sill and heaved it inside. It was growing worryingly light. Hopefully John would have good news for him – perhaps another job – and he'd be able to fill it again before the day was out.

'Here.' He handed Pepper the last of a loaf of bread, followed by an apple. 'Eat.'

Pepper hesitated for a second – glancing surreptitiously at the meagre remains Noll had left for himself – before tearing into the food.

He was too skinny, Noll thought vaguely, as he quickly saw off the last of a hard chunk of cheese. He was short, too – far too short. Noll supposed that was the effect of living rough and eating too little for too long. Pepper was around nineteen years old – at least, they assumed this was the case, as neither were sure of the exact date of Pepper's birth – but was reedy and stick-thin.

With luck, Noll's fortunes would change, and he would be able to keep him safe and warm and, most importantly, *fed*. Pepper's own pitiful wage was not enough. Perhaps once they had the means Pepper would catch up with his peers. Although that, too, was risky. Pepper's slim stature and stunted growth was a boon that would not last forever.

Noll rummaged through his pack, skimming his fingers over his meagre possessions: a dagger, a coin purse, the package he'd picked up two days prior, a bone comb, and his clothes.

He quickly turned out the contents of the purse into his hand. A ring fell out with them.

He'd kept it all these years. He'd told himself it was because he could sell it. But he hadn't. Even in the worst depths of poverty he hadn't, not even when he was injured and convalescing, when he'd needed the money most.

Something had forced him to keep it. Doubt, he supposed. Hope. Stupidity.

He shook those thoughts from his head, and without hesitating any longer poured both coins and ring back into the purse. Once he was ready, they headed out. The city's streets were thick with people, shouting in English and French and getting in each other's way. He pressed himself close to Pepper's side, a wall against the crowd. He looked away as they passed the pillories. He easily could have known the man within them.

'Alms, sirs, please—'

Noll hesitated. There was a man slumped against the wall of a nearby building. His skin was wrinkled, loose on his bones. He was coated in dirt and God knew what else. His eyes were clouded.

Noll didn't stop to think. He reached into his purse, pulled out a coin, and handed it to the old man.

'Why did you do that?' Pepper demanded, once they were out of earshot. 'You have *nothing*.'

Noll shook his head. '*He* has nothing. Now he has a little more.'

When Noll had first arrived back on English shores as a penniless escapee, he truly had nothing – nothing but the clothes on his back. Even his *name* wasn't his anymore. He'd cast it aside like he had everything else, forced to give it up. Those first, hard months, he'd turned not to begging, but to stealing. He could have charmed people into handing over their money willingly, but through thievery he could gain far more than they would ever have given through charity alone.

And besides, it was easier to steal – easier on his pride, and a soothing balm to his anger. He had been abandoned by those who loved him, those who had the money and comfort that he no longer did. Those who could have saved him but had chosen not to.

He was aware, with every purse he stole or ring he slipped from a finger, of how many people were worse off than himself. It was why he had taken Pepper under his wing. It was why, even now, he would toss a coin to a blind old man begging in the street. At least one of Noll's eyes still worked, after all.

It was his mother's heart still beating in his chest. Even when he was very young she had made him see those less fortunate than them; those not tied to wealth by marriage and blood. She was endlessly charitable, and where his brothers saw giving alms as a dull obligation, he had taken it all in.

She would have given the beggar a whole purse full of coins. But she would have had a purse of coins to give. Noll did not.

She was dead now.

Noll had agreed to meet John in his safehouse, the place he conducted all his business: a tavern-cum-brothel on the edge of town. They hurried inside, greeted swiftly by a pretty girl in a yellow hood. He gave her John's name and his own, then watched as she hurried off into a back room.

'I ought to get to work,' Pepper said, glancing around. 'Do not argue with him.'

'Why would I do a thing like that?'

'Because you're a damn fool. Come and find me when you're done. I wish to know what this is all about.'

With a squeeze of Noll's arm, Pepper headed away towards the wooden staircase that led to the rooms upstairs. Despite Noll's initial concerns when they had landed in the city just over a year ago, Pepper had flourished in the business. He'd taken on jobs as and when he was needed: serving customers in the tavern, cleaning bowls and mugs, wiping down tables. He'd made a name for himself with the girls in the brothel, too, always fetching and cleaning and carrying or – on occasion – threatening boisterous clients.

His latest role, which Noll still worried over, was far more active. But he had a set of skills – a set of tools – which made him perfect for certain clients. Between it all, he was making just enough to scrape a living; not enough to thrive, but enough to mean he didn't have to follow Noll down the path of thievery and banditry.

Still, Noll would have preferred if he could have provided for them both. In the years they'd known each other, he'd watched Pepper grow from an anxious boy into a confident – if angry – young man. He was his brother in all but blood, and while Pepper seemed perfectly happy getting his work on his knees, Noll still couldn't help but wish there was more he could do for him.

Not that he ever told Pepper that, of course. It would lead to an argument that Noll was certain to lose.

After a few minutes, the girl returned and directed for Noll to follow her into the back room. It was near empty, save for a handful of tables and there, in the corner, John. He was a large, imposing figure, his hat pulled low, his tunic straining against muscles he made no attempt to conceal. On the table in front of him sat a full mug and, Noll noticed, a shining knife. He glanced up as he entered.

'You came,' John said.

'I came. What have you got for me, John?'

'Just a little job.'

Noll took the empty seat opposite John as the girl saw herself out.

'Well?' he said.

'Onto business so soon?'

'I would rather get it over with.'

'Very well. I've received a proposition. One with a very generous compensation.'

'Oh?'

'It is a truly tragic tale. My heart bleeds for this poor family . . .'

'And their money, I would wager.'

John grinned horribly. 'Perhaps.'

'And what do they want? Riches restored? An heirloom returned?'

'If only it were so simple. They need a certain man . . . dealing with.'

'Dealing with?'

'Killed.'

Noll stared at him, aghast. 'I am not a hired killer,' he said firmly. 'I am a *thief*.'

John rolled his eyes. 'You may claim that all you like,' he said, 'but you fought in France. You were with that band of yours for years. You're telling me that a man like you has never gotten his hands dirty in this manner before?'

'Once or twice,' Noll conceded, 'but not like *this,* not for pay.'

'Then you shall be learning something new.'

'Why do they want him dead? What has he done to them? John, I cannot kill a man. Not without good reason. And *no*—' He saw John's eye twinkle. 'Money is *not* a good reason. Tell me.'

John reached inside his tunic and pulled out a well-worn letter. It bore a wax seal, with what appeared to be a hunting horn stamped into it. He placed it on the table. After a moment, he reached into the tunic again. This time, he pulled out a leather pouch.

It looked very heavy. When he dropped it beside the letter, it clinked.

'A friend of the family reached out to me. They do not know what to do and are seeking some way' – the angelic look John plastered across his face nearly made Noll laugh – 'to ease their suffering. Their daughter is being forced to wed a brute. She is a widow, with land and power. She has safety guaranteed for her in Scotland, but she cannot take it. They require someone to secure her freedom.'

'By killing her husband?'

'He is not her husband yet.'

'It just seems extreme,' Noll said desperately. '*Murder?* Why not write to her, and urge her to call the match off? Or visit her?'

John gave his best expression of contrite empathy. It was not particularly convincing.

'Ah, but they have,' he said. 'Letters gone unanswered, requests to visit unheeded. The daughter is . . . prickly, at the best of times. This family friend fears she would not respond well to him interfering in her life. His presence would force her even further into the arms of this monster.'

'Her family have had no word from her?'

'None at all.'

'They fear coercion, then. Or control.'

'That is exactly it. They are *desperate,* Noll. They would do anything for their baby girl.'

Noll raised his eyebrows. 'Their widowed baby girl who is about to enter a union with a second man?'

John grinned. 'Exactly.'

Noll sighed. 'This just seems enormously risky. I cannot—'

'The reward is extremely generous.'

Noll fell silent. He eyed the straining leather pouch beside the letter.

'How generous?'

He did not, in truth, expect a great deal. The sort of family who would request their daughter's betrothed be *murdered* rather than simply talk to the man – and wealthy enough to get away with it were their sins discovered – would likely also be the sort of family who considered a *generous reward* to be a few coins and a promise not to turn the man with blood on his hands over to the law.

'*Extremely.* They have promised money, of course; that is to be expected. And . . .'

'And?' John was drawing this out, Noll knew, attempting to pull him in like a fish on a line.

'Safety across the border in Scotland. I told them I had a man likely for the job, who was looking for a . . .' he gave a low, mirthless laugh '. . . a *fresh start.* It has been promised that the man who sees through this request . . .' he picked up the knife, and tapped the point of it against the letter '. . . will be given money and safety. A home. Employment, I would guess, should you play them right.'

Noll's chest went tight. *Safety.* That was what he wanted – what he'd been searching for all these years. He could even take Pepper with him, if Pepper agreed. It would be a chance at a new life, away from the many people they had wronged.

A chance away from the past, which still threatened to choke him. English soil and Scottish soil were one and the same. It was all just dirt in the end. But merely treading where he trod was too much, sometimes.

The border – even if it was no more real than a line in his own head – would ease that.

'May I have time to consider it?' Noll said.

John smiled. 'No.'

Noll sighed. 'Fine. *Fine.* This is hugely risky,' he said. 'It is no easy thing, to take a life.'

'If it's any incentive,' John added, 'they've paid part of your compensation already, to be given upon agreement. Presumably they think you need the tools to handle the job correctly.'

Noll had to stop himself from gasping as he looked at the money pouch beside John, realising at last what it was.

'All of that?'

John smiled. 'Only once the job is done,' he said. 'A third is yours. The rest, of course, is mine. For finding you such a lucrative opportunity.'

'Your compensation for sitting on *your* arse while *I* murder a man?'

John placed a hand to his heart. 'I am hurt, Noll.'

'Not hurt enough, I fear.'

John ignored him. 'This is *my* payment for acquiring this job for you, and ensuring the goodwill of the people who have hired you. Without me, you would not be here. It would behove you to remember that.'

Noll bristled. 'And if I don't agree to these terms?'

John played with the knife on the table. Noll tracked the shining movement carefully.

He was ready for the moment John moved, flicking the knife across the table with such speed and precision that it was barely a glimmering blur before lodging itself neatly in the wood between Noll's hands. He didn't even flinch.

'I do not think we have to worry about that.' John grinned, leaning across the table and pulling out the knife. 'Do we have an agreement?'

Noll looked at the notch in the wood between his hands. He looked at the groaning bag of coins beside John's arm.

'We do,' he said at last.

✡

Noll found Pepper waiting outside. He headed over as soon as he spotted him, eyes lit up with curiosity.

'Well?' he demanded, keeping pace with Noll. 'What did he want?'

'Not here.'

Noll managed to stay silent until they were back in their tiny room with the door bolted behind them. In a rush, he explained the whole horrible business. By the end of it, Pepper was watching him, mouth ajar.

'My God. And you agreed to this?'

'I did.'

'And who is it? This man?'

'He's an earl. John only gave me a description and told me where to wait. He does not want me knowing too much, the bastard, and frankly I agree with him.'

Pepper nodded. 'You're worried you will be traced back here?'

'I am.'

'If it is so risky, then why even do it?'

'They have offered *so much money*, Pep. And I could start again in Scotland. You know I hate it here. You could come with me.'

'Come with you?'

'You do not have to,' Noll said quickly. 'I know that you are content here, as you are, but if you *wanted* to, you would be more than welcome to join me.'

Pepper didn't respond. Noll began to panic.

'You are the closest thing I have to family,' he said. 'Damn it: you *are* my family. And I will never forgive myself if I leave and something happens to you. Besides, I owe you my life.'

Pepper sighed. 'I do not *need* anything from you, Noll.'

'And yet I still wish to give,' Noll said. 'Promise me you will think about it. I shall return for my pay once this mess is over, and we can talk about it more then. And until then . . . I have something for you. A gift.'

Pepper raised his eyebrows as Noll dug in his pack.

'A gift?' he said, cynically.

Noll pulled out the package with a flourish. 'Well, if you do not *need* it . . .'

Pepper immediately went to grab it, but Noll quickly snatched it back.

'Ah,' he said, eyebrows raised as Pepper *humphed* at him. 'So you *do* need it?'

Pepper rolled his eyes. '*Fine*. I do not need anything from you. But you cannot tease me with a gift, that is just unfair.'

Noll grinned, and this time, tossed the package across to him. Pepper caught it and hurriedly tore into it, pulling away the string and ripping away the wrapping until—

He burst out laughing.

'What?' Noll said, in faux innocence. 'You need some, after all.'

Pepper turned the bollock dagger over in his hands, still laughing. The wooden guard had been carved into perfectly symmetrical orbs, the waxed handle ending in a bulbous tip. Pepper pulled it from the leather sheath to examine the blade, his hand fitting perfectly between guard and pommel.

It was, in truth, a perfectly nondescript dagger. Noll had seen dozens of them in his time – hundreds, perhaps. But the blade was sharp and sturdy, and the sheath, which to his mind could be just as important as the blade itself, was thick and watertight. It would serve Pepper well, if he was careful, and learned to wield it.

Noll could only hope that he would be there to teach him. But if he wasn't – if accident or injury or misfortune parted them – the dagger alone would be enough to help keep him safe.

'Well?' he said. 'What do you think?'

Pepper finished examining the dagger, pushing it back into the sheath and holding it tight in both hands, as if Noll had gifted him something rare and wonderful.

'Thank you,' he said. 'It is too much, surely? How could you afford this?'

Noll waved him away. 'You ask too many questions,' he said. 'Ask me again and I'll leave you on the side of the road where I found you.'

Pepper crinkled his nose and busied himself using the straps on the sheath to secure the dagger to his belt.

'No' – Noll couldn't stop himself, leaning forwards – 'like *this.*'

As he properly attached the dagger, he thought of how correct Pepper had been. The blade had cost him the very last of his coin – the money left over from his convalescence, in fact, when Pepper had been forced to sell Noll's lute. Noll had allowed Pepper to assume that the money had been used up months ago, and had been completely unaware of the tiny stash that Noll had squirrelled away, just in case.

When the dagger was attached securely, Noll sat back on his heels.

'There,' he said. 'And do not lose it.'

Pepper laughed. 'I won't. I will protect it with my life.'

'It is *supposed* to be the other way around.'

'As you say.' Pepper looked uncharacteristically thoughtful. 'Thank you, Noll,' he said at last. 'Really.'

Noll placed a hand upon his shoulder. For a reason he could not fathom, he felt terribly sad.

✡

The birds nesting in the rafters of the building were singing far too sweetly for a day upon which blood was going to be spilled.

Noll had been waiting in the village through which the main road passed for three days. He'd given his name as William, securing a place to sleep and charming anyone who spoke to him out of questioning why he was there. It was the perfect place to lurk, catching gossip like fish in a net as travellers hurried through. It was that stream of gossip that had brought him the news that morning as he gnawed on a hunk of bread in the tavern.

The earl's party was close.

A surprise attack on the whole retinue was far too risky. He would wait for them to pass then follow behind until they inevitably stopped again. No one travelled so far and with so many people without several rest stops, and with luck Noll would be able to catch his target away from the rest of his party – either taking a walk or relieving himself.

It was poor form to kill a man while he was pissing, but the thought of that bag of coins spun temptingly in his head. He could not afford to consider *form*, right now.

After finishing his sparse meal, he hurried from the inn without a word to the innkeeper. All he left behind were a pair of coins on the counter.

He followed the main road a safe distance from the village and settled himself behind a hedge to wait. It did not take long to hear the tell-tale sounds of hoofbeats and chatter.

Noll tugged his cap as low as he could, tucking his gold hair beneath the wool, and pulled up his scarf, obscuring his mouth and nose. There was a chill in the air: at least if anyone questioned why he was dressed so suspiciously, he could claim it was to keep the cold from his face.

He waited a few moments for the retinue to pass on down the road, then scrambled from behind the hedge and followed.

It was easy to keep pace a safe distance behind, and soon – as predicted – the party halted. Two figures on horseback dismounted and headed down a lesser-trod path into the woods. Even without seeing his face, it was easy enough to judge by his fine clothes and even finer horse that one of them was the earl.

Noll slid through the trees to follow them.

Keeping away from the path, he approached from behind. The woman had a hunting bow slung over her shoulder, likely worth more money than Noll would see in half a year. He felt sorry for her, being tied to the sort of man her family had described. She was no better than a captive. He knew that feeling.

No doubt his target, too, was armed. He was an *earl,* after all. There was probably a jewel-encrusted sword beneath that fur-edged cape. Noll crept closer, keeping to the shadows.

The couple had hesitated. Noll was *fairly* sure they hadn't heard him, and had just come to a natural standstill in their walk. They were talking to each other, but positioned as he was with his bad ear towards them he couldn't make out the words.

There was a long moment where nobody moved. And then, finally, they turned away.

Now.

Noll darted from behind a tree, throwing himself forwards and colliding with his victim from behind. He wrapped his arm around his chest, angling his dagger towards his throat. The earl writhed in his grip, stronger than Noll had anticipated. He grabbed Noll's wrist, twisting his hand. Pain flared up and down Noll's arm, twinging through his fingers. He did not drop the blade.

The earl twisted again. Noll's grip around his chest loosened. The other man pulled himself around, shoving Noll off, turning to face him.

Noll froze. His thundering heart stopped, dropping through the base of his stomach and shattering. Dark eyes. Dark hair. A face of freckles. A sharp jaw. A scar, splitting that jaw in two, twisting over once-familiar lips.

Ash.

Pain burst from the space where his heart should have been.

The moment of hesitation was enough. Before he could move, he was grabbed and pulled backwards to the floor. Someone – the woman – was shouting, screaming, calling for guards. Before he could realise what was happening there was a hand yanking back his head, and the unmistakable hardness of steel against his neck.

Damn. The woman was armed beyond the bow.

He tried not to swallow, not to move, not to *breathe*. Her eyes were glinting and cold. This was not, he realised far too late, the face of a woman being forced or coerced.

He shut his eyes, better to avoid her gaze.

His single, absurd thought was how grateful he was that he'd gifted Pepper the dagger before he'd left. Even if Noll hadn't managed to say all he'd wanted to say, Pepper would know.

'My Lady?' Footsteps. Branches breaking. Swords unsheathing. 'My Lady! Good God, my Lord—'

The blade was gone. Several people grabbed him, hauling him to his feet, pulling him away.

'Get him in the cart,' the woman said. 'We will take him with us.'

There were guards all around him. Someone had an arm around his throat. He tried to call out, but his mouth was smothered by his scarf. He caught a glimpse of the woman placing a hand on Ash's shoulder before the guards pulled him away.

They shoved him in the back of a covered cart with such force that the whole thing rocked.

He was a prisoner again. He was *trapped*. Soon they would bind and gag and blindfold him. They would haul him away. Bile rose up his throat. *No, no – not again – I cannot—*

He tried to get to his knees to see outside the cart, but there were too many men in the way. A flash of red hair – the woman, talking to another guard.

'Make sure he does not escape.'

For a moment, there was only silence. And then the cart shifted and a guard appeared, a thick length of rope in his hands.

Chapter 9

Agnes

Agnes watched the guards shove the bandit into one of the wagons, the dogs barking at her heels. She should have insisted on having the guards with them for the walk. Then again, had she done so, the bandit would now be dead – a mess she was sure Barden would not wish to deal with.

Barden himself was keeping to the very edge of the party, standing beside their horses. He jumped as she approached, flinching when Litillwitte nudged at his limply hanging hand.

'Bar— Ash?'

He turned, at last. His face was *wrong*. He looked terribly pale, his freckles stark against his skin. There was a fine sheen of sweat across his brow, and his pupils were tiny, eyes darting across her face as if he was not sure she was even there.

'Are you all right?'

He nodded at her, his lips tight.

'We must return to Dunlyn,' he mumbled. 'I am . . . tired.'

She wanted to talk to him, but sensed there was no use. The attack had shaken him.

'You saw him?' he said, suddenly.

'Saw who?'

'The man who . . . who attacked me. You saw him?'

Something was wrong. 'Of course I did.'

Ash nodded thoughtfully. She appeared to have reassured him.

'I had him placed in one of the carts, with a guard,' she added, trying to soothe him. 'We can bring him to Dunlyn, and—'

His expression was icy. The relief vanished. She reached out to place a comforting hand on his shoulder.

'Ash, are you *sure* you are all right?'

'I am *fine*!'

Agnes snatched her hand back. He'd often been cynical, always grumbling, but *that* . . . that was anger, pure and, she was forced to admit, a little frightening.

She lowered her hand, but did not step away. Ash was trembling. Agnes realised that she wasn't the only one who was frightened.

'My apologies,' she said calmly. 'It should not be too much further.'

Ash ignored her, pulling himself up on the horse and tugging it away at a quick trot.

The rest of the ride to Dunlyn passed in intense silence. Ash rode ahead from the rest of the party, Litillwitte at his horse's hooves. When they stopped again to rest and eat, he refused to so much as take a bite of bread. He avoided the cart in which they'd placed their prisoner like it was a plague house.

Agnes approached Ash's steward when she was sure Ash was out of earshot to ask if he was all right. He gave her a sympathetic look.

'This is not unusual,' he said eventually. 'Since France . . .' He trailed off. 'It will pass.'

She watched Ash's departing figure, and hoped that he was right. She spent the rest of the journey riding at Sara's side – who had agreed to accompany her to her newest home – and while they could not discuss Ash's mood while travelling with his retinue it was a relief to be riding beside a friendly face.

✡

Agnes had anticipated their arrival to Dunlyn being under happier circumstances. She had been told at length about Ash's family – about his brother most of all – and she was keen to meet them all, especially Ash's sister with her unusual dressing habits.

And yet as the castle loomed at the top of a hill, she felt only dread. Ash rode ahead, looking forwards, ignoring her. Every so often, he shot a nervous glance over his shoulder, as if they were being followed.

She approached the steward again.

'I . . . am worried,' she said, watching his expression carefully. 'Could you perhaps ride ahead, alert Ash's brother that we will be there shortly? And that Ba— that my Lord will require attendance?'

The steward smiled at her. 'Of course, my Lady. I will ride ahead and inform Raff. He should be able to speak to him more plainly.'

He rode off. As he dashed past Ash, his horse at a gallop, Ash flinched away. Agnes sighed.

Steeling herself, she approached him again, this time more gently. She called to him before she was too close, and even *that* seemed to startle him. He twisted to look at her, but said nothing.

'Are you looking forward to seeing your family once again?' she asked. 'The keep is truly magnificent.'

Ash looked towards it, as if only just noticing it was there.

'It is,' he said quietly. 'And . . . I am, yes.'

He lapsed into silence once more. But now, at least, he was riding at her side and not rushing off ahead.

By the time they arrived at the gates of Dunlyn Castle, a gaggle of people had already gathered to meet them. Staff to see to their horses and things, as well as another pair of guards. Clearly the steward had informed them they had a prisoner in their party. Standing ahead of the waiting servants were two men – one tall, taller even than Ash, with a mass of curly hair, and the other shorter and stockier with a face full of freckles and long, dark hair. At once, Agnes guessed who the second man must be: Raff, Ash's brother. They looked so painfully alike that it could be no one else.

Ash seemed to sag in the saddle as they approached, as if something within him had melted. A pike, stuck through his spine, had finally been removed. He slid from the horse so quickly that Agnes feared he would fall, but Raff – and the taller man – were on him in an instant. Raff slung an arm around him, and even though Ash's expression turned momentarily thunderous, he did not shrug him off.

'Let us get you inside . . .' Raff murmured, his voice a low rumble. 'That is— ah, my Lady . . .'

Agnes too swung down from her horse. She wanted to follow them into the keep, but knew that her presence would likely burden Ash even further.

'Bring her.'

All three of them snapped around at Ash's voice.

'You ought to follow me, my Lady,' Raff said, looking apologetic. 'And . . .' He sighed, then straightened his back as best he could with Ash leaning on him. 'The bandit, was it?' he asked the steward.

'Yes, my Lord.'

'Get him in one of the side rooms. I do not care which. Lock him in the pantry if you must.'

'At once, my Lord.'

With another apologetic look towards Agnes, Raff heaved Ash towards the keep. Agnes left Sara to organise their things then hurried to follow. The other man kept pace with her.

'I am very sorry about this,' he said. 'We had hoped—' He cut himself off with a sigh. 'Forgive my rudeness. I am William. He . . . may have spoken of me?' He shot a look at Ash's back. 'I can never be sure, given the circumstances.'

Agnes tried to remember all she knew about the Barden family.

'William de Foucart?' she landed on, at last. 'The— that is, I—'

'The hostage, yes.' William gave her a devilish smile.

'Ash mentioned that the situation was . . .' She gave him a look up and down. He did not appear to be a prisoner of the family. 'Complicated,' she finished.

The grin only grew. 'Indeed it is,' he said. 'But you've time to learn. And . . . please, do call me Penn.'

She nodded. 'Of course.'

They followed Raff and Ash into the great hall. Her breath caught: it was enormous. Chandeliers heavy with lit candles hung from the vaulted ceiling; a walled-off fire crackled merrily in the centre of the room. A huge, glazed window was set into the far wall, catching the sunlight in flashes. The whitewashed walls were dark with smoke and age: once they had been painted, but the art was faded, now.

Before she could take the rest in, Raff pulled Ash into a side room, beckoning her to follow. He deposited him in a high-backed chair, tugged off his cloak, then sat beside him.

'What happened?'

It took Agnes a moment to realise he was talking to her.

'We were attacked,' she said. 'We were walking, the two of

us, and he just . . . appeared, from nowhere. He ignored me and leapt upon Ash, and I—'

'She pulled him off of me.' Ash's voice was hoarse. Penn's eyebrows rose.

'Did you now?' Raff said.

'I did,' Agnes said. 'I had to stop him.'

'Did he take anything?'

Agnes paused. 'No . . .' she said at last, 'but it did not appear that he was *attempting* to take anything, either. Were he trying to rob us then he would have gone for Ash's purse, but he did not even try.'

'Odd,' Penn said. 'Why try to kill him? What reason would he have?'

Agnes wished she knew the answer. After a long while, Ash spoke.

'I saw him again.'

Agnes did not know what he meant. Raff, however, seemed to. He squeezed Ash's hand.

'I am sorry.'

'He . . . he keeps *following* me. I thought I was—' Ash's voice broke. 'I thought I could be better,' Ash mumbled. 'He is like a ghost. He will not let me rest.'

Agnes opened her mouth to ask *who,* then immediately shut it again. *Think,* she told herself. *Think.* Before they had agreed to the match, Ash had explained to her – if not in detail – his own past. His previous vows, broken before they could ever be made by the death of the person he had vowed himself to.

She had assumed it had been a woman, snatched from the world before her time. Now, she wasn't so sure.

Pieces seemed to move into place, drawing out a pattern. The refusal to talk in more detail, the terrible sense of loss. The war.

She looked again at Ash. He looked so distraught that she could not bring herself to ask. It would beyond rude – it would be *cruel* – to ask him such delicate questions in such a state.

'My Lady?'

She turned. Penn was offering her his arm.

'Would you like me to escort you to your chambers?'

She took another look at Ash, his head down. Raff gave her a brief nod: *I have this in hand.*

'That would be very kind,' she said.

*

Penn led her to the neatly made guest chambers on one of the upper floors. Most of the things she had brought with her had already been sent up, and Sara was arranging the space and making the bed. It was a relief to see her familiar face.

'What happened?' Sara asked, as soon as they were alone.

'I am not sure . . .' Agnes said, shaking out a blanket. 'But I intend to find out.'

Once the room had been arranged to her specifications, she headed back into the hall. She spoke briefly to Ash's steward and introduced herself to Ash's housekeeper, Ellen, who was taking Agnes's servants under her wing while they settled in. It felt good to be busy: ensuring that everyone was in the right place. She found Qwippe in the kennels, waiting patiently for a feed. Everything seemed to be in order.

Raff came across her as she was making her way back inside.

'My Lady,' he said apologetically. 'I am sorry that we have not yet been properly introduced.'

'It is quite all right. Circumstances have been unusual,' she said. 'How is Ash?'

Raff shrugged. 'As well as one can expect. He wishes to speak to you.'

Agnes let him lead her back into the side room. Ash looked brighter, now. He stood when she entered.

'How are you faring?' she asked.

He grimaced. The expression was enough to tell her everything she needed.

'I will be outside if you require me,' Raff said.

He gave Ash a nod, a stiff bow towards Agnes, and left them alone. Agnes took the chair beside Ash next to the fire.

'I ought to have introduced you properly,' he said, as if only just realising his mistake.

'It is too late for that now,' Agnes said. 'Raff said you wished to talk to me?'

'I . . . yes.'

'Is it about what happened on the road? Not the attack,' she quickly clarified, 'but afterwards?'

Ash gave her a hard, knowing look.

'Sometimes I struggle with . . . memories,' he said. 'Dreams and memories. My mind confuses them. I was . . .' He took another breath. Clearly, this was not a topic he often discussed. 'You are aware that I was involved in a battle in France?' When Agnes nodded, he continued. 'I lost someone very dear to me. I watched him die. And then I was attacked myself before I could reach him. Sometimes . . .' He twisted his hands together. 'It is like I am back there. I struggle to tell what is real and what is not.' He lowered his head. 'I am sorry, Agnes.'

It all but confirmed her suspicions.

'He was your friend?'

'My dearest friend. Sometimes it is as if I have forgotten he is dead.'

Agnes placed her hand on his arm. She could not imagine such horror – such a betrayal of your own mind, to make the imagined real.

'It sounds awful,' she said at last. 'I am sorry that you are forced to face that, Ash.'

'And *I* am sorry that you were forced to witness it,' he said. 'The attack on the road . . . it was like I was back there.'

'Is there anything I can do?' Agnes offered.

Ash finally looked at her. 'No,' he said. 'But . . . thank you.' He sighed, closing his eyes, then in a swift movement got to his feet. 'Might I show you around? It would be good to get some air, and . . . I really am keen for you to settle in here.'

He offered her his arm. When Agnes took it, he placed his hand over hers. It was warm and soft. Her stomach squeezed. The smile he gave her was a little strained, but genuine.

'That would be lovely,' she said.

Chapter 10

Ash

Despite what had happened on the road and Ash's resulting fit, the afternoon passed, to his surprise, very pleasantly. Ash had never been overly invested in his father's keep, but showing Agnes around made it feel more real – the great hall, the chapel, the kitchens, out into the yard where the horses stamped in the stables and the marshal trained his men. He pointed out where the ancient building had been rebuilt and made new: windows glazed, roofing made sturdier. She seemed genuinely interested, asking questions that often he could not answer, but neither seeming dissatisfied *when* he could not answer them.

He formally introduced her to the staff, along with Raff and Penn, who found the whole farce rather funny. He even showed her, briefly, the lands surrounding the castle: the valley below, the river, the managed woodlands – a royal gift given to Ash's ancestors. The weather was clear enough for him to point out the blurred shape of Skeldale on the horizon.

The prisoner could wait. He wanted to deal with the man himself, but he had no desire for his presence to ruin the scraps of the day he had managed to salvage. Let him rot, he thought bitterly. He'd been placed in one of the towers: let him sit up there and wait for the gallows.

They shared supper with Agnes's upper staff, Sara, Raff and Penn. Ash had become used to the quieter meals in la Cleve Castle and had not realised how much he had missed Raff's presence or Penn's constant witty remarks. He began to relax, becoming more like himself. Joan the cook had put on a veritable feast with courses of boar and venison, early spring fruits, tiny little tarts and glistening fritters. Paired with the fine wine brought up from the basements and the roaring fire, it was a merry evening: light and laughter and sustenance.

Agnes seemed to be enjoying herself, too. Ash had feared that she would feel nervous in the huge keep, trapped amongst Ash's family. But she smiled widely, spoke kindly to the servants, and laughed along even with Penn's bawdiest jokes. A sort of relief settled in his heart: she would be good for Dunlyn. She would be good for the family, when he was gone.

She glanced at Ash over the table, her eyes sparkling, her hair falling in gold strands around her face and her lips sticky with honey.

Ash could not help but smile back. Something was different. Something he could not name. One truth he knew: he was glad she was there.

When Agnes retired to bed, he watched her leave, bidding her a quiet goodnight as she rose from the table. She placed a hand to his shoulder for just a moment – the touch soft yet blindingly hot.

As she disappeared up the stairs, there was a laugh from Ash's other side. He snapped around to face Penn, who quickly set his expression into contrite innocence.

'She seems very nice.'

Ash looked across at Raff, whose expression, while less cheeky than Penn's, was also set into a knowing smile.

'*What?*' Ash snapped.

'I am merely surprised that you are getting on so well,' Penn said. 'Considering how you were determined *not* to befriend your potential bride.'

'She handled the situation on the road deftly,' Raff put in. 'You explained what happened?'

'I did,' Ash said. 'She was very understanding. Lord knows why.'

'Because she is *fond* of you, you bastard,' Penn said. 'She has dreadful taste.'

Ash gave him a shove with his shoulder.

'*And,*' Penn continued, undeterred, 'I would wager that you are fond of her, too. Fonder than you had expected to be.'

'Shut your mouth.' Ash scowled. 'She is a *good choice* – that is all.'

He looked at Raff, hoping for support. But Raff's eyebrows were raised, his expression also one of disbelief.

'Not you too.'

Raff merely shrugged. 'I did not say a word.'

Ash retired to his own chambers shortly after, determined not to let himself dwell on Raff and Penn's teasing words or conspiratorial looks. Whatever it was they were imagining they were seeing was just that: imagined. It was no more real than Olly's ghost. He knew what it was to be in love. How could they imagine that this, was that?

Yet as he lay abed, Litillwitte at his feet, he could not shake the image of Agnes's face, the firelight playing on her high cheekbones, the dance of the mark below her eye. Her fox-like features, the halo of hair around her head.

It took him a long time to fall asleep, the fire spluttering into embers, and then into ash.

✡

The morning came bright, and cold, and terrible.

Ash knew that today he would need to be the earl. He put it off for as long as he could, and it was not until late that evening that he at last saw fit to attend to his final pressing duty as the earl of the keep. He needed to see to their prisoner.

With Raff at his side, he made his way to the narrow staircase that led to the easternmost tower, up towards the single room at the very top.

'I do not believe he is too great a threat,' Ash said, as they approached the locked door. 'But he *may* attempt to run. Be ready.'

Raff nodded. Ash unlocked the door and pushed it open.

A small fire had been lit at the side of the room. It was full of fading yellow light. A figure stood in the gloom.

'Step forward, man. Let me see the one who attacked me.'

There was silence. Then the man stepped into the sparse light.

Ash's skin went cold. His heart cracked in his chest.

'*Oliver?*'

He stood in the centre of the room like a ghost. Ash expected him to vanish like he had done so many times before.

Firelight from the tiny hearth played on his face. His hair was tangled where it had been bundled beneath his cap. His clothes were ragged, gambeson worn, boots thinning. He looked tired. He looked *old*.

The memory of him never looked old.

'Ash?'

Ash turned to Raff. He was staring at him, not at the ghost.

'Can you . . . can you see him?'

Raff nodded, face a mask of shock. 'I can. Ash . . . is that—'

'Oliver?' Ash could barely make his tongue move around the word. It came out like a cough.

Oliver stared at him. His expression was shattered, familiar yet so, so different.

'Is it you?' Ash's voice did not belong to him anymore. 'Is it . . . is it *you?*'

He stepped closer. He'd been taking tiny steps without ever realising, without tracking his own movement across the room. The space between them had dwindled to nearly nothing.

He reached out, brushing the backs of his fingers down Olly's jaw. Olly puffed out a hard sigh, like it pained him to release the air from his lungs.

Ash half-expected Olly to dissolve under his touch and prove that this was yet another piece of his fragmented mind made real to torture him. He would *allow* the torture – he would embrace this wild madness – if it meant getting to feel Olly beneath his hands once more, even if he wasn't truly there.

But his shape did not dissolve. He did not vanish, as he had done so many times before. Ash could feel the stubble across Olly's jaw, the heat of his skin. He was *real*. He was alive.

Ash couldn't take it any longer. His whole body *hurt,* from his fingertips against Olly's skin to his ribs around his thundering heart. *He was alive.* He was solid beneath Ash's hands – not the ephemeral ghost that had followed him around for all these years.

He pulled him into a crushing embrace, taking in the smell of him, tangling his fingers in his hair. His eyes flooded with hot tears, stinging and unstoppable. Ash felt Olly breathing against his neck, the rise and fall of his chest where he was pressed so tight against Ash's own. Ash could almost feel the beat of his heart: or was that *Ash's* heart, finally whole, finally able to beat as it should be beating?

Olly's hands moved, slowly, to come to rest upon Ash's shoulders. Ash clung to him, desperately, like a man swinging from a cliff edge, grasping at the one thing stopping him from tumbling. Olly's hands shook against him, fingers twitching.

When he pulled back – painfully, reluctantly – Olly was staring at him. His eyes were sparkling with tears, slowly trailing streaks down his cheeks. He looked lost, mouth slightly open, as if he were about to speak—

Then whatever it was, swallowed down.

Ash couldn't look away. On the road, he'd only got a glimpse of him – the flash of his blue eyes above his scarf, the noise of surprise he had made when the guards had pulled him away. Yet he'd known. He'd known, somehow, that it was *him*.

'You—' he said, his voice awkward and heavy. 'That was you? Who attacked me?'

Olly nodded, eyes huge, lips tight.

'*Why?*'

'I—' Olly's mouth moved silently. 'I did not know it was you.'

There was more, Ash knew. There *had* to be more. But a single look at him – his skinniness, his worn clothes, his tired expression – made it clear that whatever Olly had been doing had been an act of desperation, not malice.

There were so many questions. He needed answers. He needed to know why Olly had been gone so long and what had kept him away.

Why didn't you come back to me?

He could not say it out loud. Not now. Not like *this,* when his heart was still thundering and Olly looked so horribly vacant. His hands were still held loose against Olly's chest. Olly watched him, his expression so unfamiliar that it sent renewed pain through Ash's chest, a fresh wave of stinging tears to his eyes.

Then he realised what Olly was looking at, what his gaze had locked to. The scar. Of course. Olly had only ever known him with his face unblemished, his skin still whole.

He wondered what Olly thought of him, now, as ruined as he was. The scar twisted the outside, but it felt as if it went deeper, as if it was *inside* him, too, tearing through his heart, around his guts, a crack through his head from ear to ear.

He'd earned it by not being able to save Olly when he had the chance. He'd *deserved* the scar; he'd deserved more, to even begin to atone for failing to save him. Olly's blood had been on his hands as much as it had been on the hands of the French soldier who had felled him.

And now Olly was *alive*. The skin around the scar prickled. Ash found himself reaching to it instinctively. Olly's eyes tracked that movement as well.

Olly had known him young and perfect and – or at least Olly had always said – handsome. And now he was none of those things.

But he did not look horrified. He didn't look sad, either. Just *blank*.

'Olly . . .'

Olly's eyes snapped up. Their gazes met.

The force of years of grief powered Ash forwards. He kissed Olly with a hunger that he had buried, that he hadn't known in years. Behind him, as if from miles away, he heard the door shut as Raff left.

It was like coming home, like the first waking moment after a bad dream. Olly's lips were the same – the shape of his mouth, the tilt of his head. It was like Ash was a youth again, that wild boy stood on the edge of a battlefield with his heart aglow.

Olly hesitated for just a moment – a single second, stretched to a lifetime – before responding. Ash held him tighter, his lips opening, his tongue—

It was the same. It was all the same, even his *taste,* marred by however long of living rough but still *him,* beneath that.

Ash's hands were moving more urgently, now, his kisses more desperate, his lips yearning. He was clinging, touching all the places he could. Olly kissed him back with a kind of starving fervour, and Ash gripped him tighter, grabbing at his thin, worn tunic and shoving it aside so he could touch him properly.

The brush of Olly's skin against Ash's palms made him gasp – made them both gasp, Olly's caught and breathy, Ash's halfway to a cry. He was *real.* He was so warm and his skin was just as soft as Ash had remembered, as soft as it was in his dreams.

'Olly . . .' he breathed into his mouth. '*Oliver . . .*'

There was nothing in the world but Olly, and the feel of his skin, and the huff of his breath hot against Ash's neck. It was just them, locked away in this tiny space, the rest of the world outside nothing but a—

But a dream.

Ash hesitated. Olly stiffened in his arms.

He realised that he needed to talk to Agnes. That he needed to tell her . . . not all, but enough. If Agnes took offence and left, that would ruin them both. But Olly was alive. Ash could feel the heat radiating from him.

He would apologise to Agnes. He would give her anything she wanted, if it was in his power to give. He would embrace his own ruin, if she demanded it.

But not now. Tonight, he had Olly. Tonight he was no longer Earl Ashwy Barden, he was Ash – just Ashel, before war had forced him into the walking death he'd been living in for so many years.

He kissed Olly again, pulling him backwards onto the tiny pallet bed. He folded Olly into his arms, bundling him close, listening to the sound of his breathing; the irrevocable proof that he was alive. He had returned. The dreams and the wild visions couldn't harm him anymore. Ash gripped tight to Olly's shoulders, face buried into his neck, and vowed to never let him go again.

Chapter 11

Olly

Ash had fallen asleep.

Olly rolled over, dislodging himself from Ash's embrace. Ash didn't seem to notice, merely moving onto his back with a snore.

The noise was so familiar that Olly almost laughed, before the wave of emotion crashed on him, transforming it into a sob. Or a growl.

He should never have given in. He could still feel the ghost of Ash's kiss on his lips.

It was like being home, like being made whole. Part of him – the weakest part, the part he hated – had given in. It had succumbed to the feeling. *Do it,* it had whispered, in a treacherous voice. *Take it. While you can.* He'd kissed Ash back with equal parts passion and hate, the two tangled in his head. He had been ready to attempt to resist his own desires, but to his shock, Ash had never initiated anything beyond kissing, beyond holding him tight against his chest.

Now that he was able to think more clearly, the hate could triumph. Ash hadn't even *apologised.* He hadn't even acknowledged what he'd done. Describing it as a betrayal wasn't enough: Ash was a traitor, a vow-breaker, a liar to the core. And he had not even seen fit to mention it.

Outside the tiny, high window the sky was still inky black. Olly shuddered. He was no longer bound – although his wrists were marked where the rope had rubbed his skin – but he *was* still a prisoner. The whispering breeze that blew in sounded like faraway voices.

Olly slid from the bed. The guards had taken his dagger, but the pouch of coins was still tied to his belt. He pulled them out, spilling them into his hand to ensure there was enough to flee this place.

The ring fell out with them. Even in the dark, it had a glimmer to it.

He peered at it, holding it between thumb and forefinger so it reflected the dying embers of the fire.

At last he knew why he had clung onto it for so long.

His pouch was lighter but his heart was stone as he headed from the room, closing the door behind him. Outside, he hesitated, leaning against the wood. His feet stuck. It was like there was a rope tied tight around his heart, one that he thought had been severed years ago. It had never been severed, just gone slack.

Now, it was pulling him back, tugging him to return to the warmth of the bed and Ash's arms.

He had to resist. Olly pushed away from the door and headed down the stairs.

The keep seemed deadly quiet. He moved quickly but carefully, pressed against the walls, keeping to the shadows. He headed for the stables, where he picked the finest-looking horse. He was about to mount, when there was a noise from the stable door.

'What are you doing, Oliver?'

Shit.

Standing there was not, as he expected, Ash, but another

member of the household. A tall man with curly hair. Somehow, the man knew his name.

He strode into the stable, shutting and bolting the door behind him.

'You are attempting to leave?'

Olly stalked forwards to meet him. 'And what if I am? Get out of my way.'

He had been expecting the man to try to restrain him or to shout for the guards. But he did not. He burst into laughter.

This annoyed Olly more than if he *had* attempted to stop him. 'What?'

The man managed to control himself, although a smile still played about his face.

'Nothing,' he said. 'You remind me of someone else.'

'Who?'

The man shrugged infuriatingly. 'So you intend to leave?'

'You cannot make me stay!'

Olly was *fairly* sure about that. The man was taller than him, and armed with an expensive-looking dagger. He was not skinny, but not as muscular as the Barden brothers either. He would be a difficult fight, Olly suspected, but one he would win. Noblemen tended to go down easier.

'I probably cannot.' The man appeared unthreatened. 'But I can try.'

'And why would you do that?'

'Because I *care* for Ash. I was under the impression that you did, too.'

Olly glowered at him. 'Who *are* you?'

'Does it matter?'

'It does.'

The man sighed. 'Ash is . . . difficult. I know that. But I love him as a brother. Let us say that I am returning a favour to him. You *cannot* go. Not like this. He needs you.'

'He does not *need* me,' Olly said. 'Now *move*.'

He shoved forwards, attempting to push the man aside. And then there was a vice around his wrist. Before he could move, the man twisted him about, kicked a foot between Olly's boots and sent him tumbling to the floor. The horses whinnied at the sudden noise as Olly cursed, winded by the collision with the stone. The man did not pause, straddling him with his arm pinned painfully behind his back, forcing him down.

Olly blew a foul-smelling clump of straw away from his face. The man gripped him harder.

'He *loves* you, you *stupid* man,' he huffed.

Olly shook his head. 'He does not.' It was all he could manage.

The man seemed to be growing bored of him – or frustrated. 'He *does*. Come inside, come with me, and we can . . . talk.'

'Talk?' Olly scoffed, wriggling against the floor. 'Really?'

'Just talk. And if you stand by this choice, then by all means I will let you go. In fact if you do not love him in return, then I *ask* you to go, if only to save Ash even more heartbreak.'

'Of course I do not love him.'

Olly spat it out as quickly as he could, but even then, his treacherous mouth fumbled over the words. The man did not seem convinced.

'Please,' he said, exasperated. 'I will not take you to Ash. You have my word. But you cannot leave until you understand *exactly* what it is – *who* it is – you are leaving behind. *Please*.'

He seemed sincere. Olly had learned sincerity these past few years; it had saved his life more than once.

'Fine,' he said. '*Fine*. But you swear you will not take me to Ash?'

'I swear. Come.'

The man finally released him, reaching down to haul him to his feet.

'Wait . . .' Olly gave chase as the man pushed open the stable door and headed into the courtyard. 'What is your name?'

But the man was already halfway across the yard. Olly cursed, then jogged to reach him. The man didn't break his stride at all, leading him inside. As he took him through the great hall towards a side room, the promise he had made not to lead him directly back to Ash seemed dubious. He was being duped, he realised. He was being walked directly back towards his nightmare, and worse: he was allowing it.

As if reading his thoughts, the other man glanced at him, then reached out, and in a surprisingly firm grip took Olly's arm.

'Oh no,' he said. 'Don't.'

He shoved open the door of the side room. There was another person here, and Olly's first thought was that he *had* been tricked – but the man beside the fire stood and he realised at once that, despite the strong familial resemblance, this was not Ash.

'Please,' Raff said sombrely. 'Sit.'

He gestured to another chair beside him by the roaring fire. The curly-haired man finally released him and, cautiously, Olly sat.

Raff watched him. In the flash of his eyes, Olly could see Ash. It was unsettling. Finally, he spoke.

'Can I offer you a drink?'

Olly blinked. 'What?'

'A drink? Wine is all we have, though.' He gestured towards a jug sat on the opposite table. Olly eyed it nervously. 'It *is* just wine,' Raff added. 'Come, do not think I intend to poison you.'

Olly relented. 'Thank you.'

Raff did not move, but the other man quickly poured drinks for them both – and himself, Olly noted – before moving to stand again in front of the door.

Ah, Olly realised. A guard.

Raff took a drink, gesturing for Olly to do the same.

'You were trying to leave, then?' he said.

The wine was good, and strong. 'Yes,' Olly said, keeping his gaze.

'Why?'

'What?'

'Why are you leaving? Why now?'

Olly gripped the mug harder. 'He is getting married.'

Raff's knuckles, too, were turning white. 'He loves you.'

This again. Olly could nearly laugh. 'He does not love me,' he said, voice hollow.

'Do you know what happened when Ash came home?' Raff spat. 'Of course you don't. He was dragged here, his face in ruins, his body racked with rot, babbling about you, always *you*. I didn't even know who you were! But all he said, over and over, was your name. Even when we thought he was going to die, that was all he could say.'

'I—'

Raff cut him off. 'Do you know what losing you did to him? How *broken* he was? It has been years, and you follow him around like a damn ghost, and suddenly you return only to . . . what? Break him again?'

'But I—'

'I do not care for your excuses. I know . . .' Raff's voice shuddered.

There was a creak, and Olly snapped around. The man by the door had appeared to move, before thinking better of it.

'I know that whatever happened to you out there must have been

Hell,' Raff continued. 'But my duty is to Ash. I love him, and I have not watched him suffer for so many years just to sit back and do nothing as he stands on the edge of that darkness again. I refuse.'

Olly's hands were shaking. He quickly put the cup down beside the chair to prevent it spilling. Raff's words seemed sincere, but they clashed against the reality that Olly knew: the truth which clearly Ash had never seen fit to spread, for some dark reason of his own.

'I know he loved you,' Raff was saying. 'He never stopped loving you. Ever. And I do not know if you ever cared for him, or if you even reciprocated that love. Back then, I assumed you had. And now I do not know.'

Raff's words caught in Olly's chest, like barbs. He looked up. His body was trembling with bright white rage.

'You don't know,' he hissed. 'You don't know! How dare you say he loved me – that he still loves me – when he . . . when he . . .'

He was on his feet. He could not remember standing.

'When he what?' Raff was staring up at him, expression calm.

'He could have found me. He could have come for me and he didn't. He left me. I was trapped, and I was a prisoner, and he left me to *rot*.'

Olly never talked about his time in France. Only Pepper knew the true extent of it – the rest of his band only ever being privy to the barest details. And yet here he was, spilling it at the feet of the brother of the man who had betrayed him.

Raff paled. Olly slumped back into his seat, grabbing his drink. He saw it off in one go, enjoying the hot burn of the wine in his throat.

Finally, Raff spoke. 'Please. You have to talk to him. You do not know.'

Olly shook his head. 'I know enough.'

'You know nothing.' Raff glared at him. '*Nothing.* Do you love him? Did you, and now you no longer do? Because if that is the case, then I understand – I do, and I will not curse you for what your heart wants – but you cannot just leave like this. You have to talk to him.'

It was no longer a request. Olly thought he could escape the grasp of the taller man, but both, and trapped in this tiny room? It was impossible.

'Will you talk to him?' Raff asked once more. '*Please,* Oliver?'

It was the first time Raff had called him by his name. Olly had no choice, he realised.

At least this way he could finally force Ash to atone for what he had done to him.

He stood.

'Fine.'

✡

To Olly's surprise, they didn't lead him back to the cell, but up a wider staircase to a heavy oak door. Raff shot him a look, as if expecting him to flee again, before pushing open the door and shoving him inside.

The room was dark. An antechamber of some sort, Olly realised. Raff pushed him onwards, through to a second, larger room beyond. This must be Ash's bedchamber. It was huge. Olly wasn't sure why he was so surprised: Ash was an earl, now. Of course his sleeping chamber was impressive. The floor was covered in thick skin rugs, the enormous bed in the centre of the room wide enough for at least three people and hung with embroidered canopies. A fire burned too hot in the hearth.

Ash sat on the floor at the foot of the bed. He didn't look up when the door opened. In his hand was Olly's ring.

'Ash.'

Raff was the first to break the silence. Ash looked up. His gaze flicked between the three of them before finally settling on Olly.

'I thought you had gone.'

'He tried,' the curly-haired man grumbled. 'I stopped him.'

Ash gave out a choking laugh. 'Did you, now?'

'Call it a favour returned.'

'I do not know if I should be thanking you.'

'Neither do I. You will have to tell me later.'

And then they were gone, the door shut, leaving Olly locked with Ash in the flickering firelight.

Ash stood. His limbs hung limp, and as he moved the ring slid from his hand and onto the floor with a heavy thud.

He stepped forwards, close enough to touch. Olly kept his arms by his sides, clenching his hands into fists, feeling his heartbeat in them.

'You were—'

Ash reached out. There was a deep indent in his palm: a perfect circle where he'd been clutching the ring. He brushed his hand against Olly's jaw – the touch as gentle and as horrible as the first wind before a storm.

'You were . . .' Another shuddering breath. '*I love you.*'

Something snapped. Olly wrenched his face away. 'No. Ash—*No.*'

Ash was off him in an instant. 'Olly—'

'Is this all you want me for? Even whores get paid, Ash!'

There was a ringing silence. Finally, Ash spoke, voice small. 'What are you talking about?'

'Why didn't you come for me when you had the chance?' Olly demanded. 'Or do you only want me when you don't have to pay for me? When I just land in your lap?'

'Olly, what are you—'

'I could have *died* and none of you did anything! None of you! You vowed to be by my side! You swore I was yours! But I wasn't even worth a bag of coins to you. I never was!'

'Olly—' Ash strode forwards and grabbed his shoulders. 'What do you *mean*?'

He was so close. The fight fled from Olly's body, the weight of it suddenly too much.

'They took me prisoner. They sent letters to Mother. To *you*.' Each word was punched out of him. '*Demands*. They made me write them myself. It wasn't . . . it wasn't even that *much*—'

'Demands?'

'They *ransomed* me. They knew that Father was rich, and important, and they thought . . .' A silent, tearless sob racked through his body. The only thing keeping him upright was Ash's hands on his shoulders. 'They thought someone might pay for me.'

He shook himself free from Ash's grip, shoving him away.

'They were *wrong*,' he spat. 'No one even *refused*. They just ignored them. *You* ignored them.'

Ash's pained expression sloughed away. In its place was one of horror and grief.

'They ransomed you?'

'Twice.'

Ash took a staggering step backwards. He collapsed onto the bed, straight down, like his legs had given way.

He muttered something, his words lost to the crackling of the fire.

'What?' Olly couldn't help the sharpness of his voice. He glared down at Ash, heart thundering. '*What?*'

Ash swallowed. He finally met Olly's gaze, his eyes wide and haunted.

'I thought you were *dead,*' he said, voice flat. 'I saw you fall. I saw you *die.* I see you die every' – he choked around it – 'every night. I see it.'

'But—'

'Their letters never came. Olly, you *must* believe me. They never arrived. Not here, not to your mother. If I had known . . .' The noise he made was not a laugh, not quite. 'If I'd known you were alive I'd have swum across that *fucking* sea myself to get you back. I'd have given them anything. I'd have demanded Father pay, or stolen it from him, stolen it from . . . from *anyone,* Olly. I swear to you, I didn't know. I never . . .'

Ash's words died. His expression broke, his lip – his scarred, torn lip – trembled as the tears overtook him.

The anger, which had been red-hot and wieldable, suddenly had nowhere to go.

'Ash?' The word escaped Olly's mouth like a breath.

'You must— Olly, *Oliver—*' Ash was suddenly up on his feet. He grabbed Olly's arms, hard enough to bruise. Olly did not move away. 'I do not know how I can prove it to you. I will do anything, *anything* you ask.'

Olly's head was full of smoke. Ash looked distraught, his eyes manic. It did not look like a lie. It did not *feel* like a lie. But so many years of hate and betrayal coalesced still in the back of Olly's mind. The resentment. The fear. Nothing felt real: not Ash's words, not his own memory, the things he had *known* to be true for so long.

'I don't—' He struggled for words, nauseous. 'I cannot—'

'I know. I know. Please, Olly, just . . . just let me *try*—'

Olly opened and shut his mouth, trying to find his words. He was shaking, he realised; his whole body was shaking. His cheeks were wet: was he crying?

'What happened to you?' Ash asked. 'I saw . . . on the field I saw that bastard with the mace take you down, but I couldn't get to you before . . .'

His voice cracked into silence. Olly wrapped his arms around Ash's shoulders at last. He did not want to speak it aloud. But he had to.

'I fell from the horse,' he muttered. 'It was so *loud*.'

He still dreamed of that noise. The sound of metal on metal, the mace colliding with his helm. The ringing: the horrible sound that had built and built until the ringing was all that was left.

'They took me to a keep,' he continued. 'I don't remember . . . I do not remember *any* of it truthfully.'

'What about your head?'

'No wounds, thank God,' Olly said. 'No blood. No breaks. But . . .'

'But?'

He didn't want to tell him. It was desperately important that Ash did not know. But he was staring at Olly with open, terrified eyes. He deserved to know it all; he deserved to know the state of the man who had returned to him.

'My hearing,' he said. 'And . . . my eye, my right eye. It took a while, and then . . . gone.'

'Gone?'

'My right side is not as strong as it once was, I am afraid.' Olly laughed, the noise strained. 'I will never be able to aim a bow again.

I cannot hear, on this side. I am no longer the man you wished to make a marshal of.'

'Olly . . .' Ash pulled him close. 'I am so sorry. I am *so sorry.*'

Olly buried his face in Ash's tunic. The tears came freely, now.

'I went to see your mother,' Ash said. 'After.'

'What?' Olly was sure his heart had stopped.

'It was too soon. They all told me I was not well enough for the journey, but I insisted. She was . . .' Ash looked down. 'She was like a ghost.'

There was a terrible weight in Olly's chest. His mother had been all light and laughter. She had been so solidly *real* compared to the aloof God of his father. She had been something he could hold.

'We spoke for a whole evening,' Ash continued tonelessly. 'We grieved for different things, but she *understood.* It was barely even a conversation; she spoke of your youth, and I of our training together, of our squiring.

'I stayed for only a day. I slept in the servants' quarters and the next morning she came to bid me farewell. She took my hand, and—' Ash suddenly fell silent. 'Her eyes were like stone. She looked at me, but she didn't *see* me, as if I were made of mist. She said . . .' He took a breath that caught in his chest. 'She said that it should have been me. That I should have died on the field, and God should have brought you back in my stead. She was right.' His eyes were drowning in unshed tears. 'It should have been me.'

'Ash . . .'

'I already knew it, of course,' he continued, as if Olly hadn't spoken. 'I had spent *weeks* praying that it had been a dream, a dying man's last thoughts, and that I would slip away and it was *you* who'd wake up on that damned battlefield. But after talking to her . . . it built. I got it into my head that somehow

I could . . . I could *trade* myself for you. That if I returned to France I could undo it. I was completely delirious, but it seemed so *true* . . .' Ash scratched at his scar as he spoke. 'I tried, once. Raff caught me in the stables wearing nothing but my braies trying to saddle a horse. He dragged me back to bed, whilst I muttered about France and debts and *you* the whole time. He thought I had gone insane.' He chuckled, voice low, entirely humourless. 'I suppose I had.'

Olly swallowed. His chest felt hollow, his head empty.

'You tried to go back for me?'

Ash smiled – but it did not reach his eyes. 'So many times. So many arguments, so many attempts, even with a damned *sea* between us—' Something within him broke. He dropped his head, tears spilling down his face. 'Even though you were dead.'

He's telling the truth. It was Olly's own voice, but so much younger. Unruined by time and war and betrayal and death. The feeling Olly had buried for years took over. He reached out, wrapped his arms around Ash's middle and bundled him close.

For a long while, Olly just held him, listening to him breathe. Ash buried his face in Olly's neck, his breath hot and ragged against his skin.

When Olly let go, it was with a sigh, never really releasing Ash from his grip. His face was so familiar, yet so different. Olly could see all of him in those eyes: the grumpy squire, the passionate youth, the devoted lover. The man torn down in a spray of blood on the battlefield. There were strands of grey swiping through the hair at his temples. They had not been there before.

'My Ashel . . .' Olly tilted Ash's face up, his thumb pressed lightly into the scar that bisected his lip. 'What happened to you?'

'Everything,' Ash breathed. 'War. France.' His eyes dragged

shut as Olly brushed his thumb across the scar, feeling the ridges of it, the puckered skin. '*You.*'

Olly hooked his finger beneath Ash's chin and pulled him in. Now, without anger clouding his mind, he could fully appreciate his touch, the now-changed shape of Ash's lips beneath his own.

Ash pulled back with a sigh, taking Olly's hands, turning them over in his own as if amazed that they were even real. He went to raise one to his lips, then paused.

He stroked a gentle, cautious finger over the red marks left by the ropes that Ash's guards had bound around Olly's wrist. 'Is this—'

'I was their prisoner,' Olly said. 'I cannot blame them.'

Ash looked horrified. He lowered his head, pressing his lips to the marks with gentle, reverent kisses.

'I should not have let them do that to you.'

'I tried to kill you. I should count myself lucky that' – Olly shuddered, his words breaking into a gasp as Ash's kisses became more desperate, his lips opening against Olly's tender skin – 'that they did not harm me more fatally,' he managed, voice quavering. '*Ash*—'

Ash peered up at him, head still bent. His eyes sparkled. 'Yes?'

Olly could not bear for him to look at him like that. He grabbed Ash's face in both his hands, heaved him up, and kissed him properly, kissed him till neither of them could breathe.

Before, their kisses had been a rush – passion overwhelmed by anger. Olly had been too consumed with his own rage to appreciate having Ash in his arms again. Now he could.

He pushed Ash back. They stumbled over each other's feet until they collided with the far wall. Olly drunk down Ash's sound of shock as the wind was knocked from his lungs, gripping at Ash's tunic, pulling it aside.

Ash grabbed his hips, pulling him in and holding him against his body. His prick twitched between them and, unthinking, Olly slid a hand down to better feel the evidence of Ash's uncontrolled desire. He made a low, rumbling noise which became a single word:

'*Bed*.'

They shuffled to the enormous bed. Ash roughly tugged aside the hangings, and then – as if struck – froze, his hand bundled in the fabric. This was *his* space, yet he still looked a little lost. He looked around as if seeing the room for the first time, his face tense.

Ash turned, opened his mouth, dropped the curtain, and then—

'I'm the earl.'

It was so absurd that Olly burst out laughing. 'So I've heard, yes.'

'I . . . I can't be an earl.'

'I fear you've not much choice in the matter.'

'I had always thought . . .' Ash looked around the enormous room like a child sneaking around in his father's quarters. 'I had always thought when it happened, you would be with me.' His expression broke.

'Ash . . .' Olly stepped forwards, taking his hands. 'I *am* with you. I am with you now.'

'I am sorry.'

Olly sighed, rubbing his thumbs across Ash's knuckles. 'As am I.'

Ash still wore that lost expression. He was feeling awkward, Olly realised. The simple act of having Olly in his chambers, decked out in the finery of an earl, was a lifetime away from the squire he had once been who had shared Olly's cramped bed in his father's keep.

Ash needed a nudge. He needed, Olly knew, a gentle touch.

A little guidance.

This was familiar: this was a dance he and Ash had done many times before.

'Ash.'

Ash looked at him. Olly gave him his best grin.

'Come here.'

Ash did so without question or argument, letting Olly take him in his arms. He softened against him, and Olly wondered just how long it had been since Ash had given himself over like this.

He guided them down onto the huge bed, trying not to consider how he'd never fucked anyone in a bed this fine. Ash seemed a little dazed as Olly laid him down upon the sheets and slung a leg over his hips, holding himself above him.

'Are you well, my Lord?'

Ash winced. 'Don't call me that.'

'Are you well, my Ashel?'

Ash nodded. 'I— yes,' he breathed. 'Olly, *please*—'

Olly kissed him, this time careful to make it gentler, a lingering kiss that left Ash panting and squirming when he was done. He could feel Ash's prick straining at his breeches, desperate for more than just the meeting of lips.

He sat up, making Ash whine in a way that was so charmingly familiar it made Olly's heart squeeze, then began to undress him. It had often been like this, when Ash was at his most petulant or needy or fraught; Olly taking him apart, layer by layer. He started with the ties of his tunic, feeling the waxed cord beneath his fingers. Next the tunic itself, already untucked and ruched around Ash's waist, pulled up and over his head to leave his chest bare.

Something shone on a cord around Ash's neck. The ring. Ash's half of the promise they had exchanged. It was tarnished with age and oil: he must have worn it beneath his clothes since France. Since Olly's apparent death.

'You kept it?' Olly muttered, brushing his fingers against the warm metal.

'Of course I did.'

Now Ash's chest was bare, Olly could also see the true extent of the wounds that Ash had acquired in battle. The scar that snaked down Ash's face and neck twisted down his collar, too, in an uneven, broken line. Someone must have slashed at him, catching his skin at various points with the thrust.

The scars were raised and jagged. It appeared that they had healed poorly, and the deep, puckered skin bore the evidence of long-since-cleared infection. Olly could only imagine the state Ash had returned to England in, his face ruined, his body dying.

The marks still looked raw and painful. Another truth, and this one he could never deny: such wounds were not earned by a man who had tried to be rid of him.

He dragged a finger down the worst of the scars, cutting across Ash's collarbone, when Ash reached out and grabbed his wrist.

Olly froze, fingers curling. 'I am sorry,' he said, for more than just the intimate touch. 'I did not realise . . .'

Ash heaved himself up on his elbows. 'You did not know.'

Ash kissed him, one hand coming to cup the back of Olly's head, before tugging him back down.

They could have kissed for an age – the world outside them could have turned through summer and winter and spring again – before Olly finally began to continue the urgent task of getting Ash bare.

He reached down for the ties of Ash's hose and breeches, undoing them with a swift hand. It took some manoeuvring to remove the garment itself; every time he leaned back, Ash grabbed at him, pulling him back. The space between them was ringing and cold. Even like this, with Ash half-naked and eager beneath him, his eyes wide and awe-struck, he felt so terribly far away.

Olly finally removed the last of Ash's clothing with a triumphant tug. Now Ash was entirely naked, he could appreciate him more fully. He had changed over the years that had separated them; not just the scar, but his body, too. He had lost the firmness that strict training had carved into him, now plusher, softer. Olly stroked up and down Ash's chest, feeling all of him, pressing nails into pliable flesh.

Ash pulled him into a desperate kiss. Olly straddled his hips, removing his own tunic as Ash's hands roamed the planes of his chest. Olly was skinnier, now: he was no longer as well-fed as he had been in his father's keep, and he wondered what Ash made of *his* new body.

But Ash's hands had gone still, his expression furrowed in concern.

'Ash?'

Ash sat up, making Olly nearly topple from his lap, then gently pressed his hand to the terrible scar that sliced across Olly's upper arm.

'What is this?' he muttered. 'Did this happen in France?'

Olly glanced down at the mark. 'No,' he muttered. 'It was . . . after.'

Ash's expression did not change. 'After?'

'After I escaped . . . Ash, I was desperate. I did anything that could get me coin in my purse and food in my belly. Including banditry.' Olly watched him, almost daring Ash to chastise him.

But he didn't. He looked pained.

'God, Olly—' He sat up properly, pulling Olly into a crushing embrace. 'I am so sorry.'

Olly blinked at the sudden assault of emotions. His eyes prickled. 'It is quite all right.'

'It is *not* all right. You should never have been forced to do that.'

'But I *was*.' Olly sighed. 'I cannot change that.' Ash leaned back a little, staring at him. 'The scar was from an accident. A robbery gone wrong. I was too cocky. I paid for it, dearly.'

Ash examined the mark closer. 'This looks as if it turned.'

'As I said,' Olly remarked. 'I paid dearly.'

'What—'

'*Ash*. Please.'

He didn't want to be forced to talk about that now. About the stupid decision he'd made, the wound he'd been gifted through that stupidity, about the rot that set in soon after. The friends – the people who he had *thought* were his friends – who he had lost.

Ash's gaze slid from the wound to his eyes. At last, the expression softened. Olly kissed him, silencing any further questions. Ash let out a soft sigh, letting him. His hands drifted back down Olly's sides to his hips, playing in the fabric of Olly's breeches.

'This is unfair . . .' he mumbled against Olly's lips with a grin.

Olly found himself inclined to agree. He set himself to removing the rest of his clothes, and at last, they were both naked on the bed. With a little shuffling, Olly manoeuvred them beneath one of the wool blankets, cocooned in the warmth with their naked limbs tangled together and their lips brushing.

God above, he had missed this so much. He had lain with people since he and Ash were parted, and he had found pleasure in them, but *this* . . . this was like returning home, like returning to a place he had never thought he would see again. It was all so easy and familiar, none of the fumbling uncertainty that came with bedding a new lover. Ash's hand drifting down his chest and playing in the tangle of hair that trailed from his navel to his cock felt exactly as it had done all those years ago.

He wanted all of him. He wanted to draw this out and take his time. He wanted Ash *now*, hot and quick and panting. He wanted it *all*.

For the first time in too many years, part of him wondered if he could have it.

He stamped that thought down – too bright, too eager, too hopeful – and instead brought his focus back to the curves of Ash's chest, the tangle of his hair, the shimmering wetness of his kiss-bruised lips. There was too much else at play, no matter what Ash said, to ensure any kind of future. But *this* was all his. Ash was all his, at least for these few hours.

He reached between them, trailing his hand down Ash's chest and teasing his fingertips above his prick. Ash hissed through his teeth.

Olly was struck with a sudden thought. 'Do you have oil?'

Ash hesitated. 'Shit. I am not sure . . .'

Olly let him go as he slid from the bed and headed to the chest beside it. Olly was enjoying the view of Ash's bare arse too much to be *too* disappointed by the loss of his touch as he watched him look around the room.

Before France, and after they had settled into the routine of it, Olly had always made sure there was something on hand for moments like these. The result of so many years together in near-undisturbed privacy had allowed them space for experimentation, finding something that worked best and ensuring they always had some oil or tallow hidden away somewhere in Olly's chambers or in one of their packs while on the road.

Ash made his way towards a box in the corner of the room, digging through it, his searching peppered with the occasional curse. Even becoming an earl hadn't encouraged him to be any more organised, it seemed, as he dug through his things haphazardly. He swore again, then rose, chest flushed.

'Nothing,' he said. 'I—'

'No matter.' Olly reached for him. Ash obeyed immediately, taking his hand and letting Olly pull him back onto the bed.

'I will find something suitable when I am next able to,' Ash assured him. 'It was . . . linseed oil, wasn't it? And lavender?'

'No, the lavender gave you a headache.' Olly laughed, kissing his neck. 'It was the chamomile and linseed that you preferred.'

'Of course. But—'

'Ashel.'

'Yes?'

'Hush.'

Ash fell silent, allowing himself to be kissed. Olly guided him down onto his back, nestled amongst the blankets. He sucked Ash's bottom lip into his mouth, tugging but not biting – not yet. Olly's skin was aflame, his heart thudding, his cock so sensitive and hard that it felt like even a single stroke of Ash's fingers would send him over the edge. He trailed his hands down Ash's chest, across his thighs, tracing the neat line where leg met torso teasingly.

Ash writhed beneath him. Finally, giving in to what he and Ash craved, Olly reached for Ash's prick, palming it in a strong grip and swiping his thumb across the head, pressing, *squeezing*. The moan that came from Ash's mouth sounded as if it had been ripped from him, pulled from his lungs by the roots.

Olly reached up and placed two fingers against the soft pillow of Ash's bottom lip. A low noise rumbled from the back of Ash's throat.

'Open.'

Ash *whined*, parting his lips as Olly slid his fingers inside his mouth. He sucked at them, his tongue sliding over them until they were slick. Olly's cock strained between his legs, heart racing, as Ash tongued languidly at his digits, moaning around them. At last Olly pulled them out, making sure to catch the tips against Ash's lip again, before reaching down between them.

Ash lifted himself up a little to grant Olly access. Olly slid his spit-slicked fingers into the cleft of his arse, pressing against him. Ash pushed down against him with a needy noise that went straight to Olly's cock.

Olly wanted to tease him and draw it out, but he wanted *this* more. Forgoing the urge, he pushed a finger inside, then another – drinking in Ash's gasps and shudders as he breached him. He was hot and tight around Olly's fingers, like a vice. Placing his other hand on Ash's leg to steady him, Olly worked him open, enjoying watching him writhe beneath his touches.

When Ash was panting, his cock already beading with eager moisture, Olly leaned forwards so their chests were flush, finally removing his fingers. He kissed him, and Ash kissed him back like a drowning man taking in air.

'How do you want it?' Olly grinned, sliding his palm over the soft skin of Ash's inner thigh.

Ash looked as if he were about to perish. 'However,' he said. 'Any way. All ways. Olly, *please*.'

The swelling muscle in Olly's chest battled valiantly against his prick. He had gotten Ash on his knees like this so many times, open for him, eager and ready. But he needed to *see*, now. He needed to see Ash's face and feel his heart beat in his chest. He wanted to watch Ash's face as he fell apart, just to remind himself that this was all real – that it wasn't just another broken dream. That Ash still loved him, impossibly, after all this time.

He kissed him again, then trailed his lips down Ash's chest, nibbling at the tender skin around his navel. He pressed a long, languorous kiss to the head of Ash's cock, making him jerk his hips, before settling back upon his heels.

He made sure Ash was watching as he lazily spat into his hand then began to work at himself. He was already desperately hard, and even the gentle touch of his own palm threatened to force him over the edge. He wished he had something more than spit. *Next time*, he thought to himself, *next time*. No doubt he could have scrounged *something* from Ash's things – a forgotten bottle of sword oil, medicinal salve – but the thought of extracting himself from Ash's grip felt like dying. They would make do, as they had done before, as they had done so many times.

'Ash?'

'*Please—*'

He could barely refuse. He would *never* refuse. Olly gripped his hips, lifting him off the blankets, nudging at his entrance. Ash made another gasping hiss, another murmured demand. Olly positioned himself, took a breath, then pushed himself inside.

Ash was hot and tight, his whole body tensing as Olly entered him. Olly held himself there, his hands clinging to Ash's legs, fingers digging into his soft thighs. Ash let out a long, deep sigh – a breath that seemed to loosen his whole body. Only when Olly was sure Ash was ready did he pull back, then thrust again and again, feeling Ash clench around him, watching him arch on the bed, flinging one arm up to cover his eyes.

'No—' Olly leaned over him, pushing his arm aside and cupping his jaw, 'No, Ashel, I want to see you.'

Ash's mouth hung open in a wordless, desperate gasp. Olly leaned even closer, as close as he could, before reaching between their bodies. He caught Ash's prick in his hand, drawing him out, guiding him in the way he knew Ash liked best. Ash stuttered out an oath.

Olly jerked Ash's cock with unthinking haste, lost to the feeling of it. In but a moment, Ash was releasing in hot, shuddering bursts across his own stomach and Olly's hand.

Olly's thundered to his own release shortly after. He clung on to Ash's hips in desperation, all semblance of rhythm or posturing gone, only pleasure, only *Ash*.

He eased out slowly, then – in a movement like a tree being felled – he collapsed onto the bed beside Ash, breathing heavily. He felt racked with it, with the rush and release, with being back at Ash's side. He nudged closer, and Ash wrapped an arm around him with a sleepy sigh.

His skin prickled, coated in a cooling sheen of sweat. Now his pulse was calming and his hunger satiated – at least, in this moment – he could truly appreciate the finery he found himself enjoying. The sheets were absurdly soft, the bed topped with a feather tick. He hadn't experienced such luxuries in years; the last time he slept in a bed this fine was the night before they left his father's keep for France.

If he closed his eyes, he could almost imagine they were there again, locked in a warm – if somewhat sweaty – embrace beneath the sheets of Olly's bed, waiting for dawn to rise.

So much had changed since then. He'd carried around the hatred for so long. Now he realised it was unwarranted, he didn't know what to do with it. He'd cheated, somehow, to end up back in this familiar position with the worst consequence only a few, heated words and an aborted attempt at escape.

Ash started to brush his fingers slowly up and down Olly's arm. He seemed unkeen to let go, and Olly supposed he could not blame him; *he* didn't want to let go either, lest the world conspire to part them again.

He heard Ash sigh, the sound reverberating through his chest.

'I wish you had come to find me,' Ash said.

Now, in the low light with fresh knowledge of all that had happened since the battle, Olly agreed with him.

'I, too,' he said. 'But I thought you had abandoned me. I thought you *hated* me. And besides, if I *had* come to find you, it would have been to entangle myself in a scandal. Last I heard of you, half the southern counties were searching for your brother, claiming he had kidnapped or murdered some earl's son.'

Ash's hand went still on his arm. '. . . Oh.'

'Regardless,' Olly spoke quickly, needing to get it out. 'When our paths *do* cross, I hear you are to be *wed*?'

'I know it is difficult,' Ash said. 'But it is not a . . . a *love match*. It is . . .' he huffed. 'Lord above, it is business. Agnes needs a husband, and I need a wife. I have dragged my feet for far too long. The family – the *name* – needs an heir.'

'But I thought Raff—'

'You said yourself he was embroiled in scandal. He nearly *died* as a result of it. The mark against his name would be enough to put off many brides, but the wounds . . . and, well . . .' Ash hesitated. 'He is no longer the guarantee for an heir he once was.'

'Oh.' Olly was taken aback. He had never met Raff – not before this day – but Ash had often spoken of him. 'I am sorry, is he—'

'He is well.' Ash laughed. 'He is better than he has been in years. But he isn't the prize he once was, unless there is a woman out there who is seeking a scandalous cripple. And besides, I would not force him to—' He stopped, composing himself. 'He has reasons not to wed. And he has done too much for me since my return. I owe him more than anyone else.'

'And who . . . who was the man? The tall one with the—' Olly sat up and gestured around his head with his fingers, playing on the man's curls. 'Who stopped me?'

'Penn?' Ash said, only half listening. 'He's our hostage.'

Olly nearly swallowed his own tongue. '*What?*'

'*God,* that is a long story,' Ash said. 'You mentioned the scandal we found ourselves in? He is to do with that, and his father . . . It is complicated.'

That sounded right. Olly had only caught only the barest details of the story on his travels, any truth to the matter watered down by gossip and rumour. Whatever it was must have been horrific, to leave Raff so wounded and the man involved kept as a prisoner.

'But what about your family?' Ash asked, breaking through his thoughts. 'Why did you not return to them?'

'And face the same reception I feared to face with you?' Olly sighed. 'They had even greater reason to refuse to pay my ransom. After Father and Hal died out there, I assumed the others blamed me for their deaths, that leaving me to rot was their punishment. I did seek them out, when I returned. Just to see. Mother died a short while ago, and after Father's death the title had passed to Thomas. You remember him? And then . . . then he died, less than a year later. Trampled by his own horse, stupid bastard. He had no children, so the title passed to Peter. He was a poor brother but . . . but he makes a good lord, from what I can tell.'

'Why not go back to him, then?'

Olly's heart was stony in his chest.

'I could not. Not without Father. Not like this. They did not need me. And they did not *want* me, either. I thought . . .'

'The ransoms.'

'Exactly. I couldn't.'

'But now you know the truth . . . can't you go back?'

'*No,* Ash.'

'But you could still—'

'Ash!'

Ash's jaw snapped shut.

'I *cannot,*' Olly said slowly. 'I could not then. It is too late now.' He took a long, low breath. His voice quivered. 'Please, Ash. My Ashel. Do not make me talk about them. *Please.*'

'Apologies.' Ash pulled him down, squeezing him tighter. 'I . . . I know it was hard, with them. Perhaps in the future . . . ?'

Olly sniffed against his chest. 'Perhaps.'

'You have time to decide,' Ash said. 'I swear.'

Olly's grip slackened. *Time?*

'Olly?'

Olly unhooked his arms from around Ash's chest, looking up at him. 'I have time? Here?'

Ash swallowed. 'Of course,' he said. 'Assuming . . . that is, do you *want* to stay? With me?'

Could he stay? Could he stay, with Ash on the cusp of marriage?

But this was all he had wanted, since returning from France. Not Ash – he had never even allowed himself to want that, knowing that Ash had abandoned him. But a home. Safety. Safety with someone who cared for him.

'. . . Can I?' he said at last. 'What about Agnes?'

'I will need to talk to her,' Ash said. 'I cannot lie to her. But we have an arrangement. She may understand.'

It all seemed too grand a promise to be true.

'She will understand that her husband is being fucked by another man?' he said, instead of anything more vulnerable.

Ash batted at him with a laugh. 'Perhaps we do not need to tell her in quite so much detail?'

Olly gave him an incredulous look. 'You really *do* have an odd arrangement.'

'*I* am odd. She, too, although she hides it better. Although in truth, after *this* . . . I half expect she will leave. Any sensible woman would.'

'Any sensible man would tell *me* to leave, Ash. Tell me you understand that. You risk so much by my being here. If I were to go—'

'*No,*' Ash said. 'No. I will not just give up on this. On *you*.'

He looked deeply torn. An inner war, one to which Olly was not privy. A deep, cruel part of him hoped that Agnes *would* leave, keen not to be stained with Ash's sin, disgusted and insulted. But Ash looked genuinely saddened at the idea. Olly wondered what had come to pass in his absence: if the union, which Ash claimed was a mere arrangement, was somewhat more than that.

But Ash was holding him tight, rubbing his hand up and down his back, clinging to him. Ash had promised he could stay. Olly had to hold on to that. He lowered himself back down to rest against Ash's chest, listening to his heartbeat.

Warm and comfortable, he could not help but feel guilty. He needed to get a message to Pepper to let him know he was safe. John would hear soon enough that the man he had sent Olly to kill was alive and well. He would be furious, and Pepper would no doubt panic. Besides that, if Ash intended to allow Olly to stay, it meant that he had found what he had sought after anyway: safety. He could encourage Pepper to join him at Dunlyn.

'There are things I must do,' Olly said at last. 'I need to send word to my friend.'

'Your friend?'

Olly took a moment to think, before continuing. 'We worked together, for a while. He is like— no, damn it, he *is* my brother, in all but blood. He will be worried if he does not hear from me. But he cannot read more than a few words, and—'

'We can send a messenger. Someone trustworthy. At least to the next city, and it can pass on from there. What would you tell him?'

A message could pass over several pairs of lips before even reaching the town: it would need to be short enough to be memorable, yet vague enough that it should not damn either of them were the wrong person to hear it.

Something simple, then. *I am safe. Come to Dunlyn.* Safer than even that, he could give Pepper the name of the closest town and instruct him to journey there. Finding someone to watch for him then direct him to Dunlyn would be easy.

'Where is the nearest town?'

'Skeldale.'

'I could send him there. Tell him to find an innkeeper, or a bailiff, or . . . or anyone. Have someone keep watch for him and send him to Dunlyn. But only if you are sure.' Olly sat up, so he could see Ash's face. 'Only if you do not wish me to leave.'

'Olly.' Ash mirrored him, reaching out to cup his face. 'Never. I will not let you go again.'

He had to believe it. He had to hold it in his heart. Olly nodded, unable to speak. Ash's expression drifted.

'I still feel as if this isn't real,' he said. 'For you to attempt to rob *me,* of all people? It is like fate. Like someone led you to me.'

Olly stilled. Ash did not know how correct his words were. Part of him wanted to keep it secret, never force Ash to know the truth. But he would not be able to protect Ash from that forever.

He sat up. 'Ash . . . someone *did* lead me to you.'

Ash frowned. 'What?'

'It was not just luck. You were not just an easy target to rob. I was—' He had to get it out before his resolve failed him. 'I was hired,' he said, quickly.

Ash was dumbfounded. '*What?*'

'I told you I was a bandit. I have been working with a man for some time: John. He finds me work. He summoned me and he promised me riches and safety if I saw through a job for him. And I accepted. He never gave me a name, only a description, and told me where to wait . . . I never even realised it was you I had been sent after.'

'But . . .' Ash stuttered, 'but who is he? Why would he want me dead?'

Olly knew he had to tell him. He wished he did not.

'He was hired by someone else,' Olly admitted. 'But . . . I believe that will be something best discussed with your— with Agnes.'

Ash looked panicked. 'What? Surely she did not—'

'No!' Olly quickly clarified. 'Certainly, I do not believe she was involved, especially now I have spoken to you. But her family . . .'

A shadow passed over Ash's face. He looked momentarily guilty – but not shocked. 'Ah.'

'You do not seem surprised.'

'I am *not* surprised. Christ . . .' Ash dragged a hand down his face, scratching at his scar. 'They are not pleased with her choice to marry me.'

'Are you so unpleasant?'

Ash shot him a look. Olly kissed it away.

'I am sorry that I have to bring you this news,' he said truthfully.

'I suppose I should just thank God that it was *you* who was sent.' Ash sighed.

'And thank Him that I failed to kill you, too.'

Ash made a low noise: a mirthless chuckle. 'And that, I suppose.' He rubbed at his eyes. 'What a *mess*.'

'It is a little. I fear I only complicate matters.'

Ash gave Olly a thoughtful look, then pulled himself out the bed. He edged around the canopy and bent down to retrieve something from the floor. When he returned, he dropped it into Olly's palm. It was his ring.

'You *do* complicate matters,' Ash said. 'But you are entirely worth a complicated life.'

Despite it all, Olly felt drunk on it, a careless happiness he had long ago forgotten. It was easy – perhaps preferable – to pretend that the horrors of these past years were no more than nightmares. He kissed Ash again, and slid the ring onto his finger.

Chapter 12

Agnes

'Tell me again.' Agnes wiped her hands on her skirts, peering at the men sitting across the table from her. 'So *his* father shot *you*? With a crossbow?'

'Yes.' Raff seemed more amused than insulted.

'And now *you*' – she gestured at Penn, who was grinning – 'are Ash's hostage?'

'I was his father's hostage, really,' said Penn. 'I suppose given that both of the men who bargained the deal are dead it no longer stands . . . but no one has seen fit to point that out, yet.'

Agnes frowned. 'I heard all sorts of wild stories about what had happened to the Barden and de Foucart families, and yet the truth baffles me even more.'

Penn shrugged. 'If it helps at all, becoming a hostage was *my* idea. I just had to ensure Father thought it was his.'

'You *chose* this?'

'Of course.'

'Why?'

Penn shot a look at Raff. Raff looked down, his ears going red. 'I have my reasons.'

She watched them carefully. The way they were around one another did not speak to the relationship between a man and the person whose actions had caused him to be held hostage. They were clearly friends, and judging by the tale they had told her of Penn's escape from his cruel father's clutches, he owed Raff far more than just the aid he supplied when Raff's wounded arm pained him most. It was pleasing that they *remained* friends, after all that had happened; it put her in mind of one of the tales of Arthur and his band of knights, loyal to the quick, deeply enmeshed in one another's lives.

There seemed to be something more there, though. Something beyond just friendship – something like love. Both the church and society damned such a relationship, yet they did not seem to be taking great pains to hide it.

It would not do to ask. It would sound like an accusation, one that would certainly not win her any favours with the rest of the household. The pair of them seemed keen to get to know her. They were excellent hosts – Penn more than Raff, who eagerly talked while Raff listened on. Upon her entrance into the hall that morning, Raff had effusively apologised for Ash's absence the previous night after going to speak to their prisoner. His words went some way to soothing her after she asked after Ash's health, worried that he had suffered another fit.

Their sister Lily – whom Agnes was waiting to learn more of, given her own predilection for blurring boundaries – was not present. Raff had apologised again, reassuring her that no doubt she would return to the keep soon enough.

'And when she *does* return, you will meet Jo as well,' Penn added.

'Jo?'

'My sister.' Penn said it so casually that Agnes was almost unsure if she had heard him correctly. 'They own a brewery together, somewhere near Oxford.'

Agnes tried to not appear shocked. She had known that Ash's sister had such a common job but had not realised that she ran it with another woman. Penn started to laugh.

'Yes, it is rather odd, isn't it? Both the sisters of earls, now common as muck – not that I would allow Jo to hear me say so. But they're very happy, and for that I cannot judge *any* oddity.'

With every story she heard and every fact she learned about the Barden family, Agnes felt surer and surer that she had trapped herself not with a monster, but with an entire family of lunatics. She had never heard such scandal and oddness confined within one family. Two, she supposed, were one to consider Penn and his sister.

'. . . I see,' she managed weakly.

Raff gave her a warm smile across the table. 'You will get used to us eventually,' he said. 'I swear we are all drawn to each other.'

'We?'

'Eccentrics and degenerates,' Penn clarified with a sharp smile.

'Penn!'

'What?'

Before they could launch into bickering, there was a noise from the opposite side of the room. All three of them looked around to see Ash in the open doorway. He looked exhausted, his hair a mess, still wearing yesterday's clothes with great purple bags beneath his eyes. But his eyes themselves were sparkling, his head held high. He looked . . . free. As if a great weight had fallen from his shoulders in the night.

Raff stood, the bench creaking beside him as Penn wobbled on it. 'Ash—'

Ash ignored him, heading instead for Agnes. Agnes rose to her feet instinctually.

'Would you join me on a walk?' he said. 'So we may talk?'

She didn't even need to think. 'Of course.' He looked so nervous. 'Should we fetch the dogs?'

She could see the relief wash over him. 'Please.'

✡

The grounds around Dunlyn Castle were beautiful, if steep. In the early morning light, the grass still speckled with dew, they sparkled. The keep itself was built into the hill, overlooking the lands beyond, and it was a long walk down into the valley below. The valley itself was split with a long, fast-moving river overhung with trees, heavy with new leaves. It was a beautiful place – certainly the sort of place Agnes could enjoy living in.

At her side, Ash remained stoically silent. It seemed he did not want to talk until they were far away from the keep – likely to ensure they really were alone.

He led her down towards the river, watched the dogs chase each other around for a moment, and then, finally, spoke.

'Last night . . .'

She tried to help. 'You vanished,' she said. 'Was it another of those fits?'

He gave a low, mirthless chuckle. 'No,' he said. 'Not quite. Agnes . . . the man who attacked us on the road. I know him.'

Agnes's mouth hung open. '*What?*' she breathed. 'How?'

Ash looked steadfastly ahead, unblinking.

'He . . . he is the man I told you of. The man who I thought I lost in France.'

'But . . . but you said he was dead?'

'He was. When he attacked us on the road, I saw his eyes, only briefly. I thought I had imagined it. But—' His voice cracked. 'But I had not. He is alive.'

Agnes swallowed. Ash's hands were shaking.

'What was . . . what *is* his name?' she asked.

Ash took a deep breath. 'Oliver.'

'How did you know him?'

'We squired together. Or rather: I squired beneath his father. We became friends. We—' A sharp breath, pained. The river rushed noisily beside them. 'I have never known anyone like him. We were inseparable.'

Agnes stood beside him. Despite every urge telling her not to, she reached out, putting what she hoped was a comforting hand upon his arm.

'When we spoke of marriage,' she said, 'you said you had made vows to another. I had assumed it was a woman, but . . . was it him?'

Ash still stared at the water. Agnes half-suspected he was considering throwing himself in.

'We swore an oath to each other – in the eyes of God, we swore to protect each other. To share all we had. To be . . . to be beside each other.' His eyes were shimmering. He did not move. 'Forever.'

'What happened for you to believe he was dead?'

'His bloody father rode off into a petty squabble in France. Olly insisted on joining him. He wanted to prove himself. I would not let him go alone. I promised to protect him, but I couldn't. He took a mace to the side of the head.'

Agnes hissed through her teeth. 'My God.'

'He just . . . he just *fell*. I tried to reach him, but this' – he pressed a hand against the scar that twisted over his face – 'is all I earned for my efforts. They wouldn't even let me find his body.'

Agnes could feel the grief coming off him in waves. The loss.

The guilt. She joined him in staring at the water. She had one single question: the only question that truly mattered.

'Were you lovers?'

The river rushed on. She forced herself to glance at Ash. He looked broken. His lips moved wordlessly.

'I do not want to lie to you,' he said at last.

'Then don't.'

'And . . . I do not want you to hate me.'

That was as good as a confession. Agnes swallowed. 'I will not. I had assumed since that conversation that you had given your heart away some time ago. It seemed obvious. And it answered many of my questions about you, as well. To have loved someone and have them snatched away . . . it made sense. Ash, you know of my own oddities. My own sins, as others would understand them.'

'It is not the same.'

Agnes held back a retort. It was. She *knew* it was: both were tarred with the same sin against nature, of subversion. She did not say that out loud – it would not help to force herself into Ash's fear.

'In the eyes of the law I suspect it would be,' she said instead. 'Ash, I am not asking you so I can judge you. If you and he were lovers – if your vows to him *were* the same as the vows I made to my husband – then I am not intending to damn you or curse you or . . . or set the law on you. I need you to know that.'

Ash didn't look as if he believed her.

'If I were to take this to the church, or the court, then you could easily accuse *me* of the sin of pretending to be something I am not,' Agnes continued. 'We both could damn each other. I hope that neither of us want to do that.'

'Of course not.'

'Then tell me what happened, Ash.'

'I— we— yes. Fine!' He shouted the final word so loud that birds perched in the nearby trees took sudden flight. 'We were,' he said, quieter. 'He was my *world*, Agnes. He was everything. I vowed myself to him with the words of brotherhood but . . . ah, they are not so different from the promises made between husband and wife. I loved him. And they took him from me—' His words collapsed into a choke. 'If he had not come back, I would not need to tell you all of this. But now . . .'

'Things are different?'

'They are. And I cannot ask you to marry me if you do not know *all* of me. Not like this, not in a way where I could tarnish you with my own crimes.'

She swallowed. 'And *are* you lovers? Still?'

'Excuse me?' Ash spluttered. 'I have assumed him dead for years! How could we have—'

'You spent all night together.'

Ash fell silent. It was an assumption alone, but Agnes could tell by Ash's expression that she was correct.

'Let me ask again: *are* you lovers?'

'I . . .' He whispered it, like a confession. 'Yes. Forgive me. Olly . . . he was – *is* – like a part of my soul. I only ever wanted him, and after he died . . .'

Agnes thought of Nicholas. 'No one could fill that gap.'

Ash blinked at her. 'Yes. Yes, that exactly.'

She should have expected that – she *knew* that Ash had always had a piece of his heart missing, a person ripped away, even from the very start. She had known since the moment he talked of old vows. Yet to hear him say it so plainly . . .

There was a gap in Ash made for one person. She did not know why that made her feel sad.

'Oh, Ash . . .'

She reached out again. This time, she took his hand, and to her surprise she found he did not resist. Most men would never admit such dangerous truths. They would not care about the impact their secret lives would have on their wives. But Ash *did*. He did not want to entangle her in a mess she could not escape. Telling her was brave, possibly the *bravest* thing he could have done.

'Thank you,' she said. 'You could have pretended he was nothing to you. Just a shadow from your past. Just a friend.'

'And lied to you. Forced you to build a *life* upon that lie.'

She squeezed his hand, saying nothing.

'I assume . . .' his voice had quieted, now, nearly drowned out by the rushing water '. . . you will leave, now? Return to your keep?'

She turned to him, not letting go of his hand. 'What?'

'Now you know what sort of man I am, you are perfectly within your rights to leave. I will ensure everyone is made aware that the fault lies with me; you will not be made unmarriable, I swear to you.'

Agnes looked up at him. He had not let go of her hand.

'Do you *want* me to leave?' she said. 'I thought you needed this marriage as much as I do?'

'I do,' Ash admitted. 'But . . . things have changed. And while I wish we could remain as we were, I understand if . . . if you have decided I am not worthy.'

His grip loosened. She still did not let go.

'You *are* worthy,' she said. 'You have *shown* me that you are. And I understand your . . .' she swallowed '. . . oddities.'

Ash laughed at that. 'Is that what we have decided to call it?'

'It is far better than many other words I could use.'

'I suppose it is.'

'Ash, regardless of this . . . I *do* still wish to marry you. I want to see this through. But only if you still feel the same.'

He glanced at her. 'I do.'

'And . . . will Oliver stay here? Do you *want* him to stay?'

Ash looked broken. 'I do,' he said. 'I cannot be without him. Not again. But I cannot force him upon you. God . . .' He let go of her hand with a groan, rubbing his eyes. 'I do not know what I can do.'

'He knows we plan to wed?'

'He is aware, yes.'

'What does he make of it?'

'He knows that I will do anything for my family, including this. We had always assumed I would be able to force Raff into this position, but . . .'

'His arm.'

Ash gave her a strange look. '. . . Yes: his arm. And now the burden is mine alone. Not that—' He suddenly turned to her. 'Not that marrying you is a burden, you understand, it is just—'

He looked so horrified that Agnes laughed. 'The terrible burden of marrying each other is one we both must bear,' she said. 'Ash . . . you love him?'

Ash's words were a mere whisper. 'I do.'

'Then . . .' Agnes swallowed. She understood his hesitation. That same uncertainty was within her, too. She did not know if this was the right choice. 'Then he must stay. Then I grant him leave to stay.'

Ash lowered his hands to look at her. 'You do?'

'Yes,' she said, more surely. 'To have that chance ripped from you . . . I could not do it. I refuse to be that cruel.'

Ash was still and silent, for a moment. Then – much to her shock – he pulled her into a tight embrace. Agnes wavered for a moment before gripping him back.

'Thank you.' When he released her, his eyes were red. 'Thank you, Agnes. This is . . . this is a gift. And . . . I would like for you to at least be friends, if you can. When he is not attempting to murder me he can be especially charming.'

Agnes held back a smile. 'He will have to prove that himself.'

Ash sighed. He did not look as pleased as he should.

'Ash?'

'There is one more thing. Olly told me some troubling news. It was not a random attack on the road. He was hired.'

Horror gripped around Agnes's chest. 'Hired to *kill you*?'

'With handsome pay, too,' Ash said. 'And . . . God, I know of some people who would rather see me dead than alive, but he—' His face contorted into a frown. 'He seems to think that— Christ in Heaven, Agnes. He seems to think that your family may be involved in some way.'

Agnes's stomach dropped. The sudden ringing in her ears muffled the sound of the river beside them, the birds in the trees, the wind rustling the leaves.

'What?'

Her own voice sounded far away, as if echoing from across a cavern.

'He has told me that he was hired by a family looking to protect their daughter from her cruel husband. They approached a man Olly has worked with before, looking for someone to deal with him. With *me*. I—' He stopped. 'I am so sorry, Agnes.'

She managed to force her gaze to fix on his.

'Let me take you back inside,' he said. 'And you can ask Olly anything you need to. And we shall deal with this together. All right?'

There wasn't anything else she could say. 'All right.'

*

Ash had left her in a side chamber with Qwippe as he went to fetch Oliver. Agnes needed this time alone to think, yet her head was an empty, ringing void. She did not know *what* to think.

There was a knock at the door. She jerked up.

'Yes?'

'It's me.'

Ash had returned. She relaxed a little. 'Come in.'

He pushed the door open cautiously, as if worried he may startle her. He stepped inside with a hasty look over his shoulder.

And then, emerging from behind him like a fearful animal, another man. Oliver. Yesterday, Agnes hadn't managed to get a proper look at the person who had attacked them; his face and hair were covered, and he'd been bundled into the tower cell before she had been able to speak to him.

Now, in the light, and wearing clean clothes that could only belong to Ash, she could see him properly. He was of height with Ash, perhaps to the very inch, with a sort of broadness that could only have come about through many years of physical work. He was scruffy, his jaw lined with a rough beard and his straw-blond hair falling into his eyes, messy as a haystack. His face, what she could see of it, was marked with scars.

He peered around, took a breath, and then strode forwards, past Ash, towards Agnes. The effect was only a little marred by the way he crashed into the table at the side of the chamber with a curse.

Agnes found herself getting to her feet instinctively.

'*Shit*—' He righted himself, looking up at her with startled eyes. Uncharitably, he put her in mind of a cornered hare. He stood straighter, clearly trying to regain his dignity.

'My Lady.' His voice was smooth and pleasant, almost lyrical. He held his head at an angle as he spoke. 'I believe there is much we need to talk about.'

Agnes looked over his shoulder towards Ash. Ash met her eye and nodded.

'So it seems. Would you sit?' She glanced at Ash, too. 'Both of you?'

Oliver seemed uncertain. But Ash appeared at his shoulder and guided him to sit, placing himself between them. Agnes folded her hands in her lap, fiddling with her skirts.

'Ash has spoken to me about . . .' she sought, uselessly, for the right words '. . . everything,' she settled on. 'I know he has invited you to stay. You are aware that we intend to wed?'

Oliver nodded. 'I am aware, yes. And I said as much to Ash – if me being here is unacceptable to you, then—'

Agnes held up a hand. Oliver fell silent.

'I wish to repeat Ash's invitation.'

Oliver's expression dropped into shock. 'You do?'

Agnes nodded. 'I do.'

He was going to ask *why* she would make such a foolish choice. She prayed he did not: she could not put it into words. She did not know Oliver; his happiness meant nothing to her. But she liked Ash, had grown to like him, and she could not bear to see him back in that pit of despair. Even if that meant giving up something she had not even yet dared to name.

'Are you . . . are you sure? Quite sure?'

He looked terrified. Agnes could see many years of hard living, wrought into his face.

'I am sure.'

Relief melted over his face. '*Thank you.* Truly. I am sorry that these are the circumstances under which we must meet.'

The relief at not being questioned made her sag. 'Any circumstances under which *we* would meet would be complicated,' she said. 'These are . . . more so, I will grant you.'

'For quite a number of reasons, too. Ash has informed you of the people who hired me?'

'He has, yes.' Agnes sighed. This, in truth, was the harder conversation to have. Inviting a stranger into her marriage was nothing compared to the horror of her own family trying to destroy it. 'Tell me *everything*.'

Oliver shot a look towards Ash, then began his tale. Agnes recognised parts: the concerned family, the meddling friend. She was rendered speechless, her lungs squeezed empty. There was nothing to say, no thoughts that would suffice.

'To kill him seemed so extreme,' Oliver finished, clearly attempting to comfort her. 'I told John as much myself.'

Agnes sighed. 'I should have answered their damn letters and put this whole thing to rest,' she muttered. 'Christ, I should have done *something*—'

She slumped forwards, her head in her hands. There was a hand on her back.

'Agnes?'

'My God, Ash, forgive me. Had I not been so stubborn . . .'

'Do not blame yourself. You should blame *me* for having such a terrible reputation. Although I do find myself wondering *why* this friend of theirs was so sure I could only be dealt with fatally.'

'What do you mean?'

'Why did they consider me so great a threat? All they had were rumours, and the few moments your sister saw me in your keep. Surely that was not enough for them to judge me. Olly, were you told anything else?'

'Nothing.'

'They knew of the incident at your father's funeral,' Agnes added.

Ash frowned. 'Of course. I had just assumed that rumour spread fast, but . . . it is unusual for a family across the border to hear of such an event. How did you come to know?'

'I had been told by a friend of Nicholas. That is not surprising, seeing as many knew I was seeking a husband. But I am unsure how my family were told. I had assumed it was just salacious gossip spreading fast, but . . .'

'But?'

'But now I am unsure. Someone must have told them – and told them enough for them to see you as a true concern.'

'Someone wishing to cause trouble?' Oliver asked candidly.

'Perhaps. Or—' Agnes's throat tightened. 'Or to ruin the match entirely and ensure we did not wed.'

She looked up. Oliver looked thoughtful, but Ash's face too was stuck in a mask of fear.

'I think I may know—'

'That *bastard* might have—'

They spoke over each other. Oliver watched them, his eyes darting between them as they stared at each other.

'Who?'

'What do you know?'

Agnes straightened her back. 'Do you remember me telling you of Francis? I would not be shocked to learn that he is this . . . *family friend*.'

She could not help the bitterness that crept into her voice. Ash raised his eyebrows.

'Do you believe he could do such a thing?'

Agnes couldn't keep his eye. She was flung, suddenly and

horribly, back to her youth. The rolling, verdant land that cradled her father's keep. The discovery. The smell of grass. Her father shouting, after.

She said nothing, staring at the fire. She nodded, just once.

'I do not think that they would kill Ash just to secure a union with another man,' Oliver said, breaking the silence.

'They may have been able to justify the union with my death, though,' Ash responded. 'Abused and manipulated by a cruel man and reeling from his death, Agnes could have returned to the comfort of her family and the willing arms of a man who wants her as a wife.'

'I refuse to marry him,' Agnes spat. 'I will not be forced to.' She swallowed back the rest – the more forceful words threatening to spill out. 'What of *your* suspicions?' she said instead, driving the focus of the conversation onto him. 'Who is this *bastard* you mentioned?'

Ash looked contrite. 'My uncle,' he said. 'Hugh. You know already some of my *dealings* with him. Hugh is a spiteful old husk. He may be spreading rumour just to tarnish my name, encourage people to refuse me.'

'You think he could have gotten word to my family?'

Ash shrugged. 'I don't know *what* to think. Christ— I hate these *politics*. I should have been born a farmer.'

'You'd be a terrible farmer,' Oliver put in. 'You hate animals.'

'I like dogs.'

'You cannot farm dogs.'

'Fine, then, a . . . a—'

'Yes?'

Ash scowled at him. Agnes watched them both, wondering if they were *always* like this. A day ago Oliver had been a prisoner, destined for the noose. Now he was a member of the household, a fixture at Ash's side. No wonder his mood was so jovial, if his own heartbreak had matched that which she had seen in Ash.

'*Regardless.*' Ash shot a sour look towards Oliver, who winked at him, before turning back to Agnes. 'We must decide what we will do next. I suppose we must deal with the matter of the attempted murder first.'

The lightness in Agnes's chest was extinguished as quickly as it had flourished. She could not believe that her family would choose such a dreadful thing alone. The more she thought about it, the surer she was that Francis was involved in some way. He had already been pouring sweet promises into Muriel's ear: why not her parents too? He could have convinced them that murder was the only way to save her.

What if they were *still* convinced of it? Especially if Ash's uncle – a man they would trust – was the one telling them such lies?

'What if another attempt is made?' she said.

'Do you think they would do that?' Oliver asked, concerned.

'I did not believe they would do it *once*,' Agnes said. 'But they have. Or at least, *someone* has, and if it was Francis driving the force of the blow, then . . . yes. I do believe he would make another attempt, if he felt it justified. And,' Agnes said, now unable to dam back the tide of her own anxieties, 'they could still attempt to scupper the marriage. They could seek an annulment by claiming that my vows were made under duress, or that you are too mad to truly consent.'

Ash slumped back into the chair. '*Fuck*. So what do we do?'

'If we cannot be protected by laws they have already tried to break, we must find something better to shield us.'

'Such as?'

Agnes thought. Nobody – herself included – expected her to

marry for love. She would marry for land, and wealth, and protection, like all women of her status did. They would want her to be fond of her husband, and they wanted him to be kind in turn, but love? It was almost unthinkable. It was why, she assumed, Muriel was so keen for her to wed Francis.

'We could convince them it is a love match. Make my family believe that we are *truly* in love. No coercion, no manipulation. It would be easy for them to attempt to ruin a pragmatic match, but one of love? I think that would be harder for them.'

'Would that work?' Oliver spoke for the first time in a long while. 'An attempt to win over their hearts rather than their reason?'

'We can only hope so. Father is more practical, but I think the idea could win Mother over. And Muriel is terribly romantic; perhaps the notion would encourage her to drop the idea of Francis altogether. And . . .' She caught Ash's eye. 'We could marry now.'

Ash froze. 'What?'

'We have already decided on it,' Agnes said. 'Waiting longer may force those who are against the match into action. But if we wed now – or as soon as we may – then there will be at least *some* protection for us, and it will make it seem even more as if we are desperately in love.'

Ash began to nod slowly. 'We could have the first banns read today and be married within the week.'

'Can it be arranged so quickly?'

'If I can speak to the priest, I can see no reason why it should not,' Ash said. 'So long as the banns are read and time is given to contest—'

'But not *too* much time,' Agnes added. 'Just in case.'

Ash grinned. 'But not *too* much time,' he agreed. 'Yes, I see no reason why they should not accept. Father was popular with the priest in Skeldale, and we may be able to tug at his good nature a little.'

'Tell him of the attack,' Agnes said, nodding along as the plan grew more solid. 'Desperate to wed, left reeling from the attempt on your life . . .'

'. . . we wish to hurry the union lest any other bad fortune befall us,' Ash finished. 'It could work.'

'I will write to my sister and parents,' Agnes said. 'I will inform them that we have arrived safely and tell them of an unfortunate incident on the road. I can say that the horror of it has convinced us both to act quickly and wed as soon as we can. It will be a *great shame* that they could not be present, but I can then invite them to the keep to celebrate. Let them arrive *after* we are married, so they cannot interfere, and we have a better chance to show them who you really are.'

'And let them see you *both* being sickeningly in love, of course,' Oliver added casually.

Agnes swallowed. Ash had not, she realised, agreed to that idea.

'Only if you think it is wise, Ash,' she said. 'Only if you agree to it. I understand that it may be . . .' Her eyes darted to Oliver. He quickly looked away. 'Difficult.'

Ash looked pained when he spoke. 'It is . . . it is a good idea. And the only idea we *have*. I agree with you: a marriage alone will not be enough to stop whoever arranged the attack if they feel justified in a second attempt.'

He looked so unsure. Agnes felt a knot of grief in her chest. Was pretending to love her as awful as that? Or was it merely being forced to play-act when the *true* subject of one's desires was so close?

'And the matter remains of whether you wish for us to invite my family to Dunlyn,' she added. 'You would be well within your rights to refuse, considering all that has happened.'

'They are your family,' Ash said, looking serious. 'If you wish for us to invite them here, then I will stand by that decision. Just as I would stand by you if you refused to see them again. This is your choice.'

Agnes stared at him.

'I . . .' She took a breath. 'Thank you, Ash. It is not as if I *hate* them, they just . . . complicate matters. They do not— They refuse to—'

'They do not understand?'

Agnes's head snapped around. Oliver had spoken quietly, but his words had struck her regardless.

'Exactly that,' she said. 'I love them. But they do not understand me, or my choices. I want to allow them one more chance.' She clasped her hands together. 'But just one.'

'Then we can give them that chance,' Ash said. He turned, then, back to Oliver. 'You were hired by someone else? A middleman?'

'Indeed.'

'Did he tell them anything about you?'

'As far as I'm aware they do not even know my name,' Oliver said. 'I think John had intended to deal with the finer details after the deed was done.'

'That is something, at least,' Agnes mused. 'It means we will not need to hide you away lest they realise the man they hired to kill Ash is now' – blood rushed to her cheeks; she was deeply aware that Oliver was staring at her with a small smile – 'is now a part of the household,' she finished.

Oliver's smile widened. He had clearly noticed her blush. 'An apt way of putting it.'

Agnes chuckled despite herself. 'Quite,' she said. 'God . . . but I cannot spend all day here talking. There is *so* much to do.'

Ash groaned. 'There is,' he said, looking enormously unhappy. 'I will ride into town. It may make things easier if I meet the priest in person. I will speak to Hamond, too – he owns the tavern. I can ask him to watch for Pepper and direct him here.'

'Pepper?' Agnes did not know that name.

'He is a friend of mine,' Oliver explained. 'He knew what I had been hired to do and will be worried if he does not hear from me, especially once word spreads that Ash is alive. Ash has suggested that I invite him here.'

'I must also inform the steward that you will be staying,' Ash added, looking at Oliver. 'After the circumstances you arrived in, I need to make sure everyone is aware you are a guest, not a prisoner.'

'Will the staff tolerate that?'

'I . . . I suppose they must do as I say.' Ash groaned. 'I do not relish these conversations. They must think I am mad . . .'

'What will you tell them?'

'I intend to work that out as I go.' Ash sighed. 'The truth, as much of the truth as I *can* tell them. They all knew Lord Cop— They all knew of your father. They will *have* to tolerate his son – of that much I am sure.'

'And if they refuse?'

'Then . . . then we shall see.'

'You *are* the earl of these lands,' Agnes said.

Ash gave her a look. It was not sharp, or angry. He looked sad. Resigned.

'Indeed I am,' he said, voice low. 'As much good as that does me.'

Chapter 13

Ash

Agnes had hurried away to write the letters to her family. Olly, promising he would be fine, had gone to sequester himself in Ash's chambers.

And Ash, again, was alone.

He was glad for that. Olly could not see how nervous he felt. He could not see how tenuous this decision was, how much Ash would be forced to rely on the goodwill of the men who were only obliged to obey him because he was his father's son.

He set his shoulders and headed towards the treasury, looking for Michael. The rest of the staff would need to be informed as well, but with the steward aware of the situation, they would have no choice but to follow.

Or, Ash thought, with a nervous twist in his gut, Michael would refuse, leaving Ash with a mutiny on his hands.

He knocked on the door to the treasury – an old habit that even now he could not break. He still half-expected to be granted entry by his father, his booming voice rumbling through the wood.

But the voice did not come. Ash steeled himself and heaved open the door.

'Ah, Ashwy.' Michael looked up as he entered. 'How do you fare?'

'Well, thank you,' he said. 'I have some things I must speak to you about.'

Michael closed the ledger he was reading. 'Oh?'

'Lady Agnes and myself have decided that we wish to marry sooner than we had intended.'

Michael looked hugely surprised – and a little amused.

'I . . . suppose that is understandable,' he managed eventually.

'I am going to ride into Skeldale to speak to Sir Walter, the priest,' Ash said. 'If I can talk to him in person, I should be able to receive dispensation to marry sooner. I intend for it to be a simple affair, you understand, but I wanted to . . . to inform you. I . . . *we* . . . are aware that it is unusual, but Agnes is a widow, after all, and I am far past my best age as a groom. It seems sensible, especially after the attack on the road.'

'Of course.' If Michael had any further thoughts on the hasty marriage, he did not voice them, much to Ash's relief. 'Was there anything else?'

Ash braced himself. 'There is. It is about the man who attacked me, in fact.'

Ash stood straighter. He was the earl, he reminded himself.

'I have released him from the tower,' he said, voice sure. 'And given him leave to explore the keep.'

'My Lord?' Michael's expression was not anger, but fear. *He thinks I've gone mad,* Ash thought. *Perhaps I have.*

'The matter is significantly more complicated than we originally assumed,' Ash said, resisting the urge to speak with too much haste. 'His name is Oliver. Oliver Coppard.'

The steward frowned. Then, slowly, recollection.

'Coppard?' he said. 'From Lord Benedict Coppard's household? The man you—'

His grey lips snapped shut.

'The man I squired for, yes. The one who led me into war. Oliver is . . . he is his *son*, Michael.'

Michael crossed himself. 'My God.'

'Indeed.' Ash pushed some papers aside then sat in the chair opposite him. 'We were in France together. I thought him dead. His *family* believes him to be dead, too. He was Benedict's youngest son. He was captured out there, and has only just managed to return to England.'

'Captured?'

'And ransomed,' Ash said. 'But their demands never reached these shores. He assumed his mother – God rest her soul – and the rest of his family knew him to be alive. It was anger that made him hide from them, and now . . . now I cannot say what stops him, beyond stubborn shame.'

'But why attack you? Did he harbour those same thoughts about yourself, my Lord?'

Ash had already decided how to deal with these questions. No one else was to know that the attack had been an orchestrated attempted on his life – no one beyond the confines of the family.

'I am unsure,' Ash said, lying smoothly. 'But his attack on Lady Agnes and myself was truly an unfortunate coincidence. Since returning he has been forced to seek . . . less than savoury ways to support himself. Robbery and banditry included.'

'May God save him.'

'He espied us – two apparently unarmed nobles taking a stroll – and took his chance. It was *unimaginably* lucky that he did not harm us, and that I later realised who he is.'

'It truly is.' Michael looked aghast. 'It is as if *fate* has brought him here.'

Ash knew that their steward was a godly man; if he were less cynical, he would have been inclined to agree. But it was not God who had brought Olly to him: it was money and desperation and an empty stomach. He did not say so out loud, quietly sure that Michael would be discussing it all with the chaplain later.

'Perhaps,' he said noncommittally. 'But can you see why I cannot force him to go? It would go against all I know – all Father taught me. I will not allow him to starve on my account.'

'Of course,' Michael said, as if shocked that Ash would even consider removing him. 'But what will you do with him?'

'I intend to establish a role for him in the keep so he does not need to return to his previous life. We had spoken before . . .' Ash shook his head. 'We had intended, before the war, for him to return to Dunlyn with me in some official capacity. Perhaps as marshal, or even one day in the future in the steward role. But as things stand . . .'

'Things are more complicated.' Michael looked thoughtful. 'I am sure we will find some role for him.'

'Thank you.' Ash pushed a hand through his already messy hair. 'And . . . thank you for agreeing to this. It has been a difficult time.'

The steward's brow creased. 'You are the earl, Ashwy. Your decision is final.'

'You would be well within your rights to refuse to remain under the same roof as a criminal. I was half expecting you to leave.'

Michael put his hands on the desk. 'You vouch for this man?'

'I do.' Ash said it without thinking.

'Then I trust in your judgement, my Lord. I will inform the rest of the staff – and the guards, of course.'

'Thank you.' Ash stood to leave.

'My Lord?'

He hesitated with his hand on the door. 'Yes?'

'This is the right choice,' Michael said. 'This is one your father would have made, too.'

Ash gave him a tight smile. He was out in the room beyond before the steward could see the tears threatening to spill from his eyes.

As he walked across the courtyard, he tried to block out Michael's words. His father would not have made this choice, not if he knew what Ash was *really* choosing: how he was making a farce out of the sanctity of marriage that Lord Griffin had held so dearly. No doubt his father would have seen him for what he really was: a man inviting his mistress to live beside his wife.

At least Agnes understood. At least she *knew*. Marriage and all its laws and rules could go hang, but deceit he would not stand for. He would not hurt her.

He intended to speak to Dunlyn's marshal, Magnus, next – but as he strode across the yard there was a twist in his gut.

He had not spoken to Raff. Raff needed to hear the truth, and he needed to hear it from Ash's lips. He found him in the garden. For once Ash was lucky: he was alone.

'Raff?'

Raff turned from the border he was tending. 'Yes?'

Ash suddenly found his words stuck. He took a breath – but it came out wrong, like a gasp. Raff was on his feet and beside him in an instant.

'Ash?'

When Raff placed his hand on Ash's arm, fingers still stained with dirt, it all came pouring out, like a flood. Olly's apparent death, writ in more detail than he had ever told Raff before, his return. The attack, their assumptions of the force behind it.

Agnes's agreement to let Olly stay. Their decision to wed. Raff listened, never interjecting, letting him speak.

When Ash was done, his chest *ached*. It was as if his body had been in some awful battle while his mind had remained with Raff in their mother's garden.

'Would you care to ride to Skeldale with me?' he asked at last, feeling pathetic. 'I must speak to Sir Walter but . . . I do not wish to go alone.'

'Of course.'

Ash found his nerves easing as they rode. Getting out all those words – all those horrors – had been like letting blood. Relieving the pressure.

Ash's luck held as they reached Skeldale: the priest, Sir Walter, was only too glad to speak to them. Ash had been ready to use all the admittedly poor tools of persuasion at his disposal to win him over, prepared to launch into the story of the attack on the road. But they weren't needed. At the mention of *special dispensations,* and *an enormous favour,* Sir Walter's eyes had gleamed. All it took, Ash quickly learned, was a donation to the church for the matter to be dealt with in less time than it would take to see off a mug of ale.

By the time Ash and Raff left, he had the promise that he and Agnes would be wed that Sunday, and a hefty chunk had been taken from Dunlyn's purse. No matter: they could afford it, and he would ensure the steward kept an eye on proceedings to ensure the funds were being spent properly.

'I cannot believe that all it takes to dismiss papal law is coin,' Ash said, once they were back on the road. 'I should have been informed sooner – I can pay my way out of all my sins.'

'He did not even attempt to hide it.' Raff laughed beside him.

'He looked quite pleased when he realised you wanted something from him.'

Ash shook his head. 'I suppose that is *one* thing dealt with, at least.'

He peered down the road. It was quiet this morning, and the spring air felt fresh and clean. His problems were not solved – someone still wanted him dead, after all – but at least one of the hurdles had been jumped. And through fate, or God's grace, or some other divine provenance . . . Olly had returned to him. It was miraculous: a miracle Ash did not deserve yet was determined to cling to.

He glanced at Raff.

'I need to speak to Hamond at the tavern. First to his yard wins.'

'Wh—'

Before Raff had time to reply, Ash kicked his heels into the horse's flank and shot off down the road at a gallop. He caught a curse on the wind, followed by the sound of furious hoofbeats.

He laughed all the way into town.

Chapter 14

Olly

It had been decided between them that Ash should speak to the staff alone. Agnes had retired to attempt to write her letters, although she had gone cursing under her breath. Olly had been half-tempted to ask if she required assistance, but the look on her face had made him pause. Whatever her feelings towards her family, they were *her* feelings. He would not intrude.

She had allowed him to stay, despite being an interloper to her marriage. It was an enormous kindness, and he was still reeling from it. She could have insisted he go. She had not. He would not push his luck. He did not want to subject her to his presence when he was half giddy with Ash's return.

While Olly was free to do as he pleased in Ash's absence, he was still known as a prisoner. The guards and staff would panic to see him roaming about before Ash had a chance to spread word, so it was agreed he would return to Ash's chambers.

Olly had heard about Dunlyn Castle but had never actually visited, and was beginning to fear he had overestimated his sense of direction. He was *sure* Ash had brought him this way the previous day – or perhaps he had come this way with the guard who had pulled him from the cart – yet as he turned another corner, he found himself in a corridor that he could not recall.

This was why he needed Pepper with him. He had always needed Pepper more than Pepper had needed him: he certainly needed someone to be his memory when his own failed.

He wandered back the way he had come and realised that he was no longer alone. Someone was heading down the hallway towards him. Not a guard, as Olly immediately feared, but the man who had stopped Olly from leaving. The hostage. Again, his name had slipped Olly's mind. The man grinned as he approached.

'Oliver!' he said. 'I see you have escaped the tower.'

While Olly could not remember his name, he *could* remember the rest: that this man had known, somehow, the truth of his and Ash's relationship. He had known who Olly was.

'I have been invited to stay,' he said.

The man's face twitched into a smile. 'Is that so?' he said. 'I am pleased. Really, Oliver. Or is it Olly?'

'Olly,' Olly said. 'But I am afraid I do not know *your* name.'

The hostage seemed friendly enough, but it was too soon to spill all his secrets. His patchy memory was one he tended to guard more fiercely.

'Penn,' he said. 'Although you may hear some call me William. If you do, you have my full permission to strike them. Ash will tell you the same.'

Olly burst into laughter. 'I shall remember that,' he said, hoping it was not a lie. 'I admit, Penn . . . I am rather lost.'

Penn nodded. 'This place is a maze. Where are you headed?'

'I am supposed to be staying in Ash's chambers lest the guards drag me away again.'

Penn snorted with laughter. 'That sounds terribly dull. Let me show you around a little. If anyone questions us, I will tell them to fuck off.'

Being shown around Dunlyn sounded significantly more interesting than waiting around for Ash all morning. Olly allowed Penn to lead on, following close behind.

'I really must thank you,' he said as they walked.

'Oh?'

'Had you not stopped me from leaving I do not know what would have become of me. I would have gone the rest of my life hating Ash. I would have never known that he—' The words lodged somewhere in his lungs. Penn gave him a sympathetic look.

'So you *do* love him then?'

Olly wished he knew the man better so he could hit him. 'Of course I do.'

'Good.' Penn looked smug. 'I understand, in a way. To love someone and be torn from them. And *Ash,* God . . .' His expression turned far away, unfocused. 'Believing the one you love is dead? *Knowing* they are? There is no pain like that. I am glad you listened to us.'

'And *I* am glad that you stopped me.'

They spent the rest of the morning exploring the keep. Penn knew all the hidden servants' corridors and doorways, making Olly feel even more lost than he had done before. Penn knew all the staff, too – greeting people so warmly that no one seemed fit to question why Olly was even with him. He took him down into the kitchens, where the cook – Joan, Penn called her – eyed Olly warily but happily gave Penn half a dozen oatcakes, still warm.

They were eating their prize, perched on a bench in the yard, when Ash returned, Raff at his side. He approached them with a raised eyebrow.

'Why is it,' he said, as he approached, 'that I feel I should be *worried* if you two are spending time together?'

Penn gave him a sharp grin. 'I have no idea.'

'What have you been up to?'

'I have been showing Olly around,' Penn said. 'Now if you do not mind . . .'

He walked straight past Ash towards Raff, helping him down from his horse. Clearly, Ash was not going to get much more from him.

'Did all go well in town?' Olly asked, doing likewise.

'It did,' Ash said, looking relieved. 'I spoke to the priest, who was more than happy to assist, as well as Hamond. He will be keeping watch for Pepper.'

'Oh.' The sudden hurt that Ash's marriage would be so soon clashed with the relief that Ash had seen through with his promise to find Pepper. 'Thank you, Ash.'

Ash had arrived with more than he had set off with: a box slung over his horse's flank. He untied it swiftly, heaving it over a shoulder as he made his way inside with Olly at his heels.

'I found you something,' Ash said. 'A gift.'

Olly paused. 'Did you now?'

Ash pushed open his solar door and laid the box on the table. Olly had assumed it contained documents or goods – something important to an earl. Ash gestured to it.

'Open it.'

Curiously, Olly did as he asked. Ash watched like a hawk as Olly opened the lid and pulled back the cloth inside.

'What is— *Oh*.'

His heart stuttered as he peered down at the lute.

'I spotted it in the tavern when I was speaking to Hamond,' Ash said. 'And, well, it was left on the side, coated in dust, so I asked him about it. It belonged to his son, who used to play in the evenings for the drinkers, but he died last year.' Ash looked down at the dusty instrument, the faded wood. 'Neither Hamond nor his wife have been able to touch it since. It's too painful for them. So I took it off their hands. For a fair price, of course.'

Olly trailed his hand up and down the strings. They hummed beneath his fingertips.

'Is it all right?' Ash said, nervously. 'I've never been sure what kind is—' His voice caught. 'You . . . do you still play?'

Olly froze. Grief, as if it were fresh, twisted around his heart. Ash noticed at once, going to shut the lid.

'I apologise,' he muttered. 'That was foolish of me. I should not have—'

'Ash.' Olly's hand shot out, grabbing Ash's wrist. 'It has been a while. But yes. I still play. I still *want* to play. But it has proven hard, without an instrument.'

Ash nodded. 'Of course. Since France—'

'Oh, *no*.' Olly laughed. 'Not quite so long as that. I played for a while; we had a little group, musicians and thieves alike. But . . .' His fingers drifted over the lid of the box. 'We attempted to take too much. It ended poorly.' He swallowed. 'My lute was sold. We had no choice. And I have since been unable to find another.'

'You could not find one?'

'I . . . I could not afford one.'

'Olly . . .'

Olly smiled, although the expression felt hollow.

'The scar on my arm. When the wound turned, Pepper was forced to sell my lute so he could afford treatment.' His fingers shook. 'I was so unwell that I had not even realised he had done it until afterwards, until I was able to think and talk and sit up again. He had no other choice. I do not blame him. He saved me. But . . . but I have missed it.'

He lightly ran his fingers up and down the strings, as if they could bite. Perhaps they would.

'I found something else, too . . .'

Ash's voice was uncertain. Olly was immediately intrigued.

'Did you now?'

Ash moved closer, brushing against Olly's arm, then reached into the pouch at his hip. He pulled out a little jar, pressed it into Olly's hand, and opened the lid.

'Oh,' Olly said, the distinct smell of tallow and chamomile suddenly filling the room. '*Oh.* Where did you get this?'

Ash nudged him with a half-shrug. 'I have my ways. It is nothing fine, I will admit . . .'

'I am sure it will serve our purposes well,' Olly said, quickly replacing the lid and stashing away the jar. 'For now. How long do you think this will last?'

He turned to Ash with a grin. Ash went red.

'I fear,' Olly continued, leaning even closer, 'that we will soon need more. I hope my Lord can see to it.'

Ash wriggled on the spot. Olly held back a laugh: they had only been reunited for a handful of days, yet it was like nothing had changed. Ash had always been easy to tease.

'*Oliver.*'

'Yes, my Lord?'

'*Later.*'

Chapter 15

Agnes

There was ink all over Agnes's hands. All over her sleeves, too. She had tried – really – not to waste parchment. But she had failed.

It was done, at least, as well as she could manage. One thing she was thankful for: it would take several days for the letters to reach her family, and even longer for them to travel south if they accepted her invitation.

She knocked at the door of the solar. From within, she could hear scuffling – a muffled curse. And then at last, a voice.

'Enter.'

She opened the door. She wasn't at all surprised to see that Oliver was with Ash, wearing a stiff smile. They both looked red-faced. She tried not to think too much on what she had just interrupted.

'I finished the letters,' she said, placing them on the table. 'One for my parents, and one for Muriel – my sister. The one for Muriel is a little more . . .' she tapped her fingers together thoughtfully '. . . enthusiastic. My parents do not need to be told more details than is necessary, but *she* will be won over by exuberance. I have not sealed them yet, so you may read them.'

Ash hesitated. 'What?'

'Do you wish to read them? They are about *you*, after all. I do not want to say anything to them that you do not agree with.'

Ash looked unsure but took the letters anyway as Agnes sat at the desk, reaching for candle, wax and seal. He read the one for her parents first – a serious affair, detailing the journey, the attack, Ash's character, and the merits of Dunlyn Castle – before handing it back and beginning the one for Muriel. His eyebrows rose as he did, cheeks going red.

There was a laugh from behind him. Agnes realised that Oliver had been reading the second missive over his shoulder.

'It's good.' He grinned. 'I like it. Although you missed a few things.'

'Oh?' Agnes paused, heating a stub of wax over the candle beside her.

'You should have noted his skilled prowess as a lover.'

Wax dripped with a noisy hiss onto the candle, extinguishing it.

'Oliver!' Ash snapped.

'Ashwy!' he retorted.

'You are *terrible*. That will win me no favours whatsoever.'

'What? Agnes is a widow. You *are* a widow, are you not?'

Agnes attempted to seal the letter for the second time. 'Yes.'

'Then there we are. It is not as if your sister is expecting you to be a pure and untouched maiden. Perhaps she will be even more keen for you to marry if you have already lain together.'

Agnes removed the seal from the wax with carefully constrained force, then snatched the second letter back and sealed that, too.

'Ash is right,' she said, standing with the letters gripped in one hand.

'Yes?'

'You *are* terrible.' She ignored Oliver's little noise of complaint and turned to Ash. 'How did you fare in Skeldale? Did you speak to the priest?'

'I did,' Ash said. 'He was more than happy to see the marriage through quickly for an act of *charity* from the keep's funds.'

Agnes rolled her eyes. 'Of course he was,' she said. 'At least that is done, now. With luck we will be wed before these letters even reach my family.'

'One moment.' Ash sat in the chair she had vacated, pulling a ream of parchment towards himself and picking up the quill. 'I ought to write to Lily, too. I will admit that her interest in weddings is low – in fact, she does not give a damn – but I will inform her that we have agreed to a match.'

Olly frowned. 'Where *is* Lily?' he said. 'You spoke of her so often when we were young, I expected her to be here filling this keep with children. Or did your father marry her off?'

Ash laughed. 'Lily? *Never.* He tried, but that ended exceedingly poorly. She lives in Oxfordshire, now. She runs a brewery with Penn's sister.' Olly looked just as baffled as Agnes had when she had been told the tale. 'I really *will* explain that to you both,' Ash said. 'But perhaps not when someone is trying to have me killed.'

Ash scribbled out his letter, focusing intently, before blotting it and sealing it as Agnes had. In the stables, one of Agnes's servants was milling around with the stableboys and offered at once to deliver the notes across the border, apparently keen to be of use in the new keep. Another rider took the note to Oxfordshire, agreeing to pass on a message for Oliver as well.

When it was done, they retired back to the side chamber where Ash and Agnes had been shuffled after they had first arrived at Dunlyn.

'Do you think your family will come?' Ash asked Agnes, as soon as the door was shut.

'I presume so,' Agnes said.

'Then I will need to prepare the keep for guests.' Ash sighed. He leaned against the wall beside the crackling fire with a groan. 'I detest entertaining. There is always so much to do, and so many people to consider.' He grimaced. 'And now it feels as if my life may depend on it.'

'Perhaps it does,' Oliver said, cheekily grinning up at Ash from where he'd slung himself haphazardly in a chair.

Ash didn't even look at him. 'Shut your mouth.'

Agnes watched them bicker. There was no malice there, no intent to wound. They were clearly returning to old patterns, ones that she could never be part of. It was remarkable that they had done so with such speed. It betrayed a long past together: a bond that time and distance and loss had not managed to sever. There was something like grief in her chest. She had thought . . . she had *hoped*—

Or she had merely imagined.

She liked Ash – truly. He was a bastard, in his own words, but she was fond of him. His rough edges hid a soft interior, and it was clear he valued loyalty and kindness. In that alone he was all she could have hoped for in a husband: but he was handsome, too, well-built, well-edged.

But it was not to be. She had been happy with a simple arrangement when they had first met, but the longer she knew him, the less simple it all felt. She had not realised she wanted more until it was no longer available to her.

Ash clearly adored Oliver, and Oliver him. She could be happy for them, at least. She would be far, far happier in Dunlyn Castle with Ash in a marriage in name alone than she could ever have been in Scotland with Francis. It would be a *true* happiness, too, not just grabbing at the scraps she could snatch when her husband wasn't watching.

She would not let her unwanted feelings ruin that. She *liked* Ash. She did not want to see his happiness destroyed.

Her feelings towards Ash – whatever they were – would fade with time. It was that he had been kind to her, that he had seen her true self and not rejected her. That he had *encouraged* her. In time, she would realise that all she felt was camaraderie – friendship between two people with deep-buried secrets – and the feelings would pass.

Yet as she watched as Ash and Oliver laugh at one another's jokes, that pain bloomed once again in her chest.

Chapter 16

Ash

'. . . and may God bless your union, of course.'

Ash bit back a sigh as he bid farewell to the alderman standing beneath the gates. 'Thank you,' he said. 'I hope your journey is swift.'

He watched as the man rode away. The first thing he had said – and his departing remarks – had been words on Ash's upcoming marriage.

He re-entered the solar feeling deeply unsettled. Agnes and Olly looked up from where they'd been sat beside the fire, playing dice.

'How,' Ash said, as he slumped into a chair, 'does *everyone* know about our marriage?'

Agnes pursed her lips. 'Are you unused to being the subject of gossip?'

'Lord, no,' Ash said. 'Everyone sees fit to talk about the mad, wounded Barden son. But like *this* . . . I do not like the feeling that I am dragging others into it alongside me.'

'I am to be your *wife*,' Agnes said. 'It is too late for all that.'

'And you do need to plan your wedding feast,' Olly added.

Ash would rather have crawled back into the hole that Agnes had pulled him from. It must have been obvious on his face. Agnes gave him a sympathetic look.

'You know we must,' she said.

'Do not forget – you must make it seem as if you are a doting couple,' Olly added. 'You are in dire need of the practice before Agnes's family arrives.'

'Meaning?' Ash folded his arms across his chest.

'You intend to convince them that this is a love match, yes?' Olly asked. Ash nodded. 'There is the problem. You do not exactly behave as if you are quite wildly in love.'

'That should be simple enough,' Agnes said. 'Just compliments and lingering looks surely?'

'What else?'

'What do you mean, *what else*? So long as I do not beat him in the hall for being a stubborn ass—'

'*Hey*—'

'—then I fail to see why there should be a problem.'

Olly gave them both an unimpressed look. 'Agnes,' he said at last. 'Kiss him.'

'*Excuse me?*' Agnes squeaked, looking – for the first time, Ash thought – genuinely distressed.

'You do not have to—' he began, getting to his feet.

'She *will*, in fact, have to,' Olly said. 'If not when her family is here then at the very *least* during the wedding. You need to make it believable.'

Agnes seemed to have composed herself. 'That is true enough,' she said, 'but I had rather planned to . . . to . . .' She trailed off.

'Had you intended to just attempt it in the moment?'

Agnes nodded, lips tight.

'I am not *just* a thief, you know. I am a minstrel, too. A *performer*. Do you think I just leap in front of an audience and play?'

Ash could not help but laugh at that. Knowing Olly, that was exactly how he *did* play. He kept that thought to himself as Olly continued.

'No,' he said, 'I *practised*. We rehearsed. Which is what you two ought to be doing if you want your family to believe that you do, in fact, have feelings for him other than mere tolerance.'

'I do not *merely tolerate* him.'

'Then give him a kiss and show me.'

Agnes sighed, pointedly rolled her eyes, then stood and placed a kiss to Ash's cheek. 'There.'

Olly burst into laughter. Ash unfolded his arms. 'What *now?*'

'I have seen more convincing kisses from *nuns*,' Olly said. 'Again. Like you mean it, not like you are afraid you will contract some sort of awful disease from him. He is not *that* bad a kisser, I assure you.'

Agnes sighed again. She was clearly losing her patience. 'How do *you* suggest I kiss him, then?'

Olly's eyes flashed. Ash had barely time to think *oh, no* before Olly swung himself out of the chair, got to his feet, crossed the room and tugged him into a burning kiss. Ash nearly forgot where they were and what they were doing, lost to the feel of Olly's mouth, the touch of his hand to his back, the strength of his arms around him—

'Ah . . .'

Olly released him. Ash righted himself. Agnes was watching them. Her cheekbones were red.

'*That* is how you ought to kiss him,' Olly said, wiping his mouth obscenely before returning to his chair.

Agnes swallowed heavily, watching them both but saying nothing.

The dizzying feeling in Ash's stomach quickly died down, replaced with awkward embarrassment. '*Oliver*.'

'What? I was merely demonstrating.'

'I do not think that our guests will be pleased should we go on like *that* at our wedding feast.'

'Then they are very dull,' Olly said. 'What *are* you planning for the event?'

'I've no idea. The last wedding I attended was years ago, with Father. It was the usual: feasting, drinking, dancing—'

Olly snorted.

'What?' Ash demanded.

'Dancing? *You?*' Olly laughed, eyes twinkling.

'And what of it?'

'Do you recall those banquets Father used to throw?' Olly said. 'And young Susan, Lady Combe's daughter? You crushed her foot, the poor flower.'

'I did not—'

'Unless you have suddenly invested time into *dancing* since we parted, I assume you are just as poor a dancer now as you were when we were young.' Olly looked him up and down, making Ash's cheeks heat. 'Or *have* you? Are you engaging in illicit dancing in the darkness of the night?'

'Of course not.'

Olly smirked. 'What a shame. Agnes, I hope you have a pair of thick boots to wear. Or perhaps you should borrow a pair of sabatons.'

Agnes laughed as Ash sighed. He was about to insist that his dancing was not so bad, when he caught the look on Olly's face. Gone was the jocularity – the flirting from before. He looked a little sad. A little bitter.

'Well . . .' Olly said at last, 'I am sure you will have a wonderful time. And I shall find some way to occupy myself.'

Ash stared at him. 'You do not wish to attend?'

'You *want* me there?'

'I want you *here*. Regardless of the fact that I cannot stand being parted from you—' Olly made a choked noise, which Ash did not respond to, instead taking his hand. 'You *are* part of this keep, now. We have not yet discussed your future here, Olly. You *are* the brother of a lord. You may not be titled, but you are nobility. No matter of crime can erase that; if it *did*, then there would be hardly any lords at all. There are many roles in the keep you could take on. A valet, a chamberlain . . .' He clung to Olly's hand. 'If you wish for that, then these sorts of . . .'

'Performances?'

'*Events* are worth attending. If just to get my allies used to your presence.'

'Oh.'

'You do not have to decide that role now, of course,' Ash hurriedly added. 'But you *will* need to decide if you wish to attend the wedding. I—' He shot a look towards Agnes. '*We* want you there.'

Olly gave him a searching look. Apparently happy with whatever he saw in Ash's expression, he turned to Agnes.

'And you?' Olly asked. 'Would you be happy with my presence?'

Agnes looked between them. 'Of course,' she said. 'I cannot very well bar you from our lives—' Olly opened his mouth, but Agnes spoke over him: 'And *neither* do I have any desire to,' she finished, loudly. 'I am keen to get to know you better.'

Ash raised his eyebrows at that, turning to Olly. Olly's lip was twitching upwards – an expression Ash knew *all* too well.

'Well, I am sure *that* can be arranged,' Olly drawled.

'*Olly*.'

'What?'

'You are terrible.'

Olly grinned. 'So I have been told.'

Ash rubbed at his face. He hadn't even realised he was picking at the scar until there was a hand on his wrist forcing him to stop. Agnes gently pulled his hand down. She looked at him fondly – then her eyebrows creased.

'Good Lord,' she said, examining him more closely. 'I may have failed at being – what was it – *desperately in love with you* – but you *do* very much look as if someone has kissed you senseless. Let me—'

She reached out, then straightened his tunic and brushed his hair back into place.

'There.' She stepped back. Ash could still feel all the places where she had touched him. 'Better.'

Chapter 17

Olly

Something new and strange and loud had reached up from Olly's chest and taken him by the throat.

Agnes had touched Ash's face. She had stopped him from picking at himself in the way Olly had been desperate to do. She had settled his tunic and hair to make him look some semblance of an earl. It was soft, and unspoken, and *fond*—

She had touched his face.

Olly couldn't let the jealousy eat at him. Ash had promised himself to him. But he was promised to Agnes, too.

He tried to shake the thought from his head. Agnes had done nothing to make him dislike or mistrust her – nothing aside from marrying the man he loved. And that was, as far as he could tell, simply to protect herself so she would not be forced to marry someone worse. Every man was worse than Ash; that much he could agree with.

He was at war with himself. Agnes seemed *fun,* beneath a more serious exterior, and he could not help but tease her in the same way he teased Ash – all flirting and boldness. She did not seem to mind – she even encouraged it – and that, too, was dangerous. Part of him wanted to keep her at arm's length. To not treat her as a friend.

But he *wanted* her as a friend.

Ash had to see out the request from the alderman, and with little else to do and no desire to sit and discuss taxes, Olly headed back outside. The courtyard was busy this time of day, heaving with serving girls and dogs and guards, and as he sidestepped a lad with a chicken he collided with Penn, carrying a peregrine upon his gloved hand. The bird was wearing a hood, yet she seemed to know that someone else was nearby.

'God greet you, Olly,' Penn said cheerily. 'How do you fare?'

Olly tried not to look as if he had been lost in thought. 'Very well, thank you,' he said. 'Who is this?'

'Iseult,' Penn said, grinning. 'She is a bitch. Do not let her see your fingers.'

'I certainly shall not.'

'Are you busy?' Penn asked, pulling Olly out of the way of a pair of girls carrying a basket.

'I . . . suppose I am not,' Olly said. 'Ash is rather occupied, with the wedding—'

Why had he admitted that? Why had he said *wedding* and not named one of the countless other jobs that occupied Ash's time?

Penn gave him a knowing look. 'Are you *sure* you are well?'

Olly stiffened. He had tried to keep his face blank, his tone light. 'Of course,' he said, as jovially as he could manage.

Penn raised an eyebrow at him.

'It's a good act,' he said smoothly. 'But not *so* good.'

Olly felt an eerie sense of disquiet. He was not used to being so seen.

'Come,' Penn continued, not waiting for Olly to reply. 'I need assistance in the mews. You can help me clean the floors. Hurry along, now!'

He headed off at a quick trot. Olly followed, unsure what else to do.

When Olly entered the mews, a high-ceilinged room at the top of one of the towers, his first impression was of the *wall* of smells that he walked into. He coughed, eyes watering. Penn handed him a broom and gave him a sharp smile.

'Thank you.'

It wasn't until they were deep into cleaning – the birds eyeing Olly warily – that Penn spoke again.

'Truly, then. How are things?'

Olly stared at the pile of gravel and bird muck he had swept. 'Fine.'

'So you are perfectly content that the man you love is marrying someone else?'

Olly's head snapped around. Penn was looking away from him, stroking a finger down his peregrine's back.

'Shut your mouth.'

Penn did not seem offended. 'It's going that well, then?'

Olly grimaced. Truthfully, it *was* going well. But he could not stop himself overthinking, fearing the worst, fearing the sudden loss of Ash from his life once again.

'He really does adore you, you know,' Penn said casually. 'I feel as if this is some sort of divine reward for him having to live with Raff and me for so long, as well as all the horror *we* put him through.'

'What *happened* to you?' Olly asked, curious.

'Ash hasn't told you?' Penn looked genuinely surprised as Olly shook his head. 'Well, then. It is a little tricky . . . The shortest version of events is that I was supposed to marry Lily. I refused, I ran . . . Raff found me.' A small, pleased smile. Suddenly, Olly understood *exactly* the sort of relationship they had. No wonder Penn understood him and Ash so well. 'Not that he knew who I was, of course. Regardless, it all ended with him nearly getting killed for me. His arm, you know.'

'. . . Right.'

'Father shot him.'

'*What?*'

Penn shrugged, like he'd said something like: *Father offered him a cup of wine,* or: *Father insulted his horse.*

'It was a long time ago. Anyway, the reason he took such a risk is because Ash told him to. Because of *you*.' He punctuated that with a point at Olly's chest.

'Me?'

'I had returned to my father, may the Devil take his soul.' Penn spat on the ground. 'Raff asked Ash what he would have done had it been you. Ash probably would have set my father's keep ablaze if it had been you in there. I suppose I should be glad that I tied myself to the more even-headed Barden brother.'

Olly blinked. 'Uh . . .'

Penn laughed, his hair bouncing around his head. 'What I am telling you,' he said, 'is that Ash loves you. And I know all this is not what you had planned. But he *does* love you. Do not forget that.'

'Oh.' Olly blinked again, feeling off-centre. 'Thank you.'

'You are welcome.' Penn smiled. 'It's nice to finally meet you. I had a lot of questions that no one could answer . . . or at least, questions I dared not upset Ash with. I am pleased to finally have them answered.'

Olly glanced at him. 'What sort of questions?'

Penn said nothing.

'Penn! What sort of questions?'

Penn merely gave him a sharp smile before returning his attention to the bird.

Chapter 18

Agnes

Agnes had woken wrong, and the day had only gotten worse. She had dressed in haste, horribly aware of what the morning was to bring. She had barely eaten, dismissing Ash's worried looks. In the days since meeting Ash, those looks were becoming more obvious as he learned to read her better.

And now she was trapped in her chambers, standing stock-still in the new gown in the middle of the room while the dressmaker moved around her, muttering.

She shut her eyes, trying to will her soul from her body.

She was lucky, truth be told: with so little time to prepare she was having a gown from the dressmaker's stock fitted to her, rather than having one made. The dress would be sewn to size today and returned with the dawn, ready for the wedding that morning. It made the whole process quicker; yet nothing could have been quick enough for her liking.

She'd been settled in herself for the past few days, and had hoped that the feeling would last beyond the fitting.

It had not. She'd let herself down.

Once, Agnes had tried to track these days – the days where it all felt worse, where she couldn't distract her mind no matter how hard she tried. Back then, she had thought it perhaps tied somehow to her bleeds, which always left her feeling unwell. But it didn't appear to be the case: some days, she woke, and her mind rebelled against her body to leave her . . .

Like this.

She could feel every knot and splinter in the wooden floor beneath her bare feet. Better to focus on that than the gentle fall of the dress around her knees, the way it clung to her arms, her shoulders, her chest.

'If I could just check again here—'

The dressmaker approached, hands readied. Agnes didn't even think: a buried, animal-like thing took over and she leapt back. She could not let her touch her. Not again. She could *not.*

'I am sorry,' she stammered, voice breaking. 'Suddenly I feel quite unwell. I cannot . . . that is, if you could give me a moment?'

Her voice curled into a question, unbidden. It didn't *need* to be a question: she was soon to be the lady of this house. It could be a demand. It *should* be a demand. But so unsure and so suddenly fragile her usual resolve was faltering, crushed under the weight of this heavier feeling.

The dressmaker only looked shocked for a moment. No doubt she was used to such outbursts from her more noble clients.

'My lady.' She nodded, as Agnes winced. 'I think we have all we need anyway. I wish you well.'

'Thank you.'

The dressmaker seemed to understand, waiting for her to pull off the dress and handing it back to be taken in before shuffling out of the room with her assistant close behind. It was only when the door shut that Agnes collapsed onto the bed.

She tugged the blanket around herself, hiding her body until she was little more than a heap of wool.

However awful she felt now, she could only imagine feeling worse were it her mother and sisters with her in that tiny room, cooing over fabrics and commenting on her form and figure and the elegance of an endless parade of dresses. They were supposed to *love* her, to comfort her, but under their caring but misguided eyes she would have been—

She would have not been herself. They would never understand the horror of it, or worse: assume that the horror was for the act of marriage itself. They would see her distress and blame Ash, *again*.

She tugged her feet up, intending to hide beneath the blankets until necessity drove her out again, when there was a knock at her door.

'Agnes?' It was Ash.

She wrapped the blanket tighter. Still, it did nothing. Still she could feel herself beneath it, the odd curves of her body.

'Agnes, are you all right?'

'I—' Even her voice felt wrong. She muffled her face in the blanket, willing herself to be stronger. 'I am fine,' she said.

There was a pause. *Please go*, she thought.

The door opened.

'The dressmaker said you were unwe— Agnes?' Beside her, the bed sagged. 'What happened?'

'Nothing,' she mumbled. 'Nothing happened. It was just . . . just me.'

'Should I fetch the physician?'

'No, no. It's nothing like that.'

'I could get Sara?' He truly *was* desperate now.

'No,' she said. 'No. But thank you.'

There was a long pause. Ash appeared to be thinking. 'How about a jug of wine?'

To indulge in Ash's suggestion would be a poor idea . . . yet still, it appealed. Better to let the fuzz of wine blur the edges of her body than struggle like *this* with them so solid and unpleasant.

She emerged from the blankets, feeling extremely childish for having hidden from her soon-to-be husband. She was ready for him to reprimand her when it became clear that there was nothing wrong with her – nothing physical, at least, even when the feeling was like a vice around her chest.

He didn't. He smiled at her when she pulled the blanket away, almost shyly. As she sat up, he went to put a hand on her shoulder, then appeared to realise her state of near-undress and snatched it back.

'When—' His voice caught. 'When they brought me back from France, and when I wasn't about to die, I spent weeks hiding beneath the covers in my chambers. Months, maybe.' He gave her another of those shy, self-effacing smiles. 'Sometimes it is all you can do.'

Agnes sat up properly. She reached out, now, taking his hand. His fingers were cold. Her skin prickled into gooseflesh.

'Indeed.'

'Shall I . . . ?'

Agnes nodded. 'Please.'

When Ash returned, Agnes had managed to return to some semblance of dress. She had thrown the shift aside and pulled on instead an undershirt and hose and – after a moment's hesitation – the cuirass as well. She had finished tugging it tight and was slipping a thick tunic over her head when Ash walked in.

He glanced at her, but said nothing, sitting beside her and handing her a full mug of wine.

'I . . . apologise,' he said at last, looking down into his own goblet.

'Whatever for?'

'For all of this. I hate to think that the marriage pains you. I understand that I am not, perhaps, as good a husband as you may be able to find elsewhere. And if . . .' He took a long drink. 'If you need to call off the match, or find someone else, or *leave* . . . I will understand. I need a marriage. But I will not accept one that brings you so much pain.'

Agnes realised, slowly, what he meant. He had recognised the symptoms of panic and fear in her, knew them from his *own* lifetime suffering from them. But he did not know the cause. How could he? How could *anyone*?

It was reasonable that Ash had seen her panic and assumed it had meant she did not wish to go through with the match. That her fear was because of *him*.

Her stomach lurched. She wanted this. She wanted the marriage. She needed him to know that.

He wouldn't understand. He could condemn her. But she had been trusted with the secret of the true nature of his and Oliver's relationship, and as she had mused: perhaps such uniquenesses were not all that different.

'It is not you.'

'Then . . .'

'It was— God take you, Ash, it was that *cursed* dress.'

Ash looked utterly lost. 'You did not like it? Or the dressmaker? We could find someone else?'

'No. It was not her, it was the *feeling* of it on my skin, the sensation of them looking at me, of being paraded like something . . .' she took a sip '. . . like something I am not.'

'What are you not?' It was a cautious question.

Agnes answered the best she knew how. 'A bride.'

Ash gave a low half-laugh. 'Not *yet*, I suppose,' he said. 'But—'

'You do not understand.'

'Then *help* me understand, Agnes. Please.'

The cup was half-full. She saw it off.

'Remember when I found you in the woods? And later, when we confirmed our match?'

Ash nodded. 'I do.'

'You did not seem concerned that I was dressed in men's clothes.'

Ash shrugged. 'I was not. I *am* not. Is that what this is? Agnes, if you wish to wear men's clothes then I will not—'

'It's not that!' It came out sharp. She immediately regretted it. 'It is not *just* that. I cannot . . . I cannot explain it. I can barely explain it to *myself*.'

'Could you try?'

Reading her expression, Ash got up from the bed and refilled their mugs, then gestured towards her with his own: *go on*.

'At first it was just a game,' she began. 'Stealing men's clothes and going out on the hunt. My father *knew* – at first, it was because I wanted to join him without worrying about them treating me differently because I was a girl. I dressed in boys' clothes, pretended to be a boy, and they didn't treat me as if I was some delicate creature who needed protecting. And Father allowed it because he was pleased I was interested in his greatest love.

'But then . . . it was after my first bleed. It had never been *proper*, but suddenly it was immoral. Before, my body was like . . . blank parchment, waiting to be filled. But the bleeds meant I was a woman. I could hunt, but only if I behaved properly. I had woken up transformed, changed from a lump of clay to a woman. Were you ever told the story of Joseph of Schönau?'

Ash frowned at the sudden shift in subject. 'I do not recall it.'

Agnes rolled the cup in her hands.

'You may know of him – her, I suppose – as Hildegund?'

Another blank look. Clearly Ash was not so well versed in monastic tales as she was.

'It was a tale my nurse told me,' Agnes began. 'She was a nun, once, or at least spent some time with them. She was . . .' she sniffed '. . . a very pious woman. But she brought with her stories from the convent. Joseph was a saint . . . miracles, visions, speaking to angels . . . but the *true* miracle was his death. He predicted upon which day he would die, which as far as miracles goes was good enough, but *after* he died it was said he transformed into a woman.'

'*What?*'

'When they stripped his body they found he had woman's parts. My nurse said he was transformed at death because he was so holy: a true bride of Christ. For *months* afterwards, I prayed to God to do the same to me. I thought if it was so *easy* to change, then surely I could do it too? It never worked, of course,' Agnes added with a huff. 'A few years later I realised that he must have been born with woman's parts and simply hidden them all that time. But he was called a man, and used a man's name, and *lived* amongst men and so did that not make him a man? And he was a monk, so it is not as if whichever parts he had were ever needed to him.'

She stuttered off, face flushing. Her true confession – the endless nights of prayer to be something else, something *different* – had been buried beneath the flood of words.

Ash was staring at her. 'You prayed to be changed?'

'I did.'

'Into . . . into what?'

'Into a boy. Or at least, into something other than a woman.'

More staring. 'I cannot even *claim* that I understand . . .' Ash said. 'You . . . you *are* a woman. At least . . .' he gestured, with an embarrassed expression, at her body '. . . you appear to be?'

'And *you* appear to be a bastard,' Agnes countered, without malice. 'Yet inside . . .' she reached out before she could stop herself, pressing her fingers to his chest '. . . you are not. You are a *good* man.'

Ash shook his head, but did not push her hand away. 'It is hardly the same.'

'Very well,' Agnes countered. 'What of you and Oliver? When people see you they see a man soon to be married to a . . . a *woman*.' She had to hide a shudder, but forced herself on. 'They see a man who *loves* women, and only women. They do *not* see a man who is in love with another man. They do not even think it possible, and if they *did*, they would call it . . . degenerate. Sinful.'

'That is true enough,' Ash said. 'But I still do not *understand*. How does it feel?'

The question startled her. 'How does what feel?' she repeated, feeling foolish.

'You were so distressed. How does it feel?'

'Like my skin does not fit,' Agnes said, after a pause. 'Like I can *feel* every place my clothes touch my body, and every place my body touches itself. Like there are weights on me, all over me, pressing me. I look down and *see* myself – see my breasts – and it is like I am looking at someone else's body.' She thought again, looking for words he would understand. 'Have you ever been given a horse to ride that you are not used to? Or fought with a sword that is not your own? It may be a perfectly fine horse or a well-crafted blade, but beneath you or in your hands it feels . . . incorrect. In a way you cannot describe.'

'I see,' Ash said slowly. 'Do you . . . often feel that way?' he asked cautiously. 'Is it always?'

'Not always,' Agnes said. 'Sometimes I don't feel it at all. But sometimes it is worse.'

He appeared to be mulling over his words again. Agnes knew how this would end: shock and horror and disgust. Shouting, like she had heard from her parents when she'd tried to explain it in her broken child's words so long ago.

It was her biggest secret – the one that was the core of her, yet the one she understood least of all. And now Ash knew.

'Thank you.'

'*What?*'

'For telling me. Frankly' – Ash gave a low laugh – 'I *am* relieved that it is not that you dread marrying me. I am—' He stopped, peering down at the floor. 'I am fond of you,' he finished. 'And I do not wish to lose you.'

Agnes gave him a small smile. It was so little, as far as confessions went, but it made her heart ache regardless.

'And I am fond of you, too,' she said. 'I have chosen well, no matter what my family believe.'

'Does anyone else know?'

Agnes picked at her hands. 'Only Sara. Nicholas knew my manner of dress, and he never attempted to stop me. He was so unwell that I don't think he truly *understood*. He was just happy I was there. And my family . . .' She twisted her hands together. 'They knew of my . . . predilections towards men's clothes, as I said. Once I was older, they attempted to put a stop to it. And . . .'

She could smell the grass again, the cloying scent of summer. The way it itched against the backs of her legs. Francis's voice, his hands on her wrists, the dreadful expression on his face. Her father shouting afterwards, blaming himself, blaming *her*, having her rooms searched.

'There was some unpleasantness,' she said. 'When they realised they had been unsuccessful in those attempts. Francis—'

She stopped herself. Ash was carefully watching her, saying nothing. She needed to tell him. Not for *him*, but for *her*, so it would be out of her head at last.

'Francis found me. He was disgusted. He threatened to tell my parents. I begged him not to, and he said he wouldn't if I, if—' She took a deep breath. 'If I granted him certain *favours*.' She tried to load the word with as much hatred as she could. 'At that time we thought he was to be my husband. He said it would not matter.'

Ash made a sharp noise. She looked across at him. His expression was dark.

'I refused,' Agnes said. 'I hated him even then. He pushed. I refused again. He insulted me and told me he would ruin my name.'

'What did you do?'

Agnes smirked. 'I kicked him in the bollocks and ran,' she said. 'But true to his word, he told my parents. They were *furious*. It was why they insisted on Sara: they hoped with someone chaperoning my every movement I would be forced to stop.' She sniffed. 'They were wrong, of course.'

Ash looked down. He reached out – hesitated, corrected himself, and took her hand.

'It is hard being alone,' he said quietly.

She squeezed him back. 'It is.'

They sat in silence for a moment. Ash seemed to be thinking. 'Shall we take a walk?' he said at last.

'I— What?'

'A walk of the grounds? I find the fresh air helps when I am feeling less than myself. When I feel unwell in my mind, rather than my body.'

'Oh.' Ash was offering a part of himself to her. His own private battle. 'That sounds like a fine idea.'

'Come, then—'

'Wait.'

Ash turned. 'What is it?'

'I will need to change . . .'

Ash looked her up and down. 'Do you wish to? I thought . . . if you feel so unsettled . . . ?'

'People will talk.'

Ash stuck his chin in the air. 'I am the earl,' he said. 'Let them.'

They headed from her chambers and into the hall. Agnes was not shocked to notice Oliver seated alone at the great table, apparently deep into a game of dice against himself. He looked up when they entered, then quickly rose to his feet and hurried over.

'Are you all right? Ash told me—'

Agnes immediately twisted to look at Ash, who looked abashed. 'Uh . . .'

'Oh, do not glare at him. He told me you had been taken unwell; that was all. *Are* you all right?'

Agnes took a breath. 'As I can be,' she said, settling on the half-truth.

'We are heading out,' Ash said. 'To take in the air. We will see you *later*, Olly.'

'Wait—' Both men turned to look at her. 'You can join us, if you would like.'

'Really?'

'I would not have asked if I did not want you to.'

Oliver looked between her and Ash, disbelieving. 'Oh, well,' he said, his confusion melding into a smile. 'I would be delighted.'

'We could walk down to the river while it's still warm,' Ash mused. 'Raff tells me we will have storms soon.'

'Perfect.' Agnes smiled. 'Lead the way.'

They fetched the dogs, then took a longer route through the fields as the animals bounded along ahead. They had barely made it past the edge of Dunlyn's land when they came across another party: hunters, led by an older man on a fine, tall horse.

It was too late to hope they hadn't been seen – the rider had already spotted Ash.

'Barden!' the man called, striding away from his men towards them. 'How are you? I've not seen you since your father's—' His smile became forced and frozen. 'It has been an age, truly. How are you? I hear you are to be married?'

Agnes could tell that Ash was trying not to look at her.

'You have heard right, Lord Justin,' he said. 'On the morrow, in fact!'

'Wonderful to hear it!' Justin said. 'What of your new wife? What is she like?'

'She is . . .' Ash swallowed. 'She is extremely tolerant of what an ass I am.'

Justin guffawed. 'An extremely good characteristic to have.' He laughed. 'And what else? How does she look, boy? Is she beautiful? Is she' – he raised his eyebrows – 'naturally gifted?'

Beside Agnes, Oliver snorted. Agnes clamped her lip beneath her teeth, but it was not enough to stifle her laughter. At the noise, Justin turned.

'And who is this? I do not believe we've met!'

Ash visibly relaxed.

'This is Oliver,' he said. 'A friend of mine, and new to the keep. And this is Agn—'

Shit. Agnes gave a short, sharp cough.

'—Nus,' he finished, fumbling. 'Angus. He . . . is one of my wife's, ah, cousins. A hunter.'

'Is that so?' Justin turned. Agnes gave him a sharp smile.

'Indeed it is. I am very grateful that my cousin' – Agnes caught Ash's eye, then looked quickly away – 'has allowed me to stay with her. I was keen to extend my skills beyond the border.'

'The game here is truly very good,' Justin commented. 'Have you been on any hunting parties yet?'

'Not yet, sir.'

'Ah well, there's time yet. After the festivities are over you must join me – all of you.'

Justin swiftly drew Ash into more conversation before they were allowed to move on. Ash directed them in the opposite direction to Justin's party, heading back towards the trees in the bowl of the valley.

'You handled that impeccably,' Agnes said, grinning, as they headed towards the treeline.

'It does not feel that way.' Ash sighed. 'My *God*. Angus? What was I thinking?'

'I think it's a fine name for a dowager.' Oliver grinned.

'Do *not* call me a dowager,' Agnes snapped. 'It makes me feel like an old woman. It *is* a good name. Although maybe not the one I'd have picked for myself . . .'

'What *would* you have picked?' Ash asked, sounding panicked. 'I should have let you speak, God, I—'

'It is *fine,*' Agnes said, placing a hand on his shoulder. 'Angus is perfectly acceptable. I would have likely given him my true name and ruined everything, anyway. And it is not as if we can very well turn up to this hunting party of his and introduce me as something else. He will think you're mad.'

'I *am* mad.'

'It's remarkable really,' Oliver mused.

'What is?'

'That he assumed you were a man so quickly. You *do* look very—Well.'

'Well, what?'

'Very much like a man,' he said, with a one-shouldered shrug.

'Good.'

They proceeded down the slope towards the river. It was a fine day, the sun warm, the treetops bursting with birdsong. As they walked, Agnes noticed Oliver's eyes landing on her time and again. When he had met them in the great hall, he had not passed comment on her unusual dress, and now it seemed as if he had only just realised how strange it was.

Particularly, she noticed his eyes darting downwards at her chest. Or, the place where her chest *would* be, had she not been wearing the cuirass.

She would have thought the looks salacious, were it not for the glint of curiosity in his expression.

When Litillwitte was distracted by a darting hare, running off into a thicket of trees with Ash swearing and scrambling after him, Agnes and Oliver were left alone; she absent-mindedly fussing behind Qwippe's ears while Oliver leaned against a tree.

He was, she realised, once again staring at her chest.

'Why is it,' Agnes said, watching him closely, 'that I feel as if you have something on your mind?'

Oliver's eyes snapped from her chest to her face. 'Nothing,' he said, far too quickly.

'*Oliver.*'

'. . . It would be improper.'

Agnes raised her eyebrows, thinking on the myriad *improper* things about their situation.

'Oh, curse it.' Oliver huffed. 'I was wondering how you did . . . that.'

'Did what?'

'Did *that!*' Oliver gestured impatiently at her chest. 'How did you—' He made another, cruder gesture with both hands. 'I mean, they—'

'You are asking how I flattened my chest?'

Oliver blushed. She'd never seen him blush, before. 'Yes,' he mumbled.

'It is a kind of cuirass,' Agnes said, trying to find the correct words. 'I made it myself. I simply put it on and tighten it and it . . .well. Presses.'

'A cuirass?'

'Yes, it's quite simple really. And about the only thing I've ever used my years of needlework for,' she added, with a laugh. 'Why so curious?'

'No reason,' he said, although he was looking thoughtful. 'Truly, just that: just curiosity. I suppose it is to make shooting easier?'

Agnes frowned.

'You use a bow,' Oliver said. 'I have heard that they' – another crude gesture – 'get in the way.'

'Was that something you learned on the road?' she asked.

Oliver barked out a sharp laugh. 'It makes sense,' he protested. 'I was once told this story – I met a man in France. We were both prisoners, both trying to get home. He was a *poet,* he said. Why he'd seen fit to become a military man I cannot say, although he was very loyal to the king. He told me this tale he'd heard of a whole *country* of fierce warrior women in Scythia. They were led by a mighty queen – I forget her name – but they were all skilled marksmen.' He paused. 'Markswomen. Regardless, they favoured the bow, but their womanly assets often got in the way. So they cut them off.'

Agnes pictured it – the blood, the shine and slice of the knife, the carved body. While visceral, the image held no horror.

'Both of them?' she said at last.

'Just the one,' Oliver said. 'I presume for—' He mimicked pulling back a bow.

'Oh.' Agnes considered this. 'And they *all* did this?'

'I am unsure. My friend did not elaborate.'

She let the thought hang in her mind. A whole *tribe* of women, not mutilated, but *freed*. It was intriguing. She wondered what it felt like, how much it hurt. If it was worth it, afterwards.

Soon after, Ash reappeared, half-dragging Litillwitte beside him, whose fur was now full of burrs.

'Stupid hound,' he muttered, letting him go and watching him bound down the path. 'What have you two been discussing? You look guilty.'

'Nothing,' Agnes said quickly, just as Oliver said: 'Breasts.'

Ash looked between them. He opened his mouth. He closed it again. 'I regret asking.'

They continued on. They'd only gone a little further when there was a noise from up ahead: a laugh. Ash stilled, Agnes and Oliver coming up sharp behind him. And then, from the trees, burst a pair of familiar figures.

It was Ash who spoke first, his shoulders relaxing. 'Greetings.'

Raff and Penn froze as they realised that they were not alone. Penn was ruffled, and Raff's tunic was slung over his arm, his undershirt slipping from one shoulder. There was a fresh, dark, bruise nestled just below his collarbone. His eyes darted towards Agnes and then, skin turning pink, he quickly tugged the undershirt up.

It was all the confirmation she needed.

Perhaps this was why Ash had thought she would fit within his family. Perhaps it *was* as Penn said: they truly were all eccentrics and degenerates. All of them were blurring the rules of sex – changing between *man* and *woman* – herself and Ash included.

'We were just heading back to the keep,' Penn said, while Raff stood by looking awkward.

'Oh indeed?' Ash said. 'Do not let us delay you.'

As they went to pass her, Agnes shot out a hand, grabbing Penn around one of his skinny wrists.

'One moment—'

He turned an appeasing smile on her. He knew he was caught.

'When you return, *do* seek out Joan,' she said. 'I believe she is baking. I would hate for you to be forced to feast on poor Raff again.'

Penn's expression went slack. Behind her, both Ash and Oliver burst into unconstrained peals of laughter.

Penn blinked at her. 'Uh—'

She maintained her sure smile. 'We shall see you later, I am sure.'

Without another word, he and Raff dashed off.

'That was *wonderful*.' Oliver approached from behind. 'My God, his *face* . . .'

'You were aware of their— of them?' Ash asked, he too holding back laughter.

'I had suspected there was something more between them than a simple friendship, yes,' Agnes said. 'They . . . are not very subtle.'

Ash gave her a conciliatory look. 'That they are not. God's

bollocks, I am happy to have it *out*, now, at last. Now everyone knows everything: everyone who matters, that is. No more secrets. I had intended to tell you,' he added quickly. 'Or insist one of *them* told you. Just in case.'

'It is not a secret easily given,' Agnes reassured him.

'That it is not.'

They didn't need to walk much longer before Agnes could hear rushing water. The path was rough and footworn, little more than a track through the brambles. They emerged onto the bank of the river, the sunlight sparkling from the water and low trees hanging above it, branches drooping.

Olly rushed ahead, already making quick work of his tunic and undershirt. Before Agnes could look away, he'd shucked off his hose and braies as well, throwing them aside and leaping into the water with a splash. Ash called after him, his words utterly unheeded.

'He will be at this for hours,' Ash said. 'Come, join me . . .'

He perched on a low bough facing the water, shuffling along the mossy wood to grant Agnes room. The tree sagged as they sat, leaves rustling above them.

They watched Oliver turn neat lines through the water, cutting through the flow of the river like it was nothing. His arms were strong and powerful, even if the sight of his firm muscles betrayed how poorly he'd been looking after himself for far too long. Scars littered his chest and arms, as well as perhaps a dozen bruises all over his right side.

Despite his cockiness, Agnes found that she *liked* Oliver, too. He was charming, annoyingly so, and appeared determined to either win her favour or drive her utterly mad. Thus far, he had succeeded in both. It was because he was so deeply unserious, she suspected; he treated most things as if they were amusements.

'Do you intend to join me?' he called, pausing to float. 'Or will you be sitting there all afternoon?'

Ash laughed, heaving himself from the bough. He, too, began to strip. Agnes watched as he removed his clothes layer by layer: tunic, undershirt, hose, breeches. His body was softer than Olly's, with thick, strong-looking arms and legs furred in wiry, dark hair. Like this, she could see that the scar did not stop at his jaw, but grazed across his chest as well.

Her heart beat out of time, a stuttering thing between her ribs. With the soft sunlight dappling Ash's skin, she could not tell if the feeling was something cautious and gentle, or something voracious, wanting to *bite*.

Ash stopped at his braies, leaving them about his waist as he threw his clothes aside and stepped into the water with a muffled curse at the cold. He entered the water with far more care than Oliver; a choice that was utterly wasted when Oliver immediately swam over to him, grabbed him, and pulled him beneath the surface. Ash remerged red-faced and spluttering, and a childish splashing war began. Agnes watched as they spun around each other. Like this, she could see where they had been trained in the art of war: skills now used, apparently, for thievery and water fights.

'Agnes! Will you join us?'

She looked up to see Ash standing, watching her. The water barely reached his thighs, and the expensive linen of his braies – which he had no doubt kept on in an attempt to maintain some sense of propriety – had become entirely transparent.

She swallowed heavily. She tried, truly, to keep his gaze. She failed magnificently. He was hard beneath the fabric, no doubt the result of such fervent contact with his lover.

'Agnes?' he said, entirely unaware of her predicament. 'Are you all right?'

'Get *down.*' Olly grabbed him from behind and pulled him into the water. 'Or do you truly mean to speak to her with your prick on show? There are *ladies* present.' He shot a look at Agnes, a wild, cheeky grin. 'Allegedly.'

Ash went *scarlet.*

'Actually, Oliver,' Agnes said haughtily, 'I had not even noticed.'

Oliver caught her eye. He raised a single, suggestive eyebrow.

'Of course not,' he said. 'Terrible of me to suggest otherwise. *Will* you join us?'

Agnes rose tentatively from the branch and placed herself at the edge of the water. The chill of it seeped into the fabric of her hose. For a moment her hands went to her laces. But that clawing feeling inside of her whispered – *Do not. Do not make me look. Do not make me be like that.*

She lowered her hands, took a deep breath, and flung herself into the water between them.

Chapter 19

Ash

In a muddy clearing in France on the edge of a blood-ready battlefield, Ash had made his vows. He had sworn himself away, dedicated his body and soul and all he owned to one person. He had exchanged a promise, a kiss, and a ring.

Today, outside the church of the town he had grown up beside, he would be making vows again. He wondered if God could sense his lies.

All eyes were upon him. Him and the person who was to be his wife.

Since the announcement they were to be wed, word had spread, and the churchyard was full of people: some he recognised, many he didn't. He missed that field in France – silent save for their words, and the words of their marshal, and the gentle sound of the trees in the breeze above them.

Agnes squeezed his hands. Perhaps she could tell he was nervous. She, too, seemed out of sorts. She had spent all morning twisting her hands in her skirts, jumping out of her skin every time someone brushed past. Ash was not sure if it was nerves for the marriage, or the same affliction that had troubled her the previous day.

He squeezed her hands in return. Their mutual anxiety was

likely making them *both* feel worse, but it was reassuring to know he was not alone.

They stood in the door of the church, the priest between them dressed in his holy finery. Ash felt the reassuring presence of Olly behind him – in full armour, no less; something Olly had insisted upon himself.

'Should anyone try to steal your bride away,' he had said, making Agnes laugh and Ash roll his eyes.

The priest announced them, as if anyone present did not know who they were, then began the long process of reading the vows: the words handed down from God to bind them together. Ash found them washing over him without ever touching him, already bound by promises he had made so long ago.

The words hung between them like clouds. Their own unspoken vow – Agnes's allowance of Olly's presence – the heaviest of all.

They spoke with confidence, eyes upon the other. *Yes. I will. I do.* Agnes never let go of his hands.

They were declared married with a kiss – the kiss given from the priest to Ash, and from Ash to Agnes, a light, chaste thing that barely brushed the corner of her lip.

And then it was done.

The road back towards Dunlyn was one Ash had trodden before; one he had walked not so long ago, the imagined smell of smoke in his nostrils, his face throbbing and his heart hollow. The man who walked that path then, with Raff keeping him upright at his side, would never have imagined that this was the way he would walk this path next.

That day, he was sure that the next time he was taken down this road he would be travelling the other direction. He was sure that he would be alone.

Today, he was not. Agnes stayed at his right side, their arms linked, her own nerves clearly abated now the ceremony was complete. To his left strode Olly, the perfect picture of a knight. Raff came behind, and behind *them* the allies who had seen fit to join.

The procession arrived beneath the outer gates of the keep to a chorus of cheers from staff and servants. He was sure that for many of them, their joy was feigned – a way to win his favour.

Despite the terribly short notice, Joan and Ellen had pulled together a grand celebration for the event. As they headed into the great hall, he could not hide how impressed he was: the central fire was burning, rushlights burned on every surface, and the chandeliers hanging from the ceiling shone with candles. They had found a band willing to play on short notice for a hefty fee, who struck up a happy jig as soon as the party entered the room.

Ash was met with a parade of people eager to congratulate him. The mug in his hand emptied, but never for long. On his arm, Agnes smiled at him. At his side, Olly kept his ear full of filthy jokes. It was not, Ash realised, as awful an event as it could have been.

Chapter 20

Olly

It should have been more momentous. It should have felt like the end of something; like a door slammed shut, Olly's fingers trapped in the frame.

It did not. Ash and Agnes had married in front of what appeared to be the entire county, and nothing at all had changed.

At least the wedding feast would soothe his anxieties. After removing his armour – *better for dancing,* he had said – Olly stood with Ash on his left, so he could hear him above the din, and peered around the room. He had not been a part of such excitement in *years,* and he was determined to make the most of it.

His attempts were waylaid, however, by the overwhelming number of people who were determined to greet the new couple. Olly had not yet really seen how *important* Ash was, and here it was as clear as the red beard that prickled across Ash's chin. Everyone wished to speak to him, and those who had nothing of import to say wanted to greet him anyway, likely to ensure he remembered them and would continue to do so.

'I do not know how Father managed all this,' Ash said, when they were granted a moment of peace.

'You will get used to it,' Agnes said. 'If only because you have no other choice.'

'Wonderful,' Ash huffed. 'Thank you so much.'

'Don't look so *sour,*' Olly said. 'You are supposed to be enjoying yourself.'

Ash gestured to his mug. 'Is this not enjoying myself?'

'You have not even danced yet.'

Ash did not move. 'Good.'

An evil little thought bloomed in Olly's mind.

'Come,' he said. 'This is your wedding feast. Everybody will think you are a poor match if you do not even *dance* together.'

'You said yourself I have no skill in it.'

'And?' Olly exclaimed, 'Neither does he!' He gestured to a man crossing the hall uneasily, hoisted up by the people dancing on either side of him. 'Yet that does not stop him.'

'But—'

'Go! Dance!'

Ash shot a sideways glance at Agnes. She, too, looked unsure.

'As much as it pains me to admit it,' she said, 'he *is* right.'

Ash looked between them with an expression of betrayal. 'I hate you both.'

Agnes took his hand. 'Come, the sooner we can get this over with the sooner you can go back to drowning in wine.'

They moved into the centre of the hall just in time to join the beginning of another dance. They made a good pair, if only because their awkwardness was matched in the other. Neither of them looked particularly keen, either; at least that way they could claim it was a shared dislike for dancing rather than a dislike of each other.

Not, Olly thought, that anyone *would* assume they disliked each other. It was clear that they were fond of each other, and they made a good couple; Agnes's practical nature was an effective ballast against Ash's more tempestuous one. As they shuffled around the other dancers – Agnes wincing as Ash stepped in the wrong direction – something hot and acidic rose in Olly's throat.

They were wed, now. And while they were only friends, he had known too many people whose marriages had started on bedrocks far less certain but had still bloomed into love. For Ash, of course, Olly knew himself to be lost: how could anyone *not* love Ash, as he did? How could anyone not want him? Agnes, too, was fair and bold and, Olly had no qualms in admitting, pleasing to look at. It was natural that, given time and proximity, their relationship would bloom into more.

Part of him wondered if it had not already happened – or at least had for Agnes. He recalled the way she had so gently stopped Ash from picking at his scar. She looked at him with a fondness that Olly was all-too familiar with.

He had pushed them to dance for little more than his own devilish glee, delighting in watching Ash be forced into something he detested. And now, as they moved together around the hall, he regretted doing so.

What would become of him if Ash and Agnes's friendship *did* become more?

The one jealousy that Olly allowed himself, while watching Ash step on Agnes's foot and then quickly and effusively apologise, was the fact that *their* relationship would always be real. In the eyes of their family and friends and of God Himself, it was an unbreakable union. There was no recognition for him and Ash – not beyond the vows they had made to each other before entering the battlefield, and those would only ever be recognised as a comrades' bond. They were knights, brothers-in-arms, soldiers. Not lovers. Not *joined* in the way Ash and Agnes were.

At least that bitterness was not directed at Ash or his new wife. It was directed at the world around them, at the God who had made him *this,* made him *other,* and then rejected that otherness and made it a sin.

Ash had insisted that he would not leave Olly again. That they would never be parted. That he loved him, as desperately and rawly as he had done all those years ago. Olly believed him: Olly would *always* believe him, after seeing the pain in Ash's eyes when he'd tried to leave, and after hearing the full and rotten truth of his life since Olly's apparent death. Given all he'd been through, the fact of Ash's love felt like the only solid thing he could cling to, and so cling to it he did.

Ash had kept the ring, after all.

All Olly could do was hold on to the twin facts that Ash loved him, and that Agnes tolerated their relationship. *More* than tolerated. It was another mark in her favour: she saw Ash for who he was and wanted him to be happy. Another wife would have forced Olly away. Another wife would likely have never known about her husband's tryst with his oldest friend regardless, forcing their love into the shadows, breaking it through a thousand tiny blows.

The musicians – who were, by Olly's high standards, very good – stopped their song. It was the sudden silence that roused him from his thoughts, looking towards Ash and Agnes as the minstrels began readying for the next tune: a carole. Ash gestured towards him, reaching out his hand. His expression was amused and daring.

Olly would rarely turn down a dance: especially after cajoling Ash into the act himself. He had practised enough to see off some of the clumsiness that had plagued him since his injury, and besides: in such close quarters he would be less likely to trip. He saw off his drink and rose to his feet just in time to join. Ash handed him off to Agnes, placing himself on Olly's other side. Olly swallowed, half-amused that he was about to dance with the wife of his lover. It was a farce: but one that only *they* were privy to, making it all the more amusing.

He took her hand with a low bow, fluttering his lips over the backs of her fingers. 'My Lady.'

She gave him a half-annoyed smile. He edged closer, so only she and Ash could hear him.

'My *Lord Angus,* how pleased I am for this dance.'

That got a reaction from her – the smile split into something far warmer and more real. Her cheekbones flushed.

'I hope you are a better dancer than him,' she said, gesturing over Olly's shoulder towards Ash.

'*Far* better.'

The dance began. Agnes's skin was warm, fingers calloused from her bow. Her hand was smaller than his own, but her grip was firm. Like Ash, she was unsure of the dance, forgoing the more complicated cross-steps. Unlike Ash, she hid her uncertainty well, where Ash continually forced himself to attempt steps his legs could not keep up with, tripping himself – and Olly – over.

When the dance ended, the other attendees politely clapping or complimenting each other, the call for another coupled dance began. Expecting to be dismissed again, Olly went to turn away, but to his surprise found Ash gripping his shoulder, preventing an escape.

'You were quite right,' he said, speaking so closely to his ear that Olly's skin flourished into gooseflesh. 'I *am* a dreadful dancer. Quite a danger. It is your turn.'

With that, he spun Olly around in a manoeuvre Olly was sure was from their training days, directly into Agnes's arms.

'Be *good*,' Ash muttered, as he pressed their hands together.

'Aren't I always?'

'I was talking to *both of you*.'

Agnes shook her head at him as Ash headed towards the edge of the room and was immediately pulled into a conversation by a wealthy-looking woman. Olly refocused his attention on Agnes, leading her into the next dance.

With a competent partner, Agnes's own uncertainty was less noticeable. Olly found her easy to move and redirect as needed, and she seemed happy to follow his lead, only redirecting him when his bad eye nearly sent them crashing into another couple.

He had not been this close to her before. She was a good head shorter than him, forcing him to peer down at her as they danced. Her tight dress emphasised the width of her shoulders: he had not noticed how strong they were. He could sense rather than feel the muscle of her archer's arms beneath the silk.

Her hair, as always, was tied into a complex series of plaits crowning her head. Today, she wore a fine mesh of gold studded with little jewels atop it. It made her hair glow, imbued with some fiery magic. How had he not already appreciated how striking she was?

Unthinking, he reached up to tuck a strand of hair behind her ear. Was it the heat of the hall and the wine in his blood making his cheeks flush, or something else?

When the music ended – a moment later, a lifetime later – it took several seconds for him to realise, only releasing Agnes's hand when she gave it a little squeeze.

Feeling distinctly unsettled, Olly was grateful for the sudden appearance of a gaggle of women, all keen to be introduced to the earl's bride. He made awkward introductions as best he could before leaving Agnes with them – but not before giving her the brief nod he had always given to his co-conspirators in these sorts of situations: *will you be all right?*

Agnes had given him a small but confident smile, and he had left her to it.

The night was long, the room dim and smoky. Ash, for his part, appeared to be doing a fair job in his new role: he spoke to the right people on mundane topics like taxes and crop yield and weather. He never looked like he was *enjoying* himself, and Olly was sure those he spoke to could see that, but at least he was not shouting at anyone.

Not *yet,* anyway. Ash's latest conversational partner – a man named Roland wearing a feathered hat that Olly immediately envied – was certainly doing his best to rile him.

'What are you still doing down here?' he said, after Ash had greeted him. 'You should be bedding your lovely new wife.'

Ash's face twitched. 'I have *work* to do as well, Roland, as you well know.'

'Begetting heirs is work, boy! A much more pleasant kind of work, too.'

Ash's expression had settled into a pained grimace. Olly quickly stepped forwards.

'And who is this?' Roland said, noticing him at last. 'I do not believe we have met, although you and your brother are always showing up with strays.'

'This is Oliver,' Ash said, with a relieved sigh. 'He is to be a new fixture at Dunlyn. I've known him since we were both troublesome boys. I intend to elevate him, once I can work out what role he deserves to be elevated to.'

Roland guffawed. 'Quite right, too. When I first came into my house I immediately sent word to my friend in Norfolk. *Richard,*

I said, *you get your arse here and be my marshal or there shall be Hell to pay.* He was only too happy to, of course. It pays to have those close to you be your friends. No one is better suited to lend you their hand when you need it most. Or' – Roland gave Olly a conspiratorial look – 'to tell you when you are being an unreasonable bastard.'

'I tell him that often enough.' Olly laughed.

'Good! I am sure he needs it. Regardless . . .' Roland turned back to Ash. 'Ash, I've been meaning to find you all night. I need to talk to you. Let me fetch us some drinks and find us somewhere quieter . . .'

As Roland hurried after a servant with a jug of beer, Ash turned to Olly.

'I suspect Roland will desire to talk in private,' he said. 'I can ask if you may stay, but . . .'

'No, no, this is *earl* business,' Olly said, laughing as Ash scowled. 'Terribly dull. I can amuse myself with Agnes until you are done, I'm sure.'

'A keen idea,' Ash agreed. 'I certainly do not want her to be cornered by . . .' He paused. He peered around. 'Where *is* Agnes?'

Olly, too, turned. He had assumed she was with the group of women he had left her with. But now her tightly wound crown of burning red hair was nowhere to be seen.

'*Shit,*' Ash muttered. 'I should look for her . . .'

'*I* can look for her,' Olly said. '*You* need to be playing at earl, not chasing lost brides.'

'Very well.' Ash sighed. 'Come and tell me if you cannot find her. I can invent some sort of emergency to get away.'

'Losing your wife does not count as an emergency?'

Ash said nothing, merely shoved him away as Roland appeared with a serving girl carrying a jug of wine. He gave him a playful swat, low on his back where Roland couldn't see, then returned to the throng of people.

Agnes really did appear to be gone. She wasn't at the side of the hall, nor was she caught in conversation with anybody. Even Sara did not know where she was. Olly felt a little guilty for not having realised Agnes was no longer with them. The previous day she really had seemed distressed, and while neither she nor Ash had specified the *form* her distress took, it was clear that she had been left feeling fragile.

She had probably returned to her chambers. On his way towards the staircase, hurrying down the quieter servants' corridor, he heard a little *thud* from the buttery.

He hesitated. 'Agnes?'

Silence. Then, so quiet he almost didn't catch it: 'Oliver?'

'Yes, it's me. We quite lost you . . .' A breath. 'Are you well?'

More silence. Then the sound of a bolt being slid across. The door opened, just a crack. Taking the invitation, Olly slid inside.

Agnes was sitting back down on an upturned crate, looking utterly miserable. Olly locked the door and hurried towards her,

'What in God's name is the matter?'

She stared at the cracked stones in the floor.

'Do you need to return to your room?' Olly asked. 'Or I can fetch you something to drink?'

'I just need . . . time. To breathe.'

Olly lowered himself to the floor beside her, sitting a careful distance away.

'Is there any way I can help?'

She shook her head, lips tight.

'Is it the banquet? The heat?'

'It is *me*,' she spat.

'You?'

'It is . . . my illness from the other day. I thought I was recovered, but . . .' She sighed, frowning. 'Clearly not.'

'If you are feeling unwell, you should return to bed. I do not want you vomiting all over the floor.'

'It is not that sort of illness.'

Olly knew at once what she meant. The grip of one's own mind, the horrors it could conjure through the simple act of existing. The previous day she had slipped into one of these fits, and today it had returned, snarling and striking like a beast freed from a cage.

He knew that feeling far too well. It was sibling to the feeling he'd been burying in his *own* chest: the heave of jealousy and the fear of being left. He thought, again, of how he had to hate her. How by all rights he should. But she was so curled in on herself in a way he had never seen before, so *vulnerable*. She had done so much for them: allowing the relationship, whatever her feelings on the matter.

He could not hate her. Even had she *not* been like this – scared and frantic and hidden in the buttery – he could not hate her.

He reached out across the cold floor and took her hand. She did not react, but she did not let go either.

A thought struck him. It was not a *new* thought, but it was growing more certain. Agnes had been seeing the dressmaker when the fit had begun, and afterwards – when they had retired together outside – she'd been wearing . . . well. She had been wearing men's clothes, along with the strange garment that flattened her breasts.

Olly had listened. He'd *watched*. He told her of the captive poet's warrior women, and gauged her response: interest, not horror. When they'd run into that lord in the woods and he'd assumed she was a man, she hadn't been offended. It had almost been the opposite:

she'd taken it in her stride. When Ash had given her a man's name, she'd enjoyed it.

He'd suspected, then. It was why he'd used that name again as they danced.

She was like Pepper. He was almost certain of it. He'd seen but not experienced that pain, that sense of wrongness: he'd helped Pepper dress properly and cut his hair, spinning tales about a hereditary line of late bloomers to explain his hairless chin. He'd been there for Pepper's first bloods, hiding all trace as best he could.

Through all of it, Pepper had been *Pepper*. There was nothing else he *could* have been. He remained the too-skinny, too-clever lad who played the fiddle like the devil and could charm a horse into allowing itself to be stolen.

There was no real way to ask, not without insulting her if he was wrong. But he had to try.

He plucked at the fabric of her dress, pooled around her.

'Is it because of this?' he asked.

The look Agnes gave him was a mix of horror and surprise. 'What did Ash tell you?'

So Ash knows. Olly tucked that thought away.

'Nothing,' he said aloud. 'Truly, nothing.'

Agnes examined him disbelievingly. And then she heaved a sigh, wrapping her arms around herself, digging her nails into her arms.

'It's . . . it is *wrong*. It feels wrong,' she said.

'Wrong?'

'I can hardly describe it. It is like I can *feel* my skin. Like it does not fit. It is . . .' She wrung her hands. Olly found himself tracking the movement. 'I feel so *aware*. Of my body, my clothes, all of it. I want to step out of myself.'

'How can I help?'

Agnes glanced at him. 'What?'

'You are distressed. How can I help?'

'You cannot. I simply must . . . wait. Until it passes.'

'Could you change clothes?'

Agnes sniffed. 'Oh, of course, I shall change into the tunic and breeches I have hidden in here.'

'Take mine.'

'*What?*'

'Take mine. You are clearly distressed, and I do not want you to have some sort of fit.'

Agnes's mouth hung open. And then, despite everything, she burst into laughter.

'What?' Olly insisted. 'I am being serious!'

'You are not.'

'I *am*. Truly, that dress is very fetching, I do believe the colour would match my eyes quite beautifully.'

'*Oliver—*' She could barely breathe, now.

'And it would be such a shame for it to go to waste. At least on me it would go some way to serving its purpose.'

'Which is?' Agnes choked.

'Delighting and seducing the earl, then ending up in a heap on the floor of his chambers this evening.'

Agnes *cackled*, bruising her eyes with the heels of her hands to stop the tears that were streaming down her face.

'We *cannot*.'

Olly grinned, leaning his elbow on the crate she was perched on. He hadn't been bluffing – had she agreed to his absurd plan, he would have thrown off his doublet and donned her gown. It would not have been the first time he'd worn a dress, after all. But the point had never been to truly swap clothes – just to shock her enough that the panic subsided. It was a method he'd used countless times before: with friends, with fellow thieves, even with the people he robbed from. Most of the time, it worked.

'You know the worst of it?' Agnes said, at last.

'What?'

'I do not *hate* wearing dresses, and looking like—'

'Like a woman?'

She shot him a look. Neither of them had said quite so boldly what sort of affliction was troubling her, and to name it out loud had been dangerous. But she did not look cross.

'Quite,' she said. 'I do not hate it all the time. But sometimes . . . sometimes I wish I could grab all of the things that paint me *woman* and rip them away.'

Olly nodded. He had heard similar things before – most virulently once a month, when Pepper was at his most resentful of his body.

'How do you understand all of this?' Agnes asked. 'You just . . . you just seemed to *know*.'

Olly paused. 'Have I told you about Pepper?'

'Not very much.'

'He is . . . well, he is as good as my brother. We ran together for a time. He saved my life. I worry about him *so damn much*. He's a stubborn little bastard and I fear it will get him killed.'

Agnes was watching him, curious but confused.

'He . . .' Olly continued, rubbing at the back of his neck, staring at the floor, as if that could tell him the words he needed. 'He is a woman. No: that is entirely wrong. He has a woman's body. But the rest of him – his heart, his *soul* – is a man. *He* is a man.'

'And you . . . you call him your brother?'

'He *is* my brother.'

'Even though he—'

'Even though.'

'Oh.'

'You know, I often have wondered if his condition is more common than people think. You hear all sorts of stories, of course; like Hildegund, who was—'

'Joseph of Schönau, yes,' Agnes interrupted him. 'I know the story very well.'

'And of course there's Yde.'

Agnes looked up. 'Yde?'

'Oh, it's a *marvellous* story. I made a song of it for Pepper's sake. It's very long, lots of courtly adventures, but at the end of the whole thing Yde – who starts as a woman – is turned into a man, cock and all.'

'Oh.' Agnes sniffed with a sardonic little smile. 'I fear it all comes down to *parts,* in the end.'

Olly hummed noncommittally. 'I would not be so sure of that. Pepper's got a cock. He keeps it under his bed.'

Agnes choked on her own breath. *'Excuse me?'*

'In a little wooden box,' Olly continued. He peered across at Agnes, who was now staring at him incredulously. 'What is the matter?'

'You cannot tell me this man keeps his cock in a *box beneath his bed* and refuse to tell me the rest. What in God's name are you talking about?'

'It's made out of leather and wood. He lies with people with it.'

There was a pinkness creeping around Agnes's neck. 'Lies with people?'

'Men, women. Anyone who pays. It has these straps, he showed me once, where he ties it around his hips and . . . well. Does what one *does* with a stiff cock.'

'Oh.'

She appeared to be thinking this through, which had rather been the point.

'I cannot imagine how such a thing would even *work*,' she said at last.

Olly racked his memory, trying to recall Pepper's much-prized false phallus.

'The inside was carved wood,' he said thoughtfully. 'For stiffness. And then he padded wool around it – or was it cloth? And then made a kind of . . .' he gestured with his hands '. . . a kind of *sleeve* that went around the whole thing.'

'Good Lord.'

'I believe that is what his customers say.' Olly grinned. 'He *made* himself a man. Is that . . . Agnes, is that what you want? To be a man?'

Agnes sniffed. 'Sometimes? But . . . it is not always like that. Nothing so *simple*, more's the pity of it. There are times when I am quite content as I am, and others when I *detest* it. Often it is as if I am floating, trapped in a current, being pushed this way and that . . . Sometimes I wish I could just be *man* and be done with it. But sometimes . . . more often, really, I wish I was simply . . . something else.'

'Something else?'

Agnes nodded. 'A third thing. Something *beyond*. When I was a girl my nurse always told us about those who chose to devote their lives to God, the brides of Christ, and they were women and men alike but they were something else, too. Something beyond either of those things. I never considered myself *holy*, but something about that life . . . I wanted it.'

Olly nodded. 'I never understood all of that,' he said. 'But . . . I can see it.'

Agnes gave him a small smile. 'Thank you,' she said. 'For allowing me to speak. For *listening*.'

'You do not need to thank me. I am your *friend*, Agnes.'

'You are?'

She looked so suddenly afraid.

'Of course I am.'

✡

Olly was not sure how much time had passed when there was a quick, sharp rap on the door. Both of them froze – Agnes with her feet propped up on the crate, Olly juggling turnips.

'Olly? Agnes?' They immediately relaxed at Ash's voice. 'The door is bolted . . . Let me in, for God's sake!'

Olly dropped the turnips all over the floor then rushed to open the door, pulling Ash inside.

'What in *God's* name are you doing?'

'Looking after your wife,' Olly said simply.

Ash peered at Agnes over Olly's shoulder. 'She looks fine to me.'

'I was not when he found me,' Agnes said, removing her feet from the crate and standing. 'I was . . . in a state of distress.'

'Oh.' Ash looked immediately guilty. 'Well, then— I am glad he found you. Although I have been going mad looking for you both.'

'What did your friend need from you?' Olly asked.

Ash's expression fell. 'He wishes to discuss *business*. Land, trade, vassals, tenancies . . . He's very keen to tell me some traders he has met from the east.'

'He wanted to discuss all of that at your *wedding*?' Agnes asked, mouth agape.

'Thank God, no,' Ash said. 'But he has asked me to join him

tomorrow to go over it all. I suppose you will have to find some way to amuse yourselves without me.'

'I am sure we can cope,' Olly said, leaning on him. 'I would far rather be in the castle than forced to discuss tenancies.'

'As would I.' Ash sighed. 'People *are* asking after you, you know,' he said, looking towards Agnes.

Agnes cursed. 'Then we ought to return to the hall.' She stood, smoothing out her skirts. 'Come, before I lose my nerve once more.'

Chapter 21

Ash

Upon their return to the hall, Agnes was immediately met by Sara, who looked deeply concerned. After reassuring Ash and Olly that she would be fine, Agnes let Sara drag her away to the corner of the hall, where they appeared to be deep in conversation.

'I think I worried Agnes's friend,' Olly said, pulling Ash to sit at a low bench and handing him a cup of wine. 'I hope Agnes will be all right.'

'As do I.' Ash sighed. 'Thank you for looking after her. I should have been there.'

Olly gripped his arm. 'You were busy. She does not blame your absence.'

'What was wrong?'

Olly took a while to reply. 'I think it was the same affliction that troubled her yesterday.'

Ash opened his mouth. Shut it again. He was surprised Agnes had told Olly so much. It was *her* secret to share, of course, but before it had been something shared between just them. He didn't know what to make of it.

'Oh,' he said. And then, truthfully: 'I *am* glad you were with her. I worry about her— her affliction.'

Ash tried to put it out of his mind. He swirled his wine,

considering when he was permitted to begin shooing people out of his home. And then the shouting began.

'The bedding!'

Shit. A sense of dread settled low in Ash's stomach. Olly put down his mug, looking amused.

'I had forgotten about this.' He grinned.

Ash shot him an acerbic look but could not launch a retort before he was surrounded by a group of drunk guests, being led by Roland, who appeared to be having a marvellous time. Just behind him Ash noticed Raff, looking hugely embarrassed, and Penn – on the verge of laughter.

'Come on, my boy,' Roland bellowed. 'Time for the best part of the night!'

Ash spotted Agnes across the room, surrounded by women. Sara was at her arm, whispering something to her. She appeared unamused by the whole affair: likely because she had already gone through this rigmarole with her late husband. She saw him watching her from across the hall and gave him an apologetic look.

They were shepherded by their respective groups to the centre of the room. The priest, who had been watching proceedings from afar, joined them. Ash's sense of dread became even heavier.

He glanced at Agnes, who gave him a small, supportive smile. And then someone pushed him from behind, and they were being led up the staircase towards his chambers.

'Sorry about this.' He looked around. Raff had joined him at his side. 'But it *is* tradition.'

'I am not sorry at all.' Penn appeared at his other side. 'This is wonderfully fun. I can only assume you are very glad I never managed to marry your sister now.'

Ash grumbled at him, but before he could launch an insult

back – or push Penn down the stairs – they reached his chamber door and he was shoved inside. They placed him on one side of the bed, Agnes on the other. He looked across at her, attempting to silently convey a barrage of thoughts: *I am sorry. This is ridiculous. You do not have to—*

The priest raised a hand, and the rambunctious crowd at last fell silent. He muttered a prayer in Latin over the bed. Ash shot a look out of the corner of his eye towards Olly, who appeared to be doing his very best not to laugh. Someone passed Ash a goblet of wine, which he took gratefully. It was only when Olly nudged him – and he heard giggling – that he realised he was supposed to pass it across to Agnes to drink from too.

The giggling became laughter, which melded into shouting once again. Ash glanced across at Agnes, who was now looking pink about the ears, as their guests called out words of encouragement and – much to Ash's displeasure – marital hints.

Someone pushed him onto the bed, and then Sara grabbed Agnes's arms, forcing her down beside him. There was a moment of complete confusion, then the hanging curtains around the bed were pulled closed, locking them both in darkness.

'Good luck!'

Ash and Agnes shared a look as Olly's voice rang out amongst the others, and then, at last, the door shut and silence fell.

Ash collapsed backwards onto the bed with a sigh.

'Last time,' Agnes whispered, 'they undressed us. It was *awful*.'

'That sounds dreadful,' Ash said. 'I would be subject to teasing for *months*. Every time I saw Roland he would ask me about my prick.'

Agnes leaned back against the pillows. 'Do you think they are outside the door, listening?' she whispered.

Ash groaned into his hands. 'Oh Lord. Probably. Is that what one does at these things? To ensure consummation?'

'It is not as if they can check if I bleed,' Agnes said. 'Ash . . . ?'

'Yes?'

'Thank you. It has been a good day, even if it is all for show.'

Ash had not been expecting that. 'You are welcome,' he said.

'I know that our arrangement is unusual,' Agnes continued, 'but I cannot think of anyone else who I would prefer to have such an unusual arrangement with. Truly.'

She reached out and took his hand. A frisson of *something* sparked up Ash's spine.

'Nor could I,' he said. 'Given all that has happened . . . I am glad it is you here with me.'

They sat for a while longer, Ash wondering exactly how long it would take to convince the guests and well-wishers that they had done their part, and then there was a knock at the chamber door. They both froze. Ash waited for a suitable amount of time before calling out.

'Yes?'

'It is me!'

He relaxed at once. 'Olly,' he hissed towards Agnes. 'Come in!' he called, pulling the bedcurtains open.

Olly slid in, opening the door just a crack.

'You know,' he said, as he sauntered over. 'There was a little crowd determined to stand outside and listen to you. I saw them off.'

Ash made a disgusted face as Agnes laughed. 'I told you they would. Thank you, Oliver. Are they still out there?'

Olly shook his head, picking up the discarded goblet from beside the bed and helping himself to wine.

'There are a few left in the hall, but now the fun of it is over most have headed home, or bedded down for the night.'

'Marvellous.' Agnes stood up, straightening out her skirts. 'That means I can finally retire and be out of this gown.' She turned back to the bed. 'Again, Ash: thank you. I really am glad to be your wife.'

As she left the room, she walked past Olly. She paused, laying a hand to his arm.

'Remember,' she said, 'it is your lord's wedding night. Do make it a good one.'

Olly looked as stunned as Ash felt as Agnes left the room, shutting the door behind her.

'Well,' he said, making his way over to the bed. 'I suppose she is the mistress of this keep, now.' He settled himself on his knees at Ash's side. 'I ought to do as she commands.'

Ash looked up at him. He could already feel himself twitching into life in his breeches. He swallowed.

'I think you ought.'

Chapter 22

Agnes

Agnes headed to her own, new rooms. She was still getting used to them, most of her things in chests after being moved from the guest chambers to the lady's chambers in the room beside Ash's. Attached was a single-roomed servant's quarter which was, she had been informed, no longer in use.

It had been suggested that she staff the room with a lady's maid, but she hadn't yet seen fit to do so. She *ought* to acquire a lady's maid soon enough – until now, she had only been assisted by Sara – but she was aware how useful such a private room could be. She could use it to store her men's clothes, for one: or as a space to make more.

She stretched out her arms. Her body felt worn and heavy, her limbs settling into an ache, but her mind was still awake. Not wishing to attempt sleep, she grabbed a candle from the fireplace, pushed open the door to the servant's chamber and headed inside.

She peered around, eyes adjusting to the dark as the door shut behind her. She could make out furniture: a chest, a table and stool, a bed pressed against the furthest wall. The room was utterly *filthy*, but usable. She would need to air it out, but it was a good size. Perfect for her needs, in fact.

Happy to have found some way to keep herself occupied, she headed back to her chamber, intending to use one of the chests to prop the door open to begin the long process of removing the years of built-up dust.

Agnes pushed the door. It did not move. She twisted at the iron handle. Still nothing. She cursed under her breath. So many years of disuse had clearly taken their toll. She pushed harder, twisted firmer, but the door remained steadfastly shut.

Her heart was beginning to race. She shut her eyes, willing it to calm, as she took a long, deep breath.

And then: a noise. Footsteps. A man's voice.

Was someone in her room? Surely not: she had locked the door, and no one would dare enter the chambers of the lady of the keep without explicit permission.

But there it was again – a low timbre, the creak of floorboards. She edged away, looking around.

The noise was not coming from her chambers, but the corner of the room. She walked towards the sound, candle raised. Finally her eyes focused, and she realised what she was looking at. Another door, half-hidden behind stacked crates. As she made her way around the boxes, she could see low light spilling from beneath it.

And then she grasped where she was. This room was not *just* to serve the bride's chambers. It joined her chambers to Ash's – a way for servants to tend both lord and lady. That was his chamber, beyond the door – those sounds were him and Oliver.

A way out, at last, and if *this* door too was stuck, she could hammer on it until they noticed her and came to fetch her. They would laugh about it. She could already picture the look on Oliver's face when he realised what she had done.

The door was ancient, the wood swollen and warped with age.

It barely fit in the doorway any longer: it jutted from the stone, as if trying to escape. Even the wood was cracking, knots and holes speckling the surface like tiny stars in the dark. No wonder she could hear their voices so clearly.

She was about to beat her fists against it and call to them, when she heard Ash speak.

'Are you quite done? It's freezing.'

'You should come here, then, if you are so cold.'

Agnes stilled. Her heart thudded a little harder. There was a *tone* to that voice. It was commanding, but playful. It was a voice that dared whoever it was turned on to disobey.

She heard shuffling, footsteps.

'You are quite right . . .' That was Ash. 'It *is* warmer here.'

She should call out. Call out *now,* before this could go any further, or return to the other door and try once more. Hide beneath the covers of the disused bed and plug her ears.

But she did not. She lowered the candle and knelt down until her eye aligned with one of the holes in the ancient wood.

The crackling fire lit the room in glistening golden light. On the fur beside the hearth lay Ash and Oliver. Both were stripped to their braies.

Agnes's mouth went dry, her lips suddenly parched. They were lying together: Oliver leaning back on his elbows, Ash holding himself above him. As she watched, unable to look away, they met in a gentle kiss – one that melded into eager hunger. She remembered asking Oliver to make Ash's wedding night a good one.

He heaved himself up, wrapping his arms around Ash's middle, tugging him closer. Ash let himself be dragged down as Oliver kissed him furiously. As Agnes stared, Oliver broke off, trailing kisses down Ash's scar, across his neck. He traded lips for teeth, sinking them into Ash's flesh. Ash gasped, drowning out the muffled noise that escaped Agnes's own lips.

Their bodies seemed to fit together in a way Agnes had never known possible. They moved as one, as if their bodies had been carved for it, as if God had made them for each other and no one else. When Oliver moved, Ash chased him. When Ash ducked his head to lave his tongue across Oliver's chest, Oliver leaned back to let him, not a word passing between them.

Ash did something to the crook of Oliver's neck – Agnes couldn't tell what – and Oliver arched back, his lips gently parting in a silent escape of breath. He, too, was beautiful. Agnes knew he was *handsome,* knew that his cocky demeanour crossed the fine line between outrageous and attractive, but like *this* he looked like something else entirely. He grinned, the firelight making him glow. He resembled a mischievous spirit, sent to doom them all.

Oliver trailed his hands down Ash's sides to the ties of his braies. Agnes needed to leave – to turn away, to close her damned eyes – but she could not. There was a tight ball of anticipation in her chest, bundling around her heart, spreading downwards. Oliver slipped his fingers beneath the fabric, pulling at it, and the feeling expanded, filling Agnes with heat.

Oliver tore away Ash's braies with a swiftness that betrayed a well-practised hand, leaving Ash entirely bare. Agnes swallowed heavily, gaze trailing down Ash's body before she could stop herself. His cock jutted from the thatch of hair between his legs, and even from such a distance Agnes could see how stiff and eager he was for Oliver's touch. Oliver did not wait to give him what he so clearly desired, wrapping one hand around the back of Ash's head and his other around his prick as he pulled him in for a ferocious kiss. He squeezed, and Ash whimpered.

Agnes pressed her thighs together.

They remained like that for a moment – Oliver kissing the life from Ash's lungs, his hand wrapped tight around him. And then, as if something within him had snapped, Ash pushed Oliver down, and before Agnes had a moment to register what was happening had tugged Oliver's braies off as well, leaving him naked and sprawled on the fur.

'Eager,' Oliver breathed, watching Ash from the flat of his back.

Ash didn't reply, just bent down, licking along Oliver's chest, covering him in toothsome kisses. Agnes watched, the hot tension between her legs near aflame, as Ash moved lower and lower until he reached Oliver's cock. He paused for but a second before taking it into his mouth all at once and with such ease that Agnes knew he had done this a hundred times before.

Oliver leaned back, a sigh escaping his lips. 'Ash—'

Ash pressed one hand down to Oliver's hip. Oliver gasped, bucking upwards, his jaw hanging open, his hands tugging Ash's hair.

'Ash, God, *Ash*—'

Ash released him, his now-shining cock springing free, stiff against Oliver's belly. Ash grinned – his teeth flashed in the dark – before sliding back up Oliver's body and capturing his mouth in a kiss.

Oliver hummed. 'I know what you want.'

Ash made a low, rumbling noise. Agnes swore she could feel it, vibrating along the boards and through the door and up her legs. Oliver pressed a sharp kiss to Ash's lips, then extracted himself and headed towards the bed. Agnes watched, eyes fixed on him, as he grabbed something before swaggering back to the furs and getting to his knees. He was holding a little jar. He tossed the lid aside and scooped out some of the contents, which glistened in the light.

He was staring at Ash with a hungry, smug expression. He reached down, and slowly wrapped his hand around his own cock, slathering it in the slippery stuff. There was a lump in Agnes's throat and a tight pressure in her core, tingling through her legs. She dare not move, dare not disturb the feeling lest it overwhelm her. She squirmed on the spot.

Finally, Oliver spoke, breaking the thick silence. 'Knees.'

Ash did as he asked, getting to all fours. Oliver grinned, sliding a still-slick hand down Ash's back, teasing at the cleft of his arse. Ash let out an impatient-sounding curse. Agnes pressed herself so close to the door that the wood scraped her skin.

She couldn't see all, but she could see enough. Oliver bent low, pressing a kiss to Ash's back, then righted himself and took Ash's hips in a firm grip.

Ash let out a long, low sigh as Oliver pushed inside him. Agnes's legs shook. Her tongue wet her lips. Oliver paused, brushing a hand up and down Ash's back, murmuring something Agnes could not hear. He pulled back, then thrust into Ash with such force that she half-expected them both to topple over. Ash muttered something, low and needy.

That appeared to be all Oliver needed.

He thrust into Ash again and again, speed building. Ash swore into the fur, one hand gripping at the rug and the other reaching underneath himself, taking his cock in hand.

Now was the time to go. Now, while they were both distracted, while they were both panting and gasping and cursing into the air.

Yet it took all her willpower to move, to force her stiff legs to unfold. She spared one last, lingering glance through the crack in the wood then rose unsteadily to her feet, hurrying for the door. It still stuck, but now with adrenaline coursing through her she paused – waited for a moment of noise – and heaved against it.

The door opened at last. Agnes shut it as carefully as she could. She leaned against the wood, heart pounding, thighs slick.

She shouldn't. But the dredges of her self-control were used, now, utterly spent, leaving only a hot and urgent sense of *want.* She made her way to the bed in a haze, sitting on the very edge. She felt every place her clothes touched her body – not in the painful way they did so often, but like being wrapped in a blanket on the hottest summer day.

The dress crumpled to the floor.

Agnes fell backwards in a messy heap onto her bed. The image of Ash and Oliver flooded her mind, the sounds they had made in her ears. She could still see it: Ash greedily taking Oliver's prick in his mouth, the slow and languid way Oliver had coated himself in slick, playing with himself, before making them one.

Her hand moved almost of its own accord, slipping lower, moving through the curls between her legs to the place between them. She was already wet – she had been wet just watching them – but now with the attentions of her hand her body was reacting twice fold. She gasped as her fingers brushed against the sensitive spot below the hooded flesh, a sound that was nearly a name: nearly two names.

What if she had walked in? What if she had *been* there, with them, watching? Placing a hand to burning skin, her lips to slick flesh. She jerked her hips upwards, sliding her fingers lower – one, then another. The images were painted to the insides of her eyes, real enough that she could be back there, watching Oliver fuck her husband with reckless lust.

When she finally broke, a wave like none other washed through her in great, shuddering crests. She lay panting on the coverlet for a long while, not moving, barely breathing, only thinking.

As she gathered herself and tugged the blanket over her body, it began to rain.

Chapter 23

Olly

Olly woke up aching all over – a pleasant feeling, even if it tempted him to drift back to sleep. Morning light flooded the room, dulled only a little by the weather outside. He wanted to remain here forever.

But no matter what he *wanted*, the reality was far crueller. Ash extracted himself with reluctance.

'You *know* I must speak to Roland today,' he said. 'And then I will be yours all night.'

That was a pleasing promise, so Olly allowed Ash to rise from the bed and dress, grumbling all the while.

His departure left Olly and Agnes alone, not that Olly had seen Agnes that morning. It was odd: she appeared to be an early riser, sitting in the hall already by the time Ash and Olly rose with the countenance of one who had been awake for hours.

She was probably still feeling shaken after last night. She had seemed happy enough when he and Ash had retired to bed, but he knew more than anyone that a cheery face could be false.

With little else to do, Olly took himself on another walk of the grounds.

It was never *quiet* in the keep, not with servants and grooms and soldiers always running about. After two full laps, he decided to head to the gardens. As he made his way inside, he realised that he was not alone. Here, at last, was Agnes: head bent, nestled in the furthest corner of the garden.

'Good morning.'

Agnes jumped from her skin. 'Oliver!'

'How do you feel?'

Agnes was not meeting his eye. Her skin seemed blotchy. 'Good.' And then, too late: 'Thank you.'

'I am pleased to hear it,' Olly said.

There was something shuttered about her expression. She was mulling over something. Perhaps she *had* been avoiding him. Perhaps she had decided that she could not bear his presence after all.

Or . . . he looked more closely at her face, at her bagged eyes, her messy hair. Perhaps something was troubling her. Olly's suspicion that Agnes really *did* harbour feelings for Ash could be correct; it would explain her demeanour.

'Well, I ought to . . . that is, I—' Agnes swallowed heavily. She stood. 'I shall see you later, Oliver.'

He was right: she *didn't* seem like herself. He was determined to discover why, especially if it *was* his fault. Besides: he had nothing else to do to pass his time, and once again that nagging thought returned: he *liked* Agnes. He did not want to see her sad.

'Where are you going this morning?'

Her whole body was stiff. 'Just for a walk of the grounds.'

'Lead on, then.'

She hesitated. She did not appear to wish for his company, but neither did she insist he leave her alone.

'Very well.'

She headed away at speed, leaving Olly to chase after her as she moved towards the fields that lay around the keep in a misshapen patchwork. She did not speak, and once again Olly felt a shadow over them, something she was not saying.

'Agnes.'

It took a moment for her to respond. 'Yes?'

'Are you quite all right? You may tell me to go if you do not wish for company.'

Agnes stopped so suddenly that he walked directly into her.

'I have a lot on my mind.'

'Oh . . . ?'

She looked as if she was about to speak – her lips opening, her eyes downcast. And then she righted herself, returning to that stiff-backed posture.

'It's nothing, really.'

Olly decided to ignore the lie. There was no point pressing; she would speak if she was ready, and if she wanted to.

'How about a challenge?'

That seemed to take her by surprise. 'A challenge?'

'Indeed; it can take your mind off whatever is worrying you. And, frankly, I fear I will die from boredom if I do not do *something* with my time.'

'What do you intend to challenge me in, then?'

'I do not care.' Olly shrugged. 'Anything.'

Agnes glanced out towards the fields. 'Archery?'

Olly gasped at her 'Cruel! I had no idea you were such a cheat. My poor, dear Ash, shackled to one so treacherous.'

Agnes ignored the insults. 'How so? Are you so bad with a bow?'

'I am *terribly* bad with a bow,' he scoffed. 'Typically one requires *two* eyes to fire one with any accuracy.'

Agnes peered at him. He could see her own eyes flicking between his, taking him in. Clearly Ash had not told her of the extent of his injuries: she was surprised. But she was assessing him before saying something foolish.

'I was not aware,' she said. 'That is, I cannot tell at all. Which is it?'

He gestured towards his right eye. '*No one* can tell,' he said. 'I am lucky enough, I suppose, that the wound is on the *inside*. My eye was not plucked from my skull. I was struck in the head.'

'My God. And you lost your sight?'

'My hearing too.'

'How?'

Olly thought on it. 'Slowly.'

Agnes nodded. 'Then the bow *is* unfair.' She looked out back at the sky. 'The weather feels as if it is about to turn again regardless.'

'What do you suggest instead?'

She appeared to be thinking. 'How are you at chess?'

'Fairly good.'

'Excellent. I have needed a suitable opponent.'

'So I have heard,' Olly snorted. 'Shall we make a wager?'

They stepped into pace as they headed back towards the keep. Agnes, Olly could not help but notice, placed herself on his good side.

'What would you wager?' she asked. 'Money?'

'What use have I for money? Until Ash finds some role and wage for me, he has promised me any I may need. No, it must be something neither of us can gain by other means.'

'Then what do you suggest?'

Olly didn't even think. He always wagered the same thing.

'A kiss,' he said. 'If I win, you grant me a kiss.'

He was sure that the look of outrage Agnes launched towards him was entirely false.

'Oliver,' she gasped. 'You do understand that I am married to your Lord, yes?'

'And I am bedding him. I fail to see your point. Call it a kiss of peace, if you like.'

Agnes rolled her eyes. 'And what are we declaring peace over?'

'Over Ash, of course.'

'Do you intend to go to war for him? Against *me*?'

'Do *you*?'

It was a joke, yet tension thrummed between them. And then it snapped as Agnes sighed at him.

'I harbour no ill will towards you, Oliver. I really do hope you know that. You are good for Ash. You can see it just to look at him when you enter a room. Ash and I began this arrangement with the understanding that it was practical only. And while I—' Her mouth snapped shut. Olly raised his eyebrows, but it appeared that she had swallowed whatever she had been intending to say. 'I am not going to attempt to send you away, or prevent you being with him. I need you to know that.'

Olly stared at her. Her words were tinged with a sadness she was doing her best to bury.

'I . . . thank you,' he said, unsure what else would suffice. 'Really. I—' This would not do. This was too close to the wound still threatening to reopen in his gut and spill his insides out. 'A kiss of *agreement*, then.'

Agnes laughed through her nose. 'Very well. A kiss. And if *I* win?'

'Then I must give *you* something. You may have a kiss too, if you like.'

Agnes was staring steadfastly ahead. Olly didn't know her well enough yet to tell if her thoughtful silence betrayed her shock, or the fact that she was considering it. Her ears were a little pink.

'If I were to ask for that as a prize,' she said at last, 'then there would be no point at all in the challenge. We may as well forgo the chess and go directly to the kiss.'

'Well, if you insist—'

She raised a hand to silence him, although her expression was amused.

'I am not sure if you have anything that I *want.* You certainly have little enough as it is . . .'

'Come, tell me what I can do for you. Make it a chore, if you wish; have me cleaning out the kennels or restringing your bow.'

Agnes raised her eyebrows. 'You are asking me to trust the one-eyed man to string the instrument that requires two eyes to use properly?'

'You *are* cruel!' Olly gasped again. 'And you very well know, I have *two* eyes. It is simply that one does not work. Think on it while we walk. Besides: I intend to beat you, so you will never have a chance to demand your prize regardless.'

After retreating inside, it did not take long for the weather to turn. Agnes headed into the common room to set up, while Olly went to find something to eat and drink from the kitchens.

When he returned, she was ready and waiting for him, the board set, her expression confident.

'You can take the first move,' she said, as he sat.

Olly was keen to make her regret that.

As they played, it became clear that Agnes's weeks of playing against Ash had cursed her form. She had grown used to his inability to concentrate, making her either let down her guard or simply not put as much thought into the game as she otherwise might have.

There was an opening; clearly, she had not spotted it, or she would have strengthened her defences. Olly maintained his calm expression and made a move towards her king. Still, she did not notice.

He *did* enjoy this dance, even if he usually preferred something livelier. He relished the feeling of knowing something that someone else did not: of tricking someone, of having the upper hand. It was why he had done so well as a thief.

It took only a few more moves before he seized his chance. Agnes moved a bishop, and Olly swooped in, taking her king in a quick, easy win.

'Well done,' she said, looking mildly surprised.

'Are you shocked I bested you?'

She pursed her lips. 'I am, although I am beginning to realise how foolish I was to underestimate you. You are a keen player.'

Olly grinned. 'What high praise.'

'You have not been attempting to play with Ash for the past few weeks. He is *dreadful*. I've missed such a strong opponent.'

Olly laughed. Ash *could* be thoughtful and cautious when he wanted to, but faced with a task he did not enjoy he never had the patience to sit and think. He had been the same as a youth: even simple games of dice would inevitably be lost when Ash became overly bored and under enthusiastic.

'So.' Olly stood, as Agnes began to reset the board. 'I have won.'

'That you have.'

'Which means I am owed a prize.'

Agnes gave him a long, searching look, then rose to stand beside him.

'Very well,' she said. 'Never let it be said that I do not keep my word.'

She gave him a teasing smile. Clearly if he wanted his prize, he was going to have to take it himself.

He took a step closer, wrapped an arm around Agnes's middle and pulled her into a firm yet tight-lipped kiss. Her mouth twitched into a smile against his. He wondered what it would be like to open his mouth a little more, to play, to give her a *real* kiss . . .

But she was Agnes, and Ash's wife, and she was *Agnes.* He stepped back. She looked flushed, but not unhappy.

'Satisfied?' she asked, eyebrows raised.

'Very. Another match?'

She barked out a laugh. 'On the same terms?'

'We can make another wager. Or none at all: now you know I am a true contender, perhaps you will try harder.'

Agnes spluttered at him. 'Oh, is it to be like that? Very well; sit, let me show you a real game.'

As the afternoon drew slowly into evening, the rain beating against the castle walls grew heavier. A rumble in the distance announced the arrival of a storm, and through the slit window Olly watched great bolts from the heavens lighting the clouds above the fields. The storm stalked closer, filling the sky with blackness and fire and thunder. It seemed to approach from all sides: two great clouds colliding over the castle.

Distantly, a church bell began to chime. Oliver shuddered.

'Are you all right?' Agnes said, watching him closely.

Oliver fiddled restlessly with the piece he had been about to move. 'I am—' A resounding clap of thunder silenced him, the noise rumbling over the keep. When the noise abated, he spoke again. 'I cannot say I care for storms.'

He had no desire to admit to the way his heart was thundering in his chest, or the prickling of the hair on the back of his neck. He did not want her to see his true feelings. But, he suspected, she could tell regardless.

'Perhaps it will pass soon,' she said.

He gave her a sardonic look. 'Perhaps.'

The noise of the storm battered at him. Agnes beat him soundly and quickly – a defeat that he should have foreseen and defended against. But she did not gloat with her victory.

'It is late,' Olly said, desperately wishing to be somewhere safe. 'I should . . . I should retire. I feel unusually tired this evening. My apologies.'

A neat line appeared between Agnes's brows. 'There is no need to apologise. Are you—'

He did not give her a chance to finish before he was on his feet and out of the room, the door shutting behind him with all the resounding noise of the thunder above. Even the staircase that led to Ash's chambers seemed to be imbued with it, the steps beneath Olly's feet shaking with every clap.

He prayed it would pass soon.

Ash's bedchamber felt wrong without Ash there. But Olly tried not to think of the aching space where the other half of him should have been as he pulled off his boots and tunic and scrambled beneath the woollen blanket.

Another clap of thunder shook the walls as Olly huddled deeper beneath the covers. He *knew* it would pass, that it was simply a storm, yet still that tight pit of fear nestled low in his gut. He wished Ash would return soon – although the thought of Ash riding home in the dangerous weather made him shake, too.

He had always hated storms, that fear hardened by his time as a prisoner in a ramshackle building as storm-shaken as the castle was this evening. It was the noise. As a boy, the crash of thunder had made him run for cover. As a grown man, it made his head and stomach lurch with the sickening memory of the blow to his temple.

There was a thud from somewhere beyond the room. He wasn't sure if it was his imagination, or if something had been knocked loose from the walls. When he thought of the latter scenario, it made his decision to burrow beneath the covers feel even more sensible. He chose to ignore the noise, whatever it was.

'Hello? Oliver? I knocked, but . . .'

Olly froze. That was Agnes's voice. He emerged slowly to see her approaching him from across the room, a jug and a pair of mugs in her hands. She must have let herself in.

As he emerged, a resonant crack sounded from the heavens and lightning flashed through the shutters of the window across the room. He jumped, clawing the blankets closer.

No. This was stupid. He could already hear his brothers laughing at him, and his father chastising his cowardice. He attempted to sit a little straighter.

'Are you all right?' He addressed Agnes quickly, trying to hide his fear. 'Is everything all right?'

Agnes took the liberty of sitting beside him. 'All is well,' she said, as if his question wasn't absurd from his position hiding in the bed. 'Truly. Aside from the courtyard threatening to flood.' She shot him a smile which he returned, weakly. 'I went to the kennels to check on the dogs, and I thought . . .'

Oliver sat up as she gave a sharp whistle. Qwippe and Litillwitte padded over. Qwippe sat obediently beside the bed, but Litillwitte, as soon as he spotted Oliver in his master's place, leapt up onto the mattress and settled himself down by Oliver's feet.

'Oh.' Oliver stared at Litillwitte then up to her. 'Thank you.'

'Is all well with *you*?' Agnes asked. 'I felt rather guilty leaving you.'

Oliver gave a one-shouldered shrug. 'As well as can be while God Himself is attempting to tear this castle down around my ears.'

Agnes winced as the storm raged. 'Would you care for some company? The more this continues . . . I admit, the less keen I am to lie awake alone listening to it, wondering what it may do. And it is not like I will be *able* to sleep regardless, not with this noise.'

She had come to check on him. Olly doubted that she was anxious *at all* – she certainly did not seem it. Which meant she had sought him out for the simple purpose of soothing his fears. To look after him. Olly wasn't sure what he had done to deserve such treatment.

'I would be happy for you to join me,' he said, sitting up properly and leaning against the wall. 'Here—'

He patted the empty side of the bed beside him. Agnes raised her eyebrows.

'What?' he said. 'Or do you intend to perch there like a nun all night?'

'We could sit by the fire? On chairs?'

Olly pulled the blanket tighter. 'And leave the warmth of this bed? I can see no benefit in that.'

Agnes stared at him, keeping his gaze. He smiled. Agnes heaved a huge sigh, placed the jug beside the bed, tugged off her boots, and slid into the space next to him. Qwippe curled up on the sheepskin beside the bed as Litillwitte lifted his head to regard her.

'Much better.' Olly grinned. 'You sitting there made me feel as if I'm some sort of invalid.'

Agnes shuffled beneath the blankets, keeping a careful distance between them. 'Have you always been afraid of storms?'

'As long as I can remember,' Olly admitted. 'There was a huge one, when I was a boy, and this great bolt struck a building in the village . . . It was awful. My brothers . . .' His smile faltered. 'My brothers used to tease me about it. They used to tell me stories about these monsters in the sky who would come and tear me to pieces. Even after I learned they were lying, the fear stuck.'

'Siblings can be . . . difficult.'

Olly did not meet her gaze. 'That they can be. Ash used to sit up with me or distract me until the storms passed.'

'Then I shall have to see what I can do in his stead. What did he do?'

'He usually just kept me entertained with filthy jokes, or mindless talk about . . . well, about whatever we had been up to that day,' Olly said. 'And when we were older . . .' He looked away, cheeks ruddying. 'Let us just say that I do not believe that *that* is the sort of distraction you had in mind.'

Agnes's eyes flashed. 'You are not about to ask me to kiss you again, are you?' she teased.

'Only if you lose another wager.'

'No more wagers!'

'How *dull*.' Olly pouted at her. 'Pass me a drink. What is it?'

'Wine,' Agnes answered, pouring them both a generous helping. 'I thought it would be best to find whichever was strongest, given the circumstances . . .'

'A wise choice indeed,' Olly said, taking the cup from her. 'I can see why you are such a good prize as a wife.'

She laughed, although she rolled her eyes at him as well. The wine she had found was good, *and* strong; even if it didn't ease the fear still coursing through him, it muffled it. It was good to do something with his hands, and the comforting warmth of a body beside him quietened his anxiety. He realised that he was glad she was there.

It was a moment before Agnes spoke again. 'I really do need to thank you, Oliver.'

'Whatever for?'

'For being so understanding when you found me at the feast. It has not been easy.'

'What *is* easy?' Olly chuckled. 'But you are welcome. I do not like seeing you so distressed.'

'And thank you for that, too. By all rights you should hate me.'

Olly supposed she was right: she *was* married to the man he loved. But the feeling should be mutual, if his estimations of her feelings were correct: *he* was bedding the man *she* loved.

'And *you* should hate *me* for fucking your husband. I enjoy our truce.'

Agnes laughed. 'As do I.'

Olly shuffled a little closer. She did not move away. They were alike, Olly realised; if only in their shared feelings for a man who drove them both into fits of anxiety. He reached over her for the jug of wine. As he did, the knot of scars in his arm twinged, the stiffness exacerbated by the storm raging above. He flexed it out with a wince after refilling his mug.

'Another war wound?' Agnes asked.

Olly gave her a half-smile. 'Nothing so bold,' he said. '*This* was given to me on the road. We targeted a town whilst we were posing as minstrels. I decided the brewery would be an easy goal.' He pressed his fingers to the old wound. 'I was stopped. This terrifying woman came out of the shadows with a sword and caught me on the arm.'

Agnes winced. 'Is that the one that turned?'

'The very same.'

'But you survived. And kept the arm.'

'I did, but it was luck more than anything else that saved me. And Pepper.'

Agnes mulled it over. 'It sounds awful. You *were* lucky, extremely so.'

'It was my own damn fault. I earned this wound through my sins. Had I not been trying to rob that family I would have been unharmed.'

'Or you would have been harmed by some other misfortune,' Agnes countered. 'How long were you living like that?'

'Like a thief? I cannot say. From the moment I set foot on English soil I became an outlaw. It was the only way I could survive.'

For a moment, it all passed again: the journey, the hopelessness, the loss. Those endless, grey days after the injury in that god-cursed brewery where he lay, unsure if he hoped to recover or simply pass in peace. He tried to force it away. He was safe, now. He had to believe that.

'It is done, now. All of it, if Ash really does intend to keep me here. Although I have no notion what he intends to do with me.'

'You could be a minstrel,' Agnes said, eyebrows raised. 'Or a fool. A resident jester: I am sure we can find you a cap.'

'Only if you promise to fit it with bells,' Olly said. 'Although you have not heard me play; I may be dreadful.'

'Even better,' Agnes said, swirling her wine. 'A good singer is only good for singing. A *bad* singer is good for entertainment.'

Olly laughed. 'Very well. Pass me that—'

Olly gestured to his lute. Agnes did as he asked – with a little grumbling, as she slipped from the warmth of the bed – and handed the instrument over. It was a fine thing: not as well made as some he had seen – as some he had *stolen* – but sturdy, and it produced a pretty, mellow sound.

He ran his hand down the neck, feeling out the strings, the vibration within them, and the music within those vibrations. He shut his eyes, enjoying the feeling. He had always loved this: no matter the instrument, if he had been able to get his hands upon it he would pick it up and play it. His father had always been disinterested in his musical talents, preferring instead to dote on his brothers' more military prowess, but his mother had encouraged him from the time he was old enough to pluck a string.

His first impulse was to play something slow and melodic, something beautiful yet sad. But he was done with sadness. He was done with death and living in fear.

He fiddled with the strings, then launched into the bawdiest song he knew. It was a simple tune detailing the adventures of a nun upon freedom from her convent, and the various men she had those adventures with. Agnes burst into laughter as soon as she realised what he was playing, the dogs looking up in startled confusion.

It was a merry tune, with a chorus written to be easy enough for a crowd of drunkards to repeat, and it only took a little cajoling to convince Agnes to join in, faltering over the words she was unfamiliar with.

When he was done, finishing with a passionate if less-than-artful flourish on the strings, there were tears shining in Agnes's eyes as she struggled to regain her breath from laughter.

Buoyed by her joy, and flushed from the wine, Olly felt the familiar urge in his chest to *impress*. To show her his real talents – not just his ability to keep a note and remember the obscene lyrics to a song about a nun fucking her way across Normandy. He tried to think of the best songs, the ones that Agnes would most favour. The answer came quickly. The song he had written for Pepper about the exploits of Yde: the woman who became a man.

He strummed the first few chords, trying to remember them. Songs, he found, were harder to lose: names and dates and those little maps that everyone else seemed to carry about in their heads were as ephemeral as smoke, but *songs* tended to stick.

'Many men have proved themselves
With deeds which made them whole,
But I bring you the noble knight,
Whose body changed to match his soul . . .'

It was an odd song, somewhere between bawdy and ballad. It delighted in Yde's exploits as a knight and the beauty of Yde's wife, while taking great pains to describe the disconnect of his body. It touched on the glory of the transformation in words Olly had carefully chosen to feel right and holy and *good* . . . but he had also allowed himself several stanzas to describe Yde's new body as a man, with *great* detail on the size of his cock.

When he was done, ending on the birth of Yde's son, he finally looked at Agnes. She was watching him with awe, her eyes red. He wondered if she had rubbed tears away when he had not been looking.

'That was . . . that was lovely, Oliver.'

Olly lowered the lute to his lap. His cheeks were hot. 'Thank you.'

He'd often been complimented on his music: it was how he'd made them profitable as a travelling minstrel group. But something about Agnes's words felt different. Here they were, together, in the bed of the man they shared, hiding from the storm.

It felt dangerous, somehow. A sliver of Olly's heart was

clamouring at him, and he couldn't understand it. He didn't want to listen to it, either, lest it prove something he didn't want to know.

Agnes seemed to sense his hesitance. She pulled her legs up beneath the covers, knocking their shoulders together.

'Has Ash told you of how he and I met?'

Olly grabbed at the lifeline. 'He has not.'

Agnes's eyes lit up. 'Then *I* must. Perhaps you can put it in a song.'

Chapter 24

Ash

Ash dragged his leaden legs up the wide staircase to his chambers, head ringing. Roland was a good man, but God above, he could talk.

And drink too, Ash thought ruefully as he reached the top of the stairs. Matching the speed with which Roland imbued wine may have been a mistake.

The storm had done little to ease either the swirl of alcohol in his gut or his feeling of bone-deep exhaustion. Roland had offered him a room for the night, but Ash had refused. He wanted to be *home*.

There was a slice of yellow light beneath the door to his chamber. Olly must have kept the fire burning for him. That thought buoyed him, at least. Olly's closeness was a constant reassurance, one that he'd gone without for far too long.

He heaved the door open, expecting to be met by warmth and the soft sound of Olly sleeping, but instead was hit with the sound of . . . of *laughing*.

In front of him, buried beneath his covers with faces red from laughter, were Olly and Agnes. A dark little thought somewhere in the back of his head stirred. Blinked. And then – dissipated.

I should be jealous, he thought blandly. *But . . . but I am not.*

Olly noticed him first, his expression lighting up even more when he spotted him standing there, mouth open.

'Ash!' He spoke too loud, bursting into further peals of laughter. 'You look as if you have been drowned. Agnes has been telling me about how you met.'

Ash could only blink. Beside Olly, with a mug in her hands, Agnes's laughter had died away. Unlike Olly, she looked up at Ash with wide eyes and a worried expression – as if, he realised, she was waiting for him to start shouting at them.

Olly's new lute rested across his lap. He quickly lowered it to the floor, then patted the space in between him and Agnes.

'Come,' he said. 'There's room for another.'

Ash was so tired. And his head was reeling – although now he could not tell if that was because of the wine or because he had found his wife and his lover in the same bed.

Exhaustion won out. He kicked off his boots, tugged off his damp tunic, clambered over Olly – who made absolutely no attempts to move for him – and slid into the empty space between them.

Despite his soaking hair and the chill still permeating his skin, he was red-hot, as if his face were aflame.

'So . . .' he said, trying to make sense of it all. 'What—'

'We are waiting out the storm,' Agnes said.

'And waiting for you,' Olly added, on his other side.

Ash remembered Olly's fear of storms. It had plagued him even when they were young – cowering beneath the covers of his bed, gripping Ash tight enough to bruise, waiting for it to pass. He was glad that Agnes had been there in his stead.

'Oh . . .' Ash wasn't sure what else there was to say. 'I take it you found a way to distract yourselves in my absence?'

'We took a walk of the grounds before the storm began,' said Agnes. 'I had intended to hunt, but the weather won out, so we played chess.'

'And we kissed.'

Ash twisted around beneath the covers. Olly watched him with a glint in his eye.

'Oliver!' Agnes snapped, hauling herself up to look at him.

'What?' Olly asked innocently. 'Surely you did not intend to keep it from him?'

'Of course not,' Agnes shot back. 'But I had planned to tell him at a more appropriate time!'

'Such as?'

'Such as when he is *not drunk!*'

'Now may be the best time, if he is drunk.'

'Oliver—'

'Please, call me Olly.'

'You—'

'Enough!' Ash shouted over them. They both fell quiet. 'You kissed?'

There was that odd prickle in the back of his head again. He should have felt jealous. Perhaps he *did*, although not in the way he expected.

His mind conjured an image, bright and vibrant across the back of his already furred skull: Olly and Agnes, tangled beneath the furs of the bed, their lips locked, the air around them full of heat and sighs.

He blinked it away. Olly was watching him closely.

'We did.' Agnes sighed. 'Truly, Ash, I *was* going to tell you.'

'. . . Why?'

It seemed, as soon as it had passed his lips, a truly stupid question. It was easy enough to guess at *why*. They were alone, and bored, and Olly was the singularly most handsome man Ash had ever seen, and Agnes—

He had been trying not to think on it too hard, but Agnes was especially striking, with sharp, pleasing features. Ash could see why Olly would find her a suitable partner for kissing – amongst the other things trying to force themselves into his head.

'It was a wager,' Agnes said, slumping back against the pillows.

That had *not* been what Ash was expecting. 'A wager?'

'I challenged him to chess,' Agnes explained, 'and *he* decided it would be more interesting if we included a wager.'

That certainly sounded very much like Olly. As a youth, he had enjoyed making preposterous bets – coin and services from his friends and family, kisses and favours from Ash.

'If I won, she was to give me a kiss,' Olly said smugly.

'I may have been overconfident,' Agnes conceded. 'After all, I have grown used to a less experienced partner. I had assumed that he would be equally poor at the game. I realised my mistake as soon as he had made his second move. Although it was not an *easy* win for him.'

'It *was* a win, though.'

'It was. And so, I had to maintain my end of the bargain. A kiss for a fair win.'

'I suppose that is only right,' Ash managed. 'It sounds as if you have had an . . . interesting day.'

'Very interesting!' Olly agreed, with a sharp laugh. 'I found Agnes hiding in the gardens this morning, and I knew it would not do.'

Agnes's laughing expression faded. 'I was not hiding. I was simply spending some time alone.'

'You certainly seemed bothered by something,' Olly pressed. 'I am glad I could bring some levity to your day, that is all.'

Agnes looked sombre.

'Agnes?' Ash said, growing concerned. Finally, Olly noticed too.

'I apologise,' he stuttered. 'I did not mean to offend you.'

'It is nothing,' Agnes said quickly. She was gripping the blanket in her hands.

Ash turned back to her. Her knuckles were turning pale. Ash placed his hand atop hers. She snatched it away.

'I . . . I must confess something,' Agnes said at last. 'To *both* of you.'

'Whatever is it?'

Agnes looked distraught. 'Do not hate me. You *will* hate me. God's teeth, I did not mean to—'

'To *what*?'

Olly sat up too, staring at her across Ash. Her eyes darted between them like a frightened animal, her face bright red.

'I saw you,' she whispered at last.

Ash was baffled. 'What?'

'I *saw you*,' Agnes spoke louder, now. More desperately. 'Together. After the wedding.'

There was a leaden feeling in Ash's stomach. Agnes gestured towards the door of the servant's quarters.

'I was wondering what use I could put the servant's room to, but the door caught behind me and I could not open it. I did not even realise what was happening until it was too late. And then—' Her voice croaked into silence.

'And then?' Olly pressed closer to Ash's side.

'And then I heard a noise. I realised it was you both, and thought perhaps you would be able to help me open the door, so I . . .'

Ash realised what she had done. 'So you looked.'

Her hands went still. 'So I looked.'

There was a dull ringing in Ash's head. Agnes had seen them, seen them *together,* seen him at his most vulnerable. She had seen Olly take him apart.

The first thought: horror. The horror of a lifetime hiding himself, decades of caution, even when he and Olly were at the height of their relationship. The horror of their cove of safety, carefully carved and kept, being broken into, being discovered, being *invaded*.

But this was *Agnes*. Agnes who had asked if he and Olly were lovers. Agnes who had not cared when he answered with the affirmative: who had encouraged him.

He had nothing to fear from a secret already spilled.

And something else, something beneath it. Wanting to know more. Wanting to know *what* she had seen, and how much: if it really had been the whole sordid, sweaty affair. If she had watched Olly prepare him and take him, if she had seen him on his knees.

He couldn't form the words, couldn't find a way through the tangle of emotions.

But Olly could. 'What did you see?'

Ash tried to stop him. 'Olly—'

'I am curious! You cannot chastise me for curiosity.'

'You should be *furious*,' Agnes cried. 'You should throw me from the keep or refuse to ever speak to me again.'

Ash swallowed. 'I will not do either of those things.'

Agnes's wobbly smile was telling; she did not believe him.

'If you will not allow me to ask what you saw,' Olly said, his tone growing keener in a way that Ash had learned not to trust, 'then may I ask you something else?'

'I am in no position to refuse *anything* you ask of me.'

'You will regret saying that,' Ash muttered. Olly ignored him, speaking quickly.

'*Why* did you look?'

Agnes frowned. 'I heard a noise—'

'And went to see what it was, yes. But clearly you took more than a glance. I would be willing to bet that you saw . . . something. Everything, perhaps. Would I be correct?'

Agnes was chewing on her lip. Her cheeks flushed. 'I . . . Yes.'

'Well!' Olly sat back, triumphant. 'My question stands! Why did you look for long enough to see such things? Why not run as soon as you realised what you had stumbled into? Why not entreat us for help, as you had intended to do?'

Agnes's mouth opened and shut wordlessly. Olly watched her with an intent expression, leaning against Ash's arm. Ash would be lying if he denied that he, too, wanted to know what had caused Agnes to linger so long.

He thought of it again: of her watching them, of her knees to the floor and her face pressed to the ancient door. Something stirred within him: the same beast that had stirred when he considered her and Olly in his bed, the things they could have been doing in his absence.

'I do not know,' she said quietly.

Had she stayed there for long? Had she watched, intent? Perhaps it had been shock and revulsion freezing her to the spot, forcing her to watch.

Perhaps it had not.

Silence fell. Ash didn't know what to say – didn't know what to *think*. Olly took over once more.

'Agnes—' They both turned to look at him. Ash couldn't tell what he had planned, nor read his expression. 'Why don't you take that' – he nodded at the empty jug – 'and fetch us more wine?'

'What?' Agnes said, looking dumbstruck.

'When you return, we can talk about all this. It is pointless to pretend it did not happen.'

Ash sniffed. That had rather been what he *did* intend to do – certainly the way to move forward with fewest complications. Yet Olly clearly had other ideas, and Ash supposed that he was right. Agnes swallowed, giving Olly a look of outright suspicion.

'All right,' she said. 'Give me . . . just a moment.'

'Oh, and one more thing . . .'

'Yes?'

'Could you return the dogs to the kennels? There's barely enough room in here as it is.'

Agnes gave him an odd look but did as he asked. She grabbed the jug, summoned the dogs, then with a final look towards them left the room, closing the door behind her. Ash stared at the wood.

'I cannot believe she saw us,' he said at last.

Olly pressed closer. 'Are you angry with her?'

'I was. But . . . but briefly. It is not as if she did not already know that we are lovers. My first instinct . . . it was like we had been *invaded*. As if she had taken something I had not given her. But . . .'

Olly nodded. '*But*. A powerful word.'

'I—' He glanced at Olly, feeling his skin flush. Of all people, *Olly* he could trust with this. 'I keep thinking about it. About *her*. About her watching us. Why would she do that? Why did she not *leave*?'

'I can see no other reason for her to have watched than because she *enjoyed* watching,' Olly said.

The heat in Ash's chest built. 'Surely not.'

'There is nothing so unusual in it. I have seen it myself.'

'You have?'

'You forget how long I have been living on the edge of the law, Ash. You would shudder to think how many brothels I have worked and lived in. There is *always* someone who simply wishes to . . . watch. And . . .' he gave a long, languid smile '. . . there are others who enjoy being watched.'

Ash swallowed. His body was alight. 'Do . . . do you mean *yourself*?' he managed.

Olly gave a half-shrug. 'I had never really considered it. Not until now.'

'And now?'

'I cannot say I dislike the idea. At first I was shocked. I felt invaded, as you said. But after thinking on it . . .'

Ash swallowed heavily. 'It feels different.'

Olly looked at him through his lashes. 'It does.' He ran a gentle hand across the blankets. 'I think of it like this: you and Agnes are wed, yes?'

'Yes.'

'And what of me?'

'You will be here. With me. Always.'

'Exactly. No matter what happens . . . we are tied together. All of us. Even more so once we begin to navigate, well—' He ducked his head, muffling a laugh.

'Navigate what? Navigate *what,* Olly?'

'The thing that married folk *do.*' Olly laughed, breath tickling Ash's neck. 'I do not think you'll have much luck in the realm of heirs if the only one you are bedding is *me*.'

Ash swallowed. He kept the truth of it to himself; the way he had planned for any heirs to never truly be of his blood. Olly would not understand, and besides, it was too painful a thought to ruin this moment with.

Olly noticed his hesitance, clearly assuming it was fear of a different kind.

'It is something we need to traverse *together.*' He held Ash's gaze. '*All* of us.'

'Are you suggesting we invite her into our bed?' Ash said, aghast.

'I am suggesting we propose she . . . watches. And if she dislikes it, or if *we* dislike it, or if it is a horrible farce, then we never do it again and we blame the wine.'

Ash wasn't sure what to say. 'Oh.'

'And if it *does* go well . . . then we stand a little stronger. Arrangements like ours are more solid when everyone is happy. Perhaps *I* can watch *you* when you go about the terribly important business of filling this castle with children.'

Ash laughed. 'Does that mean you are proposing that *I* watch you and—' He found his lips halting. He thought again of finding Agnes and Olly in his bed.

Olly noticed immediately, pressing closer with a sly smirk.

'You were thinking about it, were you not? When you heard we had kissed. I saw your expression. Agnes does not know you as I do, so she could not tell. But *I* could.'

Ash's face heated. Had it been so obvious? It must have been to Olly, who always seemed to know what Ash was thinking – certainly, at least, pertaining to matters of the prick.

'I was not—'

The image assailed him again. Them, in *his* bed, under *his* sheets. The jealousy was nowhere to be found, the blood that should have rushed to his muscles to ready him for a fight rushing elsewhere, instead.

Olly rolled closer, sliding a hand over Ash's chest with a low laugh.

'Weren't you?'

His hand snuck lower, trailing down Ash's stomach, below his navel, his fingers teasing and twitching and *searching* until—

Ash hadn't realised how hard he was until Olly wrapped his fingers around his cock. Ash let out a sharp curse. '*Olly*—'

'So you *were* thinking about it,' he said. 'Interesting.'

Ash's eyes fluttered shut, his skin tingling, now unable to think of much else apart from Olly's hand. 'Olly . . .'

'Hmm?'

'We should not— Agnes—'

'Perhaps we *should*, given all we have found out.'

'Olly—' Ash gasped against his lips. 'No, we must . . .'

'Spell it out?' Olly kissed him again. 'Sit down, sign a contract, make a binding pact of what we are about to do?'

Ash had not been about to propose anything so formal – but his arguments died in his throat with every kiss Olly placed upon his lips.

'I thought not,' Olly said. 'Let me . . .'

He slid a hand under Ash's undershirt, tracing his fingers across the band of his breeches. Ash let out a soft gasp as Olly stroked his skin, a gentle touch – no firmer than a breath – with the promise of more.

Ash wasn't sure how Olly had done it; one moment they were side by side, then he was on his back at the foot of the bed, Olly above him, pressing his hands down above his head and staring at him with an eager, hungry gaze.

He was caught, willingly. Olly squeezed his wrists, a sure message: *I have you. You are trapped*. Ash let out a low, shaky breath as Olly grinned down at him, pinning him in place. He loved this feeling: he beneath, unguarded and eager. It had been like this for as long as he could remember, and he had not realised how much he had craved it – how much he had *missed* it – until Olly had returned.

He gave a cursory wriggle – a test of unflexed strength. Olly pressed harder, gripped tighter. Ash let out a low, hungry noise that rumbled right from his core and out of his mouth.

He was about to speak – to beg for more – when the air in the room changed. He sensed the door opening more than heard it. There was a noise. An intake of breath.

This had been a terrible idea. This had been too much, too soon. Agnes would be horrified. He needed to push Olly off him and apologise and scrub them all clean of this—

'My Lady,' Olly drawled, still pinning Ash beneath him. 'How kind of you to join us.'

Ash could not see Agnes's face. Was she shocked? Disgusted?

Or had she stumbled into something akin to a dream? Did she feel the same sudden stuttering in her chest that Ash did, that same building feeling in his heart, that same tightness creeping hotter and lower and swirling in his gut?

He wanted to speak, but his lips were dry, his tongue as trapped as the rest of him. Olly glanced down at him, and then away – back towards Agnes, Ash assumed.

'Do you wish to stay?'

From across the room, Agnes made a soft noise. It was as if that single sound filled the chamber. It struck Ash's body like the lightning outside, going straight to his prick.

The door shut. Above him, Olly relaxed. Ash had not even realised that Olly was nervous about this, too.

Footsteps. The soft sound of fabric.

'Please.' Ash could not quite place where her voice was coming from; but it was enough to know she was there. 'Continue.'

Olly didn't need telling twice. He lowered himself down, catching Ash's mouth in a kiss. He dragged it out, sucking at Ash's bottom lip, biting it between his teeth. Ash arched against him, the little sting of pain enough to bruise but not break, enough to thrill but not harm. Enough to leave him wanting more.

Olly dragged his hands away from Ash's wrists. He grabbed the hem of his undershirt and pulled it off, peppering Ash's lips and cheek and the twisting scar with a hundred tiny kisses. He tugged his own undershirt away too, and the feeling of Olly's hot skin against Ash's was nearly too much. Ash grabbed at him, wrapping his arms around him, forcing him closer as if heat and sweat could meld them together.

Olly hummed, then shifted his attention. He sucked Ash's earlobe into his mouth, tugging at it with his teeth, sending a frisson of pain directly down Ash's spine. Ash let out a low moan, and – there, on the edge of hearing – he heard Agnes softly gasp as well. The sound inflamed him further.

Olly, too, seemed encouraged. He smiled against Ash's skin as he nuzzled his face into the crook of his neck. He opened his mouth, the sudden heat making Ash's prick twitch, then pressed his tongue against Ash's skin. Ash hissed, arching against him, pressing his aching cock against Olly's crotch, desperate for touch. Olly laughed low and warm, then pressed a final, fluttering kiss to the spot before sinking in his teeth.

The rumbling noise that erupted from Ash was entirely unbidden. Agnes made another noise, but so detached was he from everything but the pleasure and the pain and the heaviness of Olly on him that he couldn't tell where she even stood.

Ash shut his eyes tight as Olly deftly undid the ties of his breeches and slid his hand fully inside. Ash jerked into his grip and, emboldened, Olly shoved the fabric down and let his prick spring free. Ash groaned. From somewhere – from *everywhere* – Agnes gasped.

'Oh.'

Ash felt the weight of Olly above him shift, one hand now playfully trailing up and down the length of Ash's shaft.

'Do you wish to sit?'

He was speaking to Agnes, Ash realised.

'I . . . I cannot decide.'

'What did you do—' Olly said, breath catching. 'Last time?'

Agnes took a moment to respond. 'I watched,' she said. 'I only watched.'

'Nothing else?'

Another long pause. 'Not until after.'

Olly gasped out a laugh then ducked down, running his lips over Ash's thighs. Ash was struck with the image of Agnes locked in her chambers, the door bolted, her skirts discarded. Or Agnes on her back, her lithe archer's hands thrust beneath the fabric of her clothes, seeking, finding, pressing.

'Tell me,' Ash breathed.

It sounded so *needy*. It was too much; too fragile, too embarrassing, words that would damn him come dawn. But all he could think was how much he needed to know, how much he wanted to hear her describe bringing herself to completion.

Olly laughed again. He sucked an open kiss to the sensitive skin of Ash's inner thigh, teeth and tongue, then rose higher to brush his lips against Ash's prick.

'I say we give her something to watch, my Lord,' he teased.

Before Ash could respond, Olly took Ash's cock into his mouth. Ash arched against the bed with a curse as the wet heat enveloped him, the delirious pleasure. Agnes gasped – almost a moan.

Still he could not see her. Even had he opened his eyes, his view would only have been of the canopy above. Part of him was glad for it; if he could see her watching him, he may perish from it, from the realisation of what he was doing. What they were *all* doing, together.

He heard her take a breath. 'I returned to my chambers.'

Agnes's voice was clear but quiet. Olly stilled a little, his movements less fervent than before. But he did not pull away.

'And then I brought myself to release,' she breathed.

Olly released his prick with a soft noise. Ash groaned.

'My, my.' Olly turned his head, peering towards Agnes, Ash assumed. 'What a sinful little sodomite you are.'

'Says the man with my husband's prick in his mouth.'

'It is not *currently* in my mouth.'

'And that is the part you take umbrage with?'

Even hearing them *bicker* was enough to make Ash squirm.

'*Olly*—'

'It appears I am needed,' Olly drawled.

'By all means.'

Without further warning, Olly once again wrapped his lips around Ash's cock. Ash gasped, bucking against him. Olly laid a deft, strong hand on his stomach, forcing him back down onto the mattress, keeping him from moving.

It was so much. It was *too* much, knowing that Agnes was watching, that she was there as Ash fell to pieces. He felt Olly move, the loss of one of his hands – then a groan, a doubled sound, one from Olly's mouth that vibrated down Ash's prick and one from Agnes's, that vibrated into his soul.

Olly had taken himself in hand. Ash felt his arm move against his leg in desperate jerks, and wished he could reach down and see Olly off himself. But he could not; he was too lost as it was, too close, too trapped. He stuttered out a noise into the dark, a curse, a prayer. Olly hummed around his cock. Agnes gasped again. Ash could not see – but he could guess. He could picture it.

His pleasure peaked.

Olly made a low noise as Ash spent into his mouth. But he did not let him go, did not lean away, not until he made a muffled sound that indicated he, too, was close. Olly stiffened, and Ash felt his mouth slacken and his lips part as his spend striped across Ash's thighs.

Finally, Ash opened his eyes. Agnes was right above him, peering down at his supine form, leaning against one of the bedposts with a wide-eyed, exhausted expression. Her hair was wild about her head, her skirts in disarray about her thighs.

'I should go . . .' She started awkwardly towards the door.

'Wait—'

She hesitated. Ash turned to Olly. They shared a brief look – a tilt of the head, a raise of the eyebrows – and Ash knew that Olly approved of what he was about to do.

'You may stay, if you like,' he said. 'Just to sleep,' he added hastily, spotting her expression. 'But if you wished to . . . we would like that.'

She lingered in the doorway. Just as Ash thought she was about to dismiss him, she took a step towards the bed.

'Are you sure?' she asked. 'Both of you?'

'Of course,' Ash said, just as Olly mumbled, 'Get— *bed,*' looping an arm around Ash's middle.

'I will assume that means yes?'

Without waiting for – or needing – a response, she crept back towards them. Ash quickly wiped himself off on a discarded undershirt before getting himself and Olly back beneath the covers, watching her – waiting for her.

After a moment's thought, Agnes removed her kirtle, leaving her standing in just her loose underdress. Ash could see the curve of her breasts, the stiff peaks of her nipples.

Realising he was staring, he forced himself to look away.

She slid into the bed beside him, back into the space she had occupied when Ash first entered the room. Ash relaxed, feeling Olly shuffling closer, pressing his stomach to Ash's back and looping his arm sleepily around his middle. Ash couldn't help but melt into the touch, sliding his fingers between Olly's, keeping him close.

From only a few inches away, Agnes was peering at him. Her eyes darted over Ash's shoulder to Olly, then back to Ash. She was about to say something, when Ash quickly spoke over her. 'Sleep,' he whispered.

She gave him a nervous sort of smile – which he returned – then he tugged the fur tighter over their shoulders and let the reeling in his head overtake him, slipping into darkness.

✡

There was a tight pain, like a sharp rock, lodged behind Ash's eyeball. He groaned, then attempted – and failed – to roll over.

His body was caught in a tangle of limbs.

He opened his eyes properly, the blur around him solidifying, the confusion sloughing away like rainwater.

Agnes to one side, Olly to the other. Olly's arm was caught tight around Ash's middle, Agnes's feet slotted between his own. He shifted, almost unsure of how he had come to be here.

As he stirred, Agnes's feet twitched, moved, and then her eyes too slid open. As he caught her gaze, it came flooding back: a torrent of hot memory and blurred boundaries and sweaty, satiated lust.

'Good morning.'

Both he and Agnes jumped; Olly, clearly, was also awake. He heaved himself over Ash's body with a clammy, clumsy grip.

'Did you sleep well?'

Agnes sniffed at him as Ash rolled over. He had been attempting to shrug Olly off, but succeeded only in lying on his back with Olly now sprawled across his chest.

'Yes,' Agnes said, looking half amused, half lost. 'Quite well. Did you?'

Olly made a self-satisfied humming noise, stretching out across Ash's torso. 'Exceedingly well.'

Agnes appeared unsure. She looked how Ash *felt*: like she did not know how to navigate this new reality.

'I suppose I should return to my chambers.'

Ash found himself wishing she wouldn't leave. He and Olly could lie abed for hours, and he had half-imagined Agnes joining them for a long morning of idle chatter and slow rising. Perhaps she just needed a moment alone, if only to gather her thoughts before they were reintroduced to normal life beyond his chamber door.

She rose, clambering from the bed. She looked tousled in the dim morning light, her hair all at ends and her clothes rumpled.

'I will see you both in the hall?'

'Yes. Yes, of course.'

She gave them a smile and slid from the room through the servant's quarters, gently closing the door behind her.

'That was . . . enlightening,' Olly said.

Ash turned to face him. 'Meaning?'

'Meaning I enjoyed that very much. And I think *you* did too.'

'I did, yes.'

'Enough to do it again?'

Ash barely gave his answer any thought. 'Yes.' And then added quickly: 'If you are keen to, that is. And Agnes, of course.'

'Oh, I think she would be.'

Olly looped his arm around Ash's chest, nestling back down into the position they had slept in.

'Are you going to insist we get up as well?' he asked.

'My head hurts,' Ash replied. 'I intend to sleep until I can think straight.'

'What a wonderful idea.'

✡

When Ash awoke again, the blinding morning light now streaming in through the windows, his head felt a little lighter. He reached out, then remembered that Agnes had already left. There was a space where she should have been.

'Come,' he said, shaking Olly awake. 'It is time to rise.'

He untangled himself from Olly's grip and rose with a stretch, aware that Olly was watching his every movement. As he began to dress, he heard Olly too get out of bed, padding softly around the room.

It had been an interesting night. His head still pounded, but the fog that had settled around him had lifted. He had feared that in the cold light of day he would be gripped with guilt. But there was no guilt, no shame, no regret. Just a tingling sense of fulfilment and an eagerness to not let the feeling fade.

He did not notice that Olly had snuck up on him until he heard his voice over his shoulder.

'I think you have feelings for her.'

Ash froze with the laces of his tunic gripped in his fingers. 'What?'

'You heard me, Ashel.' Olly looped his arms around Ash's waist and rested his chin on Ash's shoulder. As he spoke, he slid a hand beneath the tunic, brushing his fingertips above the waistband of Ash's breeches. 'I think you have feelings for Agnes.'

'Do not be absurd. I love *you*. You know that.'

'That does not mean you cannot wish to bed her, too.'

'Oliver!'

'What? After what we did last night – what we *all* did, I remind you – surely you cannot pretend that you only think of her as a friend? Or as a *sister*?'

'Well, *no*—'

'You are a wonderful man,' Olly said, 'but I fear that matters of the heart lie somewhat out of your reach.'

Ash huffed. 'Does that surprise you?' he said, more bitterly than he had intended. 'I am rather out of practice.'

'But it has been *years*,' Olly said, brow furrowing. 'Surely, in all that time . . . ?'

Ash stilled.

'After France, I couldn't. I couldn't bring myself to get close to anyone. I did not *want* to get close to anyone. It was—' He shut his eyes, a useless dam against the sudden river of feeling. 'It was *you*,' he said. 'It has always been you. It *would* always be you, forever.'

Olly frowned. 'There was no one else? After?'

Ash shook his head. His lip shook. 'No. I . . . I tried, I paid for it, but—'

'But?'

'But they weren't you.' His chest was torn open, exposed, ready to be prodded at. 'It was not the same. It was *never* the same. I spent, and then after, it was like . . . it was like *nothing*. I hated it.'

'Ash . . .'

'I knew there would never be anyone else. And I did not *want* there to be anyone else. Ever. And yet now you are returned to me, and Agnes is . . . I do not know *what* she is, it's like something new has woken within me and I—'

'And you're scared?'

Ash's eyes burned. The weight of it all crashed upon him: the loss of Olly's death, the release – in more ways than one – of his return, the sudden thing that had begun to blossom with Agnes. Something Ash had never found before, apart from with Olly. He crushed his face into Olly's shoulder, hiding the tears. Olly gently moved his hand up and down Ash's back.

'It is all right,' he said soothingly. 'If it is too much, we never have to do it again.'

'I did not say that,' Ash muttered. He leaned back so he could see Olly's face and read the truth there – or a lie. 'Olly. Are you happy with this? Are you happy with having Agnes join us? Are you happy with this arrangement? Because if you are not—'

'Ash!' Olly spoke sternly. 'Ashel, my love. It was my idea to have her join us. And I may have been a thief and a peasant since returning from France, but before *that* I was a lord's son. I understand how these things are. We always knew that one day you may need to wed. And as I said, now you *are*, you *will* have to produce heirs.'

Ash hesitated. His chest hurt.

'Please tell me you had considered it, Ashel?' Olly said, exasperated.

'I did!' Ash insisted. 'But . . . not of late. And in truth . . .'

'Yes?'

'Before all of *this*, I had rather expected that whichever woman I married would find . . . someone else. My contribution would not be required.'

'*Someone else?*' Olly was aghast. 'You are telling me you would name some other man's bastard as your heir?'

'It seemed better for everyone,' Ash said, weakly. 'And . . .' he glanced at Olly, shame bubbling in his chest '. . . I did not intend to burden them with my presence for very long.'

It was a confession couched in allusion. Yet still Olly knew what he meant, his eyes going wide, his hand nervously stuttering over Ash's arm. 'Ash . . .'

'I apologise,' Ash said quickly, the shame spilling over. 'I should not have . . . I was not—'

But he *was*. He could not force the denial from his lips. Olly opened and shut his mouth a few times, eyes shining, then wrapped his arms around Ash with renewed vigour.

'My Ashel . . .' he muttered against him, not letting go. 'My love.'

There was nothing else he could say. Ash let Olly hold him, sinking into the warmth of his embrace, trying to push those thoughts back into the dark of his mind where they belonged.

'We do not have to talk of heirs. Not right now.'

Ash nodded, eyes tight shut. He felt Olly kiss his head, his cheek, the scar.

'I wish it was easy as it once was,' Ash said. 'Now . . . now it is all a tangle.'

Olly held him tighter. 'There is no one better to be tangled with.'

Chapter 25

Olly

It was the day of Lord Justin's much-anticipated hunting party. Olly and the others would be spending the day in the fields – dawn till dusk, the world their own. Agnes had appeared in her men's clothes, with her breasts flattened, in Ash's chambers just after sunrise, eager to set off. Since their tryst – if one could call it that – a week or so ago, the door to the servant's quarters connecting their rooms had found itself in quite regular use.

They had been joined by Raff and Penn today, much to Raff's delight. Raff was, Olly was learning, a skilled hunter – even if he was now hampered by his wound. Penn, with Iseult on his arm, was a force of nature amongst the little scrabbling animals of the gorse. Several times Olly watched as Iseult swung from the sky like a bolt of lightning, catching whatever unfortunate thing Penn had spotted so quickly that in a single blink the creature was dead and twitching against the grass.

With his poor eye, Olly had been relegated to Agnes's page. He was peering through the brambles, keeping watch.

There was a sound – a twig snapping. And then another blur, the flap of wings.

Agnes threw herself between two gorse bushes. Behind her, Olly crashed through the undergrowth with far less grace. There was a distant bark, and a pheasant burst from the field just ahead of them, scattering twigs and leaves as it took off into the sky.

Agnes lifted her bow, already notched, and fired off a single, clean shot.

The bird tumbled from the sky like a stone.

Olly watched on in awe. He had never seen anything like it.

'Come!' she called to Olly over her shoulder as she darted forwards to find her kill.

'I cannot believe I have been relegated to fetching and carrying,' Olly huffed, jogging to keep up.

'Would you prefer a bow?' Agnes raised her eyebrow as she examined the kill before throwing it into the basket slung over Olly's shoulder.

Olly exhaled sharply through his nose. 'Cruel.'

'You may assist Ash, if you are so bored with me.'

Agnes notched another arrow, heading back towards the gorse.

'Ash and Justin are talking about *crop yields,*' Olly said. 'If I wished to be bored to tears, I would let Raff talk me through his garden.'

Agnes grinned. 'Then cease complaining.'

As they picked their way through the patches of gorse and tall, imposing brambles they ran into another handful of hunters, men from Lord Justin's party. One of the younger men examined the basket on Olly's back, making an appreciative sound.

'Impressive,' he said, raising an eyebrow. 'And you got all of these yourself, Angus?'

'I did,' Agnes said, a little smugly.

'Remarkably clean shots,' the man said. 'Very good job.'

'He's the best bowman *I've* ever seen, certainly,' Olly said. 'Those poor creatures . . . one would almost feel sorry for them, were it not for the wonderful things Lord Barden's cook can do to a bird.'

'Do you not hunt?' someone asked.

Olly shook his head. 'I am burdened with an old wound,' he said. 'But I am more than happy to keep up with my talented friend here and collect his kills. Maybe even pass a few off as my own, if I find the chance.'

Agnes gave him a playful shove as the men around them laughed. They said their goodbyes, intending to seek out Ash to see if he'd had any luck in his own hunt, heading back towards the road where they had left him and Lord Justin. But as they approached they realised that the rest of the hunting party was no longer alone; they had been met on the road by several horses and carts.

Agnes froze, then grabbed Olly around the arm and tugged him back beneath the trees.

'What in *God's*—'

'That is my *family*,' Agnes hissed.

Olly frowned, then looked down at her. She was on the verge of outright panic. And, he realised, wearing men's clothes.

'I presume they are expecting Agnes, not Angus?'

'Quite.' Agnes gave a mirthless chuckle.

'Will they recognise you? Like this?'

Agnes hesitated. 'I do not know,' she said.

'Then best to assume they will,' Olly said, thinking fast. 'If we head the way we came we should be able to get back to the castle without them seeing us. We can keep to the trees, but we will have to make a dash across the final field— Why are you giving me that look?'

'Sometimes I forget that you spent so long evading the law,' Agnes said. 'And then you say things like *that*.'

Olly grinned, feeling proud. 'It taught me *some* useful things, at least.'

'Such as how to avoid one's family members?'

'Exactly. Although I had been doing that since I was a lad.'

Together they crept back into the woods. It was a longer route, but with luck it would avoid the main road; and besides, Agnes's family appeared to have been locked in deep conversation with Ash and Justin. Perhaps they would be waylaid.

'I hope Ash is all right,' Agnes said, breaking the silence. 'He has met Muriel – my sister – once before. It did not go well. I should have been there to ease the way the first time he met my parents.'

Olly hesitated. 'It cannot be helped,' he said. 'Unless . . . we can turn around, if you want. I suppose you must ask yourself which would be worse: them speaking to Ash alone, or them seeing you as Angus.'

Agnes huffed. 'Both are poor choices,' she said. 'We must hurry.'

They made quick time around the edge of the trees. Soon, they stepped back onto the path through the field and up towards the outer wall of the castle. With luck, Agnes would be able to hurry inside, change, and be back to greet her parents before anyone said something that they would come to regret.

'This is absurd,' Agnes muttered, as Olly hurried her along the path. 'But I do not know what else I can do. My family can be difficult. I feel awful leaving Ash to deal with them alone.'

'He will be fine. He is an earl, after all. He needs them to approve of him just as much as you do.'

Agnes sighed. 'That much is true.'

'It is not as if they can attempt to kill him on the road, after all.'

'Olly!'

They made their way down a path that wove through a thicket of unripe brambles, Olly leading the way.

'You can head in through the garden,' he said, 'and then— Ah.'

There was a man beside a horse blocking the path. He was finely dressed, and did not appear to be a servant. No doubt he was with Agnes's family. But it was too late to turn back: the man turned, spotting them.

Olly would have to hope he was not a relation. Knowing that he could not ignore the man, he instead set his shoulders and stepped out of the shrubs, pulling Agnes with him.

'My Lord!'

The man looked down at him. 'Greetings.'

'Excuse me,' Olly said. 'We were just bringing Lord Barden's catch to the kitchens for the cook to prepare, and if we tarry they will have both our heads. If we could—'

'Agnes?'

Shit.

'I do not know who you are—' Olly began.

'Shut your mouth.' The man's voice was so sharp that Olly complied, despite himself. 'Agnes, good *God,* girl, what are you doing?'

Agnes froze at Olly's side, saying nothing. Olly stepped in front of her, shielding her from his view.

'I am afraid there has been some mistake,' he said. 'I am not sure who you believe you are talking to, my Lord, but this is one of our kitchen boys. Now if you would excuse us—'

He shouldered past the man, taking Agnes by the wrist and dragging her with him. As he forced her away, he heard the man mutter as they passed.

'Degenerate . . .'

Olly did not stop until he had pulled Agnes inside the walls of the castle.

'Are you well?'

Agnes nodded.

'Who *was* that?' Olly continued, shooting a look over his shoulder.

'Francis.' Agnes sniffed.

The family friend – the one who they suspected had been crucial in hiring John's services. The one with whom Agnes shared a history that she refused to talk of.

Olly was beginning to wish he had punched the man instead of just shoving past him.

'Let's get you inside.'

He dumped the basket beside the door and shepherded Agnes inside, up the stairs, and into her chamber. She stood beside the bed, arms wrapped around herself. She looked lost.

'Is there anything I can do?' Olly asked.

'I will be fine,' she said. 'I just need a moment. Although . . . Let Ash know that Francis is here – that way he may be prepared if he sees fit to speak with him.'

'Of course.' She looked so dreadfully unsure. Olly could not bear it. 'Oh, come *here*—'

He pulled her into a crushing embrace. Her arms were flattened between them, but after a moment she wriggled them free and, finally, wrapped her arms around him in return. She let out a long, low sigh as she relaxed against him.

'Better?' he asked.

She breathed against his chest. 'Yes,' she mumbled. 'Thank you, Olly.'

When he finally released her, she looked calmer.

'I'll go and warn Ash.'

She looked up at him, tears clinging to her eyelashes. Olly was assaulted with the sudden image of storming back outside, finding

Francis, and removing that smug expression from his face with his fists.

Or perhaps his boot.

He gave her shoulders a squeeze.

'Will you be all right?'

She nodded, lips tight. Olly was not sure if he believed her, but left the room anyway, hands tingling.

Chapter 26

Agnes

Agnes stood beside her bed, waiting for her breathing to level.

She was grateful that Olly had been beside her, and even more grateful that she was not forced to explain why Francis's arrival was so distressing. She took a deep breath, allowing herself to fill her body once more.

His arrival had left her hollowed out and numb. But now the reality of it was creeping in, and into that space in her chest was seeping *anger*. How dare he? After all he had done to her? After what she was *sure* he had done to Ash?

She would not let him ruin this.

Dressed in attire more appropriate for greeting her family, Agnes headed down into the hall. There she found Sara and her parents, along with Muriel and Ada, her youngest sister, as well as Francis, seated at one of the benches looking around the space with an air of distaste. Her father spotted her first, turning and catching her as she entered the room.

'Agnes!'

Her family descended upon her, fussing and crowding.

'You look well,' her mother said, with a small smile.

Agnes thanked her, unsure whether or not to believe her. She had found relaxation at Dunlyn, and was feeling brighter in herself for it. But with Francis's invasion into her home, all she felt was anxiety, wrapped around a tight fist of anger.

At least anger could be wielded. This was *her* land. There was nothing Francis could do to her here. Francis may have thought he held the power to ruin her in her new husband's eyes, but he had no idea that she could send him to the gallows for his own, more pressing sins.

'I am so sorry I was busy,' she said. 'I had no idea you would arrive so soon . . . I assume you were greeted by Ash in the fields?'

'We were,' said her father. 'With a hunting party. He has gone to clean himself up.'

'Very wise of him,' Agnes said. 'He is a poor shot; no doubt he is covered in all sorts of unmentionable things. Was Clara unable to come?'

Her mother gave her a patronising look. 'She is *quite* busy with the new baby,' she crooned. 'It is such a difficult time, when they are so young.'

'Of course,' Agnes said, feeling like a child being chastised. 'I am sure we will have a chance to introduce her to Ash soon enough.' She smoothed out her skirts with a little smile. 'Although we may be forced to wait, should we be blessed with our *own* child soon.'

She took devilish cheer in the look of alarm on her mother's face. 'Agnes . . .'

Her father looked worried. Agnes steeled herself for what was to come. 'Yes, Father?'

'Is there anywhere we may all speak privately?'

Agnes resisted a sigh. She glanced towards Francis. He was watching her. She wanted to demand he leave. To force him to stay in the hall. To claw his eyes out.

'Of course,' she said, pushing all the vitriol down into her stomach. 'This way.'

She led them into a side room. She sat in a high-backed chair, then gestured for them to do the same. Her family took seats, Ada and Muriel perching themselves on the bench beside the fire. Francis remained standing, lurking behind her father.

Agnes sat straighter. This was *her* space.

'What did you wish to speak about?' she asked.

Her father shot her mother a nervous look. 'We are worried about you,' he said, voice low. 'We *all* are.'

Agnes did not look at Francis. 'Whatever about?'

'Agnes, do not be foolish,' Muriel snapped. 'The last time we saw each other, that *man* attacked you. And now we hear you are married to him?'

'He did *not* attack me,' Agnes said, trying to keep her voice even.

'But—'

'But *nothing,* Muriel.'

'Why has it taken you so long to respond to our letters?' her mother asked, leaning forwards. 'We have been so worried for you, just *vanishing* like that!'

Agnes felt a bite of guilt again. Not for ignoring her family, but that her inaction had convinced them even further of Ash's crimes.

'I was busy,' she said simply. 'I was navigating a *betrothal,* Mother. I barely had time for anything else. And besides, can you fault me for not wishing to engage with letters that slandered my husband?'

'You could have replied, at least,' her father said. 'Leaving us with no word for so long? We could only fear the worst.'

'And what would that be?' Agnes said.

He looked sombre. 'We feared he was stopping you from responding.'

'Or preventing our letters from reaching you,' Muriel added.

Agnes sat straighter. 'He did neither,' she said. 'So you may put your minds to rest.'

'But—'

'*Mother.*' Agnes could feel the anger bubbling in her chest. She closed her eyes, breathing through her nose. 'The letters are upstairs in my chambers. I have them all. Many of them' – she raised her eyebrows – 'still sealed. Do you wish to inspect them?'

Her mother's face mottled pink, but she would not be deterred. 'You must admit that his reputation is in tatters.'

Before Agnes could begin to deny this, Francis stepped forwards. His hand rested on the back of Agnes's father's chair.

'We have heard some truly awful things, Aggie. From people who have known him for far longer than you have. Stories of violence and erratic behaviour. The man is *mad*.'

Agnes remembered Ash's concerns: his uncle, desperate for power, and his spiteful tongue.

'And who told you such things?' she asked.

Francis gave her a wary look. Clearly he did not want to name his confidant. Unluckily for him, Agnes's father robbed him of the chance to protect them.

'Hugh Barden,' he said helpfully. 'Lord Barden's uncle.'

Agnes could have laughed at Francis's quickly hidden expression of frustration.

'My word,' she said. 'How awful. Of course, I suppose he is unhappy with Ash's conduct at the late earl's funeral' – Francis went to speak, but Agnes spoke over him – 'but we have spoken about that, and I fully understand what happened that day. Emotions were running very high. Did Hugh specify anything beyond that, Father?'

Her father frowned. 'He mentioned many incidents, compounded over the years. He said that the war Lord Barden fought in France addled his brain, made him violent. But Francis would know more than I. He has met the man many times. What else did he talk of, Francis?'

Agnes glanced towards him. His face was carefully blank, but she could tell by the constrained rising and falling of his chest that he was holding himself back.

'He mentioned that he has always been impossible. Hugh said Lord Barden became even worse after returning from France. Short-tempered and cruel. That he has shirked his duties since coming of age.'

Agnes frowned at him. 'Now that simply cannot be true,' she said. 'I cannot vouch for his behaviour before I arrived, of course, but Ash has been dedicated to his role since I have been here.'

'Hugh said that Lord Barden's brother—'

'Oh, it is a *dreadful* story, isn't it?' Agnes said, swooping in before Francis could continue to besmirch Ash's name. 'So horribly wounded. Did you know, his arm is still unhealed? Regardless: *yes*, Ash told me that – to his deep shame – Raff did take on the burden of duty for some time. Ash suffered terribly in France. When he returned, he was seriously ill. He is thankful that Raff was there to stand where he could not.'

Francis was apparently speechless.

'He was ill?' Ada asked. 'How so?'

'Ada!' Agnes's mother chastised.

'No, no, it is quite all right,' Agnes said, turning to her little sister. 'He was wounded in battle, hence . . .' She made a vague gesture to indicate Ash's scar. 'He did not seek treatment until he returned home. It made him very unwell. And . . .' she took a deep breath, finding the best words '. . . one of his dearest friends was killed. He tried to save him and failed.' Ada looked startled. 'It was a tragedy,' Agnes said. 'And its own kind of illness, one which he still suffers from now. What sort of person would I be to judge a man for such things he cannot control? Anyone would be affected by the things he has seen.'

Everyone else had fallen silent. Agnes looked at them, waiting to see if they intended to levy any more accusations against him.

'I chose to marry Ash,' she said. 'I—' She remembered her letter, how effusive it had been. She cursed inwardly: she had forgotten the act. 'I care for him a great deal. He cares for me, and he has vowed to keep me safe. He has *never* shown any violence towards me. He has only been kind.'

'Your letter . . .' Muriel began, clearly unconvinced. 'You really *meant* all of that?'

'I did.'

'I have never known you feel so *much*.'

'Yes, well . . .' Agnes glanced down at her hands. At least the embarrassment was real; the awkward flush on her cheeks was easy to mistake for love. 'It is why I wrote to you. We last saw each other on such poor terms. I wanted to reassure you. Now . . .' she looked between her parents. 'Is that all? Or is there anything else you wish to discuss?'

They shared a look. Quite clearly there *was*.

'The attack on the road . . .' her father began. 'What happened? Your letter was so short . . .'

Agnes had been waiting for this. She willed herself not to look at Francis.

'It was horrible,' she said. 'We were walking together, and the attacker burst from the trees.' She left a pause long enough to take a breath. 'He had a knife to Ash's throat.'

'My God . . .'

'How *awful*,' Ada whispered, behind her hands.

'It was,' Agnes agreed. 'Quite awful.'

'Do you know why he did it?' Muriel asked.

Francis was leaning forwards in the chair, his elbows pressed to his knees. To anyone else, he looked like a concerned friend, a man worried about the woman he claimed to love. He put Agnes in mind of a weasel waiting to pounce. She caught his eye.

'We presume he was attempting to rob us,' she lied.

She did not look away, waiting for Francis to break first. He did.

'I see.'

'Enough of this,' she said. 'It is a difficult topic, I am sure you understand. Would you like to join us in the hall? Ash must be ready by now . . .'

Thankfully, no one argued with her. When they emerged back into the hall, it was full of servants rushing back and forth, setting out food and drink, overseen by the cook. She quickly saw to them, then noticed Muriel standing aside from the family. Taking her chance, Agnes weaved through the bustle of servants, grabbed Muriel by the arm and dragged her into a little alcove in the far wall.

'What is *he* doing here?' Agnes demanded, as soon as they were alone.

'Did you truly expect one of the oldest friends of the family not to come?' Muriel said, shaking her head. 'He said he so wished to see you, and it is only right that he be here to celebrate your marriage. Besides, he has been sick with worry about you. He is our friend, Aggie. He is *your* friend!'

'He is nothing to me, and you know that.'

'You cannot hang on to the past like this—'

'Girls! What are you gossiping about?'

Agnes snapped her head around to see their mother bustling over. She shot Muriel a final, venomous look.

'Just marriage matters, Mother,' she said, putting on her sweetest smile.

She allowed her mother to lead her back to the table. Before she could stop him, Francis sat beside her. Agnes prayed silently that Ash would return soon, if only so she did not feel as if she were facing this battle alone. Thankfully, she only had to endure a few minutes of Francis's snide chatter before there was an intrusion to their conversation.

'I see you are faring quite well without me!'

She turned at Ash's voice. Her heart took a beat out of time.

He stood at the foot of the stairs, expression teasing, with nerves beneath. But he *looked* wonderful. Any traces of blood or grime from the hunt had been removed, and his hair had been combed and slicked back away from his face. He'd dressed *impeccably*: a dark red velvet doublet finished in swirling embroidery, adorned with jewellery suitable for his station: rings, brooches, even the chain he typically refused to wear along with a short capelet. His hose were tight and supple, almost indecently so. Agnes found herself blushing when he looked at her, making his way over.

Quick behind him came Olly. He, too, was dressed in finery: yellows and greens, his hood cut into dagges and edged in contrasting thread. Over Ash's shoulder, he gave her an enormous grin, and mouthed, '*You are welcome.*'

Agnes gave him a tight-lipped smile, determined to talk to him about this later. She was thankful too: Ash looked perfect, exactly like the sort of man her family needed to see. While he was clearly anxious, he did not appear particularly uncomfortable: no doubt Olly had heaped praise upon him before leaving his chambers.

She wondered just what he had whispered into Ash's ear to make him walk with such a swagger, what sort of promises he had laid out for him.

She remembered Olly's words at the wedding feast: how the dress she wore would be best put to use crumpled in a heap at the foot of Ash's bed. She wondered if the doublet and hose were destined for the same fate.

The heat in her face drifted lower, down her chest, tightening through her stomach. *No,* she reminded herself. *Do not think of that.*

Not yet, at least.

Shaking the thought, she rose swiftly to her feet and hurried towards Ash, taking his arm.

'You look wonderful,' she whispered, so only he and Olly could hear. Louder, she asked: 'Have you already been introduced to everyone?'

'Not quite,' Ash said, squeezing her hand. 'I have already made Laurence and Alison's acquaintance—' He bowed towards her parents with a smile they did not return. 'But I have yet to meet . . . Franklin, was it?'

Agnes felt herself settling, her anxiety ebbing even further. Ash looked smug.

'*Francis,*' she corrected. 'Francis mac Cainnich. He is an old family friend. I believe I told you about him?'

Ash gave her a *perfect* smile, twisted by his scar, which he turned on Francis. 'Ah yes,' he said. 'I recall. I had not expected you, Francis.'

'He came with the family,' Agnes explained. 'I was quite surprised by his arrival.'

'It seems that everyone is keen to celebrate,' Olly said, having appeared at her other side.

'*Indeed*. Oliver, might I introduce you to my family?'

This was something they had already discussed. Given that he was to be a fixture in their lives, neither of them had been keen to hide Olly away. He was to be introduced as an old friend, recently returned to the area, settling into castle life until Ash could decide upon a role for him. The family did not need to know that Olly was the man whose death had caused Ash so much pain – nor that he was the one who had been sent to kill him.

They introduced Olly to the group – even Francis, who Olly greeted with such effusive enthusiasm that Agnes had to bite her lip to stop herself from laughing – before Olly made his excuses and hurried away with a terribly overacted bow towards Ash. No doubt he was off to find Penn and Raff to gossip, preparing them for that evening's banquet.

Finally they sat, Ash on Agnes's other side. The arrival of good food and drink was a godsend; it was difficult to accuse one's host of being a monster when he had arranged such hospitality for you.

Agnes watched as Ash spoke to her father across the table. They seemed to be getting along – or playing at civility.

'Barden's cook is very good, at least.'

Agnes turned, not bothering to greet Francis with a false smile. 'She is,' she said.

Francis refilled his mug. With Ash distracted, there was no wall between them.

'I am surprised you came,' Agnes continued, attempting to pack the words with meaning: *you do not belong here.*

'Not as surprised as I was to see you,' he said, bold enough that Agnes knew exactly what he was referring to. 'But it *is* good to see you again, regardless of *circumstances*.'

'I am sure,' Agnes responded tightly.

'I do hope we manage to have some time to speak,' he drawled. 'It really has been too long.'

Beneath the table, Ash's leg bumped against her own.

'I will be extremely busy.'

'Too busy to speak to your oldest friend?'

'I suspect—'

'And what are we talking about?'

Ash, finally, had been released from conversation, and was now leaning across her, peering at Francis with a forced joviality.

'We were just discussing how surprised I was to see Francis here,' Agnes said, settling closer to Ash.

'The more the merrier,' Ash said, looping his arm over Agnes's shoulders. 'How long have you known each other, Francis?'

Francis regarded him cooly. 'Since Agnes's birth,' he said simply.

'So long! You truly are entrenched in the family,' Ash said. 'And you faced no problems on the road?'

'None at all.'

'That *is* pleasing to hear. I suppose you heard of the encounter we had on our own travels?'

Francis's expression didn't change. 'Laurence and Alison informed me.'

'Is it not terrible? I had never expected such crime, especially not against *myself*. But alas . . .' Ash gave another smile – this one bordering on smug – and gripped Agnes a little tighter. 'People cannot be judged for choices they make in desperation.'

'No,' Francis nearly growled. 'They cannot. Did you catch the fellow?'

'We did, as it were.'

'And I am sure you will see to it that the criminal gets what is owed to him?'

'Oh, I have *certainly* seen to that.'

Agnes couldn't hold back the laugh. It burst out of her in a coughing splutter.

'Apologies,' she said, trying to control herself. 'I do not know *what* came over me.'

Francis moved his cup out of her way. 'Indeed,' he said. 'Maybe madness is catching.'

'What was that?' Ash's tone was innocent and light. Agnes stilled.

'Nothing at all.'

'Would you not care to repeat yourself?'

'As I said, it was—'

'If madness *is* catching,' Agnes spat, 'then I should be glad to catch it. Better than cruelty or greed.'

'What are you implying?'

Agnes stared at him. Daring him. 'Nothing at all. Ash, I fear we have *much* to prepare for this evening's celebrations if we are to introduce our families. Would you care to join me?'

She rose from the bench. All eyes were upon her, yet she did not care. Ash was at her side in an instant.

'Of course, my Lady. I have been told my prized hunter caught several *marvellous* pheasants ready to roast for us.'

Agnes shot a last, poisonous look at Francis. 'He *did*.'

✡

By the time the day had finally dragged to a finish, the sun setting with blissful finality, Agnes was utterly spent.

The banquet had been a success, at least, in no small part due to the more outgoing members of their party: Penn and Olly had dominated conversations, keeping her family entertained enough not to start any arguments. Francis's desire to be the cleverest person in any room was thwarted at every turn by the unstoppable force of the so-called hostage, and Agnes could not help but enjoy from afar every time Penn corrected him on English court.

Concerned that they would be overheard in the solar, all three of them returned to Ash's chambers. Agnes felt like a man at war being debriefed after a day in the field. At least the blood still trapped beneath her fingernails was from the hunt and not a battle.

'How were they on the road when you greeted them?' Agnes asked, as soon as the door had shut behind them. 'Did they say anything worrying?'

Ash shook his head. 'No, although we have Justin to thank for that. I think they realised it would not do to be seen insulting me in front of one of my vassals.'

'That is *something*, at least.'

'What about you? They had you quite trapped when I arrived.'

Agnes groaned. 'They had,' she said. 'They were full of questions, asking why I had taken so long to respond to their letters. Telling me of your *poor reputation*. And to bring *Francis* here!' She let herself fall back onto the bed with a thump.

'I presume you still suspect he hired me, then?' Olly said, pulling off his boots and sprawling beside her.

'I do.'

They lapsed into silence. Ash gave her a conciliatory look, then stood from the bed and began to fiddle with the buttons of his doublet.

'I must say . . .' Agnes sat up, watching him. 'That suits you very well.'

Ash turned to look at her. He had gone a little pink. 'Oh?'

'You really look the part of the *desirable earl.*' Agnes turned to Olly. 'Although I suppose I have you to thank for that?'

'You do.'

'How in God's name did you convince him to dress so nicely?'

'I made him some favourable promises,' Olly said, with a sly smile. 'About the things I would do to him should he look his best.'

'Did you indeed?'

Agnes turned back to Ash. He looked even more flushed than before.

'I *did* wish to make a good impression on them,' he insisted. 'But . . . I will admit, it helped knowing that Olly did not think I looked a *complete* fool.'

Agnes understood that feeling. It was useful to have an ally – even if was only to tell you that you did not look as dreadful as you felt. The two men glanced at each other, and she realised that she was intruding. She should leave – return to her own chambers and wait out the long night before being forced to deal with yet more of her family's questions.

She did not want to. She did not want to be alone, that much was true, but more so – she didn't want to leave Ash and Olly. She wanted to be able to stay with them, laughing and talking and drinking them in.

But she could not. They were . . . they were *them*. She was an outsider to their happiness.

'I suppose I should leave, then,' Agnes said, 'so you may fulfil your promise.'

The two men shared another look: one which she was learning, now, how to read.

'Or . . .'

'If you—'

Ash and Olly had spoken over each other, as they so often did. She turned to Ash, giving him final say.

'If you wanted to stay . . .' he said, slowly, barely meeting her gaze. 'That would be— that is—'

'What I believe my Lord is *attempting* to tell you,' Olly said, rolling over to nudge her with his foot, 'is that while my promises to him were between *us* alone, I am sure we would be happy to have a witness to ensure I fulfil them.'

'I—' Agnes stuttered. Her first thought was to *thank* them, but that seemed absurdly formal in the circumstances. 'I would be glad to be such a witness,' she said instead, feeling her heart thud a little harder. '*Very* glad.'

'Excellent.' Olly was on his feet in an instant, and upon Ash in another. 'Let us be free of this—'

'Wait.'

Olly stilled, his fingers on the buttons of Ash's doublet. They looked down at Agnes, perched on the edge of the bed.

She took a deep breath.

'That is an expensive doublet.' Her face flushed. Her fingers twitched against the bedsheet. 'You should remove it slowly.'

Ash's eyes went wide. Olly's look of confusion became one of glee.

'Of *course*.'

He positioned himself at Ash's side so she could better see what he was doing, then began to undo the delicate buttons of Ash's doublet. His dextrous musician's fingers and lithe, clever hands made slow, delicious work of a job that could be done much faster.

He treated each individual button as if it were as rare and valuable as the finest pearl, twitching them free. Agnes could see the heavy rise and fall of Ash's chest beneath Olly's fingers, his eyes darting from Olly, to his hands, to her. His lips were slightly ajar.

Olly moved down Ash's chest until he reached the final button. He undid it with a deft twist, then reached up, leisurely sliding the doublet from Ash's arms. It fell to the floor with a muffled thud.

Ash stood in his breeches and undershirt. His neck flushed, making the stark whiteness of his scar even more apparent.

Olly turned to look at Agnes. 'Well?'

Her heart was thundering in her chest. She was warm all over. 'That too.'

Olly gave her a nod and a smile as he turned back to Ash. Olly seemed to be enjoying himself, as he looped a finger beneath the first tie of Ash's undershirt – the one closest to Ash's throat – and tugged it loose with a flourish. Ash sighed, no more than a puff of air. Agnes tensed her thighs.

Olly dragged the cord through each eyelet, brushing his fingers against Ash's skin but restricting himself to that touch alone. It was *maddening*, and Agnes could only imagine how Ash himself felt.

Finally, *finally*, and with a theatrical embellishment, Olly tugged the cord away.

Agnes let out a long breath. Again, Olly turned to her. This time he said nothing, just raised his eyebrows questioningly. Agnes nodded.

That was all he needed. Olly grabbed the delicate fabric of Ash's undershirt and pulled it up and over his head. Without the long fabric of the doublet or undershirt, she could see – clear as day – how hard Ash was.

'What next?' Olly asked, apparently enjoying the view as much as she. 'What would you bid me do?'

She took another breath. She let her imagination rule, let her reason stand aside to ask herself: what did she want?

She caught Ash's gaze. She held it.

'Kiss him,' she said steadily.

'Where?'

'Everywhere.'

Olly grinned. 'My pleasure.'

He started not on Ash's mouth, as Agnes had been expecting, but at the crook of his neck. Ash's eyes fluttered closed as Olly placed a gentle kiss there, then another, moving around his body from neck to clavicle to the curve of his shoulder.

Next he dragged his lips down Ash's arm, over the inside of his elbow, trailing down to Ash's wrists. Agnes watched enraptured at the sight of Olly's sharp, pink tongue pressing against Ash's skin, at the way Ash's head tilted back, eyes shut, lips open.

Olly grabbed Ash's hand, placing his lips to the back of his knuckles, before finally pulling him into a hard, desperate kiss. Ash made a soft little noise in the back of his throat, one that tugged at something deep in Agnes's core, as Olly gripped him. Even from where she sat on the bed, Agnes could see their mouths moving together, tongues dancing.

Agnes's own mouth went dry, her body aflame. She could barely form the words for the next instruction, but Olly seemed to know what she wanted instinctively: likely because it was what *he* wanted, too.

He undid the ties of Ash's hose with a flick of his wrist, grabbed both hose and braies and tugged at them, falling to his knees as he did. Ash stumbled as Olly pulled the hose from his feet and tossed them aside, staying on his knees as he stared up at Ash, now entirely naked.

From here, Agnes could not see Olly's expression, but she could guess at it: hungry, eager. Ash was staring at him with an expression bordering on wonder, all wide eyes and low, steady breaths. He reached out slowly, carding a gentle hand through Olly's hair. Olly leaned into the touch, and once again Agnes felt as if she were intruding.

Ash's gaze slid up to meet hers. The force of it was like a physical thing – like rope around her chest, pulling at her. His eyes were dark and hungry but soft, so soft. She swallowed heavily, her heart squeezing.

Realising that Ash's attention had been caught, Olly ducked forwards, pressed a series of fluttering kisses to his legs, his thighs, to the crease of his torso and one – soft, lingering, closed-mouthed – to his cock. Ash gasped, and Olly was back to his feet, kissing him once more.

Ash's fingers dug into Olly's tunic, leaving frantic creases in the fabric as Olly twisted them around, pushing Ash backwards towards the bed. His hands continued to roam lower, gripping and grabbing hard enough to leave little red marks in his wake.

'Wait—'

Both men paused to look at her. Olly's fingers gripped tight into the soft pillow of Ash's backside.

'Ash . . .'

Ash turned to face her. His hard cock brushed against Olly's clothed leg. And that was the problem: he was clothed.

'Undress Olly.'

Olly's eyebrows shot upwards. Agnes was suddenly concerned that she had overstepped in this dance of boundaries.

'If he wishes you to.'

Olly's look of shock melded smoothly into confidence again.

'I had not realised *you* wished for it,' he said. He appeared to be attempting to cover up his surprise.

Agnes could understand that. The link between them was Ash – lover and husband. It was reasonable for him to think her interest was in Ash alone.

'I do,' she said. 'I want to see *both* of you.'

Ash and Olly glanced at each other. Another one of those wordless conversations happened. Surprise, but not disinterest. A question. An answer.

Ash turned to her, now. 'Whatever my—'

'Our,' Olly said, with a wink.

'Whatever *our* lady commands. To me, you scoundrel.'

Ash started, as Olly had, with his overshirt, sliding his hands down Olly's chest, catching his fingers on the ties of his tunic. Olly watched him hungrily, eyes low and dark. Ash flexed his fingers, then reached up to the first tie at Olly's throat. He saw it off quickly – far too quickly for either Olly or Agnes's liking.

But before Agnes could say anything Olly took Ash's hands in his own, stilling him. He leaned forwards and kissed him, sliding his tongue boldly into Ash's mouth. Ash looked at him breathlessly. Agnes, too, felt like her breath had been stolen.

'*Slowly*, love,' Olly muttered.

He released his hands, and this time, Ash moved with more purpose. Olly's tunic was tied with half a dozen or so knots, and Ash reached for the next, looping the cord around his fingers. As he tugged it free, he looked up at Olly once more and caught him in a kiss.

He moved slowly, as Olly had instructed him, untying each one and letting it hang before finally pulling the tunic from Olly's arms. Olly's undershirt was near identical to Ash's – clearly he had pilfered it from one of Ash's chests. Ash turned now to Agnes, waiting.

Agnes nodded. 'And that.'

The undershirt went the same way as the tunic. A substantial pile of clothes was growing at their feet, one they were both ignoring. Ash moved to his breeches, removing those with even less grace than they had done Ash's, and soon they were both standing naked before her.

The air thrummed with tension. It was as if the storm from weeks ago had somehow shrunk itself and squeezed through the window, filling the room with crackles and sparks. Ash and Olly stood naked, barely touching each other, and yet even from the other side of the room Agnes thought she could feel the heat coming from them.

She wondered if they would set upon each other right there, in the middle of the chamber, leaving her to perch on the covers and watch, or if they would return to the bed.

She *wanted* them to return, she realised. Last time she had done this she had been a careful, distant observer. But now she wanted to be close: to see and hear and smell it all, to be a part, yet apart.

'Would you join me on the bed?' she asked, gathering her courage before it fled her.

Ash looked surprised, eyebrows rising, cheeks flushing even darker. Olly did not appear shocked at all, wearing that same, smug, devilish grin. They crossed the room to join her, settling themselves onto the bed side by side, Agnes still perched on the edge.

'What promises did you make to him to get him into those clothes?' Agnes asked.

They shared a glance. Agnes waited. It was Olly who spoke first. 'I told him I was going to fuck him.'

The heat between Agnes's legs flared harder.

'Well,' she said, her very *breath* feeling hot. 'You ought to fulfil that promise.'

Olly gifted her another one of those devastating smiles. He seemed to be assessing the situation.

'I've an idea,' Olly said, slowly. 'Agnes— that is, if you do not mind . . . ?'

'Please,' Agnes said, eager to know what he intended to do. 'I concede to your expertise.'

Olly grinned. 'Very good. Place yourself at the head of the bed. Ash . . .' He pulled Ash around to the foot, kissed him hard and then pushed him back. Ash collapsed onto the mattress, legs dangling.

'There. Now *stay* . . .'

Ash went still. So did Agnes. She watched as Olly sauntered to the little chest that sat atop the bedside table and opened it with a soft *click*. On the bed, Ash whined. Olly reached inside and pulled out that same jar that he had done before – the one he had used the night Agnes had watched them.

Ash, too, had his eyes upon the jar as Olly placed it just beside his head. Olly leaned over him, kissing him down into the furs, before moving to the foot of the bed. He gently eased Ash's knees apart.

'This one is a wriggly creature,' Olly said. 'Agnes, I need your assistance.'

'Yes?'

'Take his wrists,' Olly said, looking down at Ash, 'and hold him still. *Here*—'

Olly slid his hands up Ash's legs, towards his chest, then – bending over him – to his arms, forcing them above Ash's head. Agnes leaned over her captive husband.

Where it took Olly only one hand to clasp Ash's wrists, Agnes required both as she placed them where Olly indicated. She slipped into place, Olly brushing his fingers across the backs of her hands as she held Ash down.

'Very good,' he said, in a low baritone. 'But tighter.'

Ash was staring at her, she realised. She caught his eye – his gaze was needy and open. He swallowed heavily, and Agnes found herself mimicking his movements. She squeezed harder. Ash sucked in a quick breath through his teeth. His heart beat frantically against Agnes's palms.

'That's it,' Olly drawled. 'Now . . .'

He smoothed his hands back down Ash's chest, fluttering over his stomach towards his prick. He gave it a slow tug. Ash groaned, straining against Agnes's hands. Agnes's own need was growing, a tight and unmistakable wetness between her legs. She took a little breath, then immediately felt her face flush for how obvious her own arousal was.

She squeezed her legs tighter. She was desperate to reach beneath her skirts and underclothes and find her cunt, to reach that dizzying height *together,* all three of them. But she could not; least of all because both hands were currently employed in keeping Ash held down as he writhed beneath Olly's expert touch.

Olly brushed his hands up Ash's legs before reaching for the little jar. Ash's eyes slid shut, his mouth opening in silent gasp. As Agnes watched, Olly took Ash's prick in hand, slowly sliding his palm up and down the shaft, squeezing, rubbing at the tip with his thumb.

Now he opened the jar, flooding the room with a strong herbal scent. He dipped his fingers inside, coating them generously with the slick stuff within – a kind of tallow, Agnes thought, or hardened oil. It glistened as Olly coated his fingers.

'Ash?'

Ash responded with a grunt. Olly grinned, then slid his hand lower. Ash gasped out. Agnes gripped his wrists tighter, and Ash *groaned,* the sound igniting her even further. Olly worked him, one hand between his legs and the other on his cock, stroking him, muttering words of praise as Ash twisted on the bed.

Finally, he pulled his hand away. He dipped his fingers in the jar again, this time spreading it generously down the length of his own cock. When it was done, he looked down at Ash again, who was now lying back, head tilted on the mattress, breathing shallowly.

'Are you ready, my Lord?'

'*Yes—*' Ash choked.

'Agnes?'

Agnes dared to look up. Olly's gaze made her feel as if she would burst into flame.

'Yes.'

Olly grinned again. In a deft movement, he lifted Ash's legs, flung his feet over his shoulders, then eased himself inside Ash's willing entrance.

Ash made a guttural noise that seemed to come from deep within him, like water bubbling from a pool. Olly choked back a little gasp as he pushed deeper. Agnes's whole body constricted at once, every hair on her body on end, every breath a furnace. She gripped Ash's wrists even tighter, and he let out a curse into the hot air.

Olly had paused. His eyes were shut, his breathing level and controlled, his fingers twitching where they gripped Ash's leg. And then he began to move, a rhythmic, powerful thrust that made the whole bed shake. With each movement Agnes felt herself trapped in the push and pull of it, the tide of pleasure. Ash moaned beneath her hands.

She wanted it. She wanted that heat, that pleasure, that tide. She could already feel it in her blood, and now she needed to feel it in her *body*. She could not tell if it was a desire to fill or be filled – to be Ash, sprawled on the bed, or to be Olly above him, sturdy and powerful and buried inside him, fit like a dagger within a sheath.

She wanted both. *All*. She wanted everything she could get, and more.

She squirmed, attempting to reach the best spots without even moving her hands. But it was impossible. Her grip around Ash's wrists loosened. She barely even considered it as she slumped down, knees opening. One hand was enough to keep Ash trapped, she thought, vaguely, and then suddenly she was no longer pinning him, but twining their fingers together, holding his hand as her other, now freed, slipped beneath her skirts.

The relief was almost instant. As soon as her fingers brushed against her cunt that first deep thrill of pleasure coursed through her. Her body had been waiting for this, needing it for so long that even the lightest touch was enough to make her legs quake. She squeezed Ash's hand unbidden, feeling the bed move beneath them.

She gave in to it quickly and easily. Ash's gasps beside her, Olly's laboured breaths, the feel of the bed shifting beneath them, the sound of it all together in a grand, overwhelming cacophony. The air tasted of heat and sweat and she drank it in greedily as she rubbed at herself.

On the bed, Ash was making desperate, building little noises. Agnes glanced over through hooded lids to see Olly let go of one of his legs and reach between them, taking Ash's cock in his hand. Ash gasped, cursed, *growled*. Agnes squeezed her eyes shut again, unable to look, unable to do anything but press her fingers harder.

Olly went first. He sounded like a song, a melodious note that erupted from his lungs unbidden. Ash stuttered on the bed, groaning. Agnes had but a moment to think before it crashed over her, too, drowning her, soaking her in a hot, lingering burst.

Thrilled with it, body tingling all over, she opened her eyes just in time to see Ash buck and spend across his own chest, his mouth open in a wordless cry. It was so much – it was *too* much – and Agnes's hand, still in her skirts, brushed against her once more – again – again – to send her away for a second time before she collapsed onto the bed beside Ash, breathing heavily.

After a moment the bed sagged as Olly too lay down, nudging Ash aside.

They lay there, the only sound their breathing. Agnes's head was blissfully empty, her thoughts quiet. Nothing mattered beyond this room – beyond this *bed*. She could close her eyes and drift to sleep without a second thought.

Her body prickled with sweat, her heart gently returning to a slower pace. The breeze through the windows was mild, but it ghosted over her and made her shiver regardless.

'Come—' Olly had a hand on Ash's shoulder, but he was looking at her. He gave Ash a little shove. 'You are in the way, you brute. It is cold.'

With a grumble, Ash moved himself so Olly could tug back the blankets. Unwillingly, Agnes moved aside too, watching as Ash tumbled beneath the covers.

'Agnes?'

She realised that Olly was meaning for her to stay, holding the blankets up so she, too, could slip beneath. Her body was still hot and slick with sweat from all they had done; but *that* warmed her too, in an entirely different way.

She took the chance, settling in the bed beside Ash, who looped a sleepy arm around her, penning her in. She had not expected the casual touch, and she wondered if he would have granted it were he not already half-asleep and basking in the rich afterglow of his and Olly's lovemaking. His skin was warm, and in her own satiated state she could not resist leaning into him, letting her head pillow against his arm.

Olly slid beneath the covers on Ash's other side, sliding an arm across Ash's body. Their hands met in the centre of Ash's chest. Something tight and bright and good settled between Agnes's ribs as she drifted into deep, undisturbed sleep.

Chapter 27

Olly

The solar table was piled high with documents. Ash's eyes were drifting across a ledger, but Olly was sure he wasn't actually reading the words on the page. Olly was secretly glad that such dull pursuits did not fall to him: his position by the fire, with Agnes at his side and his lute in his hands, was far preferable.

It was low, hiding from Agnes's family, but given the circumstances Olly thought that he would have done the same.

He was attempting to pen something new. Agnes had been brought into the endeavour, valiantly providing rhymes when Olly's memory fogged. They were not, in truth, producing anything of much merit, but the endeavour was certainly enjoyable: especially when Ash emerged from whichever document he was reading to suggest something crude.

He was muddling over a tricky chord when there was a knock at the door. All three of them startled at the noise, and it was Olly who reached the door first. Standing outside was a nervous-looking servant girl. She peered around Olly towards Ash.

'Sorry to intrude, my Lord, but there is a man at the gates asking after you.'

Ash frowned. 'Do you know him?'

'No, my Lord,' said the girl. 'No one recognises him.'

'Did he say what it is he wants?'

'He said he needed to speak to you, and he mentioned that he was looking for a man named Noll.'

Olly's head snapped around to look at her. 'What does he look like?'

The girl looked startled to have his attention on her. 'Ah—' she mumbled. 'He's quite young, not too tall. Looks half starved.'

Olly couldn't breathe. Suddenly Ash was at his side, his hand on his arm.

'Is that him?' he said. 'Is that Pepper?'

Olly nodded. Ash's grip tightened.

'Take us to him, please. Agnes—'

Agnes was already tidying away the papers on the desk. 'Go. I shall give you some space.'

They rushed into the courtyard. Sure enough, there was a figure flanked by guards beside the portcullis.

'Pepper!'

Olly was upon him in an instant, pulling him into a hug. Pepper swore colourfully until Olly released him.

'You got my message?'

Pepper grinned. 'I did. Not that it made any sense, of course, but when have you ever made sense?'

Olly stepped back so he could properly look at him. He looked well, thank God, unharmed and unmarked and just as scruffy as he had left him. The dagger was still strapped to his hip. Beside him was a handcart, piled with things.

'What in God's name did you *bring*?' Olly asked.

'Everything,' Pepper said. 'Everything that was mine, and some besides.'

'*Everything?*' It looked like he had uprooted his entire life.

'Once John got word that you had failed . . .' Pepper sighed. 'It has been bad, Noll. Extremely bad. I gambled that it would be better here.'

Olly swallowed. 'Let us get you inside and you can tell me everything. And we'll find you something to eat. You look famished . . .'

'Stop *fussing* over me, Noll.'

'I am not fussing!'

'You—'

'Olly?' Ash finally approached. 'I presume you must be Pepper?'

Pepper gave Ash a deeply suspicious look. 'That I am,' he said. 'And you are . . . ?'

'Earl Ashwy Barden,' Ash said, matching Pepper's tone.

'Stop it, both of you.' Olly gave Ash a shove. 'Come inside, I can make *proper* introductions.'

Once Pepper's things were safely stowed away, Olly led him back into the solar. Agnes, who was nowhere to be seen, had hidden away the reams of parchments and ledgers, making the room look almost cosy. Pepper raised his eyebrows at the show of luxury around them – and the fine wine that they were brought by a deferent serving girl – but settled beside the fire quickly enough.

'So,' he said. 'What in *God's name* is going on, Noll?'

Olly took a breath. He glanced at Ash, who shrugged: *tell him what you need to.*

'Do you recall what I told you about my time in France?'

Pepper squinted at him. 'War, injury, ransom . . .' He rattled off the list like it was nothing. 'Is that right?'

'Right enough,' Olly said. 'Do you remember me telling you of my . . . my companion?'

Pepper gave him an unimpressed look. 'The one you were fucking but refused to tell me outright, for fear I would judge you? I recall.'

Olly spluttered as Ash snorted out a sharp laugh behind him. 'You *knew*?'

'It seemed rather obvious,' Pepper said. 'I thought that it was clear you did not wish to speak of him, so I never pressed the issue. From what you *managed* to tell me, though,' he added, 'it seems like he was a bastard.'

Ash laughed again. Olly sighed, leaning back.

'Pepper,' he said, gesturing towards Ash standing beside them. 'Meet the bastard. I tend to call him Ash.'

Pepper looked at Ash with an expression of deep distrust, almost hate. The air in the room became close and tense.

'You left him in France?'

'No,' Olly spoke before Ash could. 'Not deliberately, at least.'

'You said he refused to pay your ransom.'

'I did. I was wrong.'

'The ransom letters did not arrive,' Ash said, stepping closer. 'I would not have left Olly out there. *Never.*'

Pepper looked back to Olly. 'You believe him?'

'I do,' Olly said. 'And given that Ash has insisted on taking me in, I see no reason not to.'

He did not look convinced. 'You know him best.'

'There is more,' Olly put in quickly. 'The man John paid me to kill. That was Ash too.'

'*Fuck*. Is it why you could not do it?'

'I could not do it because I was overconfident,' Olly said. 'I went in too strong, and did not assume that his wife would be armed. They took me captive, before Ash realised who I was.'

Pepper nodded. 'I had heard that you failed. I had assumed . . . until I received your message . . .' His expression lost that laughing spark. 'I assumed you had been killed.'

Olly took his hand. 'I am so sorry, Pep.'

Pepper sniffed. 'We both knew it was a risk,' he said. 'But still . . . I only learned you were alive after things had already turned sour.'

'What happened?'

'John is in debt. A *lot* of debt. He took the money from your job and squandered it. When we got word that you had failed to kill Lord Barden, he flew into a rage. There was no death, so there was no more money. You told me of a family friend? The one who knew John?'

'Yes?'

'He was in town. He'd been there all that time, waiting to hear that Lord Barden was dead. He learned right away what had happened. I've never seen an argument like it. This man demanded his money back; John claimed he no longer had it. It was vicious. John tried to calm him, offered him his pick of the girls, told him they'd try again. Then the letter came.'

'The letter?'

'Lord Barden's wife wrote to her family to tell them of the attack on the road, how lucky they had been to escape with their lives and informing them that she and Lord Barden were to be wed immediately. The family wrote to the friend to let him know. He was beside himself.'

'I am sure he was,' Ash said, pleased with himself. 'Pepper . . . this man's name. Do you know it?'

Pepper barely thought about it. 'Frank.'

It wasn't shocking. It wasn't a *revelation*. But the confirmation was its own kind of blow.

'What is it?' Pepper asked, clearly registering the twin looks on Olly and Ash's faces. 'Whatever is the matter?'

'Frank – Francis mac Cainnich – is in the keep,' Olly said. 'He is under this roof.'

Pepper's eyes went even wider. 'Shit,' he muttered. 'When I left . . . I suspected that something was the matter. So . . . well, frankly, if John wants to leave his doors unlocked . . .'

'Pepper.' Olly grabbed the arms of his chair. 'What did you do?'

Pepper reached into his tunic, then pulled out a much worn, much dirtied fold of parchment. Olly recognised the hunting horn seal: the letter that John had shown him, back when he was still a hopeless murderer. He took a breath.

'Ash—'

'I'll fetch Agnes. Wait here.'

He did not take long. Agnes did not wait to be introduced, storming into the room towards the desk.

'Tell me how bad things are.'

Olly swallowed. He looked from her, to Pepper, to the letter.

'He speaks of talking to your family, and the letter repeats what John told me: a woman being married to a monster, a sister concerned for her safety. He clearly organised this with John himself. He mentions' – Olly glanced down to the paper – '*our previous conversation*. They must have already known each other and discussed the issue. I suspect that this was merely committing the agreement to paper.'

'Wonderful.' Agnes dropped into the empty chair opposite Olly. 'May I?'

She reached across the table. Olly handed her the parchment, which she took and quickly skimmed, eyes darting back and forth. Finally, she tossed it back to the table.

'It does not prove half as much as I had hoped it would,' Agnes said. 'At least he was foolish enough to sign it with his name. Is there any way we can find more information from John?'

'When I left, he had already gone,' Pepper said. 'He'll have picked up a new name by now and started again, no doubt.'

'So he is useless to us.'

'I think we have enough to accuse Francis, though,' Olly said. 'We know he spoke to John, and we know he had a problem he wished for John to deal with. *I* know that after receiving this letter, John arranged for me to kill Ash. And I know that the *writer* of the letter paid for the whole affair.'

Agnes tapped her nails on the tabletop. 'True. But what do we want to *do* with this information? Ash.' She twisted to look up at him. 'You are the one who they tried to kill. This sin is against you more than any of us. What do you want done with him?'

Ash swallowed. His gaze lingered on Olly.

'I want him gone,' he said. 'But if Francis claims we are lying—'

'Which he will,' Agnes said.

'Then it will be easy for him to turn the eye of justice onto Olly. He was the man who attempted the crime, after all. It will not be about retribution, just power,' Ash said. 'I do not wish to even *consider* starting that battle if it is one I may not win.'

'All right,' Olly said, chest tight. 'And I suppose the matter still stands of your family, Agnes. We do not know how much they are involved in this. If they asked Francis to help them take such drastic actions, or if they had no notion of what he planned to do.'

Agnes sighed. 'My family have always trusted him. Always believed his word above mine. He could have convinced them that there was no other alternative, or just assured them that he had it in hand . . .'

'If he even wanted them to know,' Ash added. 'It would have been easy to pretend that it had been a robbery gone wrong. I would be dead, Francis would have what he desired, and your family would never know what he had done. Can you speak to them?'

Agnes stared at the desk. 'I must. But if I do, and they *admit* to this . . . I do not know how I will be able to look at them again. I must talk to them. But—'

'But the uncertainty is safer than knowing,' Olly said.

Agnes finally looked up at him.

'It is . . . better, sometimes,' he confessed. 'To not know. To not ask, so they can never hurt you.'

Agnes made a sad sort of sound. 'It is,' she said thickly. 'But this is not about me. This is about us. All of us.' She reached up, placing her hand over Ash's. 'If anything else, I must know if they were part of this so I can bar them from my home. *Our* home.' Her eyes were steely. 'I will not allow them to hurt you.'

The force of her words and the cut of her gaze were like a slap. Ash looked taken aback.

'I cannot take this to Mother and Father,' she said. 'Not yet. I will speak to Muriel. I am sure she would have noticed if they were behaving oddly.'

'And what of Francis?' Olly said, leaning on the table. 'How do we deal with him?'

'We do not.'

Everyone looked at Ash.

'What do you mean?' Agnes said.

'I mean what I say. We do nothing. I would love to pull him from this castle by his hair and throw him into the river where he belongs, but to do so will only prove to them all that I *am* the monster they assume I am. Anyway, it is better to wait until we know if your family *is* involved before we throw around accusations.'

Agnes sagged in her seat. Olly raised his eyebrows.

'That . . . is extremely reasonable,' he said.

'I know.' Ash dragged his hand down his face. His fingers twitched towards his scar, but Olly grabbed his arm, halting him before he could dig at it. 'Besides, he may yet know who Olly is. It would be easy enough to learn that he was the man who attacked us if he asks Michael. I cannot imagine how maddening it would be, *knowing* that the man you hired is galivanting around the keep of the person he failed to kill.'

'Are you suggesting we wait until we confront him just to make him twitch?'

'That is not the *only* reason.'

Olly burst into laughter.

'That is quite brilliant, you know,' Pepper said, eyeing Ash critically. 'Force him to wait for the sword to drop. He may confess himself, just to get it over with.'

'Maybe he will throw *himself* into the river,' Olly mused.

Ash huffed through his nostrils. 'We can only hope. Where is Francis now?'

Agnes gave him a sour look. 'He has ridden into Skeldale.'

'At least he is not *here*,' Olly sniffed. 'One less person to worry about.'

'Indeed.' Agnes sighed, then – at last – turned to Pepper. 'Forgive me,' she said. 'I have been terribly rude to you. Pepper, is it? I have heard much about you.'

Pepper looked at Olly. 'Have you now?'

'All good things I can assure you,' Agnes said smoothly. 'I am

Agnes, although I presume you already know that. Would you like us to show you around?'

'Actually.' Olly stood. 'I thought I would show Pepper around myself. There are some things I wish to . . .' he glanced at Agnes and then away again, feeling himself blush. '. . . to discuss with him.'

'Very well,' Ash said. 'Come and find us when you are settled. And Pepper . . . welcome to Dunlyn Castle.'

Chapter 28

Agnes

Over the next few days, Ash stuck to Agnes's side whenever he could. She was rarely left alone with her family, and never with Francis, always accompanied by him or Olly. Mealtimes became a crowded affair, with Ash's family, along with Sara, taking up so much room and air that Francis rarely had a chance to make any of his typically cutting comments.

After confirming his involvement in the attack on Ash, Olly had taken to sitting at Francis's side when they ate or sat in the hall. Agnes had assumed that this was a private joke on his part, even if it made her terribly anxious. She realised, after watching Francis try and fail to engage him in conversation, that the true reason was much more amusing.

'I make sure he sits on *this* side,' Olly had said one night, gesturing to his bad ear, 'so I do not need to listen to him, and to save *you* all the burden of responding to him.'

Muriel had become impossible to corner. She was *busy*, always with their parents or, worse, with Francis himself. Those few opportunities Agnes managed to take with Muriel alone were entirely fruitless affairs. Agnes was unkeen to ask outright if she was aware of the true nature of the attack, but her less direct questions were yielding nothing. It was one evening over a week after Pepper's arrival when Agnes finally managed to find her alone, and Muriel once again refused to speak to her, giving her a weak excuse about feeling unwell before shutting the door to the guest chambers in Agnes's face.

Frustrated by her sister's stubbornness, Agnes cursed beneath her breath and stomped in the opposite direction, intending to find Ash and Olly.

She was so distracted that she did not notice Francis heading her way until she had walked directly into him. He grabbed her shoulders.

'Francis.' She froze. 'My apologies. I was lost in thought.'

He gave her a long, assessing look. 'So it seems. I presume all is well?'

She wondered what would happen if she were to hit him.

'Yes,' Agnes said, 'Quite well.'

Still, his hands were on her. She could feel his clammy touch through the fabric of her sleeves.

'You look as if you have had a fright,' he said.

'It is nothing.'

The grip tightened minutely.

'Come with me. We may talk privately.'

He was leering at her.

'No,' she said. 'Thank you, Francis.'

He did not let go. 'You do not need to lie to me, Agnes. I know your husband is—'

'There she is!'

Francis's grip loosened. Agnes took the opportunity to shake him off, turning to see Ash and Olly behind her. They both looked as if they had been rushing – faces red, a little breathless. Before Agnes could greet them, Ash stumbled forwards, pulled her boldly away from Francis, and kissed her.

Agnes scrambled to grab the front of his tunic as he ducked her down. Her heart was trying to escape her ribs, her breath utterly stolen. It lasted a moment – it lasted an age – and then he released her.

She clung to him, the ground beneath her feet feeling suddenly unsteady. He grinned down at her, eyes sparkling, lips twisting. He turned to Francis without letting her go.

'I am afraid I have need of my wife.'

Francis spluttered some retort, but Ash ignored him.

'Come on, my Lady. And you, you wastrel,' he added, glancing towards Olly.

Olly gave Francis a deep mock-bow with a grin, then took his place at Agnes's other side as Ash led her away down the corridor. As they turned the corner, Olly broke into a run, dragging them behind him until they reached Ash's chamber door, at which Olly bundled them both inside.

'Well,' Olly said breathlessly, 'that worked.'

'Are you all right?' Ash said, turning to Agnes at last. 'We noticed he had caught you, and we had to get you away *somehow*—'

Agnes's heart was pounding. It had little to do with their sprint through the keep.

'The kiss was my idea,' Olly added. 'So you may blame me, if it was unwelcome. Do not berate poor Ashel for it.'

Agnes looked between them, the feeling in her chest ebbing. It had been a ploy to remove her from Francis's company. A *good* ploy, by all means: they had successfully spirited her away, and no doubt riled him in the process. But the kiss itself was no more than a mummer's farce.

'I do not intend to berate him,' she said. 'It was . . . a keen idea. And—' Her neck was hot. She snapped her mouth shut.

'And what?' Olly said, raising an eyebrow.

Ash was looking at her a little too closely. She could not keep his gaze.

'And nothing,' she said, turning away. 'It does not matter.'

'What happened?' Ash asked.

'I tried to speak to Muriel and she shut the door in my face. I ran into Francis on my way to find you.'

The men shared a look. 'Did he do anything?' Ash asked.

Agnes shook her head. 'Nothing. Just . . . *looked* at me.' She shuddered. '*Urgh.* The sooner he is gone the better.' She dropped onto Ash's bed, flopping to her back to stare at the canopy above. 'We should remove Francis from the keep and have done with it.'

'It is a little too late for that,' Olly said.

'Unless you wish to find him now and have him hauled away,' Ash added.

Agnes laughed, despite herself. 'Perhaps.'

There was a pause. And then the bed shifted as the men sat beside her, one to either side. She heaved herself up onto her elbows just in time to see Ash and Olly looking away from one another. Ash's cheeks were red.

'The way I see it,' Olly said, glancing from Ash to Agnes, 'is that we can either follow Ash's demands and have Francis removed—'

'I did not demand that.'

'*Or* we can find some way to seek distraction until the morning, when we can attempt to find a better plan for speaking to Muriel.'

Agnes peered at Ash's mottled cheeks.

'Can I presume,' she said, speaking slowly, 'that you do not mean a game of chess?'

'Do you *wish* to play chess?' Olly asked, eyebrows raised.

'I cannot say I do,' she said. 'Ash?'

Ash glanced down at her. His eyes were dark. 'No,' he breathed. 'I think I have had enough of chess.'

Olly grinned at them. 'What a wonderful happenstance,' he said. 'So have I. Agnes . . . my Lady, my *liege*. What would you have us do instead?'

Despite now knowing it had only been an act, the memory of that kiss was still tingling on Agnes's lips. She sat up.

'Kiss each other.'

She had expected them to move – to stand, or shuffle closer to the centre of the bed. What she had not expected was for Olly to reach around her, caging her between his arms, then tug her against his chest as he placed a firm kiss to Ash's lips.

Agnes gasped, as did Ash, who clearly had not anticipated being suddenly crushed against her. She was pinned between the two men, their mouths meeting over Agnes's shoulder. She clung to Ash, Olly moving to hold on to her from behind, his hands resting at her sides.

She leaned her forehead against Ash's shoulder. Someone shifted, and then there was a soft, gentle touch against the exposed nape of her neck. Lips, mouth, *tongue*. She gasped.

'Agnes—'

Ash's voice, so therefore Olly's mouth on her skin. She gripped him tighter. Would he kiss her? Would *she* kiss *him*? Before, it had all been jokes and tests and games. But now the urge was taking her over. Her chest was tightening, the place between her legs already wet, the need growing more urgent with every touch of Olly's lips to her neck.

Her hands slipped against Ash's tunic. The fabric was in the way; it was too much, too *warm*, and without even realising what she was doing she had slipped her hands inside, flesh to hot flesh.

Ash hissed through his teeth. One of his hands made its way to her thigh.

His touch was like lightning. She wanted more. She wanted it all.

Olly pressed closer. They were kissing again, their chins digging into Agnes's shoulder. She felt every movement, heard every soft noise.

She breathed out low against Ash's chest. She wanted it – she wanted *him* – more than she had thought was possible. She had not known *any* of this was possible, not when she had lain with her previous husband, not when she had pleasured herself, not when she and Sara had played beneath the sheets.

She wanted Ash. She wanted Olly, too, although she oughtn't, knew that giving in to such lusts made her sinful.

But she was *already* sinful: sinful for being herself, for being *other* than the lines of her body. What was one more sin?

Besides, Ash was her husband. It was a sin *not* to lie with him. Why not now? Why not *here*, with Olly besides?

She could feel Ash's prick, already hard, through the fabric of his breeches.

'Ash—'

She mumbled his name, hands sliding against his skin. She drifted lower, fingers playing in the coarse hair that coated his chest and stomach, delighting in the softness of his skin, the plushness of him. She hesitated at the band of his breeches.

'You will need to go lower than that.'

Olly's voice sent shivers down her spine. She had not realised they were no longer kissing, nor that Olly knew what she was doing. She let out a breath.

'Oh?'

'Indeed,' he muttered, lips ghosting over her ear. 'Perhaps you require some assistance?'

In truth, Agnes did *not* require assistance. She knew full well how to pleasure a man, or at least coax him into hardness – not that Ash needed her help in that regard. But the idea of it, of Olly guiding her, and in turn them *both* pleasuring Ash, was too delicious to resist.

'Please,' she muttered, twisting her head around so her lips brushed the edge of his cheek.

One hand still wrapped around her middle, Olly reached between them so his hand rested on Agnes's. He guided her down to palm Ash's cock, fingers folding into the taut linen of his braies.

Agnes pressed harder, feeling as much as she could. She and Olly moved as one, hands roaming, sliding beneath the fabric. When she wrapped her fingers around his prick, it was hard and hot. Ash groaned, thrusting helplessly into her hand. Behind her, Olly laughed languidly.

'So *keen* to bed your wife, my Lord,' he said. 'Or do you intend to spend into her hand?'

Ash leaned backwards. His eyes were dark, pupils wide, lips parted. He turned his gaze upon Agnes: a question.

'Kiss her, you dolt.'

At Olly's words, they both froze. Then Ash did as he was told, capturing her mouth beneath his own. She still had her hand on his prick as he hummed into her mouth, wetting her lips with his tongue. She squeezed him a little harder. He groaned again, grabbing at her sides, hands bunching in her dress.

That *damned* dress. Not only was it *wrong* on her body, now it was in her way as well. She released Ash's cock then reached to tug it away.

'Olly,' she said, reaching behind her back, 'the ties—'

'With *pleasure.*'

He undid the ties down her back with swiftness – unsurprising, really, considering how adeptly he could undress Ash – then pulled the overdress up and over her head, tossing it aside. Beside her, Ash was also hastily undressing, pulling off his tunic and undershirt, followed swiftly by his hose, till he kneeled beside her on the bed in only his braies. She could see him through the fabric, hard and eager. She wanted him. She heaved herself onto his lap. He bundled his hands in her underdress and pulled.

Cool air kissed her skin. Ash's hands went to her hips, Olly's upon her back, coming around, cupping—

She froze, head spinning, body suddenly fraught and uncooperative. Both men noticed.

'Agnes?'

'What is—'

She covered her breasts with her hands, wrapping her arms around her chest, forcing herself flat. She had been *fine*, she had been happy, and then suddenly the old, familiar, treacherous feeling had struck her like a thunderbolt.

'My apologies,' she stuttered, 'I just . . . all of a sudden, I feel quite—'

Ash pushed himself up on his elbows.

'The same as before?' he asked, not needing to say anything else.

Agnes nodded wordlessly.

'One moment—'

The bed moved behind her. Olly was up, grabbing for their pile of discarded clothes.

'Ash,' he said, holding up an undershirt. 'How fond are you of this?'

'I believe that is *yours*,' Ash said, frowning. 'But I suppose—'

His words were drowned out by the sound of Olly tearing the undershirt in two.

'What in *God's name* are you doing?' Ash said, sitting up so suddenly that Agnes found herself nearly toppling from his lap.

Olly grinned. 'Helping.'

He slid back onto the bed behind Agnes. 'Arms up,' he said.

Every fibre of Agnes's being was urging her not to listen to him – to keep herself hidden. But he seemed to have a plan, and part of her, a little voice buried beneath the anguish, wanted to see what it was.

She lifted her arms. Olly wrapped the shredded shirt around her chest several times, positioning it *just so,* then tied it at the back with a deft, easy hand.

'How—' She ran a hand down her flattened chest then turned to face him. 'How did you manage that so *quickly*?'

'Practice.'

Now her heart was calming and the overwhelming sense of *wrongness* was easing, she was returning to herself, the position she was in atop Ash's lap.

'Better?' he asked, his hands pressed lightly against her thighs.

She nodded. She could not speak, could not find the words, so instead kissed him again, hoping he understood. He kissed her back, hard and desperate, tongue exploring her mouth. The force of it pressed her against Olly's chest, and he shifted behind her, placing himself so she was sat between his legs. He nuzzled into the divot of her neck, his breath tickling at her skin, throwing it into gooseflesh.

He put a hand upon her flattened chest. It felt *good,* felt right. When she did not twitch away, he took the other, roaming down her stomach to the place between her legs. She made an eager sound against Ash's lips, unable to bear the tension of it as Olly's fingers slid lower.

When he touched her for the first time, she was afraid it would feel wrong – the same wrongness that had filled her when she undressed. But all she felt was pleasure, the hot rush, the intense little centre of bliss where he rubbed against her.

'My *Lord . . .*'

He whispered in her ear as he slid a finger inside her. It was already nearly too much. She bucked, thrusting against Ash, arching against Olly, trapped between them in a wonderful vice.

She reached out, this time feeling more confident, pulling aside the loose fabric of Ash's braies and sliding her hand inside in a single, swift movement. Ash moaned into her mouth, then quickly backed away as he removed those too.

'Ash—' It was all she could say. 'Ash, I— *please*—'

He was upon her in a moment, his skin warm and slick. She wrapped her arms around him and clung there, holding on to him like a lifeline. His prick rubbed against her thighs.

Olly moved his hand away. Agnes gasped as he did, desperate for more. Ash pressed closer. His cock nudged at her legs, at her mound, at her cunt. She spread her legs a little more, Olly's hands upon her knees.

Ash ducked down, kissing her hard against Olly's chest. She moaned into his mouth.

When he entered her, it was slow and sure and deep. Agnes hissed, her breath coming in a low gasp. She pawed at his back, nails digging into his flesh. Behind her, Olly made a little noise. She felt his cock digging into her arse.

Ash breathed out her name. 'Agnes—'

'*Yes.*'

He thrust into her slowly, surely, his face buried in her neck, mouth open against her skin. She couldn't speak, couldn't *think* – the only thing she could focus on was the feeling of him inside her, the heat of his skin against hers, the brush of his lips.

He settled into a rhythm – although a little unsure, a little unpractised. She moved with him, trying to match him. They were *both* unpractised, she realised. She let him guide her, matching his speed. He thrust deeper; she wrapped her legs around him.

Ash's speed built, his movements becoming more urgent, his pacing faltering. Agnes gripped onto him, her nails biting into his back, her own pleasure building and coalescing. She gasped out, so close, so *close*.

'Ash—' She grabbed him harder, legs twitching. '*Ash* . . .'

He made a rumbling noise against her throat, shuddering into climax. He thrust into her one final time, body jerking into a sudden stillness as he spent. He breathed against her, gasping for air, slumped against her chest.

Agnes's body was still taut with unspent tension as Ash slowly pulled out of her. She tingled all over, her body *aflame*, eager for more.

She had almost forgotten Olly still behind her, even as she lay almost atop him. He moved beneath her with a low sort of laugh. His cock pressed against her backside.

The feel of it urged the flame in her stomach even fiercer, the heat in her core. She ground back upon him, his clothed prick rubbing against her arse. He gripped her tight, his legs twitching where they bracketed her in. He peppered her skin with little kisses, a drag of teeth, a *huff* of air as he laughed.

'My Lord,' he drawled, reaching out towards Ash. 'Would you mind *terribly* if I fucked your wife?'

The sound Ash made was barely even a word. His eyes were wide, pupils blown. He looked *debauched*.

'Only if she will have you.'

Olly grinned. 'Well, Sir Angus? Would you mind?'

Agnes's mind was sparks and lightning. Her throat and tongue were thick. 'Not in the slightest.'

'*Wonderful*.'

Olly took the lead, which suited Agnes fine. He shuffled beneath her – pulling his prick from his braies.

'You tell me if I displease you, my Lady,' he said. 'My *Lord*.'

Agnes nodded silently. Olly reached beneath her buttocks, hoisting her up. He was *strong*: she had not realised quite how strong before. The thought thrilled her even more.

He shifted, positioned her, and then – with a low noise – lowered her down onto his prick. Ash was watching them, entranced. What was he thinking, watching them like this? What was going through *his* head, to see his wife and his lover entangled, Olly's prick buried deep inside her?

'Agnes . . .'

He put his hand on her arm. He was there, as he always was, supporting her, holding her. Olly moved into her. Agnes moaned, the sound mirrored by Ash. She leaned forwards and grabbed his shoulders, shuddering as Olly thrust into her again and again.

She felt full and hot, her pleasure building, growing within her. She needed release, needed it *out*, needed it like she needed air.

'Ashel . . .' Olly stuttered, his voice cracking. 'Ashel, touch her . . .'

Yes. Agnes caught Ash's eye – *please*. He reached between her legs, one hand still supporting her, feeling for the sensitive nub above her entrance. When he found it, touch light, Agnes let out a little cry. Encouraged, Ash pressed harder, letting his fingers slip wetly over her. Agnes felt herself tightening, Olly cried out behind her.

Her climax crashed over her with such fierce pressure that her vision swam. She gasped, falling against Ash's chest, Olly still thrusting into her. He continued to move, Agnes's mouth hanging open, her breath punched out of her with each thrust.

She let out a long curse – a curse mirrored by Olly who, at last, spent with a final, jerking thrust.

For a long while, there was nothing but heat and silence. When at last Olly pulled from her, it was as if her whole body had turned boneless, her energy spent, her skin prickling. She slumped against Ash's chest, Olly swift to join them.

They lay against the covers, breathing together. No one spoke. No one needed to.

✡

It was Ash who awoke first. He rose and dressed swiftly, cursing and complaining as he went. Agnes watched him as he fettled around the room, Olly snoozing quietly beside her.

When dressed, Ash made his way to Olly's sleeping form. He gave him the lightest touch, Olly's eyes flickering open.

'Is it morning?'

'It is. I must go. I will return soon.'

Ash caught him in a kiss, which Olly drank in deeply. Agnes's chest squeezed. It was so gentle. So untouchable.

She sat up as Ash moved around the bed towards her. He hesitated as he reached her side. She reached out, taking his hand.

'Try not to be away all day.'

His fingers were rough and warm. 'I will try.'

He lingered there, as if unsure. Then he let her go, heading for the door. She watched him leave, feeling an old ache in her chest. She pushed it away. She did not need to feed it. She went to lie back down, to hide beneath the bedclothes for a little while longer, when she noticed Olly awake and wide-eyed.

'Olly?' She shuffled closer. He looked as if he were on the verge of tears. She reached out towards him. 'Whatever is the matter?'

'I cannot— I—' Olly's voice cracked. 'I cannot continue like this.'

Agnes stilled. 'Like what?'

'Like— like *this,* waiting for it all to crumble.'

Anxiety wrapped around Agnes's lungs. 'Waiting for *what* to crumble? Olly—'

'You love him.'

Agnes went still. Her heart was in her throat. 'What?'

Olly sat up, blankets falling away. 'Ash. *Your husband*. You love him.'

Agnes's mind was swirling. 'I do not—'

'Of course you do!'

Agnes's eyes were burning. 'I don't see why that should matter,' she said stubbornly.

'Why *would it not* matter?' Olly shot back.

'Because he loves *you!*'

Her shout echoed from the stone walls. The sound of her own voice shocked her. She brought her hand to her mouth, as if she could push the words back in.

'He loves *you,*' Agnes muttered, inhaling sharply. 'He loves you, and you he, and whatever my *feelings* . . . they do not matter. They *cannot* matter.'

She stared at him, hands trembling. She could not allow herself that feeling, could not indulge it, could not speak it aloud. She needed to ensure it did not exist.

'Why not?' Olly asked.

'Because—' She turned away from him, ashamed. 'Because I could not put that burden upon Ash. We have always agreed, *always*, that ours was just an arrangement, nothing else. I will not ruin that agreement by being *foolish*.' She spat out the last word like a curse. 'I care for Ash, yes,' she continued, now unable to stop. 'And I care for— I *like* you, Olly. I do. I do not want to ruin what you have. I would never be able to forgive myself.'

She finally looked around, meeting Olly's gaze. 'My feelings are what they are. And our *reality* is what it is, too. So I must simply . . . wait.'

'Wait?'

Agnes forced herself to smile. 'It will pass.'

'Agnes . . .'

'I am sorry, Olly. I really am.'

He sighed. 'You have nothing to apologise for,' he said. 'I have been *so scared* since I found Ash again. I have been terrified that he will realise he feels more strongly for you than he thinks, and that . . . that you will be the obvious choice. What if he comes to his senses and sends me away? What if he leaves me again?'

'He did not leave you before.'

'I struggle to remember that,' he said. 'After everything . . . sometimes it still feels like he may slip away.'

The bed felt very small. Agnes's reason urged her to leave. The rest of her – her soul, her heart – wanted her to stay. A thought struck her, as she threaded the edge of the blanket through her fingers.

'Oliver . . .'

Olly gave her a look. 'I mistrust you calling me that.'

'Last night,' she said slowly. 'Did you want that? Truly? I hate to think that we . . . that *I* . . . forced you into something you did not want.'

Olly looked a little surprised. 'Oh,' he said. 'No— Agnes, this you must believe: if I do not want to do something, I do not do it.'

'And last night?'

'I wanted it. Very much.'

'But . . . but everything you said! About Ash and me, about my . . . my feelings, and your fears—'

'Are apparently incomparable to the strength of my desire,' Olly said, with a half-smile. 'Believe me, I am well aware of my senselessness, where that is concerned.'

'Do you want me to stop joining you?'

'Do *you* wish to stop joining us?'

Agnes was ready to say yes. She *ought* to say yes. But she *didn't* want to. She did not want to let it go, whatever it was.

Olly noticed her silence. He shuffled closer, until their shoulders rubbed. His naked skin was warm.

'Do you?' he repeated.

Agnes gripped the blanket tighter. When she looked up, he was watching her.

'No.' It came out on a breath. 'I do not wish to stop. I . . . I enjoy what we have. What *all* of us have. I can barely understand it, but . . .'

'But you want to explore it?'

Not for the first time, Agnes was reminded how astute Olly was.

'I do. But *not* if it brings you pain. I will not do anything that makes you unhappy.'

'There we are, then,' Olly said, leaning back against the pillows with his arms above his head.

'What?'

'*You* wish to continue. As do I. And, I can only assume, so does Ash, given how willingly he partakes.'

'But—'

'*Agnes.*' His voice was so suddenly stern that Agnes turned to face him without thinking. Before she could speak, he'd closed the tiny gap between them and was kissing her.

It was swift and short. Yet still her head was reeling when he released her.

'You *are* like him,' he breathed. 'Too many worries.'

Agnes couldn't speak, lips tingling. The cocksure look slid from his face.

'Bollocks, Agnes, I should not have— Was that too much?'

She shook her head slowly. 'No,' she managed, pulling the word from her chest. 'No, just . . . I feel a little guilty. What about Ash?'

Olly visibly relaxed. 'I have kissed him plenty of times. He kissed *you* plenty last night.'

'Only because you told him too,' Agnes said bitterly.

'Only the first time,' Olly countered, grinning.

Agnes's mind was at odds with itself. She wanted to find the route out, the sensible option, a way to untangle it all. The triple threads of she and Ash and Olly, interwoven and braided and knotted. The ropes of her family, the chains of Francis, the taut string of her freedom.

Perhaps the tangle was good. Perhaps there *was* no untying it, now. And perhaps . . . perhaps she did not want to.

Chapter 29

Olly

Olly could not decide if he was stupid, or just incapable of thinking with anything other than his cock.

Likely both, he concluded, as he watched Agnes leave.

Their conversation had not truly revealed anything to him that he did not already know. He had suspected that Agnes harboured stronger feelings for Ash for some time, and her denial – and then her sad acceptance – had only proven that. He'd expected to be jealous, to be *angry* – to try and scare her off. But he hadn't. He'd opened his heart and from it had poured fear, his secret anguish.

He teetered, mind changing with every moment. Did he believe her insistence that she would never get between them, or did he fear her ruining what he and Ash already had?

It would have been easier were he not so terribly fond of her.

Were he *not* so fond of her, he would have been more inclined to see her as a villain: a witch stealing what was his. But as it was, he saw her for what she was: a little afraid, stubborn as an ass, and more concerned with Ash's feelings than her own.

And, as his overactive imagination and *treacherous* prick were reminding him, she was exceedingly fine to look upon, was desperately engaging, had shoulders he could worship and was – as a final insult to his self-control – an exceptional lover. It would have been easier were it *just* Ash, or *just* Agnes. Both of them made his head spin.

He wondered how he would behave were their roles reversed. If it was he who loved Ash from afar, in secret. Would he have kept that within his ribs as well, if he feared that to voice those feelings would lead to destruction? Would he have accepted lying together – mutually slaking desire – without the rest?

Of course he would have.

It was his fondness for her that had led him to ask Pepper for a favour the day he had arrived. Another mistake, in truth, but one he was seeing through regardless. It was a *good* idea – a sinful idea, as all the best ones were – and she had *sworn* to him that she would not stand between Ash and himself. He had to let himself believe her.

It was no great hardship for Pepper, especially given how he had little else to do, and Olly had offered him hefty pay from Ash's coffers – not that Ash knew about it. The idea had come to him some time ago, but Pepper's arrival had spurred him to act. If *anyone* knew how to make the gift he intended to give, it was Pepper.

Olly had an expert on his hands and was keen to use him.

He went to seek him out a few days after he and Agnes's conversation, to see how he was progressing. He wanted to give Pepper as much time as possible – partly to ensure he got the job done well, but also because Olly had no desire to overburden him with demands and orders. Pepper was his guest. He did not want him to think he had to earn his keep.

He found him in the great hall, to Olly's surprise, playing a complicated dice game with Sara. He watched with interest as Pepper leaned a little too close to Sara's shoulder, pointing at the dice on the table. Sara looked up with a smile, nibbling on her lip as she laughed at whatever it was Pepper was saying.

'Am I interrupting?'

Pepper and Sara turned at the intrusion. Sara's cheeks darkened.

'I have need of you, Pep.' He gave him a broad smile. 'Unless you are otherwise occupied?'

Pepper shot him a dark look, but joined him regardless, promising to return to Sara once Olly was done with him.

'You certainly seem to be settling in very well,' Olly said, as they walked away.

'Shut your mouth.'

Olly led him into the private side chamber from the main hall. With the castle so busy, Pepper had no sleeping chambers of his own, and Olly felt distinctly uneasy about taking him to Ash's chambers, not least of all because there was never any guarantee who may be in there.

'What did you wish to speak about?' Pepper said, falling into a chair with his legs dangling over one arm.

Olly rolled his eyes. 'Could it not be that I simply wish to ask how you are?'

Pepper snorted. 'Go on then: ask.'

'How are you?'

'I am very well. Now ask me what it was you *really* wanted to ask. I promised Sara I would join her for dinner.'

'It is about Agnes's gift . . .'

Pepper's eyes lit up. 'Oh, *that*.' He sat up straighter. 'Don't worry, Noll, I have not forgotten.'

'And you have not told anyone?'

'No one at all.'

'Not even Sara?'

Pepper looked for a moment like he was about to argue, before relenting. 'No,' he said. 'Not even Sara. Although . . .'

'Please do *not*,' Olly said, covering his ears, 'do *not* tell me if you are about to describe how much she enjoys it herself.'

Pepper burst into laughter. 'Rest assured, I would not know.'

'Good.'

'Yet.'

'Oh Lord.' Olly sighed. 'Have you everything you need? Let me know if there is anything you require. I am sure I can find a way to procure it for you.'

'Your earl will certainly know all the best traders.'

'I— ah . . .'

If Pepper's ears could have pricked up, they would have. 'Oh?'

'I have not told Ash,' Olly said, feeling himself flush.

'Is he not paying for it?' Pepper said, eyebrows raised. 'Or has he granted you a wage?'

'You know he has not. He has simply indicated that I may spend his coin as I see fit. *If* I see fit.'

Pepper smirked. 'So you are a kept man, then?' he drawled.

'Envy is a sin, Pep. You ought to remember that.'

Pepper shook his head. He was not incorrect: until Ash decided a role for him, Olly was wholly reliant on him. In truth, he did not mind. Such security was a relief after so long on the road, and he trusted Ash entirely. Ash would have given him *anything*, had he asked.

'I am surprised you have not told him,' Pepper said, bouncing his leg. 'Does this mean it is a gift for them both?'

Olly's face was burning, now. 'And what of it?'

'It is sweet of you,' Pepper said, smugly. 'Really. What a good . . .' He paused, frowning. 'Well, I do not know how to describe you. A good friend? A good husband? A good *lover*?'

'Two of those things I certainly am,' Olly said.

'And you are the third in every way that matters,' Pepper retorted. 'So who is this for *really?*' Pepper said. 'Agnes? Lord Barden? *You?*'

'Pep—'

'All I am saying,' Pepper drawled, 'is that you are going to great lengths to ensure that the person who is, in most people's understanding, your *rival,* feels comfortable. And can fuck your lover as well as you do.'

Olly choked on his own spit. *'Excuse me?'*

Pepper looked entirely innocent, as if he had passed comment on the weather.

'Is that *not* what you are doing?'

'Well, I—'

'But I certainly don't think you are attempting to replace yourself. No, you love him too much for that.'

'Pepper.'

'And I think – although I know you do not want to hear this – you love *her* too much for that too.'

Olly got to his feet. 'That is not true.'

'You know, I have never seen you in love,' Pepper said, as if nothing were amiss. 'I have seen you in *lust* . . . but I've never seen you give your heart away. It must be hard, giving it to two people.'

'That is not what I am doing.'

Pepper raised his eyebrows. 'Is it not?'

'No. I—' Olly took a swift step back. 'This conversation is over.'

He reached the door as Pepper called after him: 'So is that to say you wish me to stop work on Agnes's gift?'

Olly stopped with his hand resting against the doorframe. 'No.' And then he strode away.

✡

Pepper's words nagged at him over the next few days. He found himself shrinking away – from Ash, from Agnes, from the life they had tentatively built around each other. When he looked at Agnes across the hall, when he saw her lean against Ash as they walked, when he watched her curled against the sheets of Ash's bed – of *their* bed – in deep sleep, he thought of Pepper's words.

He thought of them in burning clarity when they lay together, when her lips parted in a sigh that could have been Ash's name or his, when her hands brushed against his skin, through his hair. When Agnes watched, lingering beside them as Ash and Olly worked each other to pieces.

Who is it really for?

He didn't know. He thought he had known, but Pepper had thrown that certainty into disarray.

Whatever his feelings, they – like Agnes's – were unimportant. Francis was still beneath their roof, Agnes's family were still being difficult, and no progress at all had been made towards discovering their involvement in the attempt on Ash's life. However frustrating it was for him and Ash, the toll it was taking on Agnes was undeniable. She wavered between distress and anger every time she so much as *looked* at Francis, and as the days passed she became plagued with headaches and sickness, her food untouched, retiring to sleep early more often than not. She returned to her own bed, something that surprised both him and Ash.

It made it harder to deny what Pepper had said, too. He *cared*. He worried. On more than one occasion he and Ash had hovered outside her door, not knowing what to do.

Life in the keep continued as normal – as much as it could be described as normal – with the unwelcome presence of Agnes's family and Francis. With no progress made on the matter of the attack, he was truly losing his mind.

It was over a week after he had spoken to Pepper that his unsure grip upon it was threatened to be lost entirely. They were sitting for a morning meal, preparing to ride out for the afternoon, when the outer doors to the great hall burst open.

Olly did not recognise the man who strode from the blinding sunlight towards the table. But beside him, Ash stiffened, his knife clattering down. Before Olly could ask, Francis – sat beside him – was on his feet.

'Hugh!' he bellowed. 'How wonderful to see you!'

Chapter 30

Ash

'Please, join us, let me fetch you a drink—'

Ash's world was crumbling around him.

Francis gestured to a serving girl then sat back down, face smug. His unwelcome guest took the seat beside him without being bidden to sit.

Ash stared at Hugh across the table. His uncle smiled at him, expression sharp.

'Francis said he would be in the keep,' he said, taking the mug from the serving girl. 'I happened to be in Skeldale and thought I should like to pay you all a visit.'

'Indeed,' Ash growled, teeth clenched. 'I had not expected to see you again so soon. How is Simon?'

The last time Ash had seen Simon his face had been dripping with blood. He wondered if he had broken his nose.

'Simon is doing very well,' Hugh said. 'He is courting a lovely girl from the west. We are very pleased for him.'

Ash struggled with a smile. 'You must send him my best wishes.'

The only solace was the mug in front of him. He saw off the wine and refilled it with haste. Olly tensed beside him, but nothing was said.

Behave.

Was that Olly's voice, in his head? Was it Agnes's? Was it his father's? He could not tell. He did not care; he drowned it with wine.

By the time the meal was over, Ash's head was gently spinning. He was aware of Agnes and Olly sharing a look around him. It was Agnes who grabbed his arm, pulling him up.

'Ash,' she said, 'I think I need some air. Will you walk with me?'

Something his fogged brain could recognise – Agnes was unwell. She had joined them for the meal, despite how tired she looked. He stood, refusing to let her down.

'Thank you, love,' she said. 'Oliver, would you . . . ?'

Olly stood at his other side, and together they headed out into the open air. They only released him after they had crossed beneath the portcullis and away from the castle, their only companions the spring breeze and the determined little birds swooping above them. Ash leaned against the outer wall, watching them. He felt as if his bones would meld into the cold, hard stone.

'I cannot believe Hugh is here,' he muttered. 'This is no coincidence.'

'I agree.' Olly sighed. 'Francis must have sent word to him to come.'

'That must have been why he has spent so much time in Skeldale,' Agnes said. 'No doubt they have been meeting since he arrived.'

Ash shook his head. 'He seeks to undermine me,' he said. 'And he *will*, I know he will. Whenever he speaks to me I am reminded of what I am. A mad, angry, violent—'

'You are none of those things,' Olly snapped. 'Ash, do *not* allow him to make you think like that. Hugh is a bastard. He is a bitter, twisted little man. He has fed Francis a pack of lies through spite alone.'

'And through that spite encouraged somebody to attempt to kill me,' Ash said.

'You think they worked together?' Agnes asked.

'I cannot say,' Ash admitted. 'If Hugh wanted the title, he would need both me *and* Raff to be gone. I cannot imagine him trying anything so horrible.'

'Let us hope you're correct.' Olly reached out, gripping his arm. 'Do not let him win. Do not let him get under your skin, Ash. You are better than him.'

Ash did not believe that. The darkness was creeping back in. 'Olly—'

'You *are.* Please, Ashel. Do not let him make you believe otherwise.'

Ash gave him a weak smile, saying nothing.

There was a leaden ball of dread in his stomach. A rock that had solidified as he walked, turning his insides hard. Spring sunlight brushed his cheek, but it felt cool, despite the brightness.

It was too much. Hugh would be waiting for him when he returned, Francis at his side, both men aware of what he really was, in his core, in the horrid dark centre of his soul.

If only Francis's plan had played out how he had intended. If only Olly had pressed the knife deeper. Ash stared ahead at nothing at all.

The familiar feeling was like greeting an old friend. He looked at his companions – his wife and his lover, the two he had vowed his life to – and buried it down.

Chapter 31

Agnes

It was nearly mid-morning by the time Agnes finally stirred. She had retired early, feeling unwell, the churning in her gut made even more fierce by Hugh's sudden and unpleasant arrival. Her stomach knotted to consider how she had left Ash with him; but at least he still had Olly by his side.

She rolled over. The bed beneath her transformed into a great, open, empty plane. She was grateful that they had left her alone during her illness – *especially* these past few days – but the loss was gnawing at her.

She rose reluctantly and headed to the basin at the side of the room. She splashed the cool water on her face, then got to work cleaning herself up. As she had expected, the bloodied marks on the linen rags she pulled from between her legs were light, near invisible. That was one less burden upon her, at least, although her head still pounded.

She had often felt out of sorts when confronted with things she did not wish to confront – she had been so anxious before meeting Nicholas that she had spent a full day and night vomiting into the basin beneath her bed – but rarely did it feel so all-encompassing.

At least Francis, and her family, would be gone soon. And

then there would be no reason for her to ever see Francis again. That thought alone was enough to soothe her.

Regardless, her stomach still churned, so she quickly dressed and headed down into the kitchens. Whilst there was nothing at all she could do about Francis's continued presence, she *could* deal with the blasted nausea.

The kitchen was, as ever, a hive of activity. One of the girls showed her where Joan kept the various dried herbs, and soon Agnes had a little square of cloth bursting with fragrant stalks and leaves. She threw them into a pot of wine to stew over the fire, then finally crept back to her chambers, a warm jug in her hand.

Not wanting to return to bed, she sipped at the wine, vaguely making plans for the next iteration of her cuirass. The medicinal drink helped immensely, and soon the nauseous feeling had settled.

There was a sharp knock at the door. Before she could call out, her unspoken question was answered for her.

'It is me!' That was Sara's voice. She didn't wait to be asked to enter, opening the door and sliding quickly in. 'Are you well? Pepper told me you were in the kitchens looking for medicine.'

So she was the subject of gossip, now? Agnes supposed she could not blame Sara – she and Pepper were growing terribly close.

'Much,' Agnes said truthfully. 'But it is just a passing sickness.'

Sara gave her a long look as she sat opposite her.

'What?'

'Agnes.'

Agnes sighed. '*What?*'

'I have known you *far* too long for you to think you can simply *not tell me*.'

'Tell you what?'

'Are you with child?'

Agnes nearly choked on her mouthful of wine. 'Sara!'

'What? Are you not?'

'Of course not!' Agnes said. 'My bleeds came on a few days ago.'

Sara seemed unconvinced. 'You must admit it seemed terribly likely, given how unwell you were.'

Agnes knew she was right. It would not have been *impossible* for her to be with child. When lying with Ash and Olly, she had not been thinking about begetting children, only chasing pleasure.

'Perhaps,' she admitted at last.

What if she *had* been with child? She had Ash's stalwart support. When her body felt wrong, he soothed her. He allowed her to be *herself*. But his support was nothing compared to the horrors of her own mind. She forced herself to imagine if she were pregnant: the changes she would go through, the new form her body would take, the final and irrevocable way she would be named *woman*.

She had never had to face the reality of what bearing a child would entail. That was ignorant of her, she now realised. That lurching, skin-crawling feeling was already threatening to overwhelm her. She dug her nails into her palms. Had she missed her bleeds, she knew how to bring them on once more. But could she make that choice that without Ash's knowledge?

She needed to talk to Ash and Olly. Damn Hugh and Francis: this was more important, especially if they continued to lie together. It was not a conversation she relished. But it had to be done.

'Sara . . .'

Sara took her hand. She must have been closer than Agnes realised. 'Are you well?'

'I must speak to Ash.'

She headed from her chambers intending to seek them out. As she walked the corridor, she heard a door down the hall slam – the guest chambers within which Muriel was sleeping. Agnes paused.

She could not imagine bringing a child into the mess of her family: a baby whose grandparents hated their father, who may have tried to have him killed. Would a child even be *safe* in such a family?

There was another conversation she needed to have before she could seek out Ash and Olly. For the first time, it was the preferable choice. She strode towards the guest chamber door, knocked once, then shoved it open.

'Agnes, what *are* you doing—' Muriel spluttered, as Agnes pushed past her.

'I need to speak to you,' Agnes said.

'Can this not *wait*?' Muriel huffed.

'No,' Agnes said. 'It cannot.'

Muriel hesitated a moment, then relented. 'Fine. What is it?'

Agnes sat on the chest at the foot of the bed. 'I need to know if you have heard anything, *anything*, about the attack on the road,' she said.

A small line appeared between Muriel's brows. 'The attack on Lord Barden?'

'Yes. We . . .' Agnes took a breath, unsure of how much of the truth she could trust Muriel with. 'We suspect that the attack was no coincidence. It was planned.'

Muriel did not seem concerned. 'Are not all crimes planned?' she said. 'A wealthy party, travelling by road? It is not unusual to attract bandits.'

Agnes drummed her fingers against the chest. Soon enough, it would all come out: it was not a secret that could be maintained forever. She needed to trust Muriel, for Ash's sake. She saw the love he had for his siblings: perhaps she could find it with her own as well.

She took a deep, calming breath.

'I believe Francis arranged the attack,' she said, keeping her voice steady. 'As a way to prevent the marriage.'

Muriel's face was entirely blank. And then she barked a harsh, discordant laugh.

'Do not be *absurd*, Aggie! What, you claim that Francis paid this bandit to have Lord Barden killed?'

'That is precisely what I claim.'

'That is *madness*.' Muriel began to pace the room. 'You cannot simply accuse a man—'

'I am not accusing him,' Agnes said, 'Not yet. All I need to know is if Mother and Father—'

'You think *they* were in league with him, too?' Muriel looked horrified. 'This has gone too far. You cannot say such things about Francis just because you do not like the man! He has only ever been kind to you, and *this* is how you repay him?'

Agnes closed her eyes. She focused on the feeling of the old wood beneath her fingers, calming herself, before speaking again.

'This is not a baseless accusation,' she said slowly. 'And that is all I will say on the matter. I just need to know if you have been made aware of *anything*, if Mother and Father have been acting strangely, or if they reacted oddly when the news reached them.'

Muriel sighed. She looked almost sad. 'Agnes, this is absurd.'

'*Please*, Muriel.'

Muriel looked at her like she was a stranger.

'You are *wrong*,' she said. 'Mother and Father were horrified to hear of the attack. They have been behaving precisely as they always do. Which is far more than I can say about you.'

Agnes tried to remember the letter. She tried to remember Pepper's words, Olly's confessions. She was not mad. This was *true*.

'Muriel . . . if we could *talk* . . .'

Muriel took a step away. She opened the door. 'I think it is best if you leave.'

'But there is still so much to—'

'You should leave, Agnes. We can discuss this with Mother and Father later.'

Agnes's stomach turned to lead. 'No,' she said quickly. 'Do not mention this to them. If Francis learns—'

'*Enough*.' Muriel stood aside. 'When they return we will talk. But *now*, I need you to go.'

There was nothing else to be done. She stood, then moved towards Muriel to leave her with a parting embrace, at least.

Muriel swiftly stepped back.

Agnes did not chase her. She nodded, eyes down, and left the room.

Chapter 32

Ash

Perhaps, Ash thought, upon reflection, hosting a wedding feast had been a calming and pleasurable experience. It was, at least, preferable to playing host to Laurence Forrett, Francis and Hugh.

They had spent the morning hunting, although the sport was in name alone. It had been declared a *men's* outing: Agnes had been barred, which Ash found deeply irritating not only because of Agnes's unique relationship to manliness, but also because it meant she was not there to deflect Hugh or her family's odious friend for him. She had brightened this past day or so, and he resented wasting time when he could have been with her and Olly instead.

After their so-called hunt, they had been sequestered into the side chamber. Francis and Laurence had gone to fetch more wine, leaving Ash and Olly alone with Hugh.

'And how *is* your wife?' Hugh said, as if sensing his thoughts.

'She is much improved,' Ash said. 'It was only a passing sickness.'

Hugh laughed derisively. Olly bristled at Ash's side.

'May God grant me the foolishness of youth,' he said. 'Did your father teach you nothing?'

'Excuse me?'

'Sickness is one of the first signs a woman is with child.'

Ash's skin went cold. 'What?'

Hugh glanced at him. 'Ah, I see you truly had not considered it. Apologies if I may have ruined any surprises.'

Ash couldn't see his face. His vision swam.

'I . . . I—' His ears rang, muffling all sound.

'Ash?'

The room fell away, leaving only fog. He could hear shouting. *Screaming,* coming from the very walls themselves. He was a child, a tiny child, and the keep was full of panic.

His mother had screamed when Raff was born, too, but that had been different – different in a way his child's mind couldn't describe. *This* screaming bit into him, shot into his bones, twisting and cruel and horrible. But the silence, the silence after had been worse. A ringing, empty, sucking silence broken only by the whining cry of his baby sister.

It rang in his ears, echoes of the past and the future. There were binds around his chest, squeezing the air out of his lungs. All that was left was fear, blind, naked fear, vibrating up his spine and into his skull.

'Ash?'

That voice was another memory. In the fog, he couldn't quite recall if it really *was* just a memory, or if it was real. If it had ever been real.

'What is happening?'

That voice was not as familiar, but he knew he should fear it. He flinched back.

'I do not know . . . *Ash.*'

He couldn't breathe, let alone talk. He heard his name again, through rushing ears. A hand wrapped around his own.

'I cannot lose her,' he managed, gripping tight. 'I will not—I cannot let it happen. *God,* Agnes, I am sorry—'

'Ash, *breathe*. It is me; it is Oliver. You are safe.'

Oliver. His Olly. He was a part of this, too. He was tied up in them. How would Olly survive it, when she died? Would they have each other to cling to, or would the loss drive them apart?

'Nothing has happened,' Olly said calmingly. 'It's all right, Ash. Really. Nothing has—'

'But it *will*.'

He could picture it so clearly – the sombre castle, the empty sky above, the red sheets, the red floor, the red hands of his father. *His* hands, coated in that same violent hue.

'I have killed her,' Ash said. 'It is too late . . .'

'Do not say that,' Olly whispered, gripping his arm. '*You*—' He must have been talking to Hugh. 'Fetch Lady Agnes. Alert her that Ash is unwell, and bid she find us.'

'But—'

'*Do it*.'

A door closed. After a moment – after an age – Ash felt himself slowly coming back, aware of the hard floor beneath him. Had he fallen? He could not remember.

'He's gone,' Olly said.

Thank God. Ash leaned back against the chair, breathing through his nose as the spinning stopped. The air smelt fragrant and sweet. Someone had hung herbs to dry beside the fire: lavender and sage. He pulled away some of the lavender, twirling it between his palms, crushing the tiny little purple buds beneath his fingers. He sniffed at the overwhelmingly aromatic scent.

Olly was right. Lavender *did* give him a headache.

He tossed it aside. Olly lowered himself beside him and leaned his head on his shoulder.

'I do not want her to die,' Ash said at last.

It was all he could manage, his voice strangled around his own tongue. Olly went still.

'You *knew* you would need to beget heirs,' he said cautiously. 'Did this not worry you then?'

Ash shook his head, numbly. 'I . . . I never assumed I would be so involved in the matter. I thought . . . I thought she would resent me, or merely tolerate me, and so it would not matter if I was there or not. It is not as if— not as if I would have feelings for her. Not as if I had so much to fear.'

'"Her"?' Olly repeated. 'Do you mean Agnes?'

Ash shook his head again, more fiercely now. 'No, not Agnes. Just . . . *her*. My wife.'

'But she *is* your wife.'

'She is. But I did not expect to care . . . not like this.'

Olly took his hand. They sat in silence until Ash's heart calmed.

Chapter 33

Olly

Was that a confession? Olly could not say. But it *felt* like one. He had never seen Ash so scared.

Ash had spoken only briefly of his mother and her death, the topic always out of reach, the subject one that Ash refused to entertain. Olly knew she was dead, and he knew how she had died. But he had never asked, never wanted to risk Ash's ire *by* asking.

Now he wished he had. If he had, he could have understood this more.

The fear had consumed Ash. It had rendered him utterly insensible, his skin flushed and sweaty, his chest heaving. Olly had only been able to sit and watch as Ash had muttered about being the cause of Agnes's death.

God, if only he had asked sooner. If only he had thought to ask sooner.

Nobody who did not love someone would have that reaction to hearing that they were doomed to die. *Nobody.* Ash loved her, and she him, and—

And Olly needed to work out where he fit into that.

He wondered if his own reaction to Hugh's assumption had been its own kind of confession. Not horror, not *anger* that Ash and Agnes's marriage would soon be sealed so conspicuously, but something far brighter than that. Something bordering on joy.

Olly was not stupid; both Ash *and* he had lain with Agnes, both of them had spent inside her. In flesh alone, any child she bore could be from either of them. There was no way of knowing, not unless the babe was born with blue eyes and yellow hair. Yet that did not seem to matter, not in any material way.

He had never considered the idea of children. As a youth, he had expected to gain his knighthood and spend out the rest of his days at Ash's side. After his return from France, the thought was never one he entertained, taking pains to ensure nothing he did would beget children. It would be too cruel to both them and the woman who would be their mother.

And now the idea had been thrust upon him, a new world in which it was no longer a vague thought for the future but a more certain promise of what it held. It was shocking – but shocking like an unexpected gift, like reaching the peak of a hill and seeing out across a beautiful landscape one had not realised was there. Like waking from a good dream to see your lover sleeping beside you.

Like waking to see both of them sleeping beside you.

He dared not voice this aloud, not while Ash was so anxious. Once Ash had calmed, perhaps Olly could infect him with his own joy. But before he could even try, he needed to make Ash safe. He could not do it alone.

'Stay here,' he said. 'I am going to fetch Agnes.'

Ash barely registered he had spoken. He bolted from the room and barrelled directly into Hugh, who was lingering outside. He caught his eye as Olly hurried past.

'What a shame you had to witness that, young man,' he drawled. 'To see your lord's nature writ so terribly.'

Olly halted so quickly it was like a wall had sprung up in front of him.

'Don't you *dare*—' Olly growled, advancing upon Hugh. 'Do not speak in such a way. This man is *scared* for his *wife*. Do you understand that? Do you understand why? Can you not think why he may fear this, considering what happened to his mother?'

Hugh, to Olly's surprise, backed away. It was as if no one had ever challenged him before.

'He is unstable—'

'He is *afraid*! My God, man, have you no care for your own blood?'

'But—'

'Lord Barden was cut down in war, watched his closest friend die, *heard* his mother die, and now fears the same fate for his wife! Do you not see how those things could affect a man? Could make him less than his best self?'

Hugh had gone quiet. 'It is no excuse—'

'No,' Olly spat. 'It is no excuse to treat your own nephew so terribly, or to say such *heinous things* about his siblings.' Hugh looked shocked. 'Yes, Ash told me what he heard. Frankly, I think you should be pleased that all he did was send Simon home with a few bruises.'

'It was *more* than a few—'

'Do you know what your *venom* has done?' Olly demanded. 'I do not know if you are cruel, or stupid, or both, to put into motion the attack on Ash on the road.'

Hugh frowned. 'I do not see how that is relevant.'

'Do not play the fool with me,' Olly said. 'Ash may be keen to assume you would not stoop so low, but *I* have no such qualms.'

'I have no idea what you are—'

'It was a deliberate attempt on Ash's life, and you well know it!'

Hugh went silent. His mouth opened and shut like a great fish. 'What?'

'You heard me, you bastard.'

'An attempt on his— He was trying to *kill him*?'

'He was *paid* to kill him!'

Olly hissed the last words. Hugh had gone very pale.

'I had no idea,' he mumbled. 'I did not . . . I had no idea . . .'

Olly launched forwards and grabbed Hugh by his collar. '*Swear it.*'

'No . . . I . . . never. I swear to you, I would never— That is *a crime*. That is the worst crime, to kill one's own kin? No, no, I swear I did not—'

Olly stepped back. Hugh slumped down, rubbing at his throat.

'You are sure?' he breathed.

'Entirely sure. The attacker was sent to kill Ash in the woods like a dog.'

'*Why?*'

'Because of *your* poison. Your stupid, spiteful words dripped into the wrong ears.'

'What— but, who—'

'Francis mac Cainnich.' Olly turned to see Agnes standing behind him. She must have been alerted by the noise and come to see what was happening. 'Francis mac Cainnich paid a man to find Ash and have him killed.' She strode forwards like a warrior. Olly stepped out of her way. 'Francis was told – *by you* – that Ash is a cruel, violent, unpredictable man. And as he already had his eyes set on his *prize* . . .' she sneered the last word '. . . he used your lies to ensure it would be his.'

Hugh gaped at her. 'I had no idea. I did not know—'

'No,' Agnes said. 'You did not know. You did not know that

spreading spite and hate could get your nephew killed. And yet it nearly did.'

'Ash is a good man,' Olly said. 'He is *loved* by his allies, not merely tolerated. Whatever you think of him, whatever you *thought* of him, you will keep it behind your teeth where it belongs.'

Hugh nodded, wordlessly. 'Yes, I . . . I did not mean to—'

'No,' Agnes said. 'You *did*. You meant to spread doubt about him, to turn his allies against him, to seclude him just for the bitterness in your own soul. You just did not mean to get him killed. The difference is not so great as you seem to believe.'

'But—'

'I would advise you to leave my keep, Hugh Barden,' Agnes said. 'Before you can cause any more harm.'

'May I speak to Ash? To apologise?'

'I can pass on any message you may have for him,' Agnes said. 'If he wishes to speak to you, we will send word.'

Hugh looked between them. 'Tell him . . . tell him I apologise. And pass on my congratulations. To you both. I will pray for your health.'

He left with his head down, at speed. Olly watched him go, glad to see the back of him.

'What happened?' Agnes asked, once he had disappeared. 'Hugh sent a servant to say Ash had been taken unwell, but did not say anything else.'

'It was a sort of . . . attack,' Olly said, unsure what else to call it. 'He lost himself. He could not breathe; his eyes were glazed. I think he could hear things.'

Recognition dawned on Agnes's face. 'I have seen that before.'

'You have? When?'

'When you attacked him.'

Olly swallowed back the urge to vomit.

'Olly . . . What did Hugh mean?' she asked.

'What?'

'He wanted to pass on his congratulations. What did he mean by that?'

'He . . . we . . .' Olly closed his eyes. Took a breath. 'Agnes. Are you with child?'

She stared at him. Her expression drifted, like clouds. Then she grabbed his arm and led him back into the side chamber where Ash was beside the fire, staring at nothing. She knelt beside him, taking his hand. Olly sat on his other side, waiting.

At last, she spoke, loud enough that both of them could hear.

'I am not.'

Oh. Olly was not sure why it felt so terrible.

Ash finally looked at her. 'Are you sure?'

She nestled closer, leaning her head against his knee. 'I am entirely sure.'

Ash said nothing. Olly took his hand. They sat together in silence.

Olly wondered if they were feeling the same sense of grief that he was.

✡

A heaviness seemed to have settled over the keep. Once Ash was calm, Agnes hurried off to see if Francis had been made aware of Ash's attack, ready to smooth the situation over. Olly led Ash upstairs, leaving him in his chambers. Ash asked him to fetch Raff. Olly could only comply.

He felt oddly hollow as he headed from Raff's room. He had

only been a father for a few moments. Yet it was as if something had been taken from him.

Would he have been a father? In the mess of it all, where would he have stood? Would he have been second again to the holy union, an outsider, cursed to watch a child grow up without him?

It was too much of a burden to place on Ash's shoulders, and to speak to him *or* Agnes would lead to conversations that Olly was not ready for. Which left one person.

Pepper would be smug about being right – if he even *was* right – but he was open and honest and would tell Olly if he were being a fool about the whole thing.

It was pure luck that he found Pepper in the servants' quarters, even if he were not alone. Sara's face snapped around as Olly entered, blushing.

'Pepper?' he said, trying to ignore whatever scene he had wandered into. 'I wondered if we could talk.'

Pepper grinned devilishly and cast a quick glance towards Sara.

'Important business, my Lady,' he said with a wink. 'We will speak later.'

As they made their way to an empty room, Olly resisted the urge to tease him. It would make him a hypocrite, given his own rather tenuous situation. Pepper seemed to realise this as he shut the door behind him.

'Noll? Are you all right? I heard that Lord Barden was taken ill, but I did not realise . . . Is he well?'

Olly leaned against a wall, staring at his feet. He felt Pepper's eyes upon him.

'I do not know how to phrase it . . .'

'Then you are a poor minstrel. Phrase it *badly*, if you must.'

Olly sighed. 'You are aware that Agnes has been unwell? We – Ash and I – realised that she could be with child.'

Finally, he looked up. Pepper was staring at him.

'And is she?'

'No.'

Pepper chewed on his lower lip. 'I . . . am sorry to hear that,' he said.

Olly had been expecting Pepper to laugh or say that Olly had been lucky. He had been expecting a quick dismissal – not this. He was not sure what to do with it.

'Thank you,' he said quietly. 'Although I am not sure if I am allowed your sympathy.'

'Noll. You *have* my sympathy, whether or not you believe you are allowed it. Was Ash unhappy to learn she could be with child?'

'He was *scared,*' Olly said. 'I do not think he was angry or unhappy, but after his mother—' He took a deep breath. 'His mother died while Lily was being born. I do not think he realised how deep that wound runs.'

Pepper nodded. 'I really am sorry, Noll.'

Olly realised his eyes were wet with tears. Pepper came to stand beside him, wrapping an arm around his shoulders. Olly slumped into the embrace. Pepper rubbed a hand up and down his back.

'You need to talk to them,' he said, after Olly's shoulders had stopped shaking.

'I do not know how.'

'You will find a way,' Pepper said. 'You are *Noll.* You've always been able to find a way.'

Olly smiled into Pepper's shoulder. He hoped that he was right.

Chapter 34

Ash

Ash needed to get up, but he could not quite find the energy to move. Litillwitte snored beside the chair, his legs in the air, his paws twitching.

He felt vaguely hollow. The panic had passed, leaving him empty.

There was a knock at the door.

'Enter.'

Raff appeared, a jug in one hand and mugs in the other. 'May I come in?'

Ash sat up. Raff shut the door behind him with his foot and sat beside him. He lifted the jug towards Ash: an offering. Ash shook his head.

'How do you feel?' Raff said, pouring himself a drink.

'Tired.'

Raff gave a brief laugh. 'But otherwise all right?'

'Otherwise all right,' Ash parroted.

'What happened?' Raff said.

Ash looked at his fingers, already regretting refusing a drink.

'I panicked,' he said.

'Why?'

'I thought Agnes was with child.' There they were again: the echoes of screams. 'Were you too young to remember Lily's birth?'

Raff's lips were tight. 'I remember.'

The memory surrounded them like a soap bubble. The shared loss. The shared horror.

'I thought— I *knew* that it would happen to Agnes, too. It was as if she were doomed, and there was nothing I could do to save her.' He took a breath. 'I do not want her to die. I do not want to be the *reason* why she dies.'

Raff reached over, wrapping a warm hand around Ash's wrist. 'She will not,' he said.

'How can you know that?' Ash snatched his arm away. 'None of us know. It is too dangerous, I should have never—'

'*Ash.*'

'Do not pretend it is not true. If she dies, it will be *my* doing. I should—'

His words lodged in his throat. *I should remove myself, to save her.* Those thoughts again returned to tempt him.

'Ash?'

He was shaking, his fingers numb. 'I thought it was better,' he said, lips tingling. 'I thought *I* was better. Why am I still— Why do I still want it?'

Raff stared at him. 'Want what?'

Ash clasped his hands together, trying to stop the shaking. 'To die.'

There was a heavy, horrible silence. Ash immediately regretted letting the words pass his lips. He should have kept them locked in his mouth, kept them inside his head, where they belonged. He should have never voiced it aloud, for fear that if it did come to pass, they would know the terrible sin he had committed. It would tar *all* of them, the whole family doomed.

'Raff, I did not—'

Raff threw himself forwards, wrapping his arms around Ash's shoulders. The sudden onslaught of care was too much, and Ash attempted to push him off, but Raff clung harder.

'I am so sorry,' he said, refusing to let go. 'I did not realise. I thought—' A breath. 'I did not know.'

'You should be cursing my name.'

'Never, Ash. Never. After France, you always seemed so close to an edge I could not see. I did not realise you were still there. I should have been able to tell.'

'You have been rather busy,' Ash said. 'After running away and getting shot.'

Raff leaned back. Tears clung to his cheeks. '*I should have realised,*' he repeated. 'If there is anything I can do for you, *anything*, you only have to say. I— *we* will stay here with you as long as you need.'

'But—'

'But?'

'I did all of this for you. You and your hostage.'

Raff frowned at him. 'What do you mean?'

'I knew that if I remained unwed and childless when I died' – Raff made a little noise, which Ash ignored – 'the title would pass to you. And you would become obliged to marry and have heirs *yourself*, to avoid the title falling into Hugh's hands, and to ensure Father's legacy could continue. And do not *argue*,' he added, spotting Raff's expression. 'We both know you would have felt like you had no choice in the matter. You would have married and had children and ruined the happiness you have worked so hard to achieve.'

'Ash . . .'

'I do not know what being forced to do that would do to you, *or* to Penn. I do not know how you could survive it. And I could not—' He took a great, gasping breath. 'I could not go without knowing you were safe from that fate.'

'So finding a wife . . .' Raff said, disbelieving, 'you did it just so I would not have to do it myself?'

'Yes.' Ash nodded. 'And ruin what you have with Penn.'

Raff's expression shattered. He lunged forwards again with another hug. 'Thank you,' he said.

'You deserve it and more, for all you have done for me,' Ash said.

Raff leaned back, taking his hands. 'You must promise me, Ash,' he said, 'that you will not go. Even if Agnes *does* have children.'

It was too huge a promise. 'I can try,' he said.

Another tear rolled down Raff's face. 'That is enough,' he said. 'Do you still feel the same? That the marriage is just to ensure heirs and the title and *my* stupid happiness?'

Ash looked down at their clasped hands. He shook his head silently.

'Do you love her?' Raff asked. 'Do you love her as you love Oliver?'

Ash's breath caught in his lungs.

'Raff . . . is it even possible? Can you love . . . can you be *in love* with two people?'

The silence was deafening. Raff's face was unreadable. The longer they stayed there trapped in that silence – seconds that felt like minutes – the surer Ash was that Raff thought him cruel, or insane, or some kind of monster. Raff, who had such a steadfast devotion to his own love, his *only* love. He would tell Ash what he already knew: that he could *not* love two people. That he would have to choose. That his broken mind was broken in this, too.

Eventually, Raff took a breath.

'I do not know,' he said. '*Are* you?'

*

Ash emerged from his chambers not long after Raff left him, the hound at his heels, seeking Olly and Agnes. He found them in the hall, trapped in conversation with Agnes's family. They looked up when he entered, Olly's face breaking into a smile and Agnes's into relief.

'Ash,' she said, wrapping her arms around him. 'Are you well?'

Ash looked down at her. His heart felt full and tight and painful. 'As I can be.' He shot a look towards her family, still sitting with Francis. 'Do they know?'

Agnes sighed. 'Some of it.'

She looked so *exhausted* with the whole affair. Not angry, not saddened – just worn, spread too thin.

Enough.

Ash took a step away from the long table.

'My dear family—' The Forretts looked up at him as one, even Francis pausing in his conversation with Muriel to peer at him. 'I would like to speak to you. In my solar, if you please.'

Everyone rose. Olly rushed to Ash's side.

'What are you doing?'

'What needs to be done,' Ash said. 'Agnes?'

She gave him a hard look. 'Do it.'

Ash strode forwards, leading them into his solar. Before he could stop him, Francis threw himself carelessly into the high-backed chair behind the table. *Ash's* chair. No: Ash's *father's* chair, from where he had ruled his lands and attempted, often without success, to teach Ash to be a good man.

'So—' Ash began.

'My Lord.' Francis cut him off. 'I had wondered, in fact, if I may speak to you first.'

Ash did not like this. But he would allow Francis a chance to say his piece: perhaps he would incriminate himself after all.

'Yes?'

'I worry that we have no trust between us,' Francis said. 'Which saddens me greatly, considering how close Agnes and I are.'

Agnes snorted incredulously. Francis ignored her.

'I *do* hope we can become friends, Barden,' Francis droned. 'I know Agnes better than many. She is spirited, that is true. I can ensure you know best how to tame that spirit.'

Olly tensed at Ash's side.

'Meaning?' Ash said.

'Meaning that she has a sharp tongue, and an . . . active imagination,' said Francis. 'One would hate for either to cause her problems.'

He knows, Ash thought. *He knows that we know what he did.*

'One would,' Ash said, pretending to agree. 'Although I cannot think what you could possibly mean by that.'

'She can get carried away,' Francis said. 'Especially regarding those she does not hold in high esteem.'

Ash said nothing. Francis clearly wanted a response: he would not give it to him.

'I just wish to ensure she does not find herself in trouble.'

Further silence. Francis was beginning to twitch. 'Especially important,' he said, now leaning closer, 'considering how much she courts trouble already, given her oddities in her choice of dress.'

'Francis, *please*.' Agnes glared at him.

'Whatever is the matter?' Francis continued smugly. 'I was so shocked to learn that you had not grown out of that distasteful habit. I must ensure your husband is aware of it too, so he can put a stop to it. A woman in London was tried and punished not so long ago for dressing in such a way. You ought to remember your sex.'

'You do not know what you are talking about.'

'I am only telling you these things so you may be a good wife. I am quite sure your new husband would agree with me. He does not need his wife parading about like a degenerate.'

'Enough.'

Francis fell silent, yet unafraid. Ash remembered all the things Francis had been told about him – the lies about his nature, about his violence, about his madness. He rounded on him, towering above him in the high-backed chair that was not his.

'Shut your *stupid* mouth before I shut it for you.'

'What—'

'That is my *wife*.' Ash snarled the word out, letting the rage fill him, letting it spill out of his mouth. 'And you will treat her as such.'

Francis's mouth hardened. 'If she dresses and behaves like a degenerate sodomite, then I see no reason why I should not treat her as *that* instead.'

Ash snapped. He reached down, grabbed the collar of Francis' doublet and hauled him to his feet. And then *everyone* was on their feet, Agnes behind him, her family behind Francis.

'Get out of my castle,' Ash said. 'Get off my lands. *Now*.'

'What in God's name do you think you are—'

'Oliver!'

Olly was by his side in an instant, one hand on the knife at his belt, looking gleeful.

'Yes, my Lord?'

'Get this man out of my sight.'

'With pleasure.'

Francis spluttered out the start of an argument, but Olly was already on him, pinning his arm behind his back and shoving him out of the room.

'You cannot—'

'I can, in fact,' Olly said, twisting a little harder. 'Come, now, let's not have any problems.'

'Agnes, *please*—' Muriel started, as Olly manhandled Francis past him and through the door. 'You cannot allow this.'

'I can and I do,' Agnes spat back, pushing Ash aside as she bore down on her sister. 'I want him out of my sight. You should never have brought him here.'

'But—'

'If you are so keen to have him by your side, please feel free to join him in *leaving my home*.'

Muriel fell silent. Her parents watched on with wide eyes.

'Go on! *Go!*'

The moment snapped. Agnes's family left the room without any further argument, the door shutting behind them with a deadly finality. The tension fell from Ash's shoulders as if a rope keeping them upright had frayed and fallen.

'Ash . . .'

Agnes turned to him. She looked flushed. Triumphant.

She kissed him. Ash had the briefest moment to breathe – a small, stifled gasp – before he deepened the kiss, his hands finding their way to Agnes's hips.

He thought, for just a second, of Olly's attempts at tutelage so long ago. Of their shared awkwardness. He gripped Agnes's hips tighter, stroking one hand up her side, as her lips moved over his with gentle ease. When they had kissed before – once to wed, once to pull her from Francis's grip, and many times as they twisted together with Olly – it had felt different, somehow. One had been law, one had been play, and the rest . . . the rest had been desire, pure and easy.

This was different. Her lips played against his, gently opening his mouth, seeking entrance. Her tongue slid against his own, hot and warm, and he could feel *everything*, every nerve in his body alight, every beat of his heart in tune with hers.

When she pulled back, he chased her, lips desperate for more. She left him with another, lighter kiss and a smile.

They stared at each other for a long moment. Ash could still feel the tingle of Agnes's lips on his, the warmth of her hands where she'd gripped his arms.

'Oh—' Ash said stupidly. 'I . . . that—'

Agnes smiled at him, still clinging to his arms. 'I quite agree.'

Nothing else existed. Ash ducked his head low, intending to kiss Agnes once more, when suddenly the door slammed open with such force that they leapt apart.

'What—'

'It is Olly.' Raff stood in the open door, panting heavily. 'It's Olly, he's been hurt. You *must* come, now!'

✡

Ash burst into the courtyard in a run, ears ringing, vision already blurring. He barely registered the figures standing around, the huddle of men to one side, the shouting, the shouting—

There was someone lying on the ground.

He was beside him in a moment. His knees screamed in agony, but he ignored the pain, ignored the sharp dig of stones into his skin.

'Olly— Oliver, *Oliver*—'

There was someone next to him, pressed against him, hot grips around his wrists.

'Ash, *breathe.*'

That was Agnes.

'Breathe. You need to breathe.'

He tried to do as she said. Olly, lying on the ground in front of him, swam in and out of his vision.

'He is all right. Ash—'

He could still hear shouting. Shouting, and crashing from far away – like waves, or wind, or clashing steel.

'Ash.'

There was a firm, familiar hand gripping his own. He focused, as much as he could.

'There you are.' Olly smiled up at him.

'You . . . you were hurt, Raff said—'

'Just a scratch. Really, I'm—' Olly winced. The panic gripped Ash again in the face of Olly's lie, swirling in him, pulling him back down.

Something was tugging their hands apart. No; not apart. Loosening the grip. Agnes's calloused hands sliding between his and Olly's, becoming part of them.

'You are hurting him.' She whispered it, leaning against his side, lips near his ear. 'There. *There—*'

As she eased them apart, Ash realised his hands were shaking. He looked down: his knuckles were white. Olly's fingers were pink where he'd gripped them so hard.

Tears sprung into his eyes.

'I . . . I . . .'

'It's all right.' Slowly, the world started to come back. Olly, still on his back, grinned up at him. 'I really am unharmed.'

Agnes rolled her eyes at him. 'There is blood on your tunic.'

'Only a little.'

Ash finally dared to look down. They were both correct: the bloodstain across the pale fabric was minimal. Agnes tugged away the tunic and undershirt – both sliced neatly through. There was a gash of about a hand's-width across his side, long but shallow.

'See?' Olly said. 'Nothing. I have had far worse.'

Ash let out a breath of relief. It came out half-choked, his throat tightening around it.

'What happened?' he managed.

Olly attempted to sit. Ash quickly helped, supporting him as he heaved himself up onto his elbows.

'The bastard tried to stab me.'

He gestured with his head. For the first time since rushing outside, Ash looked over towards the huddle of men. Penn and a pair of guards were holding Francis between them, keeping him still. His face was scarlet, nose bloodied.

Penn was sporting a fresh black eye, looking tremendously pleased with himself.

On the ground was a bloodstained knife.

Ash was on his feet in an instant.

'You come into my home. You insult my wife and wound my man. This is to say *nothing* of all you have done before you even stepped foot within my keep.'

Francis's eyes went wide. 'I do not understand what you are talking about.'

'Yes,' Ash spat, 'you do. And be grateful that I do not intend to involve the law in this. You leave, *now,* or I will be forced to repay your behaviour in kind. *All of it.* Do I make myself clear?'

Francis flushed even redder. He scowled, the expression contorting his face. He said nothing.

'Then we have an agreement,' Ash said. 'Leave. *Now.*'

He turned on his heel.

'They were all right, you know! Your uncle and the rest! At least you are suited for each other: the madman and the degen—'

Ash swung with such force and speed that no one had time to prepare themselves before his fist connected soundly with Francis's jaw. The guards holding him jumped back in shock as he crumpled to the ground.

Francis spat red onto the dirt, immediately struggling back to his feet. But before Ash could act, Agnes was upon him. A well-placed kick knocked his arm from under him, toppling him back down.

Agnes's family, watching from aside, gasped. Her mother cried out. Agnes swung on them, too, leaving Francis on the ground, cradling his arm.

'If you find yourselves in agreement with him, you may leave as well. I understand you do not approve of mine and Ash's union, but I *chose him*. He cares for me. He treats me kindly. If you agree with Francis's words about him – his words about *me*' – Agnes made a hiccupping noise, the words stuttering in her throat – 'then you may leave, and think of me no more.'

'Agnes—'

'I am asking—' Agnes took a deep breath. Ash rushed to her side. 'I am *telling* you, for the last time. You must choose. Him or me.'

'But—'

Agnes's shoulders slumped. Ash couldn't tell if her family noticed – if they saw the way her expression shifted, a minute change to the tilt of her eyebrows, the hard line of her lips. He took her hand.

'Agnes . . .'

She turned to look at him.

'Let us go inside.'

He led her towards Olly, who was now rising to his feet, his hand clamped to his side. Agnes seemed to steel herself, giving Ash's hand a tight squeeze before releasing him and heading towards Olly to help.

Ash realised belatedly that Francis was still standing in his courtyard.

'I demanded you leave. Why are you still here?'

'You cannot expect me to go *now*. It will soon be sunset—'

'Skeldale is not that far away. Stay in the inn.'

'And travel in the dark? On these roads? What about bandits?'

Ash sighed, then bent down to pick up Francis's dagger. It was stained with Olly's blood. He took a breath and handed it to him. 'Then you will be needing this.'

'But—'

'Enough.' He gestured to a pair of guards. 'See to it that he gathers his things. Escort him to Skeldale, if he is so concerned about travelling alone. Raff.' Raff stood straighter, looking – Ash thought – proud. 'Please see to Agnes's family as they decide how they wish to proceed. We shall take Oll— Oliver inside and assess if we need to send for the physician.'

Raff nodded. Ash turned his back on them all and followed Olly and Agnes into the keep.

*

They bundled Olly into the side room. Each step Ash took shifted beneath his feet. But Olly was beside him, standing and walking and talking – talking *so* much. He would be all right.

They propped him on a chair, then began to remove Olly's clothes to better assess the wound.

'See?' Olly said, leaning back as Ash removed his undershirt to reveal the neat, thin cut. 'It is fine.'

He was right – it wasn't so bad – but it would still need to be cleaned and bandaged.

Ash took the remains of Olly's undershirt and started wiping away blood. Agnes positioned herself at Olly's other side, watching closely.

'Is that *really* necessary?' Olly asked, wincing.

'Yes.'

'It isn't so bad,' Olly began. 'You—'

'Shut your mouth.'

Agnes and Ash had spoken in unison. She looked across at him with a small smile.

'Is he always this stubborn?' she asked.

'Yes.' That was Ash and Olly's turn to speak together.

Agnes chuckled, guiding Olly to lean back again. Her fingers lingered on Olly's chest, lightly grazing his bare skin.

'There.'

Ash watched them both, finally able to breathe again. Olly turned to look at him, expression concerned.

'Ash?'

Ash could do nothing more than lean forwards and kiss him. It was brief, but he hoped it told Olly what he needed to know: the fear and the relief.

When he leaned back, Agnes was peering at them. She, too, looked relieved; but her eyes were shimmering with something beyond that as well. Ash thought of the moment they had shared before they were interrupted, of the way she had looked at him, the lurch in his heart that had threaded down to his stomach, down to his toes.

He glanced again at Olly, who seemed to know what he was about to do, then took Agnes's jaw and tilted her forwards. Their lips met for only a moment. When he released her, she sighed against his lips.

'So is that how it is?'

They both turned to face Olly. He was looking between them with a curious expression.

'Olly—'

Olly ignored him, reached out, placed a hand to Agnes's nape and pulled her into another kiss. It was a little fiercer than the one Ash had shared with her, a little deeper, a little more daring, much like everything Olly did. When he let her go, her face was wholly pink.

'I think we have much to discuss,' Agnes said, once her breathing had levelled.

Olly looked between them. His smile spread from ear to ear.

'I suppose we do,' he said. He reached out so he could take both of their hands at once. 'I—'

'Ash!'

'God's *pendulous bollocks*—' Ash stood, stomped across the room, and flung the door open. 'What is it?'

Penn stood in the doorway, looking embarrassed.

'You are needed,' he said. 'Or, I suppose, *Agnes* is needed. Your family is unhappy.'

Agnes joined Ash in the doorway. 'Are they displeased about Francis?'

'That is one way to describe it.'

She sighed. 'Fine. *Fine.* We need to sort this mess out. Better to do it now. Ash?'

Ash nodded. 'I agree. Come—'

'Wait!' Olly was tugging his tunic back over his head. 'Wait for me—'

'Olly, you need to *rest*. You were hurt!'

'Only a little . . .' Olly was on his feet now, throwing his tunic over the undershirt. 'You cannot propose I miss this?'

Ash relented. 'Penn, just . . . make sure he does not injure himself further.'

Penn grinned. 'Of course.'

He headed inside, looping an arm around Olly's middle to keep him upright.

'You know,' Olly muttered, as they left the room, 'he did not wound my *leg*. I can walk perfectly well.'

'If you faint and crack your head open, Ash will have me flayed.'

'He is correct, you know,' Ash called over his shoulder.

'Fine, *fine*.' Olly huffed. 'That was an exquisite punch, by the way.'

Ash grinned as Penn laughed.

'I know.'

Chapter 35

Agnes

There was fire burning beneath Agnes's skin. No matter what her family said, no matter what denials they gave her or insults they hurled against Ash, she would not stand down.

They were gathered in the great hall, looking nervous. Servants milled around, the steward standing carefully to one side. Everyone was watching.

She did not let them speak.

'Have you decided to stay?'

He father stepped forwards. 'Agnes, we need to *talk about this*—'

'No.' Agnes stood straighter. 'We do not. *I* am going to tell you what has happened, and *you* may decide what you wish to do with that information. Do I make myself clear?'

Her mother joined her father, taking his hand. 'Agnes, please. You are being unreasonable.'

'Unreasonable?' Agnes repeated. '*Unreasonable?*'

'Francis only worries about you.'

'Is that why he tried to have my husband murdered?' Silence fell. Agnes felt the eyes of everyone in the hall upon her. She did not care. 'Well? Do you have nothing to say?'

'Agnes—'

'You *stupid bitch!*'

Muriel. She shoved their parents aside, advancing upon Agnes. Their mother gasped. 'Muriel!'

'Why must you drag Mother and Father into this?' Muriel shouted. 'They did not need to know!'

Agnes's tongue was thick. She could not make sense of Muriel's words. 'What?'

'Francis *knew* you would behave like this, he *knew* it, and I said it would be all right, but I was wrong.'

There was a cavern in Agnes's chest. A dozen wounds, opening and reopening.

'You knew?' she managed, at last. '*You knew?*'

'Of course I knew! Francis was right: he told me you were walking into a trap, and you had your eyes wide open as you did. You had to be stopped for your own good!'

Agnes's father placed himself between them. 'What are you talking about? Both of you!'

Agnes swayed on the spot. Thank God, Ash spoke first.

'Francis hired a man to have me killed,' he said, voice remarkably calm. 'The attack on the road was not a robbery. It was an attempt on my life. We have proof,' he added, as Agnes's father opened his mouth. 'This is not mere speculation. This is *fact*. And it seems that Muriel was aware of it.'

Agnes's father looked aghast. 'It cannot be true.'

'We can show you the evidence,' Agnes said, finally managing to find her tongue. 'We have the man who was hired to do it. We have the letter confirming the deal. We know how much money he offered.'

'I cannot believe Francis would do such a thing . . .' Agnes's mother breathed, face pale. 'After all this time . . .'

'You knew of this?' Agnes's father turned to Muriel. 'You knew?'

Angry tears stained Muriel's cheeks. 'I told Francis what was happening. He needed to know. He needed to help stop it.'

'But *why?*'

'Because Barden is *wrong,*' Muriel cried. 'He is cruel, and violent, and mad, and I saw—'

'You did not see anything!' Agnes shouted over her. 'Has all of this been because of a misunderstanding? Ash and I were merely talking. I tried to explain to you and you did not listen! You *never listen!*'

Muriel shook her head. 'You are blind to it,' she said, near hysterical. 'You cannot *see*. He will only hurt you. But Francis *loves you*, you stupid, *stupid* creature. He loves you and you have thrown that in his face!'

'Francis does not know what it *is* to love someone,' Agnes said. 'I do not care what he thinks he feels for me. Ash is worth a dozen of him. A hundred. He is a good man. He loves me.' It was not true. She said it anyway. 'And I . . . I love him. And I will not have you – *any* of you – come between us.'

Muriel was silently crying. Agnes's parents looked sick and ghostly.

'I think it would be best if you went home, Muriel,' Agnes said. 'Find Francis, go home, and forget all of this. Do not let me see him upon these lands again, for I *will* take retribution upon him.'

'Agnes—'

'Go.'

There was a moment of hesitation. Then Muriel dashed past them, up the stairs and away. Agnes stared at her parents.

'I apologise for . . . for everything,' she said. 'You must take her home in the morning.'

'I cannot believe it,' her mother said. 'You are sure? *Entirely* sure?'

Agnes nodded. 'He wanted his way, as he always has. He took the stories of Ash being poorly tempered and twisted them for his own purpose. Once the deed was done he would have *insisted* I marry him instead. And' – she looked between them – 'I suspect you would have agreed.'

Her parents' guilty faces confirmed what she already knew.

'As I said . . . I am sorry. I am sorry that it came to this.' She did not trust herself to look them in the eye. 'I will see you off tomorrow morning. For now . . . I must rest, and attempt to put this mess behind me.'

She turned on her heel. Knowing that Ash and Olly would follow, she did not turn back as she made her way out of the hall.

✡

'I wish we could have seen all that through *after* supper,' Olly said from the chair beside the fire. 'I am *famished*.'

Agnes rolled her eyes at him. They had convinced him to allow them to clean and dress his wound, but he had complained bitterly about his hunger the whole time. Ash had gone to fetch food, keen for some way to keep himself busy.

'How can you even *consider* eating?' Agnes said, fiddling with the ties of the tunic she had changed into. 'I feel as if I will be sick every time I think about it.'

'Then do not think about it.'

There was a thump at the door. She pulled it open, revealing Ash carrying a wide tray in both hands. It was piled high with dried meats, bread, cheese, and cakes. The sight did little to settle her stomach.

'How was Joan?' she asked, as he edged in.

'Very well,' he said. '*Everyone* is aware of what happened. She was sympathetic, said I could take what I needed, and that she hoped my Lady Wife was well. She even asked after *you*, Olly,' Ash added, placing the tray on the table. 'She heard you were wounded.'

Olly was too busy to answer, his mouth already stuffed with bread and cheese.

'How *do* you fare?' Ash asked Agnes, taking a bite from one of the honeyed cakes. 'Are you all right?'

Agnes shrugged. 'As well as I can be having just thrown my parents from my home and learned that my sister was complicit in the attempted murder of my husband.'

'You should eat,' he said, putting an arm around her.

Agnes leaned her head against him. 'Must I?' she grumbled.

He pushed the half-eaten cake into her hand. 'You must.'

She nibbled at it. Ash was right: she did not realise how hungry she was until she began to eat. It tasted good, sweet and sticky and filling. She licked the honey from her fingers mindlessly as Ash took another for himself.

'What you said to your family . . .' he began.

The sweetness turned sour in her mouth. Of course he would want to talk about that; of course he would *need* to. They had lain together, and they had kissed, and they had shared a bed, but that did not mean his feelings matched her own.

'I apologise,' she said quickly. 'I did not know what else to say to make them believe me. And *most* of it was true. You are a good man. The *best* man. And I . . .' She could deny it no longer, not now the words were out: 'I love you.'

Ash stared at her. 'You do?'

'I do,' she said simply. 'I have loved you for longer than I would wish to admit. But you have Olly. I did not want to ruin that.'

Now she had started, she could not stop. It was a relief to finally get the words out of her chest, even if that relief came edged in pain.

'I didn't want you to know,' she said, laughing at herself. 'I thought if you never knew, it would be better.' Olly had risen from the chair to stand beside Ash. 'I did not want to ruin what you have. What *we* had. And I dreaded hurting either of you, or getting between you in some way . . .'

'You will not.' Ash reached out, taking her hand. 'You will not get between us, Agnes. You are . . .'

'You are part of us,' Olly said, supplying the words where Ash could not.

Ash blinked, as if Olly had espoused some revelation.

'You are,' Ash said. 'And you were right. You were right to tell them I love you. I . . . I should have agreed with you then, but with all that was happening . . .'

'You do?'

Ash held her a little tighter. 'I think . . . I think I do. That is, I have only ever loved one person, and I do not know how it feels to love someone else, and I—'

'Oh just *kiss her,* you useless bastard,' Olly piped up, shoving him closer.

Agnes laughed, stifling it when she realised how distressed Ash looked. She pushed herself up onto her toes and kissed him before he could say anything else. Ash gasped, then wrapped his arms around her, kissing her back with deep, slow urgency.

When she let him go, she had forgotten how to breathe.

Ash grinned, looking dizzy himself. 'I love you. I love *both* of you,' he amended, looking towards Olly as well. 'I did not even know if it was possible, if it was *permitted,* but . . . but I do. I am sick of running from it. I have run from myself for long enough. I cannot run from this. I want to find some way to . . . to *be*. All of us.'

He looked between them. His expression was unguarded and raw. Fear and joy mingling. Agnes wrapped her hand around his.

'I want that too,' she said. 'I do, Ash. This . . . whatever *this* is . . . it is all of us.'

'Olly?' Ash reached out towards him.

His name was all Ash had needed to say aloud. The rest was a look – a simple look. A question. And now Agnes could interpret them as well as they could.

Olly stepped into Ash's waiting arms. Ash pressed a kiss to his lips, a reassurance, a promise.

They stood, all three a tangle, their breath mingling between them, an odd crisscross of limbs. No one spoke for a long while. It was Olly who detached himself first, looking thoughtful. He stared down at Agnes and then, at last, appeared to make a decision.

'I have a gift for you.'

That had not been what Agnes was expecting. 'A gift?'

'You may call it a marriage gift, if you like,' Olly said, kneeling beside the bed. 'Although it is far too late, and while I suppose you may both make use of it, it is more for you than Ash.'

He emerged holding a small box.

'What in God's name is that?' Ash asked, looking perplexed. 'How long have you been hiding that under there?'

'Only a day or so. You ought to take better care of your chambers, Ash.'

Ash shook his head as Olly pressed the box into her hands.

'Here.'

Having no idea what he could have procured for her, Agnes gave him one last look before opening the lid.

She gasped. Or, perhaps, she laughed – the two mingling over each other into a snorting, croaking choke.

'*Oliver!*'

'What is it?' Ash said. He turned to Olly. '*What is it?*'

Agnes reached into the box and pulled out a perfectly formed, perfectly weighted phallus.

'Good *God,*' Ash said. 'Is that a . . . is that a *cock,* Olly?'

'Not a real one,' Olly said, as Agnes turned it over to get a better look at it.

It was, she realised, much like the one that Olly had described to her before. It was made of dark red leather. When she wrapped her hand around the shaft – eliciting a noise from both men that she did not miss – she found it hard beneath her palm. Inside was no doubt wood, or perhaps bone, wrapped with something softer to ensure it remained pliable.

It did not feel *entirely* like a real cock, but it did not feel entirely *unlike* one either. The base of the thing was sewn to a kind of girdle, along with two long, soft-feeling straps.

'Is this—' She laughed at herself, at the false phallus. 'Is this to be *worn?*'

'Of course.' Olly grinned, as if it were the most natural thing in the world. 'And you can wear it wherever you wish.'

Agnes had the sudden image of her strutting around the fields, breeches – or skirts, for that matter – tended with an illusory erection. She raised her eyebrows at him.

'Oh, *no,* not like *that,*' he said, gesturing at it. 'I had Pepper make it for me. For *you.* You can remove the rod inside and wear it like that. Make it—' He drooped dramatically with his arms. 'One does not always stand to attention, after all.'

Agnes looked down at the cock. She imagined herself wearing

it – wearing it stiff or tucked away beneath her clothes. Sparks ran up her spine: not the thrill of desire, but the elation of something else, something she could not name.

It was hers. It felt, somehow, like a part of her.

Olly took a step forwards, taking her arm. His expression was open and sincere. Despite his laughing, despite his lewd jokes, she could read in his eyes that this was true. This was not a joke at her expense, not an insult to the way her soul and body clashed.

'You do like it?' he asked. 'If not, we can pretend this never happened. Throw it in the river.'

'No.' Agnes shook her head. 'No, I like it very much.' His hand still lingered on her arm. 'Thank you, Olly. Really. It is . . . I hesitate to call it *lovely*, but . . . I do love it.'

Olly's lips parted a little. He looked terribly unsure. He looked how *she* felt, too: as if there was something just out of reach, something that she was sure she wanted, but was too scared to take. She didn't know what it was. She wanted to find out.

She edged closer and pressed a light kiss to his mouth. Olly's eyes fluttered, his tongue darting out to wet his lips.

'You do?' he said, his voice strained.

'Yes,' she muttered, their lips brushing. 'I do.'

Olly looked from her to Ash. 'Do you wish to try it on?'

None of them were too sure what she should wear *with* the piece, before deciding that the best course would be to strip up to the waist, her hose and braies abandoned in a pile beside the bed. There was a moment – a brief moment that drew out – when Agnes insisted that if *she* were disrobing then they should as well, leaving them all to become distracted while the phallus sat unused on the bed. By the time they remembered what they had planned to do, Olly was utterly naked aside from the bandage around his middle,

Ash in only his undershirt, and Agnes quite ready to push them onto the bed, cock or no.

It took all three of them to work out precisely how to attach it, devolving into a short argument between Ash and Olly as they threaded the straps between her legs, trying to find the best place to tie them. The belt around her waist tightened perfectly, and together – with much shuffling and moving and grabbing – they managed to secure it in place.

Agnes stood, legs a little apart, the cock – *her* cock – jutting heavily in front of her.

It felt . . . *right*. It was unwieldily upon her body, but not in a way that made her shrink away. She felt the heaviness of it, the pressure, the way it moved against her when she shifted. With a little repositioning, a little extra fabric, she wondered if she could place it in such a way that she could rub herself off against it too.

A thought to be chased later.

She sauntered to the rarely used mirror that Ash had hidden away in the corner of his chambers and observed herself in the metal.

The dark red of the prick matched the brighter colour of hair quite prettily.

Ash and Olly appeared in the mirror behind her. They, too, were observing her reflection.

'You may need tutelage if you wish to use it,' Olly whispered over her shoulder, placing a hand on her hip. 'Although much is . . .' he trailed the hand lower '. . . instinctive.'

Agnes nodded. She caught Ash's eye in the mirror.

'Well?' she said, keeping his gaze.

Ash pressed his lips to her shoulder. She could feel his cock rubbing against her arse, stiff and eager.

'I must admit to being interested,' he said.

She turned so she could see him, the *real* him, not his muddied reflection.

'In that case,' Olly said, breaking the tension that hummed between them, 'I shall fetch the salve.'

Chapter 36

Ash

When Agnes had opened the box and pulled out the thing inside, Ash's first reaction had been bafflement.

It had not taken long for him to imagine what sorts of things one could do with a false prick strapped to a pair of hips.

Agnes turned her gaze upon him. She was *magnificent*. His wife, his lord, his *Agnes* – something else entirely, something he didn't have a name for but worshipped all the same.

He fell to his knees at her feet, staring up at her, the light of the fire making her glow. Her bright hair, touch-tangled, was lit up like the sun, like a glorious vision. She stared down at him, not with derision, not with the hate Ash had spent so long coming to expect, but with soft, sure love.

Olly stood beside her like a flanking guard, like a knight. Ash edged forwards, still on his knees. He reached for her, the warmth of her skin beneath his hands like the first touch of spring sunlight.

He did not know what to do with it – with the love, with the twin looks of adoration that they were laying upon him. He did not know what to do with the weight in his chest, the fullness of his heart.

But the cock springing between Agnes's legs? *That* he was more familiar with. He did not know how to handle love, how to make it settle within him. But a stiff prick was something he had more experience in.

He nuzzled his face against the side of Agnes's cock, his lips brushing the straps, his hands gripping her hips. He was overwhelmed with the smell of fresh leather, a perfumed note above the rich scent of Agnes herself. Agnes inhaled softly, not quite a gasp, her legs twitching. He looked up at her.

'Agnes?'

Agnes swallowed. She nodded, eyes wide, lips parted.

He began along the edge of the straps; the crease of her thigh, kissing his way across leather and skin. The fabric was smooth against his lips, body-warmed and pliable, her skin soft and firm. He kissed her properly, opening his mouth to taste her. From somewhere high above he heard a breathy gasp, and a contented hum – a sound of approval from Olly.

He turned his face inwards, edging along the garter that kept the prick in place, the ties between Agnes's legs. The cock nudged against his cheek, as eager as one made of flesh and blood. Unable to resist, he opened his mouth against the shaft.

It was rich and smooth, unlike anything he had experienced before. Agnes's legs tensed, her breath hitching. She could not feel it, yet somehow her body was responding as if she could.

He laved the length of the prick with his tongue, holding Agnes still with one hand and taking the prick in the other. It had a sturdy sense of pliability to it, and as he squeezed it, he felt the hard rod within, keeping it rigid. It was a good size – big enough to fill him up. He let out a low breath at that thought, at imagining Agnes inside him, driving him to spend.

With a low, needy noise that rumbled directly from his core, he took the prick into his mouth, swallowing down as much as he could. Agnes made a startled, breathy sound as Olly *purred* from somewhere far away and up above.

'*Ash*—' Agnes's voice sounded rough and broken. 'I— *God* . . .'

She tangled her hand in his hair, tugging, pulling. He groaned around the prick.

'God, Ash, you're so good.' That was Olly, his voice piercing the fog of lust. 'Such a pious man, down on his knees.'

His words went straight to Ash's cock, already throbbing and hard between his legs. He wanted more – he wanted to feel Agnes spend in his mouth, an impossibility, a mere desire-fuelled dream. He released her with reluctance. He needed to see her face. He needed to see Olly's face, too.

Agnes was watching him, hair tousled, face red. Olly was grinning, his hands around her waist.

'*Please*—'

It was all Ash needed to say. Agnes hauled him to his feet before pulling him into a deep kiss. He trailed his hands around her waist, meeting Olly's skin on her other side. Their pricks – his flesh and hers leather – rubbed together deliciously between them. Olly looped his arms around Agnes fully, reaching for Ash, holding him. Ash could no longer tell where their bodies divided. Olly's skin was his skin, was Agnes's skin. Agnes's lips against his neck were Olly's lips, their legs tangled together irrevocably. There was an *ache* in his chest, a tightness, as if their souls had somehow mingled into a new, brighter whole.

They collapsed onto the bed in a heap. The air was pushed from his lungs as both his wife and his lover crushed him against the sheets. Olly was the first to disentangle himself, laughing as he did. The noise was so beautiful that Ash could not help but laugh along with him, the joy infecting Agnes, too.

Agnes sprawled on the bed, Olly beside her. Ash lowered himself down on her other side, his hand trailing up her leg, tangling in her undershirt. The red prick jutted obscenely between her legs, pushing aside the pale fabric. He felt her staring at him, watching him, watching *it*.

'Do you wish to try, then?' Olly asked.

Agnes's cheeks were red, her skin painted with a light sheen of sweat. She nodded. 'But—' She breathed. 'I am not sure *how*.'

'Then I shall teach you. Ash—'

Ash looked up at him. He would agree to anything. 'Yes?'

'Back on your knees.'

✡

It was nothing like he could have imagined. The *feel* of the leather prick alone was different to anything he had experienced before, the sense of fullness distinct in a way he struggled to describe.

But as soon as Agnes breached him – guided from behind by Olly – he knew it was right. She moved against him, moved within him, and he gripped at the woollen blankets and gasped and writhed and took it, her name pouring from his lips.

Face pressed to the pillows, he could hear Olly muttering soft, gentle words of encouragement to them both – *yes, like that, so good* – and then a soft noise from Agnes, a noise that grew into a gasp, a crescendo of little moans. Ash desperately wished he could see what they were doing.

The thought of it pushed his own peak closer, tension building within him. He reached beneath himself, wrapping his hand tight around his cock. As Agnes thrust into him, he thrust into his hand, mouth open against the soft pillow.

Agnes's rhythm was becoming erratic, her noises growing louder. Ash worked himself harder. Behind him, far away, *inside him,* Agnes made a sound like a dam bursting, like a star burning. Ash bit at the pillow, jerking at himself with increased urgency, then – finally, *wonderfully,* spent over the blankets beneath him.

He slumped down, body wrung out and used up. He could hear the frantic panting of Agnes and Olly, and Olly's voice, calm and quiet.

'Gentle, now, ease back— that's right, *yes*—'

She pulled from him slowly. Ash collapsed onto the bed. He rolled onto his side to look at them: both on their knees, the shiny cock springing still between Agnes's legs, Olly behind her, his hand tucked beneath the straps of the false phallus.

Olly slowly withdrew his hands, fingers lingering on the belt.

'Shall I . . . ?'

'Please.'

Olly had the straps undone in moments, carefully placing the cock to one side. As he did, Agnes lowered herself down to lie beside Ash, nestling against him with a content noise. Olly crawled up to join them, still very obviously aroused. Ash reached for him, intending to share his pleasure with Olly, too, but Olly pushed his hand away.

'*Later,*' he said, lying on Ash's other side and looping an arm around his chest. 'Lie with me.'

Ash let himself settle between them, pressed between their bodies. His skin prickled, sticky with sweat and spend.

Olly began to trail a hand up and down his chest. As he did, he started to sing a soft tune, the words barely audible. Agnes shuffled closer, listening. Ash clung to them both, drifting in the melody.

*

It was, Ash had to admit, extremely gratifying to watch Agnes shout at her parents. The previous day had been a boiling point, a pot left too long, and now the steam had cleared Agnes's even-tempered simmer was more frightening than her rage.

Her parents tried in vain to convince her to forgive Muriel. Agnes did a remarkable job of ignoring their pleas. Ash and Olly stood at the side of the room watching, even after Agnes's mother had demanded they leave to give the family some privacy.

'I *am* Agnes's family,' Ash had responded.

Olly needed to be present too, just in case the situation should turn violent as, Agnes was quick to remind her parents, it had done the previous day. Under her fierce gaze and unrelenting chastising there was very little they could do about it.

When Muriel finally appeared, red-eyed and weary, Agnes barely even looked at her before escorting them all to the retinue hastily arranged to take them home. She turned to her parents before they left, and despite the surety of her stature, Ash could tell that each word was a struggle.

'I am not barring you from my life,' she said, head held high. 'But I require you to reflect on what has happened here. I do not want my children to live without knowing you. But should such things happen again, or should you allow Francis back into my life . . . I will be forced to ensure they do not.'

She saw her parents and Ada off with a kiss. Muriel received a last parting look before Agnes turned her back on them all.

'I think I should like to go for a walk.'

They took themselves down into the valley, the dogs bounding at their heels. Instead of taking the route to the river, Ash found his feet leading him instinctively up towards the road and the great green hill on the edge of the town.

He had avoided this corner of the churchyard when he had last been here, on the day of his wedding. It had been too much for him to contemplate, too much for one man to hold. That fear was still there, that horrible yawning loss, even when flanked by Olly and Agnes. But it did not bite at him like it had before, merely lingered with him.

He stared down at the grave. Fresh green grass emerged from the dark earth in little patches. Clumps of clover sprouted in uneven bursts. Amongst the greenery shot tiny, sturdy stalks; flowers yet to bloom.

Litillwitte settled at his feet, resting his head upon Ash's boots. Olly took his left hand, Agnes his right, and the past bloomed gently into the future.

Epilogue

Two years later

Ash's solar had, these past few months, descended entirely into chaos. He leaned against the desk, piled high with papers, as Raff and Penn cooed over the baby at the other side of the room. They *had* been showing her the horses riding away through the window, but Marion had been far more interested in taking Penn's curly hair in her chubby hands and trying to pull it out.

'Is my little Onion behaving herself?' Olly asked, as Penn yelped.

'*No*,' Penn said, as the baby tugged at his hair, resolutely refusing to let go.

'This is what happens when she has not seen her favourite uncles in such a terribly long time,' Olly said, without helping. 'It is because she misses you.'

Penn hummed. 'Raff, would you—'

Raff took Marion, extracting her from Penn's hair. Penn stood up straight with a sigh of relief.

'She's a sure grip, I can tell you that much,' he said, rubbing at his scalp. The baby giggled at him, reaching back towards him. 'Although she is a delightful thing, I must admit.'

'And her *hair*,' Raff said, grinning. 'She's like a little fire.'

Ash huffed a short laugh, walking over to join them by the window. Raff was correct: she had been born with more hair than he had seen on any baby, an untameable crop of violent red that stuck all at angles.

'We're thankful for that, I can tell you.'

'Oh?'

'She looks just like Agnes.'

Raff peered back at the baby. 'That she does. Why so thankful, though?'

'We are less likely to have anyone starting rumours.'

'About Marion?'

'About her *not looking like her father,* Raff. About her coming out with blonde hair and blue eyes.'

'But . . . how?'

Ash gave a long, beleaguered sigh. Penn was watching Raff with a knowing expression on his face – amused but unspeakably fond.

'Come,' Ash teased. 'I know of late you do not exactly sow your seeds in fertile ground' – at this, Penn gave a snort of laughter so loud it set Marion squealing again – 'but you surely understand the basics of the act, yes?'

'Oh.' Raff blinked at him. And then realisation dawned on his face. '*Oh.* But I thought, that is, I had assumed that *you* were her father.'

Ash gave a one-sided shrug. 'I am,' he said simply.

'But' – Raff looked between Ash and Olly – 'you said her hair . . . So what about Olly?'

'I am also her father.'

Raff's expression slipped into confusion once more. Ash gave him a friendly slap on the back.

'Do not worry yourself,' he said. 'If you think about it too hard, you'll give yourself apoplexy, won't he, Onion? We do not want that. Penn would be far too melancholy to deal with.'

Marion babbled in delight. Ash really was thankful that the

matter of her father remained uncontested: the pregnancy had been anything but easy, and it had taken some time for them to reach the point where seeing it through even felt possible. There had been a slip: just once. They had been too blinded by lust and thoughtless overconfidence, and the world had crumbled around them as they waited for the sticky concoction – tansy and pennyroyal and wine – to take hold. They'd been more cautious since, so when the signs returned, they were more prepared.

Even so, it had been a long, difficult time. Physically, all had gone well, but by the day Marion entered the world Olly had been the only one of them with a full grip left on his sanity. Somehow they had seen it through together, and Marion was as a light in his life unlike any he had ever known.

'We really ought to stop calling her Onion.' Agnes appeared in the doorway, a stack of letters in her hand.

'And whyever should we?' Olly asked.

'Because I called her *Onion* in my last letter to Mother, and did not realise until she responded asking what I meant. I was so tired I did not even notice . . .'

Olly snickered, then cut himself off at Agnes's expression.

'Was she all right?' Ash asked carefully.

Agnes sighed. 'Fine, fine,' she said dismissively. 'She mentioned *that unpleasantness* again, and said what a shame it is that we have not yet visited Muriel and the baby.'

'Ah.'

'Indeed. No matter, it simply means she must wait another few months to meet our little Onio— *Marion*, damn it—' She shook her head. 'I fear it is a lost cause.'

Ash grinned at the bouncing baby. 'Perhaps. Did anything else arrive?'

'As a matter of fact, *yes,*' she said. 'There was a message from Lily: she and Jo are keen to visit again once the weather turns.'

That was good news. Lily was so busy that she had only returned to Dunlyn a handful of times since both the wedding and Marion's birth. After some initial complications – which had included three guards wrestling Lily from Olly's back when she spotted him in the yard, along with a drawn-out argument about who, exactly, he was – things had gone remarkably well. It would be good to see her again.

'Olly, there was a letter for you, too,' Agnes continued. 'I believe it is from your brother.'

Olly smiled weakly. Correspondence with his brother had been slow and cautious. No doubt the letter would go unread for several days while he gathered the nerves to tackle it.

'And,' Agnes said, shooting Ash a suspicious look, 'a rider had this for you, from the goldsmith in York.'

She pulled a little leather bag from the pouch at her hip. Ash felt them both stare at him.

'I had him make something for me,' he said. 'One moment—' He turned to Raff. 'Could you take Onion outside?'

Raff complied, Penn close behind, chatting about taking her to see the painters in the great hall or the pups in the kennels. Once the door was shut, Olly turned upon him.

'What have you been up to, Ash?'

'*Here.*'

Ash opened the bag and tipped the contents into his palm. Three identical gold rings gleamed against his skin.

'I thought, perhaps . . .'

He took the smallest ring and handed it to Agnes. She looked at the inscription inside.

'I hope you do not mind, Olly,' Ash said, as she read. 'If it is too similar, or if you do not like them, then I can find—'

'*Vōs et non alius,*' Agnes looked up. 'You and . . .'

'. . . and no one else,' Olly finished, in a whisper.

'*You,*' Ash said. 'Both of you.'

Agnes glanced between them. She slipped on the ring. 'Both of you.'

Ash handed Olly his ring. He held it between his fingers, eyes shimmering, before sliding it on.

'Both,' he breathed.

Only one band was left. Olly plucked it from Ash's palm before he could do anything. Agnes took his hand. Together, they pushed the ring onto his finger.

'And no one else.'

Author's Notes

Before anyone starts yelling: the ceremony between Ash and Olly in the prologue is a real thing. You can read more about it in *The Marriage of Likeness* by John Boswell, which is a fascinating look into queer histories. I'd also recommend reading *Seeing Sodomy in the Middle Ages* by Robert Mills, which is a deep dive into all things queer and medieval.

For more on medieval gender, I'd recommend *Trans and Genderqueer Subjects in Medieval Hagiography*, edited by Alicia Spencer-Hall and Blake Gutt (which is where I discovered the story of Joseph of Schönau), and *The Shape of Sex*, by Leah DeVun.

If you're after some more contemporary sources around medieval genderfuckery, I'd recommend taking a look at *Le Roman de Silence, Yde et Olive, Iphis and Ianthe* (in Ovid's *Metamorphosis*) and *Tristan de Nanteuil*. The final three all follow a similar plot of a woman being transformed into a man. *Le Roman de Silence*, meanwhile, looks at gender through the lens of nature vs nurture, and could today be seen as more of a nonbinary tale.

Yes: Agnes's strap-on is real. Strap-ons are mentioned in Burchard of Worms' *Decretum*, Book XIX – a penitential from the eleventh century (a controversial source, I will admit). One is also mentioned in the trial notes of Katherina Hetzeldorfer from 1477, who was the first woman to be executed for sodomy. It's important to note that today Katherina's gender identity is a subject of debate as they presented as male, but of course this distinction isn't mentioned in the original trial notes. I learned about Katherina in *Female Sodomy: The Trial of Katherina Hetzeldorfer (1477)* by Helmut Puff.

Litillwitte is a genuine medieval dog name. You can find more exceptional examples in *The Names of All Manner of Hounds,* which lists a further 1064. I recommend reading David Scott-Macnab's *The Names of All Manner of Hounds: A Unique Inventory in a Fifteenth-Century Manuscript* to get the full list and learn more about what naming conventions were popular and why.

This is by no means an exhaustive list of the research I undertook while writing *A Vow Made Twice.* If you're interested in queer and trans readings of medieval sources, there's a lot out there: you just have to find it.

Acknowledgements

Looks like I wrote a book again. How did that happen?

There's something very bittersweet about writing this, my final acknowledgement in the Barden series. I've been in love with these characters for years, and now all their stories are told. I truly hope that all of my Ash fans out there feel like I did him justice, and gave him the Happily Ever After he deserves. I will admit: he's my favourite. Sorry to everyone else.

Oliver has been alive since I started drafting *Hartswood*. I was trying to get a feel for Ash's character and was prompted to write a short piece from his past so I could get a better grip on him. Within moments of Olly first appearing on-page, I realised that I loved him. So I brought him back from the dead. Incidentally, I'd love to know who noticed Olly – or Noll, as he's called there – in *All the Painted Stars*. I've been buzzing about that little Easter egg for ages.

As always, I have to thank my family and my friends for all their love, care and support since I started writing the Barden series. My incredible partner who has looked after me when times have been tough, supported me and taken me on little walks to calm me down when writing a book has been too difficult. Thank you to my mum, my number-one fan, and the first person who read *A Vow Made Twice*. I couldn't have done it without you both.

I also want to mention my grandad – my Pops – who sadly

passed away while I was writing this book. He was so proud of me, and he helped me become the person I am today. He will always be loved and missed.

It would be wrong to not shout-out Inber, the undisputed chair of the Ash Fan Club, who's stuck by me all these years. Without her, *One Night in Hartswood* would never have happened, and I wouldn't be here now, finishing the trilogy. Thank you for sharing the frog with me.

Thank you to all my lovely online friends, especially Dorian (who holds the prestigious title of being the first person who wrote fanfic for *Vow*) and Conny, the best artist in the world. Thank you to everyone on Discord (and . . . that other place) for supporting me and my work. A huge thank you to everyone who read *Hartswood* and *Stars*, who messaged me to tell me they loved them, and who made me realise that people do, in fact, want to read my books.

It's been a long journey – although, in the vastness of time, probably not that long at all. I'm excited to see where it takes me next.

Don't miss the enchanting first instalment in the Barden series . . .

ONE NIGHT *in* HARTSWOOD

Oxford 1360

When his sister's betrothed vanishes the night before her politically arranged marriage, Raff Barden must track and return the elusive groom to restore his family's honour.

William de Foucart – known to his friends as Penn – had no choice but to abandon his intended, and with it his own earldom, when he fled the night before his enforced marriage. But ill-equipped to survive on the run, he must trust the kindness of a stranger, Raff, to help him escape.

Unaware their fates are already entwined, the men journey north. But amidst the snow-capped forests an unexpected bond deepens into a far more precious relationship, one that will test all that they hold dear. And when secrets are finally revealed, both men must decide what they will risk for the one they love . . .

Discover the spellbinding second story in the Barden series . . .

ALL *the* PAINTED STARS

Oxfordshire 1362

When Lily Barden discovers her best friend Johanna's hand in marriage is being awarded as the main prize at a tournament, she is determined to stop it. Disguised as a knight, she infiltrates the contest, preparing to fight for Jo's hand. But her conduct ruffles feathers, and when a dangerous incident escalates out of Lily's control, Jo must help her escape.

Finding safety with a local brewster, Lily and Jo soon settle into their new freedom, and amongst blackberry bushes and lakeside walks an unexpected relationship blossoms. But when Jo's past catches up with her and Lily's reckless behaviour threatens their newfound happiness, both women realise that choices must always come at a cost. The question they need to ask is if the cost is worth the price of love . . .

ONE PLACE. MANY STORIES

Bold, innovative and empowering publishing.

FOLLOW US ON:

@HQStories